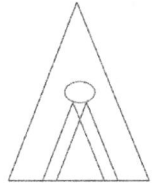

CITIES ON FIRE

C H Wilkins

Copyright © 2022 by C H Wilkins

All rights reserved.

No part of this publication may be reproduced, distributed, or transmitted in any form or by any means, including photocopying, recording, or other electronic or mechanical methods, without the prior written permission of the publisher, except as permitted by law.

For permission requests, contact C H Wilkins via charleshuwwilkins@gmail.com.

The story, all names, characters, and incidents portrayed in this production are fictitious. No identification with actual persons (living or deceased), places, buildings, and products is intended or should be inferred.

Book Cover by Lucy Redhead

ISBN: 979-8-3632-0312-1

"From everyone who has been given much, much will be demanded; and from the one who has been entrusted with much, much more will be asked."

- Luke 12:48

"And a lean, silent figure slowly fades in the gathering darkness, aware at last that in this world, with great power there must also come -- great responsibility!"

- Amazing Fantasy #15 (1962)

CITIES ON FIRE

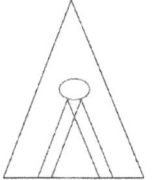

CHAPTER 1: SACRIFICIAL OFFERINGS
LOCATION: SOMEWHERE IN WASHINGTON, DC

"This is going to hurt."

THREE MONTHS AGO:

Cutting the power to the house was simple. If it were any other building, you-- 'you' being the one with criminal intent-- would target the entire electrical grid for the area, all to keep the authorities guessing which of the properties you were targeting.
Easy.
The problem was, when the death threats started coming in, the authorities circumvented the property's connection to the grid. They made it so the residence was powered by a series of generators located in the basement instead, thinking that would keep the occupants safe.
It wouldn't.
Gus Chalk and Terry Brando stood at the top of the basement stairs, flashlights raised and weapons drawn. Between them, they had thirty-four years of experience in the Secret Service, but nothing in those near three decades could prepare them for what was waiting for them at the bottom of the stairs.
"That shouldn't have happened, right?" asked Gus.
"Fucking no," replied Terry, as he checked his phone.
Gus sighed. "Call the techs, get them down here. It'll be a short or a fuse or some shit."
"… My phone's dead," replied Terry.
There was nothing but darkness in the basement. You couldn't see the generators; you couldn't see the boxes of belongings shoved

down there to be sorted through when life was less hectic. There was just the black, and it seemed to spread on forever, creating an ocean of shadow that threatened to swallow the pair whole.

"All right, let's check it out. I'm sure it'll--"

What happened next was so sudden, neither man had a chance to react. In less than a second, mid-sentence and mid-step, their hearts stopped. And that was that.

Gus had never had a heart attack before. He didn't know the warning signs or the symptoms, nor would knowing them give him a head start in preventing it from happening. There was a sharp pain, and then darkness. His legs went liquid, his head went empty, and he tumbled forward into the basement, breaking his nose and chipping three teeth when he landed face first. His flashlight shattered on impact, and his gun skittered into the darkness.

One down.

A few steps above him, and even if the details were different, the end result was the same. Terry's father died from a massive coronary when his son was a young boy, and even with that knowledge-- and a lifetime of cardio and healthy eating-- it didn't do him any favours. He landed on top of Gus, which did more damage to the man acting as a crash mat than the man crashing into him, and that was it.

Two down.

"*Weak,*" mumbled the perpetrator, rubbing his electrified hands together.

It didn't matter if the building was connected to the power grid or hooked up to some generators in the basement. Where there was a spark, the man who had stopped their hearts would find a way. It didn't matter if there were two Secret Service agents or ten. That just meant there was more electricity to pull from their bodies and redirect in the most heart-stopping way possible.

Blitzschlag cracked his knuckles and chuckled to himself. He didn't bother looking down at the faces of Gus and Terry. One of them might be an old friend. One of them might not. One of them was the insider who leaked the information about tonight's vulnerabilities to his organisation. Better to shock both men, either way.

With a bit of effort, he kicked Terry off Gus' back, and poked him in the chest, restarting the man's heart. He repeated the gesture on Gus.

If it were up to him, he would have left them to die, but his commander had told him to do the opposite. The attack would give their source in the Secret Service cover, and that meant Blitzschlag still got to hurt people, but the results would be long-term suffering and not death. That was almost preferable to a man like him.

He wasn't German, but that never stopped people like Eugene Harriman from appropriating a particularly provocative name. Electricity rolled off him in frantic, discordant waves, darting from his body and leaving contact burns on the walls as he climbed the stairs. The leather costume he wore was emblazoned with two bolts of lighting, stylised side-by-side like the insignia of the SS. Never let it be said that Neo-Nazis lacked imagination.

There were a few more Secret Service agents scattered around the house, but he didn't give them time to scream, either. When he was confident the ground floor was cleared, he made his way upstairs, his footsteps and the gentle crackle of current rippling across his costume the only sound audible in the ageing household.

The building sat steeped in darkness, apart from the one source of fluctuating light that haunted the corridors and left the stink of burning air in its wake. A walking lightning storm. A supervillain who had murder on the mind and the method and madness to follow through on it.

The door in front of him had the name of the Vice President of the United States' daughter spelt out on it with oversized tiles:

N A D I N E

"I love you. You know I love you. You're smart and cute, and that counts for a lot. But I think it's a stupid idea and I think you know it's a stupid idea," said Genevieve.

She sucked her mouth guard and took a neutral position across the mat from a much larger man dressed in a wrestling singlet and head guard. His friends were cheering him on outside the circle, while Genevieve's sole supporter was her partner-- and the target of her criticism.

"That's not a no though, is it? And do we have to do this now? I'd rather we didn't go into details in the bureau's gymnasium, y'know?"

Genevieve wasn't the tallest woman, but that had never mattered. Her deceptively low centre of gravity made her a thing of legend in her collegiate wrestling days. She held records in her weight class, and that made her a target whenever she was in Quantico. Some upstart always wanted to try their hand at taking down the FBI's own 'Queen of the Mat', and today was no different.

With close-cropped hair and dark eyes, she looked like she'd just left the Marines a month or so earlier and not slept since. In reality, she'd left a decade ago and had probably caught a few hours' sleep in that time. Her shoulders slumped and she removed her mouthguard to address her opponent.

"Hey, Bobby, you got any clue what we're talking about?"

"None, chief," replied the man, adjusting his headgear.

"Good man. You want me to go easy on you?" she asked.

"Fuck you," replied her opponent.

Genevieve grinned and replaced her mouthguard. "Fantastic."

Madison held up her whistle, ready to get things underway. The sooner she started the bout, the sooner they could continue their conversation.

Standing at 5' 8" with her wide eyes and pale skin, the brunette rarely stood out in a crowd. There was a hard edge to her jawline, but the rest of her features were sharp. From the curious lift of her eyebrows when witnessing something absurd or the subtle twist in her smile when something amused her, Madison had the uncanny ability to draw you in with a look.

If she let you get in close, you might notice the crisscrossing scars across her cheeks. They were a product of a childhood spent in the Minnesota boonies with a devil-may-care attitude toward running through whatever undergrowth stood between where she was and where she wanted to be.

She blew the whistle once and blinked. Blinking was always her mistake when Genevieve and a wrestling mat were concerned.

Bobby was somehow in the air. Like there were wheels on her knees, Genevieve had dashed across the mat faster than anybody expected, even with her impressive reputation. She was behind her opponent, then under him, hands locked around his waist, and suddenly then he was on the ground, shoulders first, the air gone from his lungs. He landed with such force his mouthguard flew out in a pathetic, spittle-filled yell, and then didn't move after Madison counted the fall.

The other agents were silent after Madison blew the whistle a second time. Bobby's friends checked on him while Genevieve brushed her thighs down. She looked at the men and said, "Come on, boys. Who's next?"

Blitzschlag licked his nicotine-and-bad-decision-stained teeth. This was what it was all leading to. He had killed dozens before this day, but this one murder would elevate him to a whole new level. The thought of it sent an excited shiver up through his thighs. He salivated, and it tasted like licking batteries.

He held his hand up and closed his eyes. Electrokinetically divining the contents of the room, he was surprised by the fact he couldn't sense any electrical charges past the door. Sure, he had knocked out the building's generators, but he still expected to feel the tell-tale tingle of a cell phone or an alarm clock. Even the minor resonance of any number of faddy kids toys or handheld game systems ticking over on batteries. But no, there was nothing. Just darkness. Just the girl.

He opened the door and took a step inside, silently moving forward toward his target. The door closed behind him with a click. It was so dark, he couldn't make out the contents of the room, other than the bed in front of him. He listened for breathing, and sure enough, the shallow, sleeping sound of a female was conspicuous from beneath the bed sheets.

For a while, he watched the movement underneath the duvet. All the planning they put into this attack, and he was stuck wondering how best to make the murder count. How best to send a message?

Better to stick to the classics, he finally made his decision. He raised a hand and began to focus his powers, drawing electricity toward his fingers like he had done dozens of times before. He could pull electricity from the air, and direct it into her bones, cooking her from the inside out. Nothing left but charcoal and burnt ends. They wouldn't even be able to identify her body when he was done with her.

As he grew increasingly excited, he bunched the bottom of the duvet up with one hand. He would pull it away and then throw the electricity gathered in his hand straight down, and then it would be over with.

Except, when he looked at his hand, no electricity crackled. No rolling, roiling lightning danced across his skin and came into focus at his fingertips. He couldn't seem to do what he had done a hundred times prior. He couldn't focus his electrokinesis into a killing strike. Half thinking, he yanked the duvet covers away, and was in for the second surprise of his evening.

"Trouble getting it up?"

A woman who was clearly *not* the Vice President's daughter aimed a shotgun directly at him.

"Oh, fu-- "

The blast caught him square in the chest. He toppled backwards and landed hard on his tailbone. The suit was bulletproof, but the wind was gone from his lungs. As he rolled onto his front, things got progressively worse.

Another woman sprung out of a nearby wall closet and bludgeoned him over the head with her baton with such force that it knocked him out immediately. He didn't have time to react, let alone think the electric thoughts that would have normally given him an advantage in such scenarios. Instead, he passed out, blood dribbling down the side of his scabbed head.

"See," said Madison, expelling the empty shells from the shotgun, "That wasn't too hard, was it?"

CITIES ON FIRE

"...Just look at this," said Madison, angling her laptop so Genevieve could see the video. They were parked outside Finnegan's Pub, an old favourite of the latter, because the former didn't drink.

"Maddie, please. *Please*. Can you drop it? First, I had to sit through another one of those boring presentations by know-nothing nerds who think a clipboard is a replacement for field experience, then, sure I got to hand several somebodies their asses and keep my rep up, but right now, I want to drink, and not talk shop. Your idea is stupid. So stupid. Who're you trying to convince?"

The trip to Quantico had been a bore, but a mandated bore, so they grit their teeth and took it. Back in the day, Madison would have loved to have listened to an extended presentation on 'Metahuman Combat Solutions', but she was older now, and being out in the world meant that theory counted for nothing in the face of practical application.

"Just *watch*, okay? Humour me."

Genevieve sighed and craned her neck. The video was one of many posted online by the Neo-Nazi organisation known as Stormhold in recent weeks. It started as they usually did, the group's logo-- a flaming swastika composed of four Todesrune-- rotating behind the word 'STORMHOLD'-- written in a font the group probably hadn't received permission to use-- with the phrase 'BLOOD AND HONOR' visible beneath that.

"Fucking Nazis," mumbled Genevieve. "Such a fucking lack of fucking imagination…"

There were four people visible in the video. The bald man at the front, Glenn Wiles, was the group's de facto leader, known as Odin. To his right was one of the organisation's lieutenant's, Eugene Harriman, AKA Blitzschlag. Behind them were the gaunt Chelmno, and the razor-sharp Skynbyrd, both of whom had experienced such extensive body modification that their identities were unknown to authorities.

Tutting, Madison scrolled through the footage until she found the timestamp she wanted.

<"...Brothers, we hear you, and we are indebted to you. Without your insight, we would be unable to complete our intended task,"> droned Odin, his eyes flitting from side to side as he read from a script off-camera. <"We know who our friends are, our allies, and--">

"There," said Madison, pointing at the screen.

Genevieve had no clue what her partner was talking about. "Yeah, sure, I see it, but for the folks at home?"

"Look at this Eugene fucker, look at his face when Wiles reads the line about 'friends' and 'allies'. The barely perceptible change in expression-- *but there is a change nonetheless*. I... well... it got me thinking."

Genevieve rolled her eyes but Madison ignored her.

"So, I reviewed all the other videos, and whenever the big guy talks about brothers, about friends or allies, his expression is different to the rest of the Neo Nazi weirdos he hangs out with. He knows something *they* don't."

"Of course," said Genevieve, half-paying attention. She knew her partner. She knew her partner was rarely wrong. She loved her like a sister, but that didn't stop her from being irritated by her enthusiasm the majority of the time.

Madison continued, picking up pace, "I ran this all by the Behaviour Analysis Unit, and they kinda-sorta see where I'm coming from, but it's not conclusive. Micro-expressions aren't the concrete science folks made them out to be in the day, but it's a start, you know?"

"Okay, so what it boils down to is that it's one of your 'hunches'," stated Genevieve. They had been down this kind of road before. "One of your headache-inducing hunches that drags me into whatever trouble that follows."

Madison nodded and rolled her eyes. "I know, I know, but this guy... I looked into him. Found out all about him. I know where he grew up, where he went to high school, who recruited him into the Aryan Brotherhood, all that shit. I know his whole damn life story."

"And?"

"I *also* know that there's a guy with a pristine record working in the Secret Service whose upbringing paralleled this creep's."

She tapped an icon on her desktop, and Special Agent Terence Brando's photo came up.

"This guy's dad died when he was a kid, massive coronary, and his mom bounced around the skinhead and pointy hood contingent looking for love. But Terry here, our pristine FBI boy, he never fell in with a bad crowd. Always rose above it. Except... he grew up in the same town as Harriman. His mom interacted with all the kinds of people that Harriman did. There's nothing connecting them on paper, but in theory..."

"...And you're the first person to put two and two together and get Neo Nazi?"

Madison threw her hands up. "He's clean! On paper, he's clean. *On paper*. But I'm convinced there's something there. But anyway, *that* got me thinking. There *is* somebody who's been leaking details about protective details to Stormhold. We know that. And it's gonna escalate. There's only so much shit you can smear in dressing rooms."

"What do you want to do?" asked Genevieve.

"I want to put all the guys who meet a certain criteria-- who *could* be the leaker-- on a protective detail that we can control. A sting operation within a sting operation. All the suspected dirty cops, the crooked agents, whoever, whatever, we get them in on it, give them a cover story, and then lay a trap of our own."

"...You've already gotten approval for this, haven't you?" said Genevieve.

"*Maaaybe?*" replied Madison. She fluttered her eyelashes at her partner, playing up the little sister angle that always worked on her partner.

"Oh, fuck off," replied Genevieve. But it was too late now. She knew she was in. She would follow Madison all the way to hell if she asked nicely enough. "When do we start?"

Strobing blue lights illuminated the exterior of the Vice President's residence as seven ambulances carried the harried victims of Blitzschlag to hospital. Various vehicles carrying representatives from an alphabetti-spaghetti of law enforcement agencies were vying for dominance, but the FBI were the first on the scene-- having been stationed just down the road throughout the entire elaborate sting.

"How's the shoulder?" asked Madison. She pulled on the Velcro strap that kept her bulletproof vest strapped to her chest. It came loose with a static rip and she let it fall limply to the ground in front of her.

Genevieve shrugged, then winced. "Guy had a hard skull. Had to put a lot more into it than usual." With her large hands, she clamped a bag of ice across her shoulder, but other than that, considering what they had just gone up against, they had done rather well for themselves.

The pair were sat on the edge of an ambulance, watching as armed FBI agents carried a sedated Blitzschlag out of the house and into a waiting vehicle. Their immediate supervisor, Assistant Director Gregory O'Bannon, found himself fielding questions from a half dozen red-faced men of differing levels of self-importance, but the inane chattering was interrupted by none other than the Vice President himself, flanked by two Secret Service agents.

"You're the two who made a mess of my daughter's bedroom?" growled Vice President Morgan Rakely.

He stood with the kind of posture that came with knowing exactly how straight one wanted their back to be in polite company, and his gait was that of a much younger man, though you'd be hard pressed to pin down the fifty-eight-year old's age if you hadn't done your research prior to meeting him.

Madison cleared her throat. "We managed to construct a rudimentary Faraday Cage without damaging the infra--"

Genevieve interrupted her partner. "That'd be us, sir. FBI, known for messing up children's bedrooms."

The Vice President nodded, his chin jutting out as he considered the pair, and then he broke into a smile. The airs of stubborn and stoic disdain evaporated, leaving behind a father who was clearly relieved that his daughter was safe. "You saved my baby girl's life. Found a gap in my detail that everybody else failed to. I'm really impressed, agents. Impressed, and indebted to you."

"We were just doing our job, sir," said Genevieve.

Rakely beamed. "And you've really impressed me. At the first sign of super-trouble, my boys here call in Aleph, and that just won't do. I want us to be able to deal with these sonsofbitches in-house, else what's the god damn point? So, I've got an offer to make. That's your boss over there, right? Let's grab him, and I'll put the kettle on. We should all talk."

<"Status check,"> crackled the voice on the radio.

"All clear here," replied Madison.

Genevieve and Madison watched as the Vice President's daughter contemplated the assorted outfits she held up in front of the mirror. Whatever mental arithmetic she was doing regarding the potential purchase had twisted the sixteen-year old's face into a mask of uncertainty, with bright flashes of interest in that fleeting moment when she held one dress up instead of another.

Nadine turned to the pair and asked, "What do you think?"

It was the third hour of moving from store to store, shopping for *something* that the pair hadn't been able to grasp yet. Outside the store were a group of surly looking Secret Service agents not used to playing second fiddle, and beyond that, and out of sight, were a surveillance team tapped into every single closed-circuit camera in the building. With zero notice and a can-do attitude, they had transformed a Washington shopping mall into a fortress. The kind of fortress with a juice bar in the forecourt, and a pretzel stand where you could see them shape the bread at the back, near the toilets.

Genevieve leaned close to Madison, so her words could only be heard by partner. "I hate you. You thought I didn't, but I do. You're so dumb and stupid and now I'm getting punished for it too. I think you know that, but I want you to doubly know that."

Madison ignored her. "The blue, not the red."

"Are you sure?" asked Nadine.

Genevieve chuckled and shook her head. "Kiddo, if you're not going to take our advice after specifically asking for it, then what was the point?"

The teenager's head bobbed from side to side as she considered the FBI agent's point then nodded in concession. "Okay. Okay! But I need to try it on. Both of them. Yeah, I should try them both on. And this one," she said, swiping another dress from the rail.

"Let me sweep the changing rooms first," said Madison.

"You've swept every changing room in the building! Every time we go into a store!"

"And the one time we don't check is when there's going to be an axe-wielding lunatic waiting for you," said Genevieve.

"Tsk. They don't have axes. They have, like, electricity powers. Or whatever. That was what the guy who you beat the shit out of had, right?"

"Firstly, language. I don't want your dad thinking we're bad influences. Secondly, yes, that one guy had electricity powers, and we didn't beat the *shit* out of him. We just beat him *unconscious*. But he-- and this is my third point-- he has a load of friends with axe-wielding powers. So, we have to be certain. Anyway…"

Madison hadn't waited around for Genevieve to finish her speech. She pushed the side of her jacket around her holster so she could pull her weapon out in an unobstructed motion if required and headed toward the cubicles. Secret Service agents had swept the entire shopping mall multiple times, this specific changing room included, but doing it again wasn't going to hurt anybody. She meticulously checked each cubicle. All the curtains were already drawn back, so she had clear lines of sight.

"Go ahead," said Madison, gesturing for Nadine to come inside.

Resuming her position at Genevieve's side, Madison quickly realised that she hadn't finished her rant, merely paused it. "We're a pair of highly decorated FBI Special Agents, and now we're doing this? And it's all because of your dumb hunches and our outstanding success rate. It's like we're succeeding downwards."

"I know, I know, you didn't sign up to be Mary Poppins, but Gen, I gotta say, you work the look so damn well," said Madison.

"Fuck off," replied Genevieve.

"You know, I don't know what I was expecting, to be honest," said Madison, an abrupt u-turn away from lobbing playful barbs at each other. "Six years ago I was in the NYPD, ten years before that, I just got out the academy. Sixteen years of ups and downs, and now we're babysitting the Vice President's daughter..."

"And it's all your fault," said Genevieve.

"You're an enabler. You've always been an enabler," said Madison.

"Blah, blah, victim blaming," countered Genevieve.

Before they could continue, an eardrum lancing screech shook the air above their heads. The pair instinctively ducked, the previously safe space around their heads abruptly savaged by a noise unlike anything they had heard previously. They couldn't see the source of the noise, but they felt the after effects, and it was worse than a tequila hangover.

"'Fuck was that?" asked Genevieve, ignoring Nadine's confusion as she pulled her out of the cubicle and kept her head down. She laid one hand flat on the girl's back, and in her other she had drawn her service weapon, ready to defend the Vice President's daughter with her life.

Madison was already on the radio, "Do we have eyes on what made that noise?"

<"We're not sure; teams are converging. Get the kid to safety.">

Genevieve took the lead while Madison brought up the rear. As the latter slipped through the door that led to the catacomb-like back corridors of the mall, she turned back and caught a glimpse of what had caused the ruckus-- it flew past the front of the store fast. The noise it was projecting was causing the glass in the windows to shake.

<"I think-- I think they're drones--"> squawked the radio.

Gunshots added percussion to the audio assault, but the FBI agents didn't have time to ask questions.

Madison reached a metal door that would lead them outside, but when she turned the handle, the door didn't open.

"What's wrong?" asked Genevieve.

"It's locked," replied Madison.

"Here's your key," said Genevieve, firing two rounds into the lock. The mangled door handle rattled to the ground along with the locking mechanism, so she threw her shoulder into the door, but it didn't budge. Something was barricaded against it on the other side.

"This passage shouldn't be blocked off," said Madison.

"I know, but we gotta keep moving," said Genevieve.

Neither agent noticed the blood flowing out from the gap at the door's base. They were already moving to their next exit. Voices continued to chirp up on the radio as the commotion back in the mall worsened.

<"They're fast! Whatever they are-- they're fast!">

"What are we dealing with?" Madison asked into her radio.

Genevieve reached another door but noticed the handle was gone, melted into slag that dribbled down into a dense, globulous mass at the base of the frame. Another blocked exit. She tried to look through the small window mounted in the centre, and her eyes widened. Though the glass was blackened by what appeared to be dirt or soot, Secret Service agent's skeletal remains were visible. The door didn't budge when she tried to push it, and her arm wouldn't fit through the pane if she smashed it open.

There was a shriek of static and metal, and the radio cut off abruptly. Instead of focusing on that, she murmured the word that had caught her attention the merest moments before. "…Drones?"

"What do you think?" asked Genevieve, gripping her service weapon as she continued to lead the three of them through the maze of the mall's back corridors. They turned a corner and came to an abrupt stop when their way forward was blocked by a large man, easily seven feet tall with a frame packed tight with muscle.

Madison recognised him immediately. Glenn Wiles, AKA Odin.

He wasn't wearing a shirt, just a pair of heavy black boots and some military trousers that came up too high at the middle of his torso, where a thick black belt held them up. Every square inch of his skin from his chest to his head was covered in tattoos. Heraldic eagles, dozens of swastikas, iron crosses and various numbers of notorious repute, all inked or scratched into his skin across the decades. A testament to his hatred.

His right eye was white and cataracted, the skin around it pocked and marred by scar tissue. Above his sneering smile was a thick black moustache that held flecks of grey, and his bald head shone under the sterile luminosity provided by the light tubes overhead. He didn't say anything. And that was enough to send a bass note shuddering down Madison's spine, a feeling that came to an abrupt halt as it bounced back up into the pit of her stomach.

Hearing about the drones should have been enough for Madison. The file she once read on the man referred to his automated, raven-shaped aerial assault weapons as Huginn and Muninn. They provided surveillance and firepower, and you didn't see him before you saw them. They scoped out the scene, and then he acted accordingly, never entering a situation he couldn't kill his way out from.

The FBI agents' radios screeched as a commotion continued to unfold back in the main parts of the mall. The drones were still picking apart the armed guards that littered the mall. The haunting, panicked sounds of people screaming and dying spat like static over the radio before cutting out completely.

"Hello, ladies," Odin said finally, his breath stinking of condescension and his voice registering an octave higher than his appearance suggested it should. It didn't matter. His words travelled with enough inherent threat and menace that it didn't reduce his malevolence one jot. He held all the cards and knew it. He began to chuckle, and the sound filled the corridor as it transformed into a full-fledged sonorous laugh.

Trying to think past his laughter, Madison focused on how his one working eye hadn't looked away from Nadine. Genevieve must have noticed as well because she stepped in front of the younger woman and held her hand up, palm front, trying to take attention away from their charge.

"Get out of the way," she said slowly.

"But I'm right where I need to be," said Odin. His singular eye focused on Nadine. "And so are you, *little girl*."

Of course. One step behind, but catching up quickly, Madison realised they'd been kettled exactly where the Nazi wanted them. Doors locked, blocked and barricaded, their colleagues dead, and the only route left to them leading the trio directly to him.

Odin rested a finger against the wall. He ran it lightly across the surface and with minimal effort scoured a trench into the concrete. He held the finger up and blew the dust and detritus away from the tip. "Now, I want you to imagine what I could do to you. With one finger. And I want you to know that I've done a thousand times worse a thousand times over."

"Yeah, we know who you are, big guy," said Madison.

"Did you lose the eye before or after you decided on such a stupid fucking name?" asked Genevieve.

Nobody had anticipated a villain of his stature being on the scene.

Odin let out a quiet guffaw, surprised by the brazen comment made by Santos. "You tell me."

"The fact that you made it this far means you're more powerful than Blitzschlag. And he was the kind of fucker who could stop folks' hearts if he put his back into it. That means you're a scary motherfucker, and that's all that really matters right now, right?"

"Sure enough," said Odin.

There was a shudder behind the group, and two silver blurs shot overhead. The twin drones that had caused such chaos back in the main section of the mall hovered over Odin's shoulders, and it was then, as they floated in place, they could see that the drones resembled birds, just as the files on Wiles said.

The automated assault drones lowered down and folded across his shoulders like heavy metal mantles, and Odin continued to laugh. Tiny wires slipped out of the aft portion of the drones and slithered toward small ports at the back of the villain's head. They snaked their way inside his skull, and he twitched ever so slightly as they latched onto something inside his head.

Huginn and Muninn. Thought and memory. They were feeding him intel based on their attack on the FBI and Secret Service agents in the mall forecourt. He was reliving their murders and clearly loving the experience. His face was twisted, with one eye half-closed and the other opened wide as he tried to enjoy the earlier rampage of his drones and keep his future victims in view.

"I said: *Get out of the way*," repeated Genevieve, aiming her weapon straight for him.

"I heard you the first time," replied Odin.

Genevieve emptied her gun against his chest-- against-- not into-- not through. The bullets pancaked on impact above his 1488 and SS Bolt tattoos, then slipped down and hit the ground with a gentle *tink tink tink*.

Odin's smile broadened. Impossible bright blue light spluttered then shot out from his uninjured eye, tearing Genevieve in half. She screamed, and for a split second, existed as two separate parts of a whole, divided by a bloody trench ridden across her torso.

Thankfully-- and Madison hated herself for thinking it-- Santos died almost immediately after that.

The two sides of her slapped the cold concrete separately, the smell of burning meat filling the cramped, stolid air. Nadine was freaking out, even as Madison put herself between the villain and his target.

Odin stepped forward, even as blood pooled toward his feet. "Y'know, I gotta kill *you* now." He shrugged, wiping the sweat from his shiny bald head. He was still twitching, his movements jarring and awkward, like he was intoxicated. "I ain't ashamed of that."

Thoughts swirled around Madison's head. Was the information being fed into his brain that good? Was he some kind of kill-junkie? How could somebody, even a monster like this, get off on the wholesale slaughter of *anybody*?

"M-Madison?" murmured Nadine, unsure of what was about to happen.

Madison tried to slow the world down, carefully, and calmly folding her thoughts down on themselves-- just like her father taught her-- and the moment slowed down to the infinite. She wasn't a superpowered being. She was just a woman. Yes, a highly trained woman, but one holding a weapon that couldn't hope to pierce the skin of a Level 3 superhuman of Odin's calibre.

She had to keep the girl safe. So, what did she know? What could she do?

One: The heat vision only came out of his good eye.

Two: Those drones of his provided surveillance.

Three: The drones fed data directly into his brain.

One-Two-Three. That was enough to work with. Madison shoved Nadine to the ground and fired two shots. Huginn and Muninn squawked as their chassis were torn into, the aft portion that had trailed wires out into Odin's brain exploding in a burst of sparks.

"You fucking bitch! Nanaaaaa--"

The villain howled in anger and pain and unleashed his heat vision wildly, but then clutched his hands to his head as the wires connecting him to his drones withdrew from his skull. Madison dragged Nadine back up, and she directed her to retreat the way they came, handing her Santos' radio as she did so.

Turning back to face Odin, she grimaced as he fell to one knee, dry vomiting at the abrupt severance between his drones and his brain. She ran forward-- she couldn't afford to mess this up. He suddenly lurched up, grabbed her left arm by the wrist, and dragged it upwards, twisting her radius and ulna into pieces. If he held on for longer, he'd tear her arm out of the socket. Instead, he released her on the upswing, so she flew into the air as he howled, "Fucking bitch fucking--!"

Plasterboard and dust billowed out as she hit the ceiling, and she screamed despite herself as she collided with the ground. Odin was still clutching his head, and though she couldn't see, at the rear of his head, translucent fluid seeped out of the damaged ports burrowed into his skull.

"Kill you kill everyone fucking fucking--"

Madison refused to stay down. Even though her left arm was completely useless and hanging an inch lower than her right, she pulled herself up and charged forward, shoving her weapon into his right eye socket just as the left eye began to spark up, ready to incinerate her. Her heart pounding like an over-produced Metallica track, she squeezed the trigger, and Odin reeled back.

With the villain staggered, Madison pushed forward. She had to keep the pressure on. She had to know if her guess was correct. Odin swatted wildly at her with one hand, and with the other, he repeatedly slapped the side of his head as if he were trying to stop a ringing in his ears.

Madison avoided Odin's chaotic swings, and when he turned his head so that the ports screwed into the back of his skull were visible, she slipped under his arm and emptied the rest of her gun's clip into the mechanism, hoping to god that her hunch was right.

One bullet flew straight through his head and out his cataracted eye, thick subcutaneous meat following the projectile as it excited. The other bullets bounced around the interior of his invulnerable skull, making soup of his not-so invulnerable brain, and he keeled over backwards.

Madison nearly retched at the sight of blood and brain bubbling out from his eye socket, but then she collapsed. Clutching at her mangled arm, she passed out from the agony in her shoulder and wrist, unconsciousness a welcome respite from the pain.

CITIES ON FIRE

CITIES ON FIRE

FBI DATABASE - METAHUMAN POWER RANKINGS
Last Accessed 10/05/2033 (US)

On Thursday, July 4th 1776, when Thomas Jefferson wrote "all men are created equal", he could not have dreamt of the concept of "metahumanity", the next stage of humanity's evolution..

The dawn of the superhuman age arrived with concepts and ideas far beyond the scope of the Declaration of Independence, and even now, the scientific field is still playing catch up, trying desperately to wrap their heads around something that, for all intents and purposes, is impossible. Brand new schools of thought are being built from the ground up every day, all to keep up with the gifts manifesting in the world's population at an accelerated rate.

The following is the generalised breakdown of the GAO RUI METAHUMAN POWER FRAMEWORK, officially adopted by the FBI and other law enforcement agencies across the globe five years ago (2028).

Level 0 - HARMLESS
Level 1 - PERSON BREAKER
Level 2 - STREET BREAKER
Level 3 - CITY BREAKER
Level 4 - WORLD BREAKER
Level 5 - COSMIC BREAKER (hypothetical)

Find resources pertaining Doctor Gao Rui's work here, including his speech to FBI Special Agents at Quantico

CITIES ON FIRE

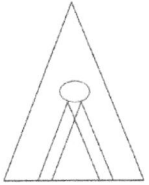

CHAPTER 2: INDUCTION
LOCATION: ALEPH ACTIVE INTELLIGENCE HQ, NEW YORK

Cold fingertips on either side of her face suddenly turned hot, and Madison jerked forward as the sensation drove rivets of pain straight into her brain. She heard a man's surprised gasp at her reaction, and spun around to see a nervous looking gentleman standing behind her, shaking out his hands as if to dislodge the same pins and needles sensation she could feel through her head.

"Ah, crap, fuck, crap," she mumbled, rattling her jaw in an attempt to regain some sense of normality in her face. "Why's my face *numb*, Jesus Christ..."

The woman sat in front of Madison smiled warmly. "Welcome back. It does get easier the more you do it. We perform psychic scans biweekly, just to ensure no one's slipped something naughty in while you weren't paying attention. Psychic worms, telepathic programming, you know, the crazy bullshit that'll start sounding like nothing special in a few months of working here. That goes all the way to the top of the food chain, not just for us grunts."

"What--? What're you--?" spluttered Madison. She looked around frantically, trying to get her bearings, but she felt utterly lost, and it didn't help that the woman sitting across the table from her looked so familiar, yet her identity remained so elusive.

The three of them were situated in an interview room, all light greys and dullness, with a large mirror reflecting her panicked expression back to her from over the woman's shoulder. There were files on the table between them that bore her name-- photos spanning her NYPD career to her present-day FBI assignment. Before-Madison and after-Madison pictures of Odin spread out for all to see.

Noting her discomfort, the woman in front of her calmly said, "I told you it would be disorientating the first time."

Madison shook her head vehemently, trying to grasp the extent of what she'd just experienced. "...The first time?"

"Your first psychic check-up," said the man behind her. He repositioned himself next to the woman so Madison didn't have to keep swivelling her head whenever his anxious voice chirped up. He was in his mid-twenties, thin-- no, *gaunt*-- with a face she once again couldn't place, but for some reason, she felt like she really should know who he was. He tried to smile warmly, but it came across as forced. "It's a delicate procedure, and like I said before, the first is always the worst, but next time it'll be a breeze."

"You're safe, Special Agent Myers. This feeling of nausea will pass, as will the temporary amnesia." She spoke with a clipped British accent, a regional accent poorly hidden behind tight consonants and harsh vowels. "I'm Kishana Muldair, this is Henry Gardner. We're with Aleph."

"Aleph? Why would the superhero-police want to take me?" asked Madison.

Kishana cleared her throat and tapped on the photo of Odin from after his encounter with the FBI agent.

"Don't worry. It'll come back to you shortly. That was the final stage of the interview process. What good would our recruits be if we permanently blitzed their brains? Henry?"

"What do you mean 'come back to me'? What's-- going-- on--"

Madison's world dropped out from under her.

An hour ago, Henry was pacing around the interview room, getting ready to get to work. Kishana had excused herself, but said she'd be back before the process started.

"Are you comfortable?" asked Henry, unscrewing the lid of his water bottle.

Madison rolled her shoulders forward and flicked her head from side to side before placing her hands palm down on the table in front of her. "As I'll ever be, I guess. Explain what you're going to do?"

Henry took a heavy glug from his water and wiped his mouth with the back of his sleeve. "It's pretty straight forward. We have to make sure you're on the up and up before we give you access to all the good stuff. We've had people try to infiltrate the organisation before, so we introduced psychic screenings. You passed the surface scans, but this is the deep dive. I'm going to go through your thoughts with a fine-tooth comb, looking for anything that might compromise us. To do this, I archive your short term memory, and I use that as the entry ramp into your long term memory. This is where we find out if you are who you say you are."

"I thought you'd already checked up on me?" said Madison.

"Oh, we have. But maybe things are going on in your brain that you aren't even aware of. And maybe somebody slipped something in since the surface scans and before this one. You could be a sleeper agent for Basilisk for all we know."

Madison swallowed hard. She hoped she wasn't a sleeper agent for any terrorist organisations. She felt like that would suck.

"Now, I'm afraid this will hurt quite a bit, but the pain won't last long. When you come out of it, your memory will have experienced a quick factory reset. You'll be confused as all heck, but that'll pass too. The first is always the worst. You won't even notice the rest."

"Sounds terrifying," said Madison.

"I'd be worried if it didn't," said Henry. He latticed his fingers and they clicked audibly as he flexed them out. "Right. This is going to hurt."

"This is a *job interview*," said Madison, her memories falling back into place, the unsettling realisation that the answers to her many questions were just out of reach in her mind's eye, hidden by a bank of mental fog, causing her to question her sanity for a split second.

"More like dotting the I's and crossing the T's," said Kishana. She took a box of tissues and offered them to Madison. "Here."

Confused, Madison touched her cheek and realised she was crying. Genevieve. Her partner. She died horribly three months ago, and Madison thought she'd been able to suppress her feelings of grief surrounding the incident. But the scan must have dislodged something, because she was suddenly overwhelmed, and the tears were followed by huge, heaving breaths as she tried to get her emotions back to an even keel.

Henry pulled a pained expression. "Emotional echoes. Any recent trauma is like a scab, and unfortunately, the scan tears them right off."

"Jeez, th-thanks for the warning," replied Madison, wiping her eyes. "Fuck…" she whispered.

Henry met Kishana's gaze and said, "I'm all done here. I've loaded everything in; so just say the word and the rest is business as usual."

"Thank you, Henry," said the woman.

Henry exited, and after he left, Madison collected herself and said, "I still don't remember your name."

"Kishana Muldair, Chief of Staff for Active Intelligence," said the woman. She extended her hand, and Madison accepted it. "Pleasure to meet you again."

"I love giving this tour."

Kishana and Madison stepped out of the interview room and arrived in a large, open-spaced office, the likes of which you'd see if you stumbled into Google's headquarters or some fresh, new tech start-up. The walls were all white, and dozens of winding corridors spread out like tentacles from the vast space they proceeded to walk through.

People moved from office to office, across the hallways and down others, jabbering, referring to the tablets they held, holding bundles of paperwork and more. It was all *go-go-go*, and there was something about the atmosphere that made Madison excited.

As she continued to speak, Kishana led Madison toward a sealed door and brushed her hand across a panel that beeped quietly in proximity. The door slid open with a hiss, and they kept going.

"Okay, so, questions and answers. That guy you just met? Henry Gardner. He's head of our psychic division and Director Stone's TPOP-- Telepathic Operative. He's responsible for making sure the secrets inside the director's brain don't get pick-pocketed by a nimble brained telepath when he isn't looking. Thankfully, for his sanity and ours, telepathy is one of those rare gifts that doesn't manifest often."

"You have a... 'psi-division'? For law enforcement? Evidence gathered telepathically is inadmissible in court," said Madison.

Kishana shook her head. "Look at you, goody-two-shoes. Of course, I know that. *'A telepath's own feelings toward a suspect, positive or negative, can affect the information gathered from their readings'*. That ruling was bullshit, but we live with it. There's more to what they do than what you think. I just wish more of them worked for us. Ours is a division of about... seven, at last count. Enough to do what we need them to do."

"What did Gardner mean by 'loaded'? What did he load?" asked Madison.

"Standard operating procedure. It's called *'Blue Boxing'*. There's a small package of data in your brain that contains-- among other things-- your logins, the customer handbook. I say the word, and it's released, and you're up to date. If I say a different word, then it's deleted like it was never there. Saves you having to read twenty-seven different piles of documentation. There are also other benefits. You'll find them out soon enough."

Madison's brow furrowed. Muldair made it sound simple. She wondered what the magic word could possibly be. And other benefits? Why did they enjoy making everything so mysterious? Didn't they have a world to protect? The Chief of Staff kept talking. While Madison was listening, she was also marvelling at the working space she was being led through. Compared to this, the FBI's New York office was the equivalent of working in a hole in the ground, all things considered.

"Director Stone's STRATOP, James Winter, is currently MIA, else you'd have met him too. He always liked meeting the new hires, even when we were at our busiest."

"MIA?" said Madison.

Kishana nodded. "Going on six months now. His whereabouts are on our active investigation board, but so far, no luck. We just hope he's gone on one of his impromptu sabbaticals, but in this business... well. We've not stopped looking."

She clicked her fingers. "That reminds me." She rummaged through the inside pocket of her jacket and withdrew a black case, the size of a smartphone. It clicked open to reveal a dark grey, domino-sized token. "We need to do this before we go any further."

"What is it?" asked Madison.

"The witches and wizards down in the Magic Department whipped it up. Then the tech boys and girls did their thing. We call it a Skeleton Key."

Madison flatly replied, "...You have a Magic Department."

"Any more surprising than a Psychic Department? You'll love Ode, Emrys runs the team, but she's who I end up grabbing a pint with after work. Drinks me under the table...."

"Things seem pretty loose around here," said Madison.

"Get the job done to the best of your ability. And when it matters, make whatever you do count. You want me to treat you like the suits treated you in the FBI or the NYPD, I won't do it. I've had enough of those kinds of arseholes making lives miserable for enough lifetimes to last. I'm sure you have too."

She remembered Detective Scott Davis, her partner from her time in the NYPD, and the positions he put her in.

He was one of the reasons she took the job with the FBI.

She was one of the reasons he was forced to take early retirement.

She cleared her throat. "Okay. Yeah. So, this thing?"

"It serves three functions." Kishana held out her hand and began counting out with her fingers. "1) It's a GPS tracker. Helps us know where you are at all times. 2) It's an ID tag, so you can access Aleph locations, be them this big bloody place or the safehouses and secure locations across the globe-- "

"If what's-his-face, James Winter? If James Winter had one of these, how come he's MIA?"

"Oh, we found his Skeleton Key. It was in a storage container headed for China on one of those gigantic Panamax cargo ships. Intact. Separate to the man. That's why we have him down as MIA and tasked a team to find him. Hopefully, he's okay. He does shit like this sometimes. But it's.... well, it's weird. James is a weirdo, but this is weird, even for him."

"You think he was kidnapped?" asked Madison.

Kishana exhaled resignedly. "We don't know. God, you ask a lot of questions. But he's one of us, and we're dedicating resources to finding him, which we'd do for any of our people. If someone was able to get the drop on him... that's scary in itself. But don't worry. We don't lose folks often. Or at all. James always had to be an exception to any given rule."

Madison suddenly didn't feel confident about her future job retention but hoped she didn't broadcast the unnerved feeling rumbling deep in her belly. She had never heard the name James Winter before, and she prided herself on knowing stuff.

Madison had spent many days combing through the metahuman data kept by the FBI during her tenure. She'd also trawled through the infinitely less organised NYPD's meta-database in the wake of her own experiences facing off with so-called supervillains during her detective days.

"Sorry. I hear jigsaw pieces, and I always want to put them in the right place, you know?"

Kishana shrugged. "It's one of the reasons we've brought you onboard. Anyway, the third and final feature of the Skeleton Key: It prevents you from being possessed. Or more accurately, it makes sure you're locked in your body, and nobody can push you out."

What did *that* even mean? "And possession... that's an ongoing concern?" Madison replied, shocked by the matter-of-fact delivery of information that seemed as other-worldly as the statement itself.

"Not yet, but we have to cover all the bases. Imagine the amount of power we wield. We're the line between humanity and superhumanity. In case of emergency, break the glass."

Kishana's head bobbed from side to side as she concerned her next point.

"Sure, the Meridian are the so-called last line of defence, but they're the last line of defence for *everything, everywhere*. Suppose there's actual police work to do, actual investigation. In that case, you think they're going to spend their valuable time doing the legwork? And if there's a problem we can deal with, without them, why shouldn't we deal with it?"

Madison nodded with a level of enthusiasm she didn't think herself capable. "That's... actually a relief to hear. Some people I've worked with, they treat superheroes as a crutch. Detectives and Special Agents, whoever, they dismiss things because they think it's something for Majestic to deal with or, uh, for Phantasma to clear up. And I hate it. I hate the idea that we've stagnated because of superheroes, that we've slowed down because of them. I'm ranting. I just hate it. And this sounds... what you've said... it sounds fantastic. It really does."

Kishana looked her up and down, and Madison could see the wheels turning in her head. "Here's a thing I think you'll understand. With the spike in metahuman manifestations, everybody is stretched thin. Not just the authorities meant to police the populace, or the corrections services tasked with keeping the worst of us locked up, but society as a whole. Like you said, a crutch. We use superheroes to hold us up, but really, having them run around is holding us down. Everything revolves around reacting to the metahuman population and not going beyond it. It's 2033! And I've read papers by scientists saying we've stagnated. We slowed down, and we stagnated, and we're decades behind where we should be as a civilisation. People say it's because everyone's more concerned with keeping the metahumans in check rather than looking toward the stars anymore. I think that's sad, don't you?"

"I guess so..." said Madison.

"So, Aleph is bridging the gap. One of the frustrating things about our operations is that we're still using tech designed by Professor Ultra back in the day. It was state of the art then, and it's cutting edge now, but everybody else's stuff is the same level. There's no advantage. Still, everything we do revolves around protecting and advancing. Keep the world safe, but if there's a chance we can parlay some of the good we do here back out into the world, we'll do it. Science Division analyses artefacts we find during investigations and postulates practical applications that can be made with them. Investigation methods we come up with on the fly become part of day-to-day policing because if it can work here, it can work out there. Even Medical are working on some stuff that will blow your mind. Aleph is here to police a threat that goes beyond our understanding, but every now and then, we claw back an inch, and we can make the world a better place because of it. That's the real question here: Do you want to make the world a better place?"

"That's all I've ever wanted," replied Madison.

"Well then, welcome to your dream job," said Kishana.

"So, what about that?" asked Madison, gesturing toward the Skeleton Key.

"Ah yes, firstly, you need to remember that it's magic. It's going inside your body, but it's not surgical. When the Skeleton Key first goes in, it feels like a pressure, but the feeling passes really quickly."

She offered it to Madison, and the new recruit reluctantly accepted it. As she closed her fingers around the domino-sized piece, the warmth of the strange material pulsed against her palm. "Why is it hot?"

"Because magic, that's why. Close your hand around it, make a fist, and think 'activation' as hard as you can. Then it'll sink into your palm and settle just beneath your wrist, between your bones." She tapped the centre of her wrist; no sign, or scar, indicating anything had been implanted. "And then it's set, and you won't even remember it's there most days."

"That sounds *horrid*," said Madison.

"Yeah, I know, I know, but it's fast," said Kishana. "Go ahead. Remember, 'activation', as hard as you can."

Madison clenched her fist and thought 'activation' thoughts. Almost immediately, there was a pressure in her hand, and she cringed. It wasn't like an injection, and that might have been preferable.

It felt like the domino-sized object was pushing against her palm with enough force that it might split the skin. She was convinced that if her hand opened, that's what she would see. Still, Madison wasn't in the mood for visible, Cronenbergian body horror on her first day at her new job.

She kept thinking about activation even as the pain spiked, pushing memories of *Videodrome* out of focus. Then the pressure abruptly ceased, and there was no more pain. She felt a fluttering in her wrist, like an itch beneath the skin that quickly passed, and then she opened her hand.

"Are you okay?" asked Kishana.

Madison held her palm up. There was a rectangular marking on her skin. It could have been the result of an object sinking into her hand or the result of holding onto something too tightly. Either way, the Skeleton Key was gone.

"That is so *weird*," said Madison.

"Check if it works?" said Kishana, gesturing toward a sealed door and the inert panel next to it.

"Are you going to possess me?" asked Madison, approaching the door. She looked at her hand again, feeling a little stupid, and then waved it at the panel. The door slid open, and Kishana walked past her into the next corridor.

"Nah, that's later."

The pair came to a halt in another domed chamber and watched as dozens of people came and went through the various corridors branching off it. There were more sealed doors with the same panels Kishana had to buzz them through earlier, while others were less sophisticated, and people passed through them with ease.

There was so much space in the open-plan design of the place. Balconies overhead that housed desks where people worked away, television screens mounted to walls that showed various international news channels. It felt like they were in a centralised hub of action and information, with everything at their fingertips if they needed it. People were walking, and some were flying. It was a hive of meta-activity, something Madison hadn't expected when she first agreed to the interview.

"This entire complex is Director Stone's headquarters. His 'castle'. Every director-- there are four, two for each division-- has a castle, a top-secret location that the other directors don't know about."

"And we're in New York?" said Madison, trying not to get

distracted by the sight of the ripped, half-naked man flapping golden wings behind her new boss' head so he could get to one of the higher offices.

"I told you it'd come back to you. For security reasons, the directors' main headquarters is classified, even to other directors. There are shared safehouses across the world, shared caches, whatever we need to get the job done in whatever part of the globe, but this is his castle, as I said."

Madison gestured toward the vast spaces and bright colours swathed across the walls. "It looks like I'm about to design a search engine or something. Does this place have, I dunno, an office pet or something?"

Muldair chuckled. "Yeah, it's a bit much, isn't it? To be fair, it beats some of the holes I've worked out of in my life. But Director Stone likes it, and considering we're deep underground, it does give the illusion we work somewhere like San Fran most of the time, so that's a relief. And no, no pets. You're a dog person, right?"

She nodded but then asked, "We're underground?"

"You don't remember the lift down? Lucky you."

Kishana indicated Madison to come to a stop in the centre of the room they'd arrived in, and then she motioned around them.

"This is the main reception. We call it the cathedral because look at that fucking dome. From here, you can get to where you need to go. You make the comparison to Google, but it's not far off. Director Stone is co-director of Aleph's intelligence side, with a focus on going out into the world and gathering it."

"...Makes sense," replied Madison.

Muldair continued, "His opposite, Director Martin, her division works' passive' intelligence. They comb through data from every single UN member's criminal database, along with the dark web, message boards, whatever... wherever... and they try to predict trouble. So, yeah, a lot of the time, it's a lot of folks wearing prescription glasses sat at computers trying to figure out what's going to end the world next."

"Uh, didn't the UK get in trouble last time they tried to do pre-crime?"

Devi Patel waited impatiently for the interstitial to finish playing so she could read the news. That's all she wanted. That's all she'd ever wanted, really, but the world seemed to oppose her at every turn, telling the news twisted into telling stories, and that was something she hated more than anything.

The producer stood behind the camera and teleprompter and began to count her down. They were going live in 5, 4…

"Good afternoon. We are still waiting to go live at 10 Downing Street, as the Prime Minister is scheduled to give an update on the accusations that the British government authorised an off-the-books metahuman program designed to invade the privacy of British citizens-- an accusation that the Prime Minister vehemently denies. This comes after an anonymous whistle-blower leaked documents to various media outlets-- *aaaand* we're being told that the Prime Minister is finally making his way to the podium-- so let's go there now:"

British Prime Minister Clive Woodingham walked briskly toward the podium outside 10 Downing Street, tamping down his tie when the wind threatened to pull it free from inside his jacket. The street was full of journalists who were edgily awaiting the man elected to govern the country, and they were all acutely aware that he was thirty-five minutes late to the press conference he himself had called.

That was nothing new.

"Good afternoon to everybody here, and to everybody watching at home. I will keep this short as we all have more important things to be getting on with: The accusation that this government has taken part in some sort of 'clandestine scheme' to build a machine to read people's minds is utter hogwash. Plain and simple. These are quite clearly falsehoods put forward by odious, bad actors. The fact that previously reliable outlets would report on such unsubstantiated and unfounded claims shows how far down the rabbit hole our own media have fallen. The British people can rest assured that thorough investigations will be made into the severe breaches of journalistic standards on display these last few days--"

The bravado spilt out of the PM as if a child had started an outdoor tap on a hot summer's day and forgotten which way to turn it off. This was audacity as chemical warfare, filling up the room with bilious misdirection and moral indignation that would cause anybody with asthma to struggle to breathe.

But then, the PM's nose began to bleed. He dabbed at his nostril with the base of his thumb, not paying it much attention, and not looking to see that his bottom knuckle was now streaked red.

"--Err, that is to say, yes, actually, yes, it's all true. I did, in fact, give authorisation to government officials to allocate funds for a project designed to-- to weaponise the psychic abilities of any metahumans they could get their hands on. When the project was a success, I directed the project leaders to begin reading the minds of people I deemed to be, err, enemies of the government, to see if there were any skeletons, anything in their closets, so to speak, that we could leverage against them to continue this party's time in power."

There was a shocked silence across the sea of journalists assembled in front of him. Before the PM's assistant could usher him away from the podium and the dozens of cameras beaming his face into millions of homes, journalists began shouting questions; and as if transfixed, as if a deer seconds away from impact with a car on a dark, wooded road, hi-vis lights on max, he stayed planted to the spot, his eyes wide and the answers flowing.

"--Members of your cabinet have gone on record saying the leaked documents were a fabrication, are you saying they were lying?"

"Yes, err, the edict from the Chief Whip-- at my instruction, of course, was to categorically and emphatically deny everything."

"--Your government has begun legal proceedings against the outlets who refused to follow the D-Notice on this story--"

"We intended for the D-Notice to shut the story down before it reached the public, but if we let its release stand uncontested then we would look guilty, which we are. Of course we bloody are. What am... *what am I saying?*"

"--Prime Minister--!"

Woodingham was finally pulled away from the podium and

ushered away from the baying crowds of journalists by his panicked assistant and unsure bodyguards. Truth, like blood, was in the water, and the media, like sharks, wanted more of it.

"--*Prime Minister--!*"

The feed cut back to the studio, where Devi Patel sat in stunned silence. The camera lingered on her while her producer waved his arms around in her direction. Her brain booted back up. Words began to come out of her mouth that she didn't have time to process. It was just what felt right to say at the time.

"That... that was the Prime Minister... admitting that the documents outlining the government's illegal superhuman experimentation were in fact real, and not fake as he, and members of his cabinet claimed. We... were also served a D-Notice by the government-- a D-Notice effectively being a 'cease and desist' on telling the news on the grounds of national security-- and capitulated to their request." Her producer was shaking his head vehemently, then made a gesture to wrap up the segment and stop speaking. "We need to hold those in power accountable for their actions, and I'm sure that this will not be the end of--"

The transmission ended, replaced immediately by a close-up on the haggard face of an unknown woman. A moment ago, households were watching the news, or a game show, or a soap, but now, without warning, their feed cut out and was replaced by this woman. A fuzz of hair, barely just grown back, covered the top of her scalp, and you could see the outline of her skull just beneath her skin. There was no meat on her, but her eyes burned with the kind of intensity that came with intent, with the need to share something with the world. The camera captured all of that, even though it only showed her from the neck up.

<*"Hello! I'm sorry to be interrupting your regularly scheduled telly. I won't keep you long. You don't know me, and I don't know you, but I wanted to fix that. You see, I'm the person who leaked all that stuff about Project Oraculum to the media. And because that didn't work, I'm also the one who just made it so that no politician, or person in a position of authority, can ever lie to us, the people, ever again."*>

<*"I lost over a year of my life because this government wanted to*

use my telepathic abilities to further their own agenda. They took us, cut us open, and did... horrible things... all so they could... they could...">

Tears began to well in those bright eyes of hers. Off-camera, someone dabbed them away with a tissue, and she looked at them thankfully, nodding in appreciation. <*"Would you...?"*> she asked.

<*"Sure,"*> came a voice just out of frame.

The camera wheeled back to reveal that the woman was lying in a hospital bed, propped up in front of the camera by a small mountain of pillows. The most striking thing about her appearance was the fact that she had no arms. Beneath the bedsheet, it was apparent that she had no legs, either.

<*"This government vivisected me, and dozens of others. They took things from us that can never be given back. All because they wanted to steal people's most precious commodity-- our thoughts, our dreams-- and use them against us. It was only a freak accident that allowed me to escape. And when I woke up, and found out what they'd done to us? I couldn't let that stand. So, yes, from this point forward, using the same technology the government planned to violate your minds with, I made it so that no UK politician can lie ever again, no matter how much they want to. This is just a small thing. I could do so much worse. You'll never see my face again. You'll never see the full extent of what they did to me and my friends. But if anybody tries to perform these kinds of monstrous acts against the population again... they will feel the full weight of my anger. I promise you that. Good night."*>

"...And it changed the face of British politics forever," said Kishana.

Madison couldn't read her new boss's expression. The 'debacle' in British politics was still ongoing, resulting from an off-the-books program that failed spectacularly and resulted in every single British politician rendered unable to lie to the electorate. After the corruption behind the rogue operation was rooted out, an emergency election was held. The landscape was flipped on its head because no matter what the politicians said, no matter what they tried to lie about or spin, all that came out was the truth.

"But that's by the by. I think everyone in politics could use a psychic shock to the system that leaves them with only the truth to back them up, don't you?"

"I guess..." said Madison.

The now-former-FBI agent rubbed her temples. This was a lot to take in, and she was already suffering from what Genevieve would call 'fuzzy brain'.

Genevieve.

As the memory of her partner in the FBI floated to the forefront of her mind, everything else finally fell into place. She remembered the aftermath of Odin's attack on the mall. The events that brought her here today. She'd jumped through whatever hoops placed in front of her by the organisation, and today was the final in a long line of trials they'd set for her. She just wondered if it would be worth it in the end.

The last two months of her life had been a whirlwind. First, she took down a super Nazi. Then she was plucked from the resulting desk assignment-- the FBI couldn't have an agent out in the field after publicly putting down a figurehead of a neo-Nazi organisation-- and arrived here.

Psych evals. Physicals. Gun ranges. Critical thinking. Every single wringer you could twist someone through, Aleph had done so. All because O'Bannon called it a fantastic opportunity for her, and it was made clear that her field career in the FBI would be-- how did he put it?-- 'limited' moving forward.

Kishana cleared her throat. "...Now, here's the thing, Madison. Incidents involving metahuman threats are automatically sent over to us. We try to take the lead on such investigations or operations, but unfortunately, due to some territorial pissing, we only found out about the threats against the Vice President's daughter from the FBI after-action report. And the bravery and ingenuity you exhibited in the face of a Level 3 threat astounded Director Stone." She paused. "Do you know what other people have done in the situation you found yourself in?"

"What's that?"

"Died," said Kishana. "After shitting themselves."

"You're joking."

"Level 3 aren't a joke. They're strong as fuck, and some can be twice as mean. You lucked out; Odin was even meaner than that. And you took him down, *pop-pop-pop*," she punctuated that last point with a finger pointed to her head like a pistol. "Anyway, your main responsibilities will involve fieldwork, investigation, that kind of thing. Active operations roll over to the other side of the coin, so you won't need to armour up and take on the end of the world, but you'll help track down whatever we need to prevent the said apocalypse."

"But what about the Meridian? How do they factor into things?" asked Madison.

Kishana held up her hands like she was reading a billboard. "The Meridian. *Earth's last line of defence against the forces of evil*. Great when the sky is falling, or aliens are invading. Incredibly good at being firemen. But do you really think Majestic is going to get down into the muck and investigate rumours of a xenobiological entity worshipping cult in Alabama? No, he'll rock up when said entity blossoms into a god-thing intent on devouring the collective human consciousness." She took a breath. "So, that's my life. And that'll be your life too if you take the job."

Without pausing for thought, Madison asked, "When do I start?"

Kishana smiled then continued to walk, leading her down another corridor to parts unknown. "To begin with, you'll be working with a two-man team of data analysts. We'll head to their office now. We search for the best and brightest minds, and these two are just that. You'll be their point man, their boots on the ground. If data needs collecting, you'll be the one with the net. Interviews. Evidence collection. Bouncing around the country and playing nice with law enforcement agencies who need their egos massaged."

Madison's brow furrowed. "… I'm capable of more."

"And you'll be utilised accordingly, but you have to start somewhere." Kishana shook her head. "'*Capable of more*', fuck me, you took down a Level 3. Like you have to remind us you're capable…"

After a few minutes, the pair reached a corridor that branched off into several open-plan offices. Madison peered inside each as they strolled past and noted that everyone inside had done something different with their working areas. She spotted standing desks, sofas, and arcade machines.

Once again, Madison was reminded of tech companies and how they tried so hard to be hip and how she kind of hated it. But that wasn't all there was to the workspaces in this place. Walls were adorned with papers, photos, post-its and pushpins, as well as wall-mounted screens that trickled data as it accumulated through the day. Case files and notes littered desks, pictures of superheroes and supervillains. She wondered how much Aleph knew about the world they policed and what the Meridian thought about it.

"Okay, here we are. Before we go any further, you were probably wondering what the activation word was for the data package sitting in your head?" said Kishana.

"I mean, sure, yeah," replied Madison.

"The word is '*discombobulate*'," said Kishana, crisp and clear, careful not to struggle over any unexpected syllables coming out of her mouth. And when the *ate* growled out from her lips, information flooded Madison's brain like it had always been there. She knew her access codes, rota, and payroll number. That was an interesting one to suddenly strike her. She knew where her parking space was, as well as a list of Aleph's secondary locations across various cities and towns.

She was suddenly altogether in tune with what was required and expected of her, and it felt good.

While the information was still processing in Madison's brain, Kishana rapped her knuckles against the ajar glass door that led into the spacious, open-plan office. There were three desks, two currently occupied and shoved next to each other, while the third was sat empty in the corner. The two desk's occupants-- a man and a woman-- looked up from where they were working almost in surprise, yanked from their focus on whatever they were working on.

"…Uh," said the man.

Madison thought he looked like he had just woken up, all small eyes and squinting, but she could see the glasses discarded on a pile of papers in front of him, which he clearly needed to put back on. He was slack jawed from befuddlement, but with a sharp elbow from his female compatriot, his bottom lip snapped shut.

The woman gave a sarcastic salute and said, "Hey, boss. I promise we've been expecting you."

The man was slight and pale, a wire brush of curly black hair atop his head that would, along with his pasty pallor, have given him the appearance of a Japanese ghost in the right-- wrong?-- light. He was dressed smartly, a shirt without the tie and a pair of pale blue trousers that he rounded out with bright red canvas shoes. Madison found herself searching, and sure enough, hanging off the end of the desk was a tie in a colour that clashed horribly with his footwear.

Taking in Madison as much as Madison was her, the woman sat back in her chair, her afro framing her head like a halo. Her face told a story of violent youth, a broken nose that never healed properly, a scar over her eye cutting through a brow that had never quite regrown. She dressed like she was going to a funeral, all black and white.

"This is Special Agent Madison Myers. She's your new field operative. Myers, this is Loretta Hawkins and James Johnson. Not as inept as they look, not by a long shot."

"Thanks?" said James.

The young man scrambled around his desk for his glasses then pulled them on, but not before dislodging a pile of papers and causing an avalanche of notes. Narrowly missing being caught in the deluge, he extended his hand, and Madison took it, smiling at the gesture. Except, he wasn't paying her any attention as he limply shook her hand. Instead, he looked at Kishana and said, "I thought Loretta and I were going to get more field time?"

"Now's not the time for that conversation," said Kishana.

"But you said--" continued James.

"Now's. Not. The time," Kishana repeated sharply.

James wanted to say more, but Loretta cleared her throat. That was enough to adjust his priorities. He looked at Madison and said, "Hawkins and I are kind of the dream team, Myers. You better not ruin our rep around here by being awful."

"Please ignore him," said Loretta. She shook Madison's hand, as well, but projected a warmth her partner lacked. "He thinks he's funny, but he doesn't have a filter. HR has a whole shelf for his screw-ups."

"Don't worry. I worked major crimes in the NYPD, so it's going to take more than awkward workplace banter to shake my confidence," replied Madison.

Loretta smiled despite herself. "Boys club?"

"At the best of times," said Madison, in an exaggeratedly forlorn manner.

"And this definitely isn't," said James, gesturing to the three women surrounding him.

Muldair shook her head. "And, on that note... IT will be down later to get you set up on the network, but I've asked this pair to get you up to speed on their current caseload anyway. As long as the world doesn't end, this next month or so will be admin heavy, and you'll be drowned in paperwork, but after that, you'll be back out in the world. Investigations report directly to me, so we'll be seeing a lot of each other. Director Stone will be down at some point, but right now, he's in Washington, briefing the President."

"Oh, what about? Anything juicy?" asked James.

Kishana sighed. It was the sigh of someone who'd gone through this a thousand times with this guy, but he never seemed to learn his damn lesson. "Mind your own, Jim. The boss wants the read book on the Tiamat situation on his desk by the time he's back, so focus on that."

"We're just wrapping it up," said Loretta.

Kishana gestured toward Madison, "Good. Lead with that. Welcome to the team, Special Agent Myers. You won't regret this." She made a swift exit, leaving the three new colleagues alone in the office.

"How's your head?" asked Loretta.

James made a beeline to the water cooler in the corner and poured her a glass. "I remember my first psychic screening. It gave both of us a nosebleed. Henry still doesn't like talking to me after that."

"Should I be worried?" asked Madison. She accepted the glass and took a sip. "Thanks."

James smiled smugly. Not maliciously mind, but not humbly either. "I have an eidetic memory. I remember everything."

Loretta laughed at his casual tone. "Don't bury the lede, man!" Still smiling, she glanced back at Madison. "He's a meta. That's his superpower. He remembers shit. He has an unfair advantage over everybody because whatever he reads, he retains. It's what makes him damn good at his job. But don't tell him I said that."

"… I'm standing right here," said James, smirking.

"God, I guess… I imagine for a psychic, it was like being hit by a ton of bricks, right?" said Madison.

"Pretty much," said James, as he bent over his desk and started rummaging through his drawers.

Loretta continued, "The screening is just searching for brainwashing, malice or the kind of invisible, telepathic sutures that can come with psychic interference. But Jim over here can't help himself, so poor Henry got a brain full. Every now and then, I still see him talking with his hands like this idiot over here."

"Wow, I'd never thought about it like that," said Madison. The idea of someone taking on aspects of your personality due to telepathic bleed-through made sense, but how disconcerting for the mind reader-- and the mind *read*-- to experience it?

"Why would you?" asked James.

"As you can probably tell, Jimmy over there is a bit of a smug a-hole," said Loretta.

"It's true," he agreed.

"But ignore him, and you'll be the better for it. Or, even better than *that*, give him a slap, and he'll quit it soon enough. I've been reading about you. About all the shit you've done in the NYPD, the FBI… you're one unlucky lady."

"What do you mean?"

"Well… I don't want to rehash your entire law enforcement career… but the Gravel arrest, for one."

Madison's shoulders ached at the mention of that. "Yeah, you learn to roll with the punches."

"Or falling off a building, yeah?" said Loretta.

"That too. But hopefully, this job won't demand *that much* of me," said Madison.

"You never know. The world might be ending tomorrow. Did you see the UN thing?"

"The Tiamat thing?"

Loretta nodded. "We're working on the read book. Gathering every bit of data we have on the situation for the powers-that-be. Contextualising the UN speech, giving background. Not that Director Stone needs it, he's been involved with them since their spymaster defected."

James clicked his fingers. " Want to take a look?"

"Sure," replied Madison. She wondered if this was how it was going to be, pivoting from one topic to another, her head spinning as she tried to keep up? She dismissed the thought. This was new but by no means insurmountable. Her track record spoke to that. She watched as James held up a television remote and turned on the large television screen behind her. The paused footage was from the United Nations General Assembly floor, the date and time stamp showing it was from the previous day.

Delegates from across the world chatted amongst themselves while others took their seats. It was a packed house for the first committee of the General Assembly of the United Nations, but Disarmament and International Security was a hot ticket in the world of international politics, and everybody wanted a piece of the action. They would be called to order soon enough, so old friends and acquaintances who hadn't seen each other in some time-- or since the last session was called-- had time to catch-up.

Before the President of the General Assembly-- currently the ambassador from Australia-- could make his way to the stage, a bright blue light illuminated the speaker's podium. The assembled ambassadors fell silent as a loud buzzing filled the air, and a split second later, a figure formed from within the light, beginning featureless, until an unfamiliar face became visible.

Members of the United Nations' Department for Safety and Security rushed forward and took up position at the base of the stage, but before they could begin barking orders for the figure to stand down, the figure began to speak.

<"I am Ambassador Donghai Sòng, duly appointed representative of the shining nation of Tiamat. This is the first and only time I will speak before the General Assembly of the United Nations, an organisation that severed ties with my homeland upon its liberation from fascist rule. An act that has not been forgotten by our glorious leader, Apsu Liu.">

Miraculously, the man's silky voice boomed out across the vast auditorium, and instantly translated into the native tongue of the listeners. It didn't matter where they were sat, or if they were amongst a group of people who didn't share a language, they heard the man crisply and cleanly-- an effect, some gathered afterwards, of the strange blue light from which he had emerged.

<"Tiamat removed itself from the stolid political cycles of the outside world upon its freedom from despotic rule and the great shield erected around our island nation is a testament to that. We stand alone, a beacon of freedom in a sea of tyranny. But we could not let another year pass where the hypocrisies of the outside world are so blatant to see with our clear eyes.">

<"We are aware of the Non-Proliferation of Metahuman Development treaty that prohibits nations from seeking out the scientific advancements that would allow the uninhibited creation of metahumans. We are aware of the lies and mistruths put forward to push this treaty through.">

<"It has become apparent that the United States, the biggest proponent of this oppressive scientific treaty, has a vested interest in ensuring the world's continued commitment. This is while its stock of metahumans continues to grow. It is convenient that the country with the densest population of metahuman-born citizens does not want any competition. Tiamat is and continues to be a self-sustaining sovereign state thanks to the exulted leadership of Apsu Liu, who pulled his people from the darkness and into the light.">

<"It is not human nature to want more? To seek out success where there was none before? Your 'American Dream', as posited by James Truslow Adams, is 'a dream of social order in which each man and each woman shall be able to attain to the fullest stature of

which they are innately capable, and be recognized by others for what they are, regardless of the fortuitous circumstances of birth or position', and does that not mean that if it is possible to become a metahuman, should those capable not do so?">

<"Know that Tiamat does not prescribe to your treaty. Know that while the world turns outside the shield surrounding our nation, that Tiamat turns as well. We will not be slowed, nor hobbled, nor made to step in line with immoral and illogical dictates from hypocrites and liars. Know that soon we will no longer be separate from, but part of, the global whole. And when we arrive-- we will not be dictated to. Thank you for your time. Peace be with you.">

The blue light snapped off, leaving a slightly scorched perimeter where Donghai Sòng had stood seconds before. The General Assembly took a moment to process that, before the uproar began. This was the beginning of something, but nobody knew what. Not yet, anyway.

Madison took a step forward and scratched the side of her chin. "Did you figure out how he got in there? Teleportation?"

James nodded. "Hologram. Satellite imaging over the island didn't detect the shield coming down, we still have no idea what's going on under there."

Madison scrunched her nose. "So *weird*. They didn't say anything when the shield went up, so everybody put it on their list of rogue nations, but that guy didn't look like he was struggling."

"No one's been able to get past Tiamat's force field since it went up. The place could be a wasteland for all we know. But imagine if that's not the case; a fully independent country, without the need for trade. The technological advancement required... I'd love to take a look someday," said James.

"But other than that, what do you think?" asked Loretta.

"That Tiamat just started a metahuman arms race?" she responded.

Madison knew the rules. After the UN instituted the Non-

Proliferation of Metahuman Development, governments weren't allowed to 'make' their own metahumans. You could recruit the superpowered-- though never deploy them during wartime, as that was now a war crime-- but genetic engineering and, more accurately, genetic *tampering* was illegal.

If any country was found to be plying their scientific know-how in the direction of *creation*, then repercussions were-- in theory-- globally catastrophic.

Abusing the metahumans under your care, as the British had with the subjects of Oraculum?

The country was still being sanctioned heavily, even though the corrupt government who created the program was long gone, consigned to the history books as monsters.

Deploying your homemade metahumans in a warzone? That would start a game of one-upmanship that could result in the end of the world. That is, if the first clash didn't result in Armageddon anyway.

This was the new Cold War. One where the real power resided in the gene code of a generation of men, women, and children, who at times could demolish whole cities with a glance.

"Beyond that," said Loretta. "What are your suppositions from his speech?"

Madison blinked. They wanted to know what she made of the speech? Made sense if they measured her. Trying to gauge her competency for this job. They did have their so-called 'reputation', as per Kishana, after all.

"Suppositions? Uh. Well. They clearly have a grudge against the US. The resentment was clear in his voice. They love their exalted Apsu, but he's Pol Pot, Kim and Stalin rolled into one, so of course, they would. Cult of personality to the Nth. Has anyone actually seen him recently?"

"Nope, we don't have a modern photo of the bastard, nothing since the shield went up," said James.

"His name is David Liu. Apsu is some made-up title," said Loretta.

"And so is David Liu," continued James.

Madison didn't track that. "Excuse me?"

James grinned. "You want to know what my favourite thing about Kim Jong-Il was? He gave himself all those imaginative names: 'Great Man, Who Is a Man of Deeds'! 'Highest Incarnation of the Revolutionary Comradeship'! 'Dear Leader, who is a perfect incarnation of the appearance that a leader should have'! Let me take a fucking breath before I continue…"

"I always liked 'Invincible and Triumphant General'," said Loretta.

"Because he went and blew himself up?" asked James.

"Exactly. I love karma," said Loretta.

"I'm sorry, but what do you mean about David Liu being made up?" said Madison.

James's smile continued to expand, so much so that it might have threatened to spill off his face. "Before the revolution, before Tiamat and before the shield, he was Li Qiang. Just one heck of an orator with a really boring name. Li Qiang is like the John Smith of the East."

"I'll take your word for it," said Madison.

"He became the figurehead of the revolution, rallied the people, overthrew the previous regime. And then he kicked out all the 'unclean' that had led to the 'once-proud culture' to 'decay'. Not long after, the shield went up. Tiamat became an isolationist nation, ruled by a lunatic who walked back on every promise he made before he took over. And the kicker? 'Liu' was the name of Chinese emperors back in the Han dynasty. It means 'destroy' or 'kill'. It's all about perception with that guy."

"Okay, so you want to know what I took from that speech? Insecurity," said Madison.

"What do you mean?" asked Loretta.

"Right, Sòng goes on about the US' metahuman population, so that's insecurity. To me, that means Tiamat doesn't have anything matching that-- or at least, they didn't. It's obvious they've been building their own. You know they have the technology. Else why would they suddenly announce it? They've been building metahumans for a while now, and they're getting ready to show the world." She paused. "But I don't think they've put themselves on an even keel with the US yet."

"How'd you get all that?" asked James.

"You think they'd make such a statement if they didn't have the know-how to follow through on it? They've already been building supers for a chunk of time, and now they're telling everyone about it. But they're not there *yet*. It's all on that guy's face. You can see it in every line of his face."

Loretta looked at James, and the former gave her a nod as he started to type. "Keep going," she said.

Madison opened her mouth to do so, but then the screen behind her switched back on. The trio turned and was collectively confused by the face of the man who appeared, someone who struck an unrelenting chord of unease with his very appearance.

"Whoa, holy fuck," said Loretta.

"What is this?" asked Madison.

"You know who that is?" said James.

"Nicholas Quinlan. That's Nicholas fucking Quinlan-- but isn't he dead?" said Loretta.

James nodded profusely. "Yeah, so what the hell is he doing on our TV?"

ALEPH BLUE BOX DATA CACHE

'PSYCHIC ABILITIES / CONTROVERSY' – SUMMARY

Over thirty years ago, Bernard Cunningham, a famed, *legitimate* psychic, was repeatedly called upon by police departments across the country to aid them in their investigations. It was his work that led to other telepaths being recruited by various law enforcement agencies. His work legitimised a cottage industry of psychic police work being performed, and for a while, everything was good.

It all went to hell when Cunningham was called in to assist the Boston Police Department with a series of child kidnappings. During that time, the things he saw both with his own two eyes and his metaphysical third were enough to drive a lesser man insane. Especially when the bodies started turning up in the state they did.

Cunningham was made of sterner stuff than that, but the urgency behind the case, the need to find the culprit before it was too late and another child was taken, led to a single catastrophic mistake that led to laws being passed to prevent telepathic evidence being used in trials, and for the regulation of psychic in law enforcement.

He became so irrevocably convinced of a man's guilt, that he projected all the ugly, deviant thoughts that had accumulated in his own mind during the investigation into the brain of the suspect. He was convinced of this guilt because the man was a metahuman, a Level 0 who's only ability was to be immune to telepathic scans, and Cunningham's gut led him astray. It was an accident, exhaustion and stress weakening the walls in his head that kept the bad thoughts separate from the rest, and the suspect went on to murder his own children after being cleared of the actual crimes.

Nobody is really sure what happened to Cunningham after that. He must've been in his seventies now if he was still alive. How could you live with yourself if you'd driven innocent men to commit the acts you were investigating? And those acts were unimaginable to them before meeting you? Teams have been tasked with locating him, but to no avail.

Where is Bernard Cunnigham today?

CITIES ON FIRE

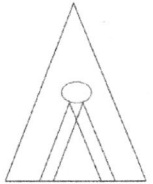

CHAPTER 3: BARELY AUDIBLE
LOCATION: BURGER DON, KIP'S BAY - NEW YORK

It was the understatement of the millennia, but Leon Cobalt 5 indeed was the product of another time. Flung from the far-off future into the-- relative to him!-- distant past, his arrival in the twenty-first century had been a rocky one, but he was never one to turn his nose up to a challenge.

Leon couldn't remember all the details of his life before his journey through time. The fall scrambled his memories and turned his existence upside down, but he tried to stay true to what felt true every day. Do good. Do right.

He didn't remember Leon Cobalt 4 or Leon Cobalt 3. He didn't know if they were his father and grandfather, a sibling or friend, or if it was a mantle handed from one random man or woman to another. But he knew he was Leon Cobalt 5, and when he tried his best to help others, that's when his soul sang.

Leon arrived with a bang in San Francisco eleven years ago. He was accompanied by his very own flying saucer and a suit of powered armour that increased his impressive physical attributes. Chasing him from the future was a time-travelling kill-squad assigned to prevent him from completing his mission.

Except, he couldn't remember exactly why he'd travelled so far down the timeline. He couldn't remember his mission. But the one thing he did know was that some disaster was coming, even if the details eluded him. He just hoped that he'd remember why he was here when it came around to it. He hoped that he hadn't missed his shot. He hoped that he hadn't ultimately failed to save the world after putting all this effort to come back to do so.

For a while, he hung around with some second-string heroes

while his memories took their time to clear up. They did good work, and he appreciated the time spent with them, but for every crisis averted, there came the celebratory bender, which led to bad decisions and worse hangovers. Even before a particular sex tape leaked to TMZ, he drank too much and acted the fool he wasn't, but eventually, he remembered enough that the tattoo he ended up with over his left nipple was even more of an embarrassing reminder of time wasted than it should have been.

He should give Ronnie a call.

After he acclimated to the past, he found himself a role at Aleph, a job that kept him on the frontlines of the good fight in all the right ways, except for this specific moment in time.

His latest assignment had led him to one of his least favourite places in the entire world. The smells physically offended his advanced future senses, causing the hairs on the back of his neck to prickle up in disgust. With his jaw set and his eyes darting around the locale, he stood ready for anything. The meta-scanner hadn't gone off on entry, but that just removed a variable from the equation. He kept it running in the background; its quiet buzz hooked up to his earpiece, letting him know if there were any changes to the scenario.

"...Sir, I don't believe this is a good idea," he said slowly.

His boss didn't look concerned. Jonathan Murray grinned as he playfully rapped his fingers across the counter of the burger joint. "Lee, you're always such a downer. You have to learn to relax a little."

Murray was the co-director of Aleph's operations division. His partner-in-crime, Zoya Zinchenko, was the other half of that same coin, and their mandate meant that they weren't allowed to be in the same room at the same time.

Those were the rules, and he liked it that way.

While Zinchenko was scarily intense, Murray was laid back, and never the twain did meet. That wasn't to say he was a pushover. After seventy arduous years as a spy, he was still as sharp as a tack and didn't look a day over fifty.

He was a frogman-- a combat diver-- back in the second world war. A young man full of arrogance and little concept of his safety, he accepted the most dangerous missions, the ones which the brass said folks wouldn't come back from. He proved them wrong time and time again.

During one mission, he was exposed to an element identified as 'Erkalite', a mysterious mineral that granted him prolonged life and superhuman abilities. As the decades went on, the more overt powers he'd received faded, but he was still a tough old bastard when he should have been a dead one.

Regardless, operations suited him simply fine, and the work was honest and honourable. You couldn't authorise an operation without intelligence, and intelligence couldn't allow an operation without doing their due diligence, so there was a careful balance between the two divisions within Aleph.

"But we didn't discuss this stop in this morning's security briefing," said Leon.

Someone sneezed, and the future warrior grimaced. Even if they weren't about to be attacked from all sides, the chance of infection from any of the children running roughshod across the fast-food establishment's shop floor was significant. What a way for them to go, after everything that got him here.

Cobalt escorted Murray to the front counter, while four agents followed shortly after and arrayed themselves across the restaurant's dining area. They tried to act casual, but who were they kidding? They stuck out like sore thumbs.

"Well, I didn't realise we'd be driving past a Burger Don on our way back from the UN security briefing," said Jonathan. His order was about to be called, and he rubbed his hands together, excited at the prospect.

Leon shook his head as he updated their itinerary to make a note of their stop. "Sir, you vetted our route of egress. You changed it before we left home base-- at the last minute, mind-- so we passed this establishment. You are a terrible liar."

Behind them, the television that had previously been playing muted music videos abruptly changed channels to show a black background behind a man who had been dead for over a decade. Leon didn't notice, but then again, his attention had to be focused elsewhere. His was a life and death business, and you couldn't allow yourself to be distracted by something like a TV show.

"You need to get out of that future man goody-two-shoes state of mind! That's why I--" Jonathan turned when he heard his order number called and smiled at the server who handed him his tray. "Why, thank you, missy."

She smiled and said something to Jonathan that was inaudible to Leon before she ignited in a flash of light, and a wave of catastrophic, destructive energy engulfed the entire building, taking all inside with it.

CITIES ON FIRE

ALEPH - PASSIVE OPERATIONS
INTERNAL CHAT TRANSCRIPT (10/05/2033)

JMURRAY (0534): HOW'S MY MORNING LOOKING?

KPORTER (0534): YOUR MORNING IS TAKEN UP BY THE UN SECURITY COUNCIL'S CLOSED SESSION. YOU REVIEWED THE TRAVEL PLANS LAST NIGHT?

JMURRAY (0535): I'M GOING TO AMEND THIS MORNING'S EXIT ROUTE.

KPORTER (0536): OKAY. THAT'S PRETTY SHORT NOTICE. IS THERE A PROBLEM?

KPORTER (0540): SIR?

JMURRAY (0541): NO PROBLEM. I JUST KNOW HOW THIS MORNING WILL GO. I NEED SOMETHING TO LOOK FORWARD TO.

KPORTER: (0541): OH, I GET YOU.

JMURRAY (0542): I'M UPLOADING THE ROUTE CHANGE NOW. PLEASE UPDATE LEON AND THE ENTOURAGE.

KPORTER (0542): YES SIR.

<CHAT TERMINATED>

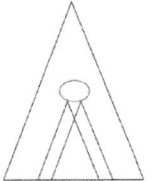

CHAPTER 4: MR STONE GOES TO WASHINGTON
LOCATION: THE WHITE HOUSE - WASHINGTON, DC

Christopher Stone checked his watch. It wasn't an expensive piece, but it kept good time, and it was a gift, so it held a place in his heart that others might not. Kishana gifted it to him when he became the director of Aleph's Active Intelligence division five years ago, and he hadn't parted with it since.

He sighed. The President of the United States was running late.

He hated these briefings. Back in the day, he would have had to wear his old USAF dress uniform, but somehow this black suit was worse. He cursed how the fabric creased at the slightest inconvenience and how he was left twiddling his thumbs until the commander-in-chief had a free slot in his busy schedule.

He'd been sitting outside the Oval Office for nearly an hour. As his security entourage wasn't allowed this close to the President, that meant he was sitting alone. The Secret Service were territorial and having security from the Aleph's Washington Office breathing down their necks caused friction, so Chris agreed to leave his bodyguards at the door.

Chris wouldn't complain. He managed to get away with not being present for one of these meetings for the better part of two years, so he probably wasn't allowed to. Usually, he dispatched James Winter, one of his senior advisors. Though the army veteran rarely stuck to the briefing notes and ended up exchanging war stories with the President instead, it got one superfluous thing off the director's to-do list. Chris didn't mind the meandering. Everything a government needed to know what Aleph was working on was made available in his organisation's daily read books.

But as it turned out, the President noticed Stone's absence, and he requested an appearance come hell or high water. Chris wondered if the others had this problem with the leaders of their home nations.

His counterpart in charge of Passive Intelligence, Delphine Martin, enjoyed entertaining the Prime Minister of France and her wife, and their briefings usually dovetailed into cocktails and a meal at a Michelin star restaurant. Jonathan Murray-- Nemo to his friends-- was a good soldier, so wouldn't complain even if you asked him to. Maybe if you ordered him, he might unload a bit, but who could say? And then there was the ice queen, Zoya Zinchenko. The less said about her, the better.

No, this was a uniquely disquieting experience for him, and as the White House Chief of Staff poked his head out from the Oval Office, Chris cleared his throat and headed inside.

"Director Stone, glad to see you," said Chief of Staff Randal Quire, shaking Chris' hand as he crossed the threshold. "Have you been well?"

"As well as can be expected, sir," replied Stone.

"Christopher!" bellowed President Hunnicutt, his arms open wide at the sight of the man.

"Mr President," replied Stone, saluting like he was still in the military. Quire lurked at the back of the room, watching their interaction unfold without saying a word.

"At ease, man, at ease. Been a long time since you were in the Air Force; there's no need for that," said Hunnicutt.

"Old habits, you know how it is," said Chris.

The President beckoned him over, and they exchanged a handshake, and then he motioned for the director to take a seat. "Listen, I know you hate this malarkey, and I can't say I blame you. But that's what comes with being the Director of Aleph. And, you know, I feel *safer* with a patriot heading up Aleph this time around. It's a shame that Jon Murray never got the job but seeing your name at the top of the list made me proud. An Air Force man, just like me, riding herd on one of the most important intelligence organisations in the world."

"I appreciate that, sir," said Chris. The same speech the President made every single time they were in the same room together. Just because it had been an age since they were in the Oval Office didn't mean Chris forgot the well-trodden path they always walked down.

"I'm sure, I'm sure. Yeah, most definitely, you're giving a whole new perspective on the issues of the day, especially considering your history with the superhero set."

Chris's lips curled. "I don't mean to be rude, sir, but was there a specific reason you asked me to brief you today?"

Surprised by the man's abruptness, President Hunicott paused before sighing. A physical weight seemed to grind into him from the shoulders down. He proceeded to round the desk and then slump into the couch opposite Stone. "Tiamat. It's about that island and the mad tin pot bastard sitting on its throne.

"...More specifically, their stance on metahuman proliferation?"

The President clicked his fingers. "That's the one. We all heard the speech their ambassador made yesterday. That's your turf, so I need to know where we stand. I've got intel coming from every department that calls the US home, but I'm getting conflicting and damned infuriating messages from every which way."

"The ambassador's comments on the floor of the UN were inflammatory, but..." replied Chris.

"Don't toe the company line with me, Stone. I want your take on it."

Stone shifted uncomfortably. "We're still compiling a read book for all heads of state. You want unbiased commentary; you wait for that. But I'll tell you this; if this government say they're growing superhumans-- if they say they're growing the next Majestic-- then we have to take that seriously. This isn't like North Korea. They paid the price for their tampering with the metagene. Millions dead. Nothing can get through that damned shield around Tiamat; that's technology beyond us, beyond the Meridian, beyond anybody. So, yeah. They seem to have the know-how."

"You don't have to remind me why all the maps show Korea as Korea again and not split North and South," murmured the President.

"Tiamat is a fortress in the middle of the sea. Wholly self-sufficient. If it weren't for their leader, we could hope for the best, but you know what Li Qiang did to get the throne. That suggests that this isn't a story with a happy ending."

The President nodded slowly, mulling over everything said. "We're going to condemn their comments today, and my ambassador to the UN tells me the General Assembly is going to adopt a resolution to condemn the situation as well."

Stone leaned forward. "Sir, this is a rogue state who managed to erect an impenetrable force field around itself, who built advanced holographic projectors capable of sending hard light copies of their representatives across the globe. Even the Meridian doesn't have access to that level of tech, and they have a base at the bottom of the Mariana Trench."

"So, you're saying…"

"Don't piss them off. Your national security advisors will tell you the same thing. Please don't give them a reason to hate the west more so than they do already. Condemn them, but don't open yourself to retaliation. It's a damn high wire act you've got to walk, but that's why they pay you the big bucks, sir."

President Hunnicutt whistled low and slow. "Well, fuck me."

"Damned if you do, damned if you don't," said Chris, leaning back in his chair.

The two men sat in silence for a time before the director's phone began to buzz-- which it shouldn't have unless it were an emergency. You don't keep your phone on for casual calls during a one-to-one meeting with the President of the United States of America.

"Ah, damn, I'm sorry," he said, taking it out of his pocket. The screen was glowing red, which meant that it was more important than anything else going on right now. Red meant urgent. Red meant danger. Kishana was on the other end of the call, and she knew better than to call him like this without reason. "I have to take this," said Chris.

"Go ahead, son," said President Hunnicutt.

As Chris stood and made an apologetic gesture toward the President, he answered the call. At the same time, Quire barged back into the room, accompanied by Vice President Rakely and several aides, who all wore the same concerned expressions. The Secret Service were suddenly very much present in the room, though they recognised Director Stone enough to give him space.

"What's going on?" Stone asked Kishana, his back to the room but craning his neck so he could see Quire whisper in Hunnicutt's ear.

Her voice was steeped in the requisite amount of drama a phone call interrupting a presidential briefing demanded. <"I'm sorry, chief. Are you able to turn on a television? You'll want to see this.">

Before Chris could speak, the giant television embedded into the Oval Office was uncovered and turned on. The President's aides had brought him up to speed as much as possible, so they were both on the same page, but it didn't take away from the gut-punch Chris experienced when the smug face of Nicholas Quinlan, the man his sister killed over a decade ago, filled the screen, and he was smiling. But Quinlan shouldn't have been smiling. He should have been *dead*.

<"**--Of you may remember me as the victim of an act of completely justified revenge at Hannah Stone's hands. You remember her, right? The vigilante Shrike? I killed her husband and daughter, and she killed dozens of my employees to reach me and end our feud once and for all. Except, what if she didn't kill me?**">

He hadn't aged a day. His receding hairline still widows-peaked toward the same point it had a decade ago. There were still the same glints of silver visible amongst his thatch of dark hair. He had pale, brown eyes and a thin nose that gave his thin lips something to aspire toward. Still in his fifties yet etched with craggy lines that came with a life spent hiding his true nature from the world. Evil managed to age even the best at obscuring their inner selves.

Quinlan allowed for a moment of silence so that that thought could settle in, tucked in tight like it was the last thought you might have before bed. As the weight of his words hit Chris, he felt his stomach turn. The man on the television screen continued, amused by his own imposed moment of quiet sobriety.

<"**Now, don't get me wrong, I really am dead. I'm recording this video the day before my-- quote-unquote-- murder, and if my algorithm works-- and if you see this, it did *spectacularly*-- then this recording will see the light of day ten years into Hannah Stone's prison sentence. But here's the thing: All that**

DNA evidence, all that security camera footage, everything that will inevitably lead to her conviction…">

Nicholas began drumming his index fingers vigorously onto the edge of the desk in front of him, building the action up to a crescendo. His drumroll culminated with grabbing the camera from its stand and swivelling it around, so the viewer could see an unconscious woman strapped to a vertical gurney. It could have been a prop stolen from any number of 90s thrillers set in psychiatric hospitals. Her eyes fluttered as Quinlan grabbed her by the chin and began to move her face from side to side so you could see who she was. Dried blood scabbed across her skin from her hairline down to her jawline, some injury obscured by her dirty blonde hair.

"Impossible…" whispered Chris.

It was Hannah. It was his sister.

<"…**I faked it all. All it took was a sample of her blood and all my resources, and I grew this simulacrum. A clone. An exact genetic duplicate. I made my very own impossible girl using impossible science to frame a good woman for an impossible crime.**">

Nicholas ran his hand through the woman's hair and revealed a three-inch surgical scar above her ear, where blood had dribbled down toward her chin. She made a whimpering noise as his fingers brushed across the wound but didn't wake up. For Chris, it was like seeing his sister for the first time in a decade, before the hell she went through after her conviction. Five years since he last visited. Five years since she let him.

<"**All I had to do was cut out the parts of her brain that provide autonomy, install a computer, and then set her loose. I've been planning this for two years. That's how long it took for me to grow this beautiful little doppelganger. What else? What next? So, I have the murder weapon right here--**"> He tapped the woman three times on the forehead with the tip of his knuckle. <"**-- How do I tie the real Hannah Stone into knots? How do I make the case against her airtight? Simple. I do it with style.**">

Chris held his phone up to his ear and said, "Track this. Trace it. Is it a recording, or is it live? How is this possible."

<"Already on it, chief,"> replied Kishana.

Quinlan continued, <"**I've hired the time-manipulating thief Kruonis to place Hannah Stone in a time loop tomorrow night. Tomorrow's the day I die, and I intend to make it a glorious spectacle and have all the blame placed at her feet. My people will take care of any loose ends; they'll bury Kruonis's corpse in the foundation of Hudson University's new library because I can't have anyone taking credit for this masterpiece other than me, and then I'll have them killed too. No loose ends. Only the crime, the victim, and the perpetrator. Me. Me. Me.**">

"Why's he doing this, Stone?" asked President Hunnicutt.

"He was mad. My sister always said so, but nobody believed her. My God, he was madder than any of us could have thought."

"Is he still alive? Is this--?" started Chief of Staff Quire.

"We don't know. But we'll find out," said Chris, cutting him off, Kishana's voice audible in his ear as she ordered the analysts around here to figure out what was going on.

Quinlan swivelled the camera back around and relaxed, shrugging off the immensity of his monologue before adding, <"**But here's the thing. Coinciding with the release of this confession, I'm also releasing the schematics of everything I ever built, devised, or dreamed of, onto the internet. Two data caches on every torrent site in existence. One unencrypted for Johnny-On-The-Street, sitting at home, harbouring aspirations toward being a big bad supervillain, and one for the powers-that-be. That second one is encrypted. Can't let you have all the fun, can I? Anyway, you want to know how I cloned Hannah Stone? It's all there. Every death ray, every nuclear engine, every piece of tech I hoarded for so long, it's all there, an Anarchist Cookbook for the new age. Because I imagine the world I leave behind is going to be boring, so why not spice things up as a final gift?**">

"Oh, no," whispered Chris.

<"Have fun, boys and girls. End the world if you can. luck, and good night."

CITIES ON FIRE

CITIES ON FIRE

FBI DATABASE
"QUINLAN, NICHOLAS - MURDER CASE (CLOSED)"
ASSORTED PRESS CLIPPINGS
NEW YORK VOICE (Friday 4th March 2022)

BREAKING NEWS: *OFFICE MASSACRE IN DOWNTOWN MANHATTAN*

NEW YORK -- At least twenty-five are reported dead in what has been described as a 'gruesome massacre' by first responders.

An NYPD spokesperson informed THE NEW YORK VOICE that the death toll is still undetermined due to the violent nature of the crimes, but at least twenty-five victims have been identified at the time of publication. The identities of the victims will be released once the next of kin have been informed.

We can confirm that among the dead is Nicholas Quinlan, billionaire founder of Endeavour technologies. A man more famous for his charitable endeavours than the work done by the company he founded, he was recently in the headlines after pledging $30 billion dollars to the World Hunger Relief Fund.

CITIES ON FIRE

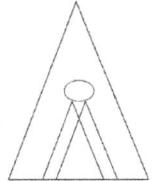

CHAPTER 5: NORTH TO SOUTH, STRAIGHT UP
LOCATION: NEVADA DESERT
FOURTEEN YEARS AGO:

"Nobody."

Inside one of the massive craters in the desert leftover from what would later become known as the Last Battle of Nevada, Hannah Stone finally caught her breath. Sand, ash, and blood covered her once pristinely white costume, worn through so heavily in parts that the black armour beneath could be seen

She was alive. She'd made it through. But how many lives were lost along the way?

"Never again."

When that thought struck her-- the fact the world had nearly ended, and she was on the front line of the battle for its continued existence-- she yanked off her Plague Doctor-styled mask and doubled over, her body shuddering with the feeling that she might need to vomit. She pushed past it, a vow from her past echoing in her mind.

"If I can, I will," mumbled Hannah, remembering the words.

The world had nearly ended-- Hell, one world *had*-- but theirs was still safe, still intact.

Her cape was long gone, so she yanked off her glove and wiped her brow. Was she going to be sick? She gave it a moment. When nothing came, she swallowed hard, then straightened back up.

"Are you all right?"

Exhausted to the bones and no longer caring that her mask was off, she turned at the familiar voice and saw the hero known as Majestic floating a few metres off the ground. How did his costume always look so immaculate? Blue inlays lined his skin-tight white uniform, accentuating his muscular physique. It was also absolutely spotless. If it was any consolation to her, his cape had gone the same way as her own, shredded and scorched by the rogue planet's monstrous ground troops.

"Uh, I heard you talking, but I didn't understand," said Majestic, careful to look away, a kindness toward the preservation of her secret identity.

Hannah didn't care. Looking at him sometimes felt like she was looking at the sun. If she looked at him for too long, she was scared she'd go blind, but he was the greatest hero of the modern generation, more powerful than any that had come before him. What was there to fear from someone who wielded ultimate power?

"Shrike? Are you all right?" he said again.

Everything.

Hannah realised she'd been so exhausted by the day's events that she'd been staring at him, slack-jawed, her face drenched with sweat. She blinked herself back into being present and replied, "Oh, you know, probably great, probably going to pass out any minute."

She discarded her mask amongst the sand and glass, making a point of letting it fall between them-- an indicator of her opinion of this man. An indicator of the trust she decided to place in him.

There was everything to fear about the hero, but the way he carried himself in that costume of his, the way he spoke to the gathered heroes in the heat of battle, there was never any arrogance or bravado. He never ordered them around, and while they may have doubted themselves, they never doubted him for a second. He was never less than the best possible version of himself, and she respected that.

He smiled and floated down. "You did well out there today."

"Easy for you to say. You held back," Hannah paused to consider the scope of what she was about to say, "Well, I think you held back a rogue Earth that was going to collide with our own? I was just fighting monsters. It looks like you did the hard work."

"I've never seen anything like it," he replied.

He was looking toward the sky that had less than an hour earlier been stained crimson as an attacking alternate Earth had burst through the dimensional walls previously keeping them separate.

The melancholy written across his face made her ache.

He sighed. "So many lives lost. I failed today."

"Umm, you held back an entire planet. *You held it back.* Instead of billions dying, thousands died. And yes, that's a tragedy. That's the worst possible thing that could happen. But at the same time, you saved the planet. You held *back* a planet."

It shouldn't have been possible, but she'd seen it with her own eyes. In a last-ditch effort to kill them all, the rogue planet was launched across the borders separating realities. If the black orchids failed, if the ensuing chaos from their blooming didn't finish the job, then all that was left was the end of everything.

Majestic hadn't hesitated. He launched himself toward the planet and stopped it in its tracks.

He defied the immutable laws of physics and held it back. Barely gave an inch. Hannah knew that the act didn't make sense. It should have been *impossible*. Did that make it an act of god? If it came down to strength alone, he would have cleaved through the planet like a hot knife through butter.

The Earth's weight, combined with the vast gravitational pull of the sun, meant that his two hands pushed against a patch of ground that should never support the sheer force needed to do the task-- but it did. That informed her that there was more to his power than simple brute strength. And that amazed Hannah more than she knew possible.

"I did what I had to do," he said.

"You did the impossible," she countered.

Majestic smiled softly. "Can't it be the same thing?"

Hannah wondered how someone could survive all that self-imposed weight on their shoulders, but then again, he could shoulder *worlds*. If anyone could bear it, it would be him.

But he looked so sad, as if he were taking every death personally. Was that a malfunction with her? When the numbers were so high, when she didn't see their faces individually, maybe it made it easier for her? She grimaced. She must do better. If there were an example to follow, it would be his, right?

"We've never properly met before, have we?" he said.

"Not before this, no. It's a bit late for introductions, but as you've seen me with my mask off, I guess you can call me Hannah," she said.

"Hannah..."

He looked at her for a stretched-out moment that hung thick in the air between them like molasses. He still hadn't landed, but as he continued to float toward her, he finally descended. When he touched the ground, his face changed ever so slightly. He was suddenly bearded, his bright eyes darker, his body looser than it had been a muscle-bound minute prior. He took one final step forward and extended his hand.

"Michael. Michael Walsh. Fair's fair," he said, a gentle accent in his voice.

She couldn't believe it. The world's greatest hero had just revealed his greatest secret to her. For a moment, she was surprised she'd never heard the name 'Michael Walsh' before, because surely someone as powerful as Majestic was *somebody,* but then it made perfect sense to her. He could be anybody. And here he was, being just that-- a man.

She stared at his hand in disbelief then clamped her own hands around it. After hearing his voice, and his accent, all she could think to say was, "Y-you're... Irish?"

"Well, yes. We all come from somewhere," replied Michael.

Shrike smiled. "Good point. Hannah Stone, then. That's me."

Michael nodded then his body shifted back to its earlier configuration. He was Majestic again.

"Hannah, we just saved humanity. I think that means something. I don't think it's a coincidence this group of heroes gathered when the shadow of that rogue planet fell upon ours. I think it's kismet-- that's what my mum would say, at least. It would be a mistake not to continue this alliance. The world needs protecting. And sometimes, it'll need saving."

"You want to make this gathering official?" she offered.

Hannah had skulked away from the others after they finally pushed the invading Earth back to the dimension it belonged. It wasn't that she was unsociable-- she was a regular party animal in the right circumstances-- but the world had nearly ended, and she was just a woman in a costume trying to do the right thing. She stumbled into the glass-crested crater near where the others had assembled and tried to gather her thoughts-- and not vomit.

An alliance of heroes borne from the near-apocalyptic threat they'd just faced? There wouldn't be a more formidable force of good in existence. But would they say yes?

Slipstream. The speedster. A man capable of travelling at speeds beyond comprehension but who never ran so fast that he overlooked the suffering of those around him. Even though they met in an apocalyptic maelstrom, he'd been kind and courteous, even when she had not been. Hannah made sure to apologise for her curtness when the day was saved, admitting that the concept of a hostile parallel universe blew her mind beyond all kinds of patience.

Adikia. The warrior. An immortal figure from before myth, who waged war like it was second nature, but whose aggression was tempered by her compassion. They'd met before, once, before the end times required their attention, and Hannah couldn't help but like the woman's swagger. Nothing fazed her, but then again, when you've been alive since the dawn of time, what could surprise you?

Tempest and Undine. The royals. Rulers of seven disparate kingdoms found beneath the oceans, the former an aquatic king and the latter an elemental witch. They were already saving the world before the attack, cleansing the seas of pollution and plastics. They were about to introduce plans to stimy over-fishing when the skies bled, and their attentions were required elsewhere. Hannah had only interacted with the pair briefly, but there was a spark in Undine that she adored, and she hoped to spend more time with her when the dust settled.

Zyj. The seer. The last survivor of the interstellar Dierlullian empire, a race that had ruled the entire solar system with an iron fist before the birth of humanity. Their arrival in the present was a cosmic fluke, but Earth could ask for no better immigrant from the universe's past. Their vast telekinetic abilities could painlessly pacify hordes of attackers, as Hannah had witnessed hours before.

Starlight. The undying. When Hannah was young, her father had shown her Tully Rogers's videos, a death-defying stuntman who wowed audiences with his ridiculous feats of fearlessness. One day, his luck ran out, but from the burning wreckage of his mangled car, he emerged unscathed. Resurrected and empowered by a cosmic force, a pair of silver bracelets had fused to his wrists, giving him access to an energy source limited only by his imagination. She could think of no better man for the job of saving the world.

Dragonfly. The marksman. Hannah knew little about the Brit, but what she did know was precise and to the point, which made perfect sense considering Dragonfly never missed a shot. She was taciturn initially, but after getting into the flow of mowing down the invading beasts from the other reality, she'd become more talkative. Enough to let everyone know she didn't want to be here and would rather be back in England, making sure nothing happened on her home turf. When Slipstream pointed out that the battle here would ensure the world's safety, Hannah noted the sharpshooter had stared at the speedster's knee for a moment longer than was friendly.

Never before had there been a group as powerful as the one assembled on that day. There had once been The Trust in the 1940s, the Community from the 1960s, and the Futurists from the 1970s. Later, you had Maximum Justice, who disappeared in the 1980s; more recently, the Revival, who faded into obscurity in the 1990s. None compared.

"Sure, why not?" replied Hannah. "What are we going to call ourselves?"

CITIES ON FIRE

ALEPH BLUE BOX DATA CACHE
MERIDIAN, THE - ORIGIN FILE

The Meridian formed in the aftermath of the 2019 parallel Earth invasion. There had been recorded instances of the Meridian's membership teaming up prior to this event, but never in this number, and never to face a threat on this scale. This is an important moment in metahuman history, and Aleph must respond accordingly.

Founding members (alphabetical): ADIKIA (2), DRAGONFLY (1), MAJESTIC (4), SHRIKE, THE (1), STARLIGHT (4), TEMPEST (4), UDINE (3), VELOCITY (3) and ZJY (3)

With the formation of the Meridian, these heroes join a long line of super-powered individuals who came together to face threats that they could not overcome alone.

It is important to note that-- other than The Trust (see: "TRUST, THE - ORIGIN FILE")-- no so-called "superhero team" has remained together longer than 16 years. The Trust was operational between 1940-1956. The Meridian are currently in their 14th year of operation.

CITIES ON FIRE

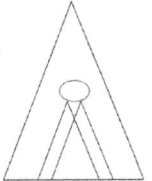

CHAPTER 6: DOUBLE DOWN
LOCATION: THE WHITE HOUSE - WASHINGTON, DC

In the Oval Office, surrounded by the President and his staff, Christopher Stone stood frozen in place. For the first time in the longest time, he didn't know what to do. And they were all looking at him, waiting for an answer to a question none of them had asked.

Quinlan had been dead for over a decade, and everyone had thought his sister had done it. Everyone but *him*.

The courts had thrown the book at Hannah before tossing her into the deepest hole available, Ziggurat Black, and then the world tried to forget about her.

It didn't matter that a week after her arrest, Aleph received a package filled with concrete evidence linking Quinlan to the murders of Hannah's husband and daughter. It contained 1) a recording of Quinlan going into intricate detail about the homicides, 2) the murder weapon still covered in the victims' blood, and 3) Polaroids he had taken of the act itself. All marked for Christopher Stone's attention.

Not only did Quinlan dispatch proof of his hands-on participation in their murders, but he also provided concrete evidence of his decades-spanning criminal career.

"Director Stone?"

Vice President Rakely's voice was distant. Chris wasn't listening. He was in a cave, lost in his own head as it filled with the implications of the reappearance of the man who murdered his brother-in-law and niece. The man who did all that and then subjected Chris' sister to ten years in hell, locked away with the knowledge she did nothing wrong.

Quinlan's posthumous package provided irrefutable evidence he was a monster. Never before had the District Attorney's Office held such unassailable proof of a criminal conspiracy. The mountains of evidence suddenly gave hundreds, if not thousands, of cold cases new life. Under pressure from dozens of social justice initiatives, the DA overturned false convictions and identified miscarriages of justice, all because of one man's ego.

All of the evidence proving how heinous Nicholas Quinlan truly was sealed it for the prosecution. If he were the violent miscreant, the evidence painted him as the bogeyman lurking in all of New York's shadows, and if Hannah Stone was the only person who tried to prove it, why wouldn't she return the favour if he murdered her family?

A situation like that would be enough to drive even the best among us to murder-- an entire world screaming that you're wrong when you know, in your heart, that you're right. Nicholas Quinlan *was* a monster.

It didn't matter how much she pleaded her innocence. Even her teammates in the Meridian couldn't stand by her side when the evidence pointed irrevocably in her direction. It didn't matter who her big brother was. She was a superhero one minute, and the next, she was a killer. There was no other scenario that the courts could believe.

So, that was that. The justice system found a hole and threw Hannah in. And that hole had a name: Ziggurat Black. A prison designed to hold the worst villains the era had to offer. Shrike was responsible for a chunk of the inmates ending up in there, and the court thought it appropriate to send her there too.

<"...Sir?"> Kishana's voice was still in his ear.

Distant again but getting closer. The cave was shrinking, and Chris was being pulled back toward the entrance, back into the world, and it was going to be new and different when he arrived. The truth was out there. The fact he always believed.

"Son, are you all right?" asked President Hunnicutt.

But she was innocent. Chris always knew. They'd thrown her into Ziggurat Black, and the inmates had done their worst. *But she was innocent.*

"I have to go," Chris said abruptly.

Hunnicutt shook his head and reached out a hand, "Christopher, wait. I'll contact the Attorney General. I'll have her out of the Ziggurat by the end of the day. We'll put her in protective custody until we sort this thing out."

"Sir, with all due respect, I'm pulling her out of there myself. Aleph has the autonomy to do so. Ten years is too long. I should never have let them do that to her. Never."

"Son, you do that, and there's a black mark against you and yours," said Rakely.

"This is about family, Mr Vice President; I couldn't give a damn about black marks," said Chris.

Hunnicutt shook his head. "Let us do this. If this is all true, then we can have her out of there and exonerated. It's not as simple as snapping my fingers, there's due process to think about, but we can at least get her out from the worst of it."

Stone grimaced. He put his phone back to his ear and asked Kishana, "Who do we have stationed at the Ziggurat?"

<"Nightshade from our side and Schwarzer Zwerg from operations,"> she replied.

"Get my sister taken into their custody. We'll coordinate with the Office of the Attorney General and have her off the island ASAP. I'm going to need a plane ready to fly from the nearest airfield within the hour. I'm going there right now," he continued.

<"Understood, Sir-- wait-- oh-- *oh my God*--"> Kishana sounded aghast, her calm tone shifting into shock and horror. <"Sir, there's been a massive explosion in downtown Manhattan-- the site was on Director Murray's updated itinerary-- it's all coming in--">

"What? What's going on?" asked Stone.

<"We can't make contact with Murray's entourage-- I'm getting in touch with his office--">

Chris was pacing, trying to process the information he received from all comers as fast as possible. His duty as Director of Active Intelligence was to develop an adequate response to the events unfolding. If asked, he would admit that the Nicholas Quinlan reappearance had shaken him up. He struggled to bear down on the facts separate from his sister.

An attack on Murray? Could it be linked to Quinlan's digital reappearance? Could it have something to do with Tiamat's statement of intent on the floor of the United Nations? What else? *What else?*

"Send an investigation team to the scene. We're taking command. I'll head back to home base, but in the interim, get my sister secure. All these events could be connected. Coordinate with the FBI and let them know why we're taking command but tell them we'll share everything. Involve the NY Field Office in the proceedings. Standard procedure."

<"Got it. See you soon, Sir.">

"Has something happened?" asked Hunnicutt.

Stone exhaled, catching up with himself after the surfeit of information unloaded on him in such a short period. First his sister, and now this?

These three events could be connected.

"There's been an explosion in New York. Cause unknown. But the location was on Director Murray's itinerary, and my people tell me we don't have any contact with him."

"Causalities?" asked Rakely.

"Unknown at this time. I'm sending people, and we'll keep you updated, but I have to go right away."

"Of course, of course," said Hunnicutt, turning away from the director and pinching his nose. He looked like he was just about to develop a stress migraine.

"What you said about my sister..." said Chris.

The President turned to his Chief of Staff and said, "Get the AG on the phone immediately, Randy. Shrike was an American hero. She was a founding member of the Meridian, and if Nicholas Quinlan framed her, then the last decade of Hannah Stone's life was a miscarriage of justice beyond the pale. We'll tread carefully, but I won't have her down in the Ziggurat while we do. So, don't start, son. I don't want to hear it. Get the work *done*."

"I-- yes-- yes, of course."

Quire pivoted from one foot to the other, his face a flustered expansion of burning red. He hurriedly exited the room while making a call, headed to parts unknown to follow through on the President's directive.

"Thank you, Sir. We'll liaise with the FBI and keep you in the loop on this. If you need anything, you call," said Chris.

"Thank you, I'll hold you to that," said President Hunnicutt, watching as Aleph's Director of Active Intelligence finally darted out the door.

CITIES ON FIRE

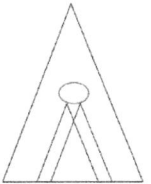

CHAPTER 7: EVEN DEEPER
LOCATION: ZIGGURAT BLACK - BERMUDA TRIANGLE

From what they could gather, Nicholas Quinlan's rogue transmission cut into every single television screen and monitor worldwide. It didn't matter where you lived. The hijacking extended from Alaska to Zimbabwe. Nicholas Quinlan's words translated instantaneously into whatever language was native to the country his signal reached. If you could access the internet or watch television, you would see his face. It didn't matter if you were browsing porn or drafting an email to your grandmother. Your experience was interrupted by the pock-marked face of a man who died ten years ago.

And that included the depths of Ziggurat Black.

In the brightly lit recreation hall where the inmates sat and watched the television, the guards knew something terrible was coming. They could feel a pressure change in the atmosphere like a storm was brewing, as if they were going to be hit full pelt with a natural disaster. The air got *muggy* and *thick*.

In all his years working in this hellhole, SCO Mulgrew never felt a change come on as fast. He was the senior-most officer on shift, and the other COs looked at him for stability. That's not what they got when they turned to him. They could all tell something terrible was about to happen when they saw the horrified expression spread across their commanding officer's face like the worst kind of rash.

He flicked the switch on his belt that activated his helmet mic and barked, "Ramp up dampening nodes in all sectors."

Ziggurat Black's guards all wore reinforced power armour designed by Professor Ultra himself. Still, they'd never had to deal with a full-on supervillain prison riot before. Sure, they'd put a few bastards in their place here and there, so there were no illusions as to who was in charge. Yes, the power dampeners did the rest, but the atmosphere, the way the inmates were getting riled up; nothing good could come of these circumstances.

This madness was not how he anticipated spending the twilight years of his career, but the pay was great, and the hazard pay even greater. After his wife left him, and the kids refused to talk to him when they saw what he'd done to her face, this job was the best he could ever dream of getting. All it took was being even more of a bastard than he had been at prior penitentiaries.

He'd been in charge since Burton was let go seven years back due to 'inappropriate conduct with inmates'.

Management didn't give any details to the guards about what that 'inappropriate conduct' actually entailed, but they suspected it had something to do with Hannah Stone and treated her accordingly.

"Everyone, get back to your cells! That is an order!" said Mulgrew, his voice piped through the speakers mounted in the walls.

"Where the fuck is she?" asked one particular inmate.

Mulgrew's brain worked overtime to remember the particulars of this particular felon. That dictated what action they could take against her-- how far they could go. Initially, he thought himself lucky to be assigned to the prison's female population, but he was naïve. Child-killers, black widows and out-and-out monsters surrounded him every single day. Most of them hid that evil behind a pretty smile, but he knew the truth.

Not Susan Cox, though. She couldn't even smile with her lack of lips and the gutted musculature around her face. The woman dubbed 'Scourge' by the media looked like a walking corpse. Her facial features had been burned away by the toxic spill that triggered the manifestation of her powers in the first place.

Her superhero origin was less than optimistic. Later studies found her to be a latent metahuman whose dormant powers triggered when radioactive waste washed across her car with her inside.

When Susan's powers manifested, she went on to murder emergency workers and first responders-- she even burnt the throat out of Johnny Iron, the retired hero who happened to be living in the area as well.

It turned out Susan Cox wasn't just an innocent victim. She didn't need superpowers to kill anybody. It came out later that before the horrific accident, her body count was already in the teens. She was a serial killer, and she would have gotten away with it too, if it wasn't for that pesky chemical spill.

Only after the intervention of Majestic and Shrike-- fresh off the investigation into the Roanoke tragedy-- had she been stopped, and ever since, she'd held a grudge. She'd been kept away from her old nemesis since the latter's arrival, but with Quinlan's admission that he framed his old rival for his murder, now there was a ticking clock if she wanted revenge!

"Get back to your cell, Cox! I won't ask twice!" barked Mulgrew.

"I want her! I want her now!" continued Scourge.

She marched determinedly toward the COs, a rabid look of violence flickering behind her eyes. Her defiance was fuelled by the baying crowds of female inmates that had started throwing furniture around the recreation room. Things were immediately going from bad to worse.

"Fucking hell, take the bitch down," ordered Mulgrew.

One of the COs raised his gauntlet and cycled the weapons systems through to non-lethal. A violet spasm of energy shot out from his wrist, but it was too late for Mulgrew to realise that just under the mask of aggression Scourge wore was something else-- eagerness.

She held up her arms, and you could see where the doctors had driven their radiation dampening control rods into her body. It was the only thing capable of containing the immense power inside her body. And they weren't working. Their black exterior began to burn white as her energy blast rode through the tips of the bio-nuclear dampening material and straight into her body.

"Oh, no," murmured Mulgrew, but it was too late.

Scourge screamed as her arms rippled with the heat from her powers beginning to flow outward from her centre. Gory trenches erupted around the rods and through her flesh, and for a harrowing, lingering moment, there was a separation between the dampeners inserted inside her and her body-- and at that moment, her radioactive powers surged.

"--Oh, fucking hell."

Both of Scourge's arms exploded; wet, blackened wads of flesh and bone spraying outward. That was followed immediately by a terrifying wave of light emanating from the stumps that shorted every electronic system nearby.

Metagene suppressing collars sprayed sparks, then either unlocked and fell off or blew deadly chunks of metal into the throats of their wearers. Scourge didn't care. In tandem with the collars, the power dampening nodes along the walls shattered too. Suddenly, all of the imprisoned supervillains were restored to their former inhuman glory, their abilities returned.

"*Fucking hell*," whispered Mulgrew.

With her arms rendered stumps just above the elbow, Scourge tried to reach out toward the senior CO as blood dribbled from her slit-nose and gummy mouth.

"C'mere... c'mere handsome..." she rasped; her throat suddenly dry with anticipation of what was still to come.

"G-get away from me!" he ordered, even though he was shuffling backwards, terrified of what the human atomic furnace in front of him was capable of.

Clawed limbs constructed from radioactive energy sprouted from the gory remnants of her old arms, and she tore out Mulgrew's Adam's Apple in one determined swipe. She turned around and looked at the other supervillains as they swarmed toward the other COs, all taking their pounds of flesh out of the bodies of their supposed oppressors.

Scourge marvelled at her new arms and then licked her lips as they started to grow back. She tore Mulgrew's arm-- gauntlet and all-- off his body as he tried to impede the bleeding from his neck, but the severity of the latest injury pushed him over the edge. With his gauntlet, the villain could open any door, which included the one leading down into solitary, where the prison kept its worst offenders under lock and key.

Outside of the confines of the prison's central areas, the pair of Aleph representatives stationed on the island watched as the riot unfolded. Correctional officers rushed around them, trying to figure out how everything had gone to hell in such a short period, while they stayed calm and still, evaluating their options.

The Aleph agents-- Henrietta Lark and Klaus Weber-- were opposites, and everything about their appearances highlighted that.

When she activated her powers, the former, known as Nightshade, was a lithe Japanese woman who would have been a dancer if it wasn't for a magical twist of fate.

Dressed in a black skirt and blazer, with a crisp white shirt punctuated by the ocean blue tie, she was firmly muscular and slender in her frame, her dark hair cut short with her fringe spirit level straight halfway across her thick eyebrows.

That stood in stark contrast to Weber-- also known as Schwarzer Zwerg-- who stood in a black and orange costume that had seen better days. But then again, so had he. The German was a stout, short man, standing at 4 feet, 10 inches tall, with a thick black beard that hung down just above his keg-like stomach. His pale grey eyes peered out from beneath his bushy black brows, and his hook nose and craggy features gave him the appearance of being carved from granite, his leathery skin French-kissed by the Sun until he had the complexion of an old hiking boot.

Lark was already on the phone with Muldair when the riot broke out. Her eyes went wide as she watched the chaos unfold across the prison, and it was taking her too many seconds to process what it all meant. One minute the agent received orders to take a prisoner into protective custody, and then this?

"... I'm going to have to call you back," she said.

All of the cameras in the recreation hall had gone down, but the ones outside showed prisoners clashing with whoever they could get their hands on-- guards or fellow inmates be damned.

<"What's going on?"> asked Kishana, her voice a tinny rattle on

the other end of the phone.

"Massive riot. We need to get down there," replied Lark. She was never one to say more than what was needed, and she was also not the kind of person to break a habit, even in the face of a superpowered prison riot. So, she said her piece, and that was that.

Naturally, Kishana didn't share her succinct sensibilities. She cursed loudly and said, <"The prisoners saw the broadcast? Bloody hell! It's going to be a god damn free-for-all!">

"Yes. I'll keep you updated," said Lark.

Schwarzer Zwerg added, "I will slave comms to my cowl. You will have eyes for the duration. Do not be concerned."

<"We'll scramble support ASAP. The Meridian will be on-site as soon as they're able. Get Shrike to safety. Make sure nothing happens to her. That's the director's priority.">

"Not the preservation of all human life on the island?" questioned Zwerg, a smug tone in his voice.

Lark and Zwerg could hear Kishana curse again, even louder than the last, but before the Chief of Staff could reprimand the latter, Henrietta said, "Understood. Lark out."

Off the phone, Henrietta cursed in her native Japanese, while Schwarzer Zwerg vehemently agreed in German.

They hurried out of Aleph's prison-based office and down the short corridor connecting them to the prison's control room to see what the COs knew.

"They've fried the knockout gas lines along with the power dampening nodes," said Braxton Pepper, the senior CO in the control room. He was trying to keep an eye on his monitor as he clambered inside a suit of power armour but struggling to do both at the same time. "So, we can't shut down-- fuck! -- we can't shut down the riot in recreation."

"What about the rest of the facility?" asked Zwerg.

"Scourge's blast only affected the immediate area," noted Lark, pointing at the screen.

Pepper nodded in agreement. "Yeah, yeah, you're right... there's a radius surrounding her last known location that's dark, but the rest of the inmates are unconscious. We'll just need to clear them up."

"How many dead so far?" asked Zwerg.

Pepper grimaced. "We won't know until we get power back up. The EMP blast-- how did Scourge do that? -- it shorted out the links between the suits and the control room."

"What about the keys in the gauntlets?" asked Lark.

"They're hardened against most energy outputs, same as the weapons systems... so they'll work..." said Pepper. "So... they'll work... *oh fuck.*"

Lark grimaced. "Stay here and coordinate the riot control efforts. We will also need you to guide us to solitary without running into the inmates."

"Path of least resistance. Nice," said Zwerg.

"What about the riot?" asked Pepper.

The short German shook his finger. "First things first. Shrike was the one who sent Scourge down for life in this hellhole. We know where she's headed, where she'll lead any other rioters with the same urge to exact revenge now there's a deadline on it. We get to Shrike before Scourge; we control the object of their, uh, misplaced anger."

"Fuck!" shouted Pepper.

"...Yes, how do you think we feel?" asked Zwerg.

"Take a step back and cover your eyes," said Lark.

"Ah fuck, fuck, fuck, *fuck,*" said Pepper, doing as Lark told him. The COs had been briefed about the pair of Aleph agents before they arrived at Ziggurat Black, and this was something he'd been both excited and terrified to bear witness ever since. You never got this kind of action at Ziggurat Blue, and there were times he missed the simplicity of working the white-collar-supervillain guard beat.

A few steps away, Zwerg turned his head, then looked back as he cupped his hand over his eyes, leaving a slat between his fingers open so he could take a peek. "I love it when she does this."

Lark cleared her throat and quietly said, "*Abraxas!*" and her entire body vanished in a flash of unnatural light. She stepped forward a second later, standing a foot taller, clad in white and purple armour. The actual mechanics of her magic word eluded her, but once spoken, it triggered the transmogrification from her mortal form to this mystically empowered avatar. And she loved the way it felt.

"You ready, Nightshade?" asked Zwerg.

Her voice two octaves deeper and reverberating with supernatural power, she replied, "Yes."

ALEPH BLUE BOX DATA CACHE
'ZIGGURAT BLACK' – SUMMARY INFORMATION

In the very centre of the Bermuda Triangle, there was an island surrounded by an energy field that scrambled signals, played havoc with radar, and generally caused misery for everybody involved. Those anti-social properties made it the perfect site for a prison designed for supervillains.

The institution's architects harnessed the esoteric energy fields surrounding the island with a series of relays that bordered the prison, distorting communication signals unless authorised. If you weren't on the allowlist and tried to make your way onto the island via unauthorised means, you simply wouldn't make it. It was the perfect prison. And it was also hell on Earth for anyone who ended up there that didn't deserve it.

There were other specially designed Ziggurat prisons across the world. Blue was a white-collar lockup, while Black was the end of the line. The place they sent supervillains who committed the most grievous acts, the site specifically designed to keep them from hurting anybody else until their final days.

CITIES ON FIRE

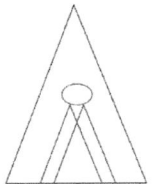

CHAPTER 8: IDENTIFYING MARKS
LOCATION: EN-ROUTE TO KIP'S BAY- NEW YORK

"First day, huh? You usually bring this kind of weather with you?"

Madison didn't respond to the woman sitting opposite her. The smug air she emanated in waves was off-putting, and there was something familiar about the woman that she couldn't put her finger on. She had been wearing sunglasses indoors, which was always a big warning sign for the former FBI agent.

Look out, it said, *I'm a douche*. That was no way to think of a new colleague, especially when there are so many psychics on the books.

Instead, she secured her holster under her right armpit, then placed her new service weapon inside, where it settled in comfortably. She made sure the pistol given to her before she was bundled into the back of the car felt right in her hand. She drew it with her left hand and held it straight forward, replacing it in the holster, then repeating the motion.

"We're about ten minutes out," said the driver.

Neither party introduced themselves, but the woman had given Madison a soft, warm smile when they'd first met, and nothing about her screamed trouble yet, so that was nice. She must have been in her early twenties, and Madison couldn't tell if her suit was an ironic statement or if it was Aleph dress code. Her coiled hair lay across her shoulders, her big eyes fixed on the road ahead.

"Thanks," replied Madison, comfortable with the smooth movement of her draw.

She holstered her gun one final time before checking the rest of the equipment the quartermaster gave her before their hurried exit.

She slipped a state-of-the-art tablet computer out from its sleeve and powered it up. When she unlocked it with a thumb press, a feed of information was already visible, containing all the limited intelligence they'd been able to gather regarding the explosion so far.

Travel plans, blueprints, posts from message boards and pertinent social media content. Nothing that she found helpful. She wanted a physical feel for the situation before making any assumptions about what had happened and why.

The driver checked the rear-view mirror then said, "Sorry, but can you please put your earpiece in?"

"Huh? Oh! Yeah, sure, sure," replied Madison.

She placed the small transmitter into her ear, and Kishana's voice piped through immediately.

<"I know this isn't how you expected your first day on the job to go, Myers, but this isn't how I expected it to go either.">

"That's fine. What's the situation?" replied Madison.

<"Massive explosion in downtown Manhattan, and I want boots on the ground that won't step on the FBI's. Yesterday you worked at their New York local field office, now you work at ours, so you get the assignment. Find out what happened.">

"What about me, chief?" asked the woman fidgeting opposite her.

She tilted her glasses down so her eyes were visible. Despite her outward attractiveness, she had a look that reminded her of the tweakers they used to throw into the drunk tank at the height of any given night's festivities. She was restless but tried to play it off, leaning back in her seat and peering out of the tinted window toward the world outside. She looked like she'd just woken up, all tussled red hair and bags under her weary eyes, and for some reason that Madison couldn't yet place, the woman looked familiar to the agent, even if she couldn't recall from where. Had she arrested her before?

<"You're there for moral support, Charlotte. What do you think?">

"But seriously," she said, leaning forward and pulling the lapels of her jacket around her chest.

<"Director Murray's travel itinerary took him through ground

zero of the blast. We've lost contact with his entourage. We need to know if this is an assassination attempt.">

"Or an assassination success?" Charlotte countered.

Kishana ignored that. <"Support teams are en-route, and the FBI and NYPD are expecting you imminently. Best behaviour. Find out if we just got walloped or if it was just a bloody coincidence. Either way, best behaviour.">

"She's talking to you. I'm Charlotte. Or Special Agent McQueen if we're super serious." She removed her sunglasses and slipped them inside her jacket before offering her hand to Madison. "But Ronnie, if we're going to be friends."

"Special Agent Madison Myers," she replied, shaking her hand. "That said, I don't know if I'm a Special Agent anymore? I didn't talk to anybody about my job title..."

Without the sunglasses, something clicked into place, and she immediately recognised the woman sat opposite her, even without hearing her name.

Charlotte McQueen used to be the Sneak, the partner and sister of Meridian member Tallyman. Her fall from the lofty heights of superheroics was the thing of FBI water cooler legend.

Madison cleared her throat. "I have to be honest; I never expected to meet you."

Charlotte smiled, thin lips melting together. "No one ever does. And if they do, they expect me to be running around in a silly little mask, drunk as fuck and high on whatever's snortable."

Sneak had been a teen hero years ago, but those golden years hadn't lasted. Drink, drugs, and even more drugs led her to drop off the map, but here she was, working for Aleph. That had to be one hell of a story, but now wasn't the time to ask about it. Maybe later if they were going to be friends.

"No, no, it's not. Honestly, it's just my world was one size an hour ago, and now it's infinitely bigger. I guess it's going to be full of surprises moving forward," said Madison.

"Well, that's nice," said Charlotte. "Most people are assholes. To me, I mean. So, I pre-empt their assholeness with my assholeness. Best to play it safe."

"Spraying wild, there," said Madison, before trailing off and saying, *"What a disgusting image..."*

Charlotte grinned. "You're an odd fucking one, aren't you? And ex-FBI?"

"As of like... yeah, an hour ago. A lot happened in sixty minutes. I guess it counts as a transfer. You don't have to work your notice in this job?"

"Yeah, I heard that. It must be cool. Listen, I'll play it straight with you because the last time I got partnered up with a norm, it was no end of hassle. Firstly, I don't speak to Tallyman anymore. I don't speak to anyone from that life unless I most definitely have to. Okay?"

"Uh, yeah, sure," said Madison. She didn't know where this was coming from, but from the sudden intensity in Charlotte's voice and the way she was staring at her through her dark glasses, it came from somewhere that didn't lurk far from the surface. "Secondly?" she continued.

"I'm clean. I haven't touched any of that shit for two years, seven months and three days. I'm clean, and I'm good, and I'm tested, and I'm good, okay?"

"Okay, you're clean," Madison repeated.

"And thirdly, yes, the video was real. Lynx is that fucking hung." She punctuated that unnecessary point by placing her hands behind her head and resuming her previous louche position.

The video. More accurately, the sex tape. Sneak and Lynx high on coke and god knows whatever else, with a third party recording the entire experience. It leaked pretty soon after and led to the public schism between Sneak and Tallyman that seemed to exist to this day. That and the punch Sneak threw at their last press conference before her exit from the media spotlight.

And if Lynx was that hung, *god damn*, thought Madison.

But that's not what interested her. None of those questions did. If she were here, she had to be straight; the drugs couldn't be in the equation, right? Her interpersonal relationships didn't matter to Madison, as long as they didn't cause an issue in the workplace. If she didn't speak to her brother, what did it matter? The thing that interested Madison, which drew her eye, was what sat holstered on Charlotte's left side. Something she'd only read about briefly but held her interest ever since.

The former superhero must have noticed Madison's eyes darting down because she un-holstered and held it up so the agent could get a better look. "You like what you see?" she asked.

Madison's eyes widened, and she quickly shook her head. "Sorry for staring. I've heard stories about that gun. Never imagined I'd see it for real, I guess."

Unlike some of her fellow agents, Madison wasn't one for magazines about firearms, nor did she read the super-gossip rags. But when she was working undercover with the Bureau, she had a very particular-- and not very flattering-- image to uphold, so found herself picking up both to keep up appearances. She'd read all about the weapon Charlotte wielded-- as well as its twin, held by her brother-- and how they didn't quite make *sense*, and if there was one thing Madison loved, it was a mystery.

Charlotte held the gun out and said, "Do you want to have a--"

She was interrupted when exterior noise seeped into the vehicle as the driver rolled down her window, and she immediately re-holstered her gun. Madison could see that the NYPD had mobilised fast, but then again, this is why they trained. After the towers fell and the black orchids took root, law enforcement agencies worldwide changed their approaches to mass casualty events. From the looks of it so far, this crime scene certainly qualified.

Though she tried to play it off as normal, Charlotte tilted her head down and replaced her glasses before anyone caught a look at her. Madison thought that was weird-- Charlotte McQueen was one of the most globally recognisable metahumans; what good was a pair of glasses?-- but it made sense she might be cagey about people spotting her in the field.

Madison looked beyond the driver as she held up her Aleph ID badge to catch a glimpse of the chaotic scene, black smoke billowing up into the sky a block down.

"Fuck," she whispered.

She'd never been smack dab at the centre of a terrorist attack before-- if that's what this was. She'd undergone the training-- both at the NYPD and FBI-- and she knew how she *should* respond to such a thing, but she felt a separation between the act and her current response to it. It wasn't *real* to her yet.

What did Kishana say? Boots on the ground?

"We're here," said the driver, having made it past the first police line and bringing the car to a stop soon after.

The pair exited the vehicle, and the driver wound down the window even further, allowing Madison to see her face fully for the first time; dark skin and delicate bone structure, freckles smattering across her cheeks. What was a woman like this doing working for an organisation like Aleph?

"I need to park up, and then I'll speak to the bomb squad. You're good?"

"As we're gonna be," replied Charlotte.

"Don't step in it," said the driver before flashing the agents a peace sign and driving off.

Half a city block was gone. Just *gone*. The buildings either side of the epicentre of the blast were gutted by the explosion, but you could trace the size of the initial detonation by the clear scorch marks that reached out from the husks of walls and road, like great, coarse paintbrush strokes that spread blistered chaos out from the centre.

City workers had been quick to shut off the gas and water mains left exposed like compound fractures jutting out of the shattered grey concrete, but the air was thick with smoke and would be for much longer than this day. Madison could smell burning plastic and instinctively covered her mouth when she caught her first breath.

Charlotte handed her a protective mask, and she gratefully accepted it. However, the smell, like the smoke, would take longer to leave than she would have wanted. It was in her now, and that was a difficult thing to shake. After putting her mask on, Charlotte shook her head. "This is bad. Really fucking bad."

"How many people died?" asked Madison. It was a question without an immediate answer. No one could give her a number right now. Questions. She always asked the questions, even when there was no one qualified to provide her with the solutions she wanted or *needed* now.

It was way past the lunch rush hour but still the middle of the day, the tail-end of Summer, and people were bound to get hungry at some point or another. That didn't even take into consideration the tourist trade. Entire groups happily hanging out in the restaurant and walking the streets outside it because nothing wrong could happen to *them*, could it? Why would you fear anything in a world where men and women could move faster than light and be more catastrophic than a splitting atom?

How many dead?

"I'm going to get a closer look at the blast site," said Charlotte. She shoved her hands into her pockets like a petulant teen and arched her neck so that her head lolled in the direction of ground zero.

"Are you sure that's a good idea? We should speak to the SAIC first," said Madison.

Charlotte's head swung around, making a dramatic show of tapping the side of her temple. "Enhanced senses. I'm more useful over there than I am out here. Go, do your thing, and I'll do mine." She went to turn again but hesitated. "And don't mention my name to anybody. It's a whole thing."

Madison sighed as the former hero hurried away. Was this her life now, or just a one-off under the tricky circumstances they all found themselves? She hoped it was the latter and not the former, but then again, this was a brave new world for her, and as much as her hunches always tended to be correct, she didn't have any of the usual feelings deep in her guts right now.

"Who even knows…?" she asked no one in particular.

Before she could think about her next move, she heard her name shouted by a familiar voice. "Myers? Is that you?"

She turned to see FBI Assistant Director Gregory O'Bannon walking over, "I thought it was. My God. Small world."

"Hey chief," she replied, extending a hand. "Long time no see."

"I saw you yesterday," he replied, shaking her hand. He gave her as much of a smile as would be polite considering the circumstances, then continued, "Shame this is where we're meeting again. You got the job then."

"Yeah, I passed their tests with flying colours. And two minutes later, all hell broke loose and here we are, right in the thick of it."

"To be honest, I don't fully understand why Aleph has a stake in this."

"The last known location of one of Aleph's top guys is that restaurant," she replied.

"*Fuck*," he exhaled.

"Do we have anything yet?" she asked. The group headed toward the final cordon between them and the smoking ruin of the former burger joint.

"We're still waiting for the emergency services to give us the go-ahead to go through the wreckage. I hate this. The waiting. Staying clear in case it's all a setup to kill even more of us."

Madison nodded. "Have any superheroes turned up?"

O'Bannon grimaced. He wasn't a fan of that question, but it bore asking whenever something like this happened in a densely populated metropolitan area.

Every Friday, O'Bannon would take his team out to the bar a few blocks down from the field office, and they would get drunk, first round on him. Get enough tequila in him, and he would go on about how much he hated the insertion of the superhero set into the world of law enforcement. What good was the due process when the likes of Majestic could hear you lying by the way your blood pressure shifted?

"…Not yet," he answered. "We've put out a call to the Meridian, but my understanding is they're unavailable. Always the case nowadays. Who's your friend?"

She looked over to where he was indicating and saw Charlotte passing through the final cordon before the still-smoking debris at the centre of the crime scene. "I don't know. But she's with Aleph. So, she's good, I guess."

Charlotte made a beeline for the nearest mask-wearing law enforcement officer and held up her Aleph badge to get his attention. "What've we got?" she asked.

Taking a moment to process her identification, he answered, "You're past the final perimeter, and we're just about to start the search for survivors, but we're not optimistic. There's no radiation, nothing mutagenic, but we still have to play it safe. We can't rush in, in case there's a secondary explosive and we're being lured into some kind of trap."

Charlotte noted that the fires were all out and then made a decision. "Caution is good, but I'm going to pop my head in anyways. I've never been known to be the 'play it safe' kind."

The office clamped his hand on Ronnie's shoulder, stopping her in her tracks. "Please, we're not moving in yet. We can't begin the search until we're sure it's safe. That doesn't exclude you."

"What's your name?" asked Charlotte. She glared at the officer's hand, then tipped her glasses down her nose with a roll of her eyebrows to look him in the eye.

"Sanchez," the officer replied, lifting his hand away from McQueen's shoulder when the full force of the look he was receiving hit home.

"Well, listen, Sanchez. Unfortunately, this badge I'm waving around gives me all kinds of permission to do all kinds of stupid shit. I have to go in there, and I have to go now. You're not liable for my life. I am."

"Fine. Fine!" said Sanchez, letting McQueen continue on her way. "But you're a fucking asshole!"

"Yup, that's me," said McQueen, brushing herself off and heading deeper into the disaster area.

What did she know? The detonation had been approximately forty-five minutes prior, but as soon as Aleph lost contact with Director Murray and his security detail, the organisation descended from up on high to take over the scene. That was her mandate, and she wasn't going to let some normie stop her from getting into the weeds of it.

This kind of thing was her job now. And with the smoke and detritus still hanging in the air from the earlier explosion, she knew she deserved every part of it. The air was thick with heat and damp in equal measure, the fire service having done what they could to extinguish the smatterings of fire left over from the initial blast.

That was interesting, she thought. There weren't many fires to deal with after the original explosion, so the idea behind it must have been about destruction at the moment of detonation and not about subsequent damage or fallout. That had to mean something, didn't it?

She clambered over the remains of the front entrance and began her survey of the explosively gutted establishment. She noted that the blast radius was almost an oval, burn marks from behind the now ruined counter to the front door. Beyond that, there were bodies. Or at this point, they were remains. Barely any flesh left on skeletons, what little skin was blackened and rendered into biological charcoal.

Away from prying eyes and possible observation, she lowered her sunglasses and wiped the tears forming from her eyes.

Adults. Children. Dozens of charred husks that had once been in the shapes of life were left disjointed and stuck in screaming freeze frames of their last moments. Walls had collapsed in on themselves, plastic and metal bending into horrible shapes that reminded her of shit modern art passed off as masterpieces in upmarket galleries.

Stepping forward and trying her best to ignore the exceedingly high death toll, she looked at where the tills had once stood and crouched down. Behind the counter, the scorch marks were intense for a short way, but moving out toward the front of the store, she could see the effects were more prolonged and just as severe.

"Directional blast?" she muttered.

She took out her handheld tablet computer and began to scribble notes with the stylus. Her marksman's eye allowed her to discern the small details, and she'd already spotted the melted remains of a 360-degree security system that had been in operation in the store. Most places like this backed up their footage, so she'd be able to get access to that at some point.

"*hhhhkkkkk*"

Charlotte jumped out of her skin at the ragged and thready voice and pulled out her gun.

It was pre-loaded for non-lethal use, but she said, "*Concussive*," just to be sure. In the span of a second, she'd un-holstered her weapon, confirmed it could knock out anybody coming at her and shouted: "Freeze!"

But who was she even calling out?

"*kkkkkkkkk*"

Charlotte tracked the noise-- the pile of debris that had a voice was ten metres away from ground zero of the blast. She tried to ignore the corpses, but with her eye and her brain, she knew the memory of the horror would never fade.

Realising the downed pile couldn't put up much of a fight, she holstered her weapon and hurried over to the debris. She began to pull at slabs of smoking fallen concrete and scalding hot twisted metal. If someone had managed to survive, then she had to do everything she could to save them. Even as her fingers burned and her skin blistered, Charlotte knew she couldn't stop. If there was a chance someone had survived, she couldn't waste any time.

Long seconds stretched out as she frantically dug, but soon enough, she moved enough rubble to reveal a severely burned man, his body a patchwork of catastrophic damage that had peeled back layers of his existence to show subcutaneous fats, bone and throbbing, aching organs. This man, whoever he was, clung to what little life was available to him as hard as he could, even if this didn't look like any life at all.

"*hhhhhhhhh,*" the survivor drawled, his mouth shredded at the corners, teeth visible through cheeks.

Whoever this was, he wore the remains of some kind of super-suit under the ragged remnants of a black three-piece, but it was the tattoo on his left pec that clinched his identity to the former Sneak. It sealed the deal because Ronnie had the same one on her right buttock.

"Holy shit. *Leon?*"

CITIES ON FIRE

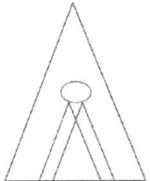

CHAPTER 9: WHO'S NEXT?
LOCATION: ALEPH ACTIVE INTELLIGENCE HQ, NEW YORK

James didn't mean to be nosey. He had two polystyrene cups of coffee from the machine down the hallway and was just trying to make it back to his office without spilling the contents down his front. Every team in the building had been re-tasked from their previous assignments to mining whatever came in from the New York blast site, including Loretta and himself.

The pair were waiting for the FBI and NYPD servers to sync up with their own so that a live stream of everything they knew fed through to Aleph, so they could begin to work through the case.

When James walked past Reggie Sandow and Julia Glüm's office, the security footage from the Shrike's decade-old murder spree was playing on their big screen. He'd personally seen it a couple of dozen times, but it stopped him in his tracks when combined with the day's revelation that the perpetrator behind the killings wasn't the Hannah Stone imprisoned for the crimes.

Floor 17 - Eastern Conference Room // Camera 1:

The Shrike arrived on the seventeenth floor of the building by breaking. Staff were working late due to a charity event Nicholas was hosting the next evening. A, the first victim, heard the sound of glass breaking and went to investigate. He had his throat pulled out for his curiosity. Blood covered the front of the Shrike's costume as the hero continued on her rampage.

Floor 17 - Eastern Corridor // Camera 3:

The next two victims, B and C, witnessed the Shrike's exit from the conference room, and attempted to intervene. B was kicked so hard in the knee cap that both his femur and tibia exploded out of his leg, which gave the Shrike time to wrap an arm around C's neck and twist. He fell to the floor instantly dead, while a palm strike put B out of his misery instantly.

Floor 17 - Eastern Corridor // Camera 2:

The Shrike continued onward. No hesitation. No second guessing. Victim D came out of the toilet to the immediate left of the hero, and had their head repeatedly slammed into the wall for their timing. In four seconds, their skull had impacted the plaster thirteen times, and by the fifth second, the man was dead, and his face resembled a dropped vat of chilli.

Floor 17 - Eastern Bullpen // Camera 1:

Victims E-K were frozen at their desks by the sound of violence. When they saw the Shrike, there was a moment of relief, then a moment of realisation. The hero's costume was mostly red now.

What happened next was yet another piece of damning evidence put forward by the prosecution, but it was also the most visceral. It took the Shrike less than forty seconds to murder seven men and women, the hero's martial prowess as indisputable as her guilt.

At this point in the trial, Hannah Stone had to be removed from the court due to her protestations of innocence.

Eleven people dead so far. The final victim count was twenty-seven.

"Why're you watching this?" asked James.

Reggie Sandow was a flinty looking man, sharp angles at his nose and cheeks, with a scratchy blond beard covering his lower jaw. His desk pointed him directly at the door to the office, so he had clocked James' arrival earlier, but said nothing.

Floor 17 / CEO Office / Camera 1

Victims L-Z were dead by the time the Shrike reached Nicholas' office. There was no white left on her costume. Only red. He was sat at his desk, and didn't move when she kicked the door open.

The Shrike looked past him, toward the window. The angle of the camera didn't cover that part of the room, nor could you see out the window itself. Then she looked back at Nicholas.

Nicholas stood. The Shrike covered the ground between them in less than a second. She pulled a knife from behind her back and proceeded to stab him to death. The violence was sudden and frenzied, the blade plunging into his chest repeatedly, again and again, as the Shrike was caught up in the rush of the act.

She didn't stop until his chest was a cavernous open wound, his internal organs spilling out in shredded fragments. Once the act was complete, she tore off her mask and spat on his corpse. Then she exited through the window.

"He really did a number on her, didn't he?" replied Reggie.

"Quinlan?" said James.

"Yeah. If she's a clone, or whatever super-science-craziness he claims, the work is impeccable," said Reggie.

Julia Glüm tapped her pen on the plaster cast covering her left leg. A Level 2 metahuman was robbing a bank she had the unfortunate luck of being across the street from. She was frantically clearing the area of civilians when the super-villain-- who was eventually apprehended by Sergeant Ross' Armoured Response Team-- threw her through a store window. Her leg was fractured in four places, but she was back at her desk as soon as the doctor cleared her. She was frizzy-haired, her dark locks matching the tired circles beneath her eyes.

"It's this though, isn't it?" said Julia, holding up a remote and skipping forward until she reached a later part of the proceedings, where the prosecutor was questioning an expert.

"Please introduce yourself to the court?" requested the District Attorney.

"Of course. My name is Gerhard Hochburg. I am the head of

Aleph's combat and defense department."

The witness was in his mid-fifties and spoke in a considered, gravelly tone that he had the misfortune of having his entire life. His face was weathered, leathery skin and multiple facial fractures having healed in various disjointed ways so as to make him somewhat unrecognisable from his parent's expectations. He had his father's pale green eyes. His mother's hard-to-earn smile.

"What does that entail?"

"I train the men and women of Aleph. Those who are the first responders to metahuman incidents." Even past his prime, he was still built like a living weapon under his suit.

Five years later he would be dead, but not for lack of trying.

"What qualifies you for that position, Mr Hochburg?"

"When I was a teenager I manifested the metahuman ability to absorb and apply any fighting style I experienced first hard. I have spent nearly forty years travelling the world, expanding my knowledge of martial arts. I am a practitioner and scholar of every known fighting style on the planet. So, what qualifies me? Experience."

"Thank you. Now, how can you be so sure it's her? Hannah Stone?" asked the District Attorney.

"Objection!" shouted Hannah's Defense Attorney. *"Assumes fact not in evidence!"*

"We're way past that, counsel. Overruled," said the presiding judge. *"Continue."*

Gerhard nodded then gestured toward the television positioned for the jury to see. *"Every martial art is like a language. Some are fluent, others can get through a conversation, and others simply cannot wrap their heads around the words being said. I have compared footage captured of Hannah Stone in action as the vigilante Shrike, and mapped her movements and competency as a martial artist against the CCTV footage taken from the crime scene. It is the same person."*

Footage flitted across the screen. Videos of the Shrike in action on the street, fighting criminals, supervillains, robots. Whatever it was that a superhero fought in their day-to-day lives, there was inevitably footage of it playing on the screen, and immediately next to that was the CCTV replay. The physical movements were identical. How the Shrike threw a punch on the street was the same way she threw a punch that night.

"Now, could someone copy those movements? Pretend to be the Shrike?" asked the District Attorney.

"Simply, no."

An alert on the big screen paused the footage. NYPD and FBI databases were now linked with Aleph's own, and data from the scene of the Kip's Bay explosion was now coming in.

"And we're ready to go," said Julia.

"Guess it's back to work then," said Reggie.

James headed back to his office, but was surprised to find that their screen didn't display the same data-feed as the other's. He handed Loretta her coffee and asked, "What's taking so long? Sandow and Glüm have already got their feed up."

James took his seat and ran his thin fingers through his curly black hair; his avian features pinched tight as he demonstrated his signature *lack* of patience. "Data's late now, right?" he said.

"Just wait," replied Loretta. She rubbed the side of her nose absentmindedly, the familiar bump of an old break providing a meditative focus. At the same time, she tried to push her feeling of serenity toward her partner. He needed constant input, else his mind would wander, and he'd start making connections that no one asked for him to make. "I'm sure--"

Kishana swooped into their room, took James' coffee out of his hand, and took a sip. "I needed that, cheers. Okay, listen, I need you on something important." She held up a small remote and pointed it at their empty screens. Information began to fill the large monitors up as data came in from whatever private server Muldair had linked to their workstations. Names. Job histories. Top secret information reserved for Eyes Only, which the pair of intelligence operatives had never been privy to before.

"Directory Murray is dead. Succession Protocol is green," said Kishana.

"Fucking hell, okay, right," said James. He sidled behind his desk and flexed his fingers. "Who's up first?"

Kishana held her hands up. "Okay, listen to me. You know by

now, but I'll repeat it for posterity: With Succession Protocol, your responsibility is to vet every prospective director of Passive Operations the algorithm spits out. You mine every single facet of their lives, working history, good deeds, and bad. You do not show bias; you do not show a preference. Everything you do goes through *me*. And then we provide dossiers to the UN Security Council. Pure data. No supposition today, people. Do you understand me? I'm going to be here every step of the way, but I'm overseeing the situation in Ziggurat Black at the same time, so no messing. Get to work."

"Of course," said James.

"Who's first on the list?" asked Loretta.

"Fuck me. '*Naasir Al-Sheikh*'?" Kishana was visibly shocked, her finger pointing at the screen as she yanked off her headset. "Succession Protocol spat his name out?"

"Uh, oh, boy. That's... that's Tiamat's former chief of spies, right?" said James.

"And that's pretty goddamn bad, isn't it?" said Loretta.

ALEPH BLUE BOX DATA CACHE
'SUCCESSION PROTOCOL' – SUMMARY INFORMATION

The following is a memo written by Arthur Galloway (AKA Professor Ultra II), Aleph's Head of Scientific Inquiry (2000-2019), relevant to the topic at hand:

From the Desk of Arthur Galloway...

To whom do we entrust the safety of the world?

I am not referring to the super-heroes. Super-heroes come and go. Since 1940, the Western world has witnessed the coming and going of The Trust (16 years), The Community (7 years), The Futurists (10 years), Maximum Justice (4 years) and The Revival (1 year).

There have been minor groups that do not operate on a global scale. There are groups formed at the behest of individual nations. There will always be super-heroes. There will always be super-hero teams of varying efficiency.

But who truly protects the world? And who holds those people to account?

Aleph.

In my nearly nineteen years as a part of this organisation, I have tried my best to ensure that Aleph is backed with the best means to protect the world. Armoured Response Team exo-skeletons. The enhanced-security Ziggurat prisons. Various armaments designed to counter the use of a multitude of meta-human abilities. But what good is a weapon, if it cannot be wielded by someone deserving of the responsibility?

What about the human factor?

I have successfully petitioned the United Nations Security Council to allow for a new method of deciding who is responsible for the direction of Aleph as we move into a new decade, something I am referring to as 'Succession Protocol'. This is the first and last time I will discuss it. Details of design and implementation are not relevant.

Understand: The protocol is online. The protocol is active. There is no going back now.

Succession Protocol is an intuitive computer virus designed to penetrate even the most hardened of databases. It does not matter if the data centre belongs to the CIA, MI5, GRU or PSIA. Succession Protocol has access. State secrets do not hold any interest to the virus.

I have designed a virus that will scour every database, civilian or military, private or public, and provide a list of candidates worthy of bringing into the fold as one of the Directors of Aleph. The United Nations Security Council will be provided the list, and vote on who should be installed. No subterfuge. No misinformation. The Succession Protocol is pure information. I will not allow an organisation such as Aleph to fall into the hands of bad actors.

This is now the way of the world.

Finally, all research and development into Succession Protocol was performed on a secured, non-networked installation, separate to any Aleph installation in existence. Since activation, there is no trace of the work done to create the Succession Protocol. You cannot find it. You cannot delete it. You cannot duplicate it.

As of this memo, I have handed in my resignation from the position of Head of Scientific Inquiry at Aleph. I trust the world is in good hands.

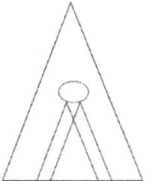

CHAPTER 10: MAN IS A ROPE
LOCATION: FBI ACADEMY - QUANTICO, VIRGINIA
FIVE YEARS AGO:

Madison would be lying if she said she wasn't looking forward to this. She'd been working at the Bureau for over a year now. Even though the Criminal, Cyber, Response, and Services Branch-- better known as the CCRSB-- head hunted her, she was itching for something more after a decade in the NYPD. The buzz word at the moment was 'meta-crime', and every law enforcement agency-- the FBI included-- was behind the curve when it came to dealing with it.

What had O'Bannon said to her after he'd gone on one of his rants? What good was a Glock 17M in the face of criminals who could chew bullets? He wasn't precisely wrong, was he?

"Can't believe you made us late," grumbled Madison.

Santos was nonplussed, trailing behind her partner as the pair entered the large auditorium. "We're not late. We're on time."

"Yeah, but I wanted to get a good seat," replied Madison. She looked around and tried to find a seat close enough to the front but found that their colleagues had already taken them. A few seconds later, she spotted two spaces, grabbed Genevieve by the sleeve and tugged her forward. "Over there."

Yanking her arm away from Madison, Santos followed but with zero good grace. She leaned in so no one else could hear and whispered, "You're such a damn nerd, kiddo. Just be glad I let you drag me to this goddamn thing."

Madison shuffled past a handful of seated agents until she reached the pair of vacant seats. "This is the future, Santos. Get on board."

Genevieve slumped down into her chair and waved her partner

off. "Yeah, it was *in* our future, too. Our session wasn't scheduled until next month, but you had to ask Greg to get us in on the first day. You're so damn eager."

"We spend more and more of our time assisting in meta-crime because state boundaries mean jack-shit to somebody who can leap across them in a single bound. If this guy can give us some insight-- and I hear he knows his shit-- then I'm all for it. Sooner rather than later."

"Okay, okay, it's starting, so quiet your enthusiasm down. Because I hate it," said Genevieve.

The lights overhead dimmed, and the stage came into sharp focus. An ordinary-looking man in his fifties stood with his hands behind his back, waiting patiently. He was dressed in a pair of old shoes cleaned well, pleated trousers pressed within an inch of their fibrous life, as well as a white silk shirt and burgundy tie tucked under a brown cardigan. He looked every part the academic, and while Madison would have been sweating under the spotlight, he was calm and relaxed, a thin smile on his lips. He glanced to his left, where a young African American academic sat behind a laptop. The second man was tall, too large for the seat they'd given him, and he loomed over the computer as he waited for the signal.

On the wall behind him, the projector displayed:

HUMANITY x META-HUMANITY.

"Good morning, everybody. My name is Doctor Wei Gao Rui, and I am a professor of metahuman science. This scientific field may be one that many of you are unfamiliar with, but as we journey further into the new millennium, it is vital. The world's established rules change every day, so we can either cling to what we thought we knew before or build a brand-new understanding to move forward.

"Before we begin, I want to share my qualifications. Who am I to speak with authority on a subject such as this? I hold numerous Masters and Doctorate degrees, covering the fields of biochemistry, bioengineering and genetics. I have spent my entire adult life researching the metahuman gene-- what are its causes, what are its effects."

"I spent four years working under Doctor Arthur Galloway, who some of you might know better as Professor Ultra. *I do not come at this subject from a place of ignorance.* To say I am qualified to speak on this subject is a vast understatement. Still, I hope this contextualises the information I am about to provide."

Santos leaned over to her partner and whispered, "This guy is going to be a barrel of laughs. I can tell."

Even though she was smiling, Madison put a finger up to her lips and mimed *shush.*

Rui gestured to his assistant. "Before we begin, please allow me to introduce you all to my associate, Doctor Joseph Sumner."

The younger doctor gave the room of FBI Special Agents and other assorted Bureau employees a gentle wave before Rui continued.

"We will be more than happy to answer any questions you might have once the presentation is over."

He gave his associate a nod, and the previous projection behind him gave way to another:

IDENTIFYING THE 'OTHER'

"In the course of our research, we have identified five types of metahuman. It's important to note that the term 'metahuman' is a catch-all for an 'enhanced person', not just those who exhibit the meta-gene. We'll expand on that later."

"We can identify a metahuman via an array of techniques. Unfortunately, we do not yet have a way to make these methods miniaturised and mobile. Therefore, they are not an option in the field, but we can reduce the metahuman spectrum to five profiles with continued study. For example, post-humans-- as they're also known-- absorb light differently. Expel heat differently. They are humans but function on a different level. We can use this information to identify who is a metahuman, but further classification is much harder. But suppose we use the Meridian as an example. In that case, we have a variety of metahuman test cases we can use to illustrate this point."

ONE: INTERNAL = ACTIVE AND LATENT

"First, we have those with the meta-gene embedded in their genetic code. We split these into two groups: 'Active', wherein the meta-gene carriers manifest their abilities naturally, without a catalyst. This activation usually occurs in adolescence, but there have been cases of pre-adolescent manifestations. Through our interviews with Majestic, we hypothesise he falls under this category, as he exhibits none of the markers consistent with the second group, which we call 'Latent'."

"This involves power manifestation through exposure to certain mutagenic properties, such as the mineral Erkalite. Tallyman, for example. His family carries the latent meta-gene, and it took exposure to Erkalite to activate it. We also know that the Tallyman's partner, Sneak, has the same genetic quirk and exposure to Erkalite has resulted in the manifestation of similar powers to her brother."

"Collectively, we call these two groups 'internally manifested metahumans'. 'Internal', as the powers came from within the genetic code, and either manifested with or without aid."

"Now, before we go any further, it's worth discussing what exactly *Erkalite* is. Formally discovered in 1926 by Professor Ivor Erkhart, it's a mineral found across the world but with higher concentration deposits across the North American and Asian continents. It's mildly-- and safely-- radioactive and interacts with a specific gene in the body to trigger the manifestation of special abilities. The meta-gene. If you do not have the meta-gene present, Erkalite does nothing."

"We believe this has been a driving force behind the proliferation of the archaic hero of myth; peoples exposed to Erkalite granted powers. Interestingly, the further into the 21st century we go, the more varied the power sets manifest. Historically, we would see powers based around strength and stamina, but now we see electrokinesis and technopathic-based abilities. It's as if when the world changes, so do the manifestations of the meta-gene."

TWO: EXTERNAL

"Second, we have 'external-type'-- those who have been gifted abilities by some outside force. Starlight wields cosmic bands that allow him to manipulate so-called 'cosmic energies'. He claims to have received these from an interstellar force that resurrected him. His identity is public knowledge-- stuntman Tully Rogers-- as is his death. I am aware the FBI have an open case on the docket regarding the veracity of his claims. And then we have the speedster Slipstream, who claims to have gained his powers after his biology was changed to allow him to manipulate his baseline speed. Again, we have no idea if this is true, but taken at face value, this allows us the designation of 'external'."

Santos leaned over to Madison' ear and whispered, "He's playing the same Pokemans game my nieces adore. Internal-type... external-type... come on..."

THREE: ARTIFICIAL

"There are metahumans who have built the mechanisms behind their power set. The Grimm is one such member of the Meridian. His exo-suit allows his great feats of strength and endurance, but without it, he's just a baseline human. Highly trained, but human. A large number of so-called supervillains fall into this category. Power armour and other devices are prevalent in that scene due to various factors. Once the genie was out of the bottle, there was no putting it back. Armoured suits were suddenly a known quantity, and their usage across the world increased. I know that some of my colleagues in the field say we should omit this 'artificial-type' of metahuman, but I believe it would be remiss to exclude them."

FOUR: ALCHEMIC

"The hardest type to qualify are those we're calling 'alchemic'-- powers based in the magic or arcane. Adikia and Penance both claim their abilities are mystical. Penance claims to be a 'Spirit of Vengeance' who feeds on energy he claims is 'guilt'. Readings taken during the use of his powers didn't give us any quantifiable information. Magic is just energy manipulation at the end of the day. Matter manipulation at its most extreme and mysterious, but still adhering to the laws of physics. Some postulate that Penance's abilities are an advanced form of telepathy, that he drains psychic energy-- actual electrical energy from the brain-- and uses it to supercharge his own. We probably won't ever know; it's not the kind of thing you can study passively. Adikia claims to be an immortal warrior from before the beginning of record time. The less said about that, the better."

FIVE: ALIEN

"The final type is somewhat of a catch-all, one we refer to as 'alien'. There are two examples of this in the Meridian. Firstly, the extra-terrestrial Zyj, AKA Wayfinder, whose physiology is wholly different from our own, and Tempest. He belongs to the underwater race known as the Homo Aquaticus. Imagine; a separate species that climbed the evolutionary ladder in a similar direction to Homo Sapiens but evolved to survive underwater. With that evolution comes adaptations that can be construed as 'superpowers' on the surface world-- eyes designed to function in the ocean's darkest depths mean enhanced vision on the surface. Skin and internal organs adapted to survive the intense pressure of the oceans means invulnerability. The oceans aren't all calm, cool, and peaceful; across the seafloor are hydrothermal vents where the temperatures can reach more than 464 °C / 867 °F. I could go on, but I think you get the picture."

"Each of these types come with their strengths and weaknesses. Some power sets are unique. Some are uniform. You cannot make any assumptions when it comes to the metahuman. Now that we can identify what we're up against, we can then begin to deal with them."

COMBATTING THE KNOWN

"Confronting a metahuman does not spell doom for the responder. It's important to note that not all metahumans are created equal. They are human with a genetic quirk that gives them powers, but they are still human. That means de-escalation techniques and negotiation tactics *can* and *will* still work. But as with all of these procedures, there is a chance that they will fail, and it's at that point, things can become a challenge."

"It's important to figure out what you're dealing with. In conjunction with national law enforcement agencies and the Meridian, we have developed the Metahuman Offenders Database. 'MHOD' contains a detailed analysis of all metahumans who have been through the system. With that knowledge, we built Ziggurat Black."

POWER SCALE

"We have broken down the metahuman power scale into six levels."

"Level 0. Meta-humans with abilities that cannot harm others. Increases in baseline strength by 1%, slightly better vision, etc. These can vary from somebody who has a knack for fixing electronics but can't talk to computers, to someone who can run an extra mile compared to the next person. Level 0s are referred to as Double Zeroes, as both their type and position on the power scale are minimal."

"Next, we have Level 1, colloquially referred to as 'Person-Breaker'. These are people with abilities that can kill. Strength to break bones, psychic abilities that can place the wrong ideas in people's heads. Dangerous, but not enough to end the world. Your standard beat cop should, in theory, be able to apprehend a Level 1 if they follow the procedure we'll get to later."

"Moving on, we have Level 2, 'Street-Breaker'. This category of metahuman concerns those abilities that can cause real damage. Telepathic power to induce a stroke, or fists that can punch through a car's engine block. We recommend the intervention of a SWAT team in these instances, as the risk to human life and property damage is high."

"Level 3s are what we call 'City-Breakers'. We're entering the territory where other metahumans would look to intervene. These are the types of threats that will draw groups like the Crusaders or the Meridian. Strong enough to shatter buildings. They are strong enough to psychically convince people that throwing themselves off the highest building they can find is a good idea. We recommend calling in the army."

"Now you're getting into powers beyond the pale. 'World-Breakers'. Level 4s are metahumans who can theoretically only be opposed by metahumans of equal ability. That is if you want to have a chance of minimising loss of human life. These are metahumans who, if they wanted, could shatter the Earth's mantle. Knock the moon out of orbit and throw the Earth's ecosystem into disarray. I think the only reason we haven't seen a threat such as this attack since the formation of the Meridian is that… what's next? You destroy the world. Where does that leave you? Contact the Meridian but know that they're probably already on their way or engaging the threat."

"And finally, Level 5, the so-called 'Cosmic-Breaker'. Anything beyond a Level 4 is something we can't think to counter as baseline humans. A Level 5 would be the end of everything. We have never known of a metahuman to go beyond Level 4. If the power levels can vary from Double Zero to Earth-shattering, then it only makes sense for the scale to go beyond that. And if a metahuman manifests powers like that on Earth, nothing we do will matter. Because we'll be dead before we even know it."

CITIES ON FIRE

FBI - MOST WANTED - KIDNAPPINGS/MISSING PERSONS

WEI GAO RUI
July 17, 2030
Bay Ridge, New York

Date(s) of Birth Used: October 21, 1970
Place of Birth: Lamma Island, Hong Kong
Hair: Brown
Eyes: Brown
Height: 6'1"
Weight: 185 pounds
Sex: Male
Race: Chinese
Nationality: American
Scars and Marks: Bullet scars across the right abdomen and collar bone. Appendectomy surgical scar.

REWARD
The FBI is offering a reward of up to $1,000,000 for information leading to an arrest in this case.

REMARKS
WEI GAO RUI frequently travelled abroad but his known itinerary did not have him leaving New York at the time of his disappearance.

DETAILS
WEI GAO RUI was last seen in Bay Ridge, New York after presenting a seminar at Hudson University. He disappeared from the faculty afterparty.

Anyone with information about WEI GAO RUI, or what may have happened to him, is asked to call the FBI New York Office at ▇▇▇▇▇▇▇▇. You may also contact your local FBI office, the nearest American Embassy or Consulate, or you can submit a tip online at ▇▇▇▇▇▇.

CITIES ON FIRE

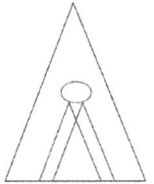

CHAPTER 11: RIOT CONTROL
LOCATION: ZIGGURAT BLACK - BERMUDA TRIANGLE

Even though Scourge had snatched the gauntlet that unlocked every door in prison, it was the grotesquely obese Valla who led the group of inmates toward the solitary wing. Wave after wave of COs were battered, beaten and in some cases slaughtered, all unable to stop the advance being made by the re-empowered and rioting bad guys.

Scourge handed Mulgrew's armoured glove to the delicate-looking nymph known as Stylostixis, whose skin was once again beginning to sprout tiny, razor-sharp needles. She was unsure of what her radioactive new arms might do to the device, and if this gauntlet was their ticket to Hannah Stone's cell, she didn't want to risk damaging it.

The guards standing between the villains' end goal tried in vain to halt their progress, but Valla's deviant physiology devoured the energy directed at them, powering her up and giving them a straight shot toward their goal.

Valla was at the front, with Chemtrail hopping around immediately behind her, transmuting the sedative gas pumped out of the walls into oxygen. She was pointing at the valves releasing the drugs into the air so that the energy blasting Dev could melt the components into slag.

From behind their massive human shield, the villains chanted and jeered. Occasionally, they threw bolts of destructive energy at the guards or unleashed whatever offensive abilities they wielded to continue their push forward.

"We're here!" bellowed Valla, gesturing just beyond the last bastion of guards in their vicinity.

The remaining COs were assembled in front of a large vault door, their power armour buzzing as they cycled their weapons from non-lethal to deadly.

Before they could even unleash what armaments they had available to them, Scourge gave the signal, and Valla released all that pent up energy in a huge kinetic blast. The armour worn by the first line of defence agonisingly collapsed, crushing the bodies within like tin cans, while the rest of the guards were sent flying away from the scene.

"Yeah, we are," murmured Scourge as she rotated her newly energised limbs, marvelling at the way they shone.

She wondered what else she could do now that her powers were released from the oppressive dampeners. Did she even need a human body anymore? How could she find out without doing something drastic?

"Y-you gonna un-unlock that?" asked Chemtrail, gently swaying from side to side. She was pointing at the gauntlet Stylostixis held, then to the large door, an excited look on her face. "You g-gonna?"

"Don't," said Scourge, holding her hand up in front of Stylostixis.

Strolling past the others, she lightly pressed her glowing fingertips against the vault door and then smiled. Her hand slipped inside the reinforced metal, melting it all the way inside, and she gutted the locking mechanism with a smooth movement downward. The vault hissed, whined, and then slowly opened, revealing the long corridor that made up the solitary wing.

And at the farthest end, in front of a vault door that presumably was another entrance to the same area of the prison, stood Schwarzer Zwerg and Nightshade, who looked like they'd been caught with their hands deep down inside the cookie jar.

"Oh, hell," said Zwerg.

"Open the door," ordered Nightshade. She started to slowly walk toward the rioting prisoners.

"What are you going to do?" he asked.

She didn't reply. Instead, she picked up speed as her walk became a jog, before breaking into a full sprint.

On the opposite end of the corridor, Valla chuckled and stepped forward, offering herself up to be the first to throw down with Nightshade. As if there were rules in this kind of fight? Before Nightshade even reached the group, Stylostixis unleashed a torrent of needles from her hand that could have torn through solid steel, but the hero vaulted forward, barrelled around in mid-air, and then grabbed Valla by the ears as she soared overhead.

Using her immense strength, she landed and, in the same motion, threw Valla heel overhead. The obese villain cried out in shock, and the ground shook on impact, but she fell silent as she was rendered unconscious, the violent concussive force of her impromptu acrobatics ping-ponging her brain around in her shallow skull.

Scourge swore loudly and pushed through the crowd of villains who were shocked by the sudden takedown of Valla, then screamed, "Chem-- Dev-- take her! Everyone, just kill her! Kill her!"

Cracking her knuckles, Nightshade grimaced as the villains swarmed her. This madness worked in her favour. Even without her magic word and the transformative power that came with its utterance, she was a fiercely trained close-quarter combatant. With both? She became a force to be reckoned with.

On top of her mystically enhanced physiology, Nightshade's powers revolved around balance, just like her sister Oleander. That meant if Valla threw a punch capable of shattering a mountain, Nightshade was strong enough to withstand it. Chemtrail sent a flood of toxins in her direction? Nightshade was immune to the worst that could be thrown at her. She hadn't faced a walking radioactive meltdown before, but with Scourge staring her down, that encounter was becoming an inevitability.

The problem was, when taking on multiple threats at once her powers became inconsistent. She had to be careful to focus on one attack at a time, even if she was being pummelled from all different directions by all sorts of fists and feet. But if all the villains dog-piled her-- like they were at that very moment-- it meant they couldn't unleash their destructive powers without injuring one another, and until they figured that out and stopped caring, she had the edge. Then they'd happily kill each other to get to her.

It was at times like this that the shattered glass voice in the back of her head would start to whisper terrible, hateful things. All it wanted was chaos and destruction, and though she rarely did what it asked, when she fed the beast, it didn't hesitate to encourage her to do more.

"Come on... come on..." said Schwarzer, as he frantically fumbled with the intricate lock on the sealed door at his end of the corridor. For some reason, the electronic keycodes transmitted from the gauntlet to the micro-computers in the prison's locks weren't enabled for solitary, and he wasn't known for his hand-eye coordination. "Damn it!"

<"What's going on?"> said Kishana, her voice crackling in his ear. There was interference in the comms line, probably due to how deep they were in this hellhole of a place. <"Do you have eyes on the target?">

"Negative," he replied.

A scream like breaking glass, and suddenly, Scourge was there, having made it past the pile-up of villains battling with Nightshade and crossed the distance between the two ends of the corridor in record time. "She's mine, she's mine, she's mine!"

She threw herself at Schwarzer in a rage, her hands crackling with radioactive energy. Before she could grab him, he ducked down, then threw his shoulder up as forcefully as possible. He caught her flush in the stomach and flipped her across his compact frame, sending her sprawling down the hallway.

Without missing a beat, the insanity fuelling the entire escapade ramping up past safe levels, she scrambled back to her feet and threw a straight punch, but her energy-construct limb splashed ineffectually against his smug face, whatever cohesion it had compromised by his super-dense hide.

"You're not going to do shit to me like that," he said. "Now stand--"

Scourge interrupted him by shoving her hand into his mouth. "How about this?" She unleashed a blast of energy inside the short-statured hero as he gagged. A split second later, his eyes rolled up inside his head as his insides were instantly turned to bloody soup.

He fell against the door, his liquefied innards spilling out of his spluttering orifices in short order.

Scourge looked back at where Nightshade was repeatedly

punching Dev in the face, then clicked her tongue impatiently. She reached her hand through the metal of the door and wrenched the slagged remains of the locking mechanism back out and then pulled the doors open wide, revealing a long hallway.

Connected to the corridor were a series of specially designed cells constructed to keep the worst prisoners under wraps, for either their own safety or for the safety of others. Usually, Scourge herself would have ended up here for the kind of antisocial behaviour she was currently exhibiting, but they were way past that now.

When it came to the reasoning behind Shrike's confinement, it was a matter of both. The villains hated her because she had put a large portion of them away, solo or alongside her friends in the Meridian. Whenever she was in the general population, the rest of the inmates took the opportunity to do their worst. For a while, the woman's life was a cycle of leaving the medical wing, getting assaulted in gen pop, going back to the medical wing, rinse, and repeat. That was before the warden finally had enough and put her in solitary permanently.

There was no love lost between her and the COs. She broke bad. She was as bad as the other prisoners, if not worse, for the hypocrisy she exhibited outside. When the prisoners had their chance to chew on her for however long they could, the guards usually let them at her. If it went too far, that's when they'd intervene, but not before. And here she was now, sat in her cell, sat in the dark, ready for the Scourge to finally kill her.

No time like the present...

Momentarily distracted by the sight of Schwarzer's empty carcass, Nightshade stumbled as Stylostixis threw a handful of needles across the hero's face. The deluge managed to cut through the mystical invulnerability she usually relied upon, and the pain was sudden and violent.

Blinded, Nightshade flailed her arms wildly and swatted the pin-cushioned meta backwards, bone breaking and cartilage popping against the edge of her palm. With Stylostixis down, Nightshade pushed forward, the most hardcore opponents who stood against her no longer conscious. None of the others posed much of a threat, and she'd already wasted too much time.

The end of the corridor where Scourge had stepped out of sight was suddenly filled with a blinding light that caused Nightshade to falter. The entire compound shook, walls to floor, and then Scourge reappeared, unconscious, and held up by the scruff of her scorched and shredded prison uniform by none other than the world's greatest superhero, newly arrived and unfazed by the chaos.

"This riot is over. Please return to your cells," said Majestic, his chest still smoking from where he'd clearly taken the brunt of Scourge's diabolical radioactive attack. His incandescently white costume was still pristine, though his blue cape was singed at the ends.

The previously rampaging supervillains fell to their knees and hooked their hands around the back of their heads. Whatever this had been, and with however many dead, it was over.

"I'm sorry I took so long to get here," said Majestic.

Majestic turned his attention to the empty cadaver belonging to Schwarzer Zwerg, and his expression darkened. Nightshade was aware that they'd worked together once, back when the German powerhouse had been 'freelance' in his superheroic career, but he wasn't aware of any profound relationship between the two. But then again, they always said Majestic had a bleeding heart.

Nightshade looked back at the surrendered villains then approached the newly arrived hero. Before saying anything, she knelt down in front of the remains of her partner. The way his indestructible, super-dense skin was the only thing left intact after Scourge's radioactive attack left a sickening impression in her mind. She noticed that she had inadvertently stepped into the thin gruel of his internal organs and shuddered at the thought of what his final moments must have felt like.

"It's fine. You ended it," said Nightshade.

He nodded even if he didn't necessarily agree. "I'll secure the prisoners."

He blurred out of sight, and then the supervillains vanished one by one, as he returned them to their cells, leaving Nightshade to consider the situation. Where Majestic had made his entrance, she could see a pair of scorched trenches burned through the walls next to the cell, all the way up to the ceiling. You could see the sun piercing through, even this deep into the island. There was a second hole, the size that would suggest a man had arrived through it. That's how Majestic had got inside, but what did the first two mean?

Answers on a postcard. Most importantly, and still behind bars, was Hannah Stone. Her hands were burned, and the sleeves of her prison uniform scorched, but she was simply sat on her bunk, her matted blonde hair obscuring her features. What had Nightshade missed?

She picked up the comms ring that Zwerg had worn and held it up to her face. When she was empowered by her magic word, she couldn't wear anything but her costume; anything else just dissolved into nothingness.

"Situation secure. Majestic is on-site," she said.

<"Schwarzer?"> asked Kishana.

"...Dead. No idea how many others. Dozens, at least. Stone is safe, though."

"She'll be safer with me," said Majestic.

Nightshade turned around and watched as Majestic bent open the reinforced steel bars of Hannah's cell. Before she could say anything, the caped hero said, "She'll be safer with me right now. The Meridian's UN charter authorises me to take prisoners into custody if I think it is in the best interest of any given situation. And considering what just happened not even a minute ago..."

"...I have my orders," replied Nightshade.

"I understand. And I respect that," said Majestic. The cell was now fully open, but Hannah hadn't moved from where she was seated. The burns on her hand had worsened, the skin peeling freely from its previously untarnished moorings, but she hadn't made a sound, nor a move. "But I'm doing this."

<"Nightshade-- do not let him remove Stone from the scene!"> ordered Muldair.

Majestic smiled and shook his head. He tapped his ear and said, "Tell Kishana I understand her concerns, but she knows where to find me. Where to find us." He placed a hand on Hannah's shoulder. "Time to go."

There was a stillness, a moment of absolute calm after all hell had broken loose on the island, and Majestic began to take to the air.

He held Hannah in his arms so delicately, and then they were gone, leaving a flurry of brick dust to swirl where he once stood. Now there was a different kind of stillness, one filled with a tension not so easily dispelled.

<"...He's gone, isn't he?"> said Kishana.

"Yeah."

<"You didn't even try to stop him.">

"There was nothing I could have *done* to stop him," she said.

There was silence on the other end of the line. Of course, Nightshade was right, and of course, Kishana had to say what she'd said, but still... Majestic had taken the director's sister out from under them, translocating to Challenger Deep, the Meridian's underwater headquarters. That meant there was little to no chance of getting her back without the super team's express permission. That was something that terrified the Chief of Staff, because what if they didn't want to give their old teammate up this time?

She exhaled and let the tension out of her body. She'd have to explain all of this to Chris, and when it came to his sister, he wasn't the most even-keeled version of himself. Finally, she said, <"We're sending an emergency support team to Ziggurat Black. They'll be there by nightfall local time. Are you able to maintain control of the situation until then?">

Henrietta sighed. "Of course. Nightshade out."

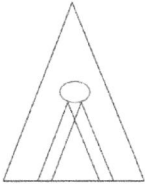

CHAPTER 12: SIT REP
LOCATION: ALEPH FIELD OFFICE, WASHINGTON

No one in Aleph's Washington office expected to see Director Stone today but considering how the world was twisting itself into knots today, they couldn't have been surprised.

Deputy Director Cross received the call from Stone's motorcade as soon as they were underway from the White House. That meant they had fifteen minutes to get his satellite office prepped and hide any nonsense her staff might have stuck on the walls next to their desks.

"Listen, don't mess around and don't try to be funny. You all saw the pirate broadcast, and the media are having a field day, so let's give him our best today, all right? It's not every day the big boss pays us a visit," she said, her small team hanging on her every word.

Wilhelmina Cross-- 'Bill' to friends and 'sir' to subordinates-- ruled her fiefdom with an iron fist. She didn't want any of her analysts showing her up in front of the director. But there came the point in their rush of preparation that she had to accept that whatever happened next would happen whether or not they were as clean and tidy as she wanted to be.

She'd turned sixty a year or so back and should have been contemplating retirement, but her daughter had recently joined up with the service, and she wanted to do what she could to make her life easier. Not that young Stevie would ever ask for help. She was her mother's daughter, and that meant independence played to extremes. But being part of Aleph meant being part of a team, so that was an exciting learning curve she wanted to watch her child experience.

Bill ran her finger across one of her analysts' desks just as Signe

Wasser, the Washington office's head of security, entered. Following closely behind were Director Stone and his entourage, who immediately began to take ownership of spare desks to get back to work.

"Good afternoon, sir," said Wilhelmina.

"Bill-- sorry to be brusque-- do you have an office ready for me?" said Chris.

She nodded and directed him toward one of the back offices, near her own. "Of course, do you need any assistance?"

"Just a live link with HQ and as much brain power on this whole Quinlan fiasco as possible," he replied.

"The New York office is working on the bombing, we're supporting where necessary, but Quinlan is Washington's focus," said Wilhelmina.

"Good. Thank you," said Chris.

He closed the door to the private office, and Cross stood there, unsure if she should wait or if she was dismissed for the time being. Deciding it was the latter, she looked over to Signe, who was removing her jacket and loosening her tie and headed over. "Busy day, Sig?"

"Not particularly. Got to drink some of that top shelf White House coffee, though, so that was a nice highlight," replied the Dane.

She was the tallest woman Bill knew, six foot six and with the muscle to match. She was one of the few metahumans Cross trusted, not that you could tell Signe was enhanced at first glance. Her cheekbones mirrored her stature, high and intimidating, and her ice-blonde hair cut short.

Wasser was a Level 1 metahuman. Her gifts included super strength and invulnerability, and she knew how to use them. In the eighties, she operated as part of Denmark's Jaeger Corps special forces, but now, coasting toward her sixties, she worked for Aleph. Whenever special guests of the organisation arrived in the city, she'd be by their side. It was her responsibility to ensure itineraries were followed, and that the visitors left in the same number of pieces as they arrived.

"Quinlan-- do we think it's legit?" asked Bill.

"Stone personally tasked a team to Hudson University and is waiting for a call back from the Attorney General about the evidence. Kishana has sent someone to the offices of the State and District Attorneys to make sure they don't fuck about."

"What about the location of the clone?" asked Bill.

"Encrypted. Codebreakers are working non-stop."

"Dammit. I remember when this used to be a lot easier."

"I don't," said Signe.

Bill chuckled. "Come on, let's bring you back to Earth with some of the office coffee."

In the private office prepared for him, Chris discarded his military uniform and slumped into the chair left for him. He tapped the computer awake and then pressed the call button on the phone. There was a moment's delay, and then he was connected to the New York office.

Henry Gardner's face materialised on Stone's screen. <"Sir, this is Gardner. I have your--">

"--Where's Kishana?" interrupted Stone. It should have been his second-in-command on the line, not Henry Gardner. And while his psychic bodyguard was a welcome voice, it wasn't the one he wanted to hear right now.

<"Ah, she's overseeing the Succession Protocol with the analysts. I have situation reports ready, but can go get her if you prefer?">

"No, no, sorry, Henry. I'm a bit frayed. Seeing Quinlan's face…"

<"I understand, sir. If what he said was true… Kruonis putting your sister in a time loop would account for the psionic schism I found when I-- ">

"Stop. I don't want to hear that right now. There'll be plenty of time for self-reflection when she's out. Where are we across the board?"

<"Tiamat's Foundation Dossier is on hold. Do you want to hear about the Quinlan investigation or the New York bombing first?">

Despite preferring to know everything about his sister's situation, Stone replied, "New York, please."

<"Right. Just gone 3pm local time, the convoy containing the director and his dedicated security team stopped at the Burger Don

on 327 W 42nd Street in New York City. Twelve minutes later, the entire restaurant detonated, taking out it and the surrounding blocks. We have a team on-site, working alongside FBI and emergency crews. So far, we only have one survivor: Leon Cobalt.">

Stone tapped his fingers across the desk. "Cobalt… do we know how he survived?"

<"Looks like his force field automatically activated at the moment of impact, but he's still a mess. We're moving him to a nearby Aleph medical facility.">

"Who do we have on-site?"

<"McQueen found Cobalt. He's with the new hire, Myers.">

"Myers. That makes sense. She's the one with the local connections," said Chris.

<"That's what Kishana thought. Hell of a first day. We don't have anything else right now. We're hoping that Cobalt might have intelligence. I'm going to head to the facility and see if I can't glean anything from his thoughts.">

"Are you sure you're up for that?"

There was a pause before Henry replied. <"…I'm the only one who can take the strain from the department. I'll be fine.">

"As long as you're sure. Have you taken your medication today?"

<"Every day and every night, sir.">

"Good. Keep me updated on New York. Have the other directors reported in safely?"

<"Yes, but it's barely been an hour; if there are follow-up attacks, they could come at any time.">

"Always the optimist. With Murray out, how is his team reacting?"

<"Hackman has taken on operational command, which is all above board, even with how it looks,"> said Henry.

"Hell. He's a wildcard. What about Porter? She's Passive Operation's Chief of Staff. Surely she's best suited for the interim directorship?"

<"It's Murray's standing order. If he's out, then it's Cobalt. If Cobalt drops, it falls to Hackman.">

Jason Hackman. Former CIA operative. Former Special Forces. Forever psychic. Back in the day, he was known for utilising his telepathic abilities to force his targets to kill themselves. Rather than get his own hands dirty up close and personal, he found it amusing to get people to commit the cardinal sin. Not that he wasn't capable of handling the killing himself, but after getting so good at it, he appreciated the opportunity to flex his brain muscles.

He looked younger than he actually was, but his eyes belonged to something dark and scary, and Chris didn't like being in the same room as him. If he was now in control of Passive Operations, then things could spiral out even faster than they were already.

"I never knew what John saw in him. What's he saying?"

<"He wants the location of the medical facility where we've taken Leon.">

"Did he say why?"

<"No, so Kishana said we should give him the run around until Leon hits surgery.">

Chris accessed his private server and began typing orders. Without looking away from the screen where Henry's face was visible, he said, "Smart. Who are our best-- and closest-- operatives trained to resist psychic interrogation?"

<"McQueen is riding with Cobalt, and Hochburg is currently at HQ.">

"Don't let them leave Cobalt's side. Have Hochburg go with you to the medical facility. As of right now, I'm ordering that Leon Cobalt remain in Active Intelligence's custody, come hell or high water. I still have the overall command of Aleph so Hackman can grit his teeth and bear it. I'm sending the official order through now."

Chris punctuated the point by pressing 'Send' on the memo ratifying the orders he'd given. It'd rub Hackman the wrong way, but Stone wanted control over the situation.

<"Orders received, sir,"> said Gardner.

"And... what about my sister? Where is she now?"

<"Unfortunately, Majestic took her into protective custody before we could secure her. Our understanding is she's been taken to Challenger Deep to prevent further attacks on her person.">

"What? What? Show me! Do we have footage from the on-site agents' body cams?"

<"Pushing it to your private server now.">

Chris typed a command into his computer, and a window opened on his screen. "Why do we only have one set of footage?" he asked.

<"Nightshade was the second operative on-site,"> replied Henry.

That shouldn't have been a surprise. Chris was aware how Henrietta Lark's armour rejected the presence of foreign objects against it, be it clothing, electronics or even low yield weapons fire. You couldn't kill her with a street handgun because the bullets would dissolve on impact, the kinetic energy spread out across her aura. A high calibre sniper rifle, though... that was something her patrons didn't count on when they wove their magics millennia ago.

The footage from Schwarzer Zwerg's chest-mounted body cam was grainy due to the depths it had been broadcast from. Ziggurat Black reinforced walls and various force field emitters were purposefully designed to prevent signals from getting in and out, and even if you transmitted on an authorised wavelength, you'd still receive this amount of fragmentation. There was a close-up on the lock of a solitary confinement cell door as stubby fingers worked to open it.

Chris fast-forwarded. There was a jerky movement, Zwerg ducking as a shape moved over him, then a struggle, an arm reaching above the camera-- a visual distortion rocked the footage, and then the German superhero collapsed.

"What am I watching?" asked Chris.

<"Scourge unleashed an atomic blast inside his mouth. His internal organs melted. Everything melted, apart from his indestructible skin.">

"Fucking hell," whispered Chris.

From where Zwerg had fallen, you could make out his empty, massless hand reaching out toward the interior of the cell. The chest-mounted camera was pointed directly toward where Chris's sister was sitting behind bars. Scourge came into frame, her ethereal arms crackling with radioactive energy. There was another spasm in the footage quality as she passed the body cam by, and Chris worried that he'd lose connection for a minute, but it normalised by the time Scourge had taken a few more steps toward the interior of the cell.

Hannah hadn't moved an inch since the door to the antechamber outside her cell had opened. She was sat cross-legged on her bunk, her thumb and forefinger touching as she meditated. Chris' brow furrowed. Is that what she did now?

"I thought I'd have forever and a day to kill you, but my timetable just changed," said Scourge.

Visibly breathing in and out and paying her visitor no heed, Hannah sat impassively, her head down, her dirty blonde hair covering her face.

"I thought, oh, the powers-that-be will let you out of this cell at some point. Eventually, given time, the guys in charge will forget who you were before this and throw you back to the wolves. I thought I'd have time to play with my meal, but I guess we're going to have to skip straight to the barbecue. No time to tenderise to my pleasure."

Scourge was in front of the cell, her hands melting the bars into molten slag where she gripped them.

"You got nothing to say? Look at you. Fucking look at you. Look how far you've fallen. This isn't even a revenge kill at this point. It's a mercy."

She reached her hands through the bars, the tips of her translucent fingers glowing even brighter, casting a shadow behind Scourge as she powered up. The camera footage flickered again as the radioactivity in the vicinity spiked. This was it-- the kill shot.

Hannah finally moved. Faster than the eye could follow, she wrenched the villain forward by the sleeves of her tattered prison uniform, smashing Scourge's face against the remains of the bars. Blood sprayed across his sister's front, but he still couldn't see her face, still couldn't discern her intent.

Scourge was rattled, but that didn't stop her from following through with the atomic burst she had revved up to incinerate Shrike. Just as the radioactive energies reached critical mass, Hannah grabbed the fleshy stumps of Scourge's arms and aimed them upwards, so the deadly energy she unleashed spilt into the wall behind her, then arched into the ceiling.

Scourge's attack shredded through the prison's reinforced walls and formed two tunnels to the outside, and suddenly sunlight burst into the darkest recesses of solitary confinement.

Unbeknownst to her, the damage took out the dampening field that was keeping help from arriving. With that bubble burst, Majestic crashed through the roof, and he didn't look happy to be there. He landed behind Scourge as Hannah kicked the villain hard in the stomach, and the villain's head bounced back against the newly arrived superhero's indestructible chest. She was knocked unconscious immediately.

"Han-- are you okay?" Chris heard Majestic ask.

Hannah sat back down without a word, gazing at the burns inflicted upon her arms.

Majestic heaved Scourge up by her lapels and then headed outside to meet Nightshade.

Chris closed the window on his computer. "Get the Attorney General on the line. Don't take no for an answer, then we're heading to the airfield. Have my jet ready. I want to be back in New York by 7pm."

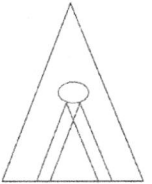

CHAPTER 13: SECOND STRIKE
LOCATION: RUE SAINT-AUGUSTIN - PARIS, FRANCE

When he wasn't wearing his heavy coat, Bilal Ikram was a visibly muscular man, with a square jaw and even squarer features. He wasn't unattractive, but it had taken a few fights for him to realise he had to protect his head, so a thin scar left over from a bottling lined his cheek, running straight toward his ear, where a triangular chunk of meat was now missing.

His hair was a tight mess of twist-curls. He was sporting a week's worth of beard growth, which he probably should have done something about before leaving his apartment for this interview. Still, if they wanted him at his best, then they would have to endure him at his worst.

Besides, who arranged a job interview for 11pm? But the message left on his machine was compelling, and while it was zero notice, the Euros they were offering made two hours to get to an interview an acceptable irritation.

He had slept most of the day after last night's patrol, and his ribs hurt like hell after he had misjudged a roof-to-balcony jump and caught the balustrade in his torso, but that wouldn't stop him from suiting up later and getting back to it. He'd been to the hospital for most of the afternoon, and they'd taped him up without asking many questions. That was nice of them, considering the sights they saw coming through their doors.

To be fair to him, he wasn't entirely sure what the job entailed, so he wasn't optimistic about it. The money on offer sounded great, but the details were quite purposely kept vague. The problem was, being a freelance superhero patrolling inner city Paris didn't pay particularly well. Membership to the Meridian wasn't coming any time soon, and his working relationship with Shrike back in the day made him persona non grata to certain other groups. When was the last time any of his former cohorts in the Crusaders had reached out to him?

"Don't focus on the past," he murmured. "Focus on the future."

But it was too late. Thoughts wandered backwards. Bilal had been a younger man, just out of his teens and looking to do some good. Hannah had helped him find his footing in the world of superheroes. When she was arrested for the mass murder of Nicholas Quinlan and one of his legitimate business enterprises' employees, he was just as shocked as the rest of the world.

But right now? He'd arranged to meet the mysterious voice on the end of the phone at Jorge's bar at 11pm.

The woman sitting waiting for him across the seat was otherworldly in her beauty. An angular jaw and cheekbones that could cut glass, her lips were pursed into a small smile, and Bilal could almost see a glow coming from her eyes. He had never met this woman before and had no idea who she was, but there was a single blue rose perched on the edge of the table. She was the interviewer, then.

But why all the cloak and dagger nonsense?

"Do you know how hard it is to find a blue rose on such short notice?" he asked, taking a seat opposite her. Poking out of breast pocket was a matching flower, though it had shed some petals during his run across the rooftops to make it here in time.

"Consider it a foot in the door. If you're not capable of rising to a simple challenge, then you won't last a day in our line of business. Hello, Bilal."

"And what do I call you?" he asked.

She smiled. "Delphine. I'm glad you came. I wasn't sure you would."

"Colour me curious. I was surprised you tracked me down, more than anything."

"Ah, yes. Your secret identity isn't public record. Would you prefer I call you Durendal?"

"Hey, keep it down," said Bilal, closing the gap between the two. "Secret identity means secret identity."

"You're worried about tabloids. Ha! If I wanted to leak your identity to the public, I'd have it go viral. TMZ, Buzzfeed. Tabloids? Hilarious."

"...Yeah, I get that, but still," said Bilal.

"You're not convinced?"

In one swift, elegant gesture, she held up her hand and clicked her fingers twice.

The entire café stopped whatever it was they were doing.

Every single person in the establishment turned to look at the elfin woman's table. Bilal was genuinely surprised and gripped the edge of the table tightly in his shock. He regretted not wearing his costume for this weird appointment. If he needed the sword though, it would come if he called, but would it be enough?

"Mr Ikram, this building is filled with Aleph agents. I'm not an idiot. And I won't treat you like one."

"So... this is a job interview?" he replied.

"It can be. Or it can be something else entirely. That depends on how our conversation goes. Drink?"

He didn't exactly know what she meant by all that, but he would be lying if he said he wasn't intrigued. "What are we having?"

"I think I'll have a '75. Order whatever you like, it's a business expense."

Demonstrating a preternatural sixth sense for being needed, a waitress approached their table and flipped open her notepad. She smiled and took down Martin's order, then looked to Bilal. "Sir?"

"Ginger ale. I have work later," he replied.

Delphine pouted. "So boring!"

"Fine, twist my arm. How about a Dark and Stormy?"

"Of course," replied the waitress, jotting it down.

Bil considered his order, then asked, "Ah, did I see a bottle of Zacapa 23 on the top shelf?"

She smiled. "You did! Would you like it with that?"

He gave her a nod. "If she's picking up the tab, then yes, please. Thank you."

Delphine pondered his request and said, "You know your spirits."

"My brother worked at La Société on Daunou. You know it?"

"I have been known to partake in one or two drinks there in my lifetime," she said.

"He used to buy the good stuff for cheap... and most definitely cheerful."

"That's interesting. You're Muslim, yes?"

Bilal couldn't read her. She was just looking-- not staring, not glaring-- just looking at him. It might have been an accusatory look if it was anyone else, but a hint of a smile appeared at the edge of her mouth. He didn't know how to take her. He knew her name, but who was this woman?

He took a breath and replied, "Was it my name that gave it away? And no, I'm not. Not anymore. When our parents died... so did my faith. And Tahir-- my brother-- he's... well. He's not doing particularly well at the minute either."

"I'm aware of his hospitalisation. Six years in a coma. You're at the hospital during the day and running across Paris' rooftops at night. You're burning the candle at both ends. I was wondering if I could help you from burning out."

Their drinks arrived but Bilal didn't touch the swirling golden liquid in his glass.

She knew about his brother.

As he sat frozen in place, Delphine thanked the server and watched as she headed back behind the bar, her gaze lingering a moment too long on the back of the waitress' head-- or perhaps backside? He couldn't be sure-- before she turned her attention back to him.

"Where was I? Yes. You've done good work in the city. You helped ease the racial tensions in the city after *Génération Pureté* turned the city inside out. And when *Grotesque* unleashed his powers in the Gare du Nord, you were the one who made him return his victims to flesh and blood. You're a true hero, Bil. Better than most."

"That's exceedingly kind of you to say. I don't mean to be rude, but what's your angle here?"

"Angle?"

"You're buttering me up. You want me to work for you? Aleph, right? Why me?"

"Because you kept fighting the good fight when your boss was locked up and they threw away the key. Others didn't. Others were too ashamed after being affiliated with Hannah Stone--"

"--Shrike," corrected Bilal.

"Excuse me?"

"They outed her. Against her will. They tore her life apart. That name shouldn't be out in the world. I don't use it. You shouldn't either. They locked her up and took everything away from her. Don't perpetuate it."

Delphine was incredibly quiet, and whatever it was she was giving him, it wasn't a look anymore. It was a full-on stare. She opened her mouth once, but no sound came out. Her mouth snapped shut, and he could tell she was trying to figure out how to say whatever was percolating in her head.

Finally, she said, "...Bilal... have you turned a TV on today?"

"What? No. I've been asleep."

"Oh, well... I have something I need to tell you--"

Before she could continue, something caught his eye and he acted without thinking and shouted, "Get down!"

He pulled a throwing knife from one of the small hilts hidden along the back of his belt and flung it straight at the waitress-- whose hand was suddenly impaled against the wall behind the bar, instead of pressing down on the detonation switch on the suicide vest she was wearing. Even if they were shocked by the turn of events, it didn't stop the agents on the scene from approaching her, their weapons drawn, ordering her to stand down.

"I thought this place was filled with your people?" asked Bilal, pulling a knife from another one of the hidden hilts strapped to his back. A dagger versus a bomb vest didn't end well for him, but it was better than nothing.

Delphine was helped up by the agent who had dove on top of her, and said, "It is. She's one of--"

The suicide bomber screamed as she yanked her hand free from where it was pinned to the wall. A slick tearing noise was audible moments before the agents who surrounded her unloaded their weapons into her head and chest.

She fell backwards against the wall-- more blood outside her body than in, the top of her head gone, bone and brain visible-- and her mouth fell open as she slid to the ground in a pile.

"Get Director Martin out of here," ordered an agent, and Delphine was bundled up by another agent.

Bilal was staring at the corpse. He watched as it twitched, as its mouth closed and opened repeatedly. And then, as the corpse said something in a deep, guttural voice-- despite the fact its skull had been turned to dust by the Aleph agents' assault-- the entire bar exploded.

MERIDIAN DATABASE - ORIGIN FILE – 'NAUTILUS STATION'

Swim out to a point equidistant between Japan and Papua New Guinea then dive ten hundred metres down. Keep going until you see the lights. If they're not the result of pressure-related visual hallucinations, you have successfully reached Challengers Deep, where the Nautilus station-- the Meridian's headquarters-- resides.

The massive base was named for the ancient creature, long dead at this point, whose shell composed the hull; a gift from Tempest when the Meridian first formed nearly two decades ago.

He carried the vast fossil on his back, all the way from the leviathan cemetery that resided on the outer edges of the undersea kingdom of Lemuria. Once it was in place at the bottom of Challengers Deep, Zyj infused the fossilised remains with their race's adaptive techno-organic super technology.

Within a matter of hours, the interior of the shell had become a hub bustling with next-level technology, a place where the Meridian could operate from with impunity. The heroes walking its intricate and winding halls continued to add what they could to the already unique environment, the programmable architecture making it the perfect launchpad from which to save the world.

CITIES ON FIRE

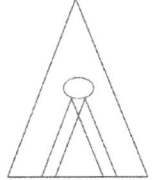

CHAPTER 14: FRIENDS REUNITED
LOCATION: NAUTILUS STATION, CHALLENGERS DEEP

Majestic and his guest had vanished from the depths of Ziggurat Black just over nine thousand miles away and instantaneously materialised on the arrival stage in the centre of the Meridian's base. Hannah's heart rate didn't change, a steady, intimidating beat marching forward. Even though it had been a decade since she last walked its halls, the space hadn't changed so much that she didn't instantly recognise where they landed. Majestic still hadn't seen his old friend's face and wouldn't use his intra-vision to peek under the tangled mess of dirty blonde hair. It seemed like an extravagant waste of his abilities, and he wanted to respect her at this delicate time.

"Are you okay?" he asked.

"ISTHATHER?" A burst of fluctuating gold light shot into the room and the distorted figure of Slipstream, the team's resident speedster, became visible. Her entire body warped from one direction to another, a living anomaly of reality that hurt to look at for any extended period. That didn't stop her from looking at Hannah and noticing that her hands were covered in radiation-induced burns. "OHGODISSHEOKAY?"

She was the youngest member of the team and had only acquired her abilities in the last year, but whatever she lacked in experience she more than made up for in perceived speed.

'Perceived', because she wasn't a speedster, per se. Her body was out of sync with the timestream, an oddity of science that allowed her to slow time down relative to herself but move normally through it. What appeared to be breaking all known laws of physics was the breaking of all known rules of time.

Her unique relationship with the timestream altered her perceptions. When she slowed native time down, she was still just moving at human-level speeds. But Slipstream didn't tire, she never felt exhausted, she just moved as fast as she needed to at any given moment.

The lactic acid build-up in muscles that athletes experienced never happened to her, because time wasn't passing when she moved. She never experienced DOMS when she ran in the quiet space between moments.

And her perception of the passage of time meant she could run ten thousand miles when her powers were active and she moved between seconds, for her no time passed at all. She lived outside the laws of space-time, and she relished every part of it.

Her predecessor had run with Shrike back in the day, but she hadn't had a chance to speak to him before his abrupt death. Unfortunately, when one speedster fell it was at that point their replacement was struck with a literal bolt from the blue and empowered, so there wasn't a chance for the torch to be passed, for an explanation about what exactly the successor's new powers entailed. Every day was a learning experience. Every day she discovered something new and terrifying and extraordinary about her powers.

"Slipstream, please slow down," said Majestic, his voice low and calming.

"OH!YEAHSORRYI'll do that, sorry," said Slipstream. Her body stopped flickering and then snapped back into a human shape. She was barely five foot two, a svelte woman with, ironically enough, a runner's body shape. Tight muscle packed in densely across her wiry frame. "Hi, I'm Lizzy. You knew the guy who wore this costume before me?"

Hannah didn't react. She held out her mangled hands toward Majestic.

"Of course, let's get you to medical," he said. He motioned in front of him and then started walking, leaving Slipstream to follow closely behind the pair. "I've already absorbed the ambient radiation left over from Scourge's touch, so there's no long-term danger. Wayfinder's healing bath will take care of the rest."

Even slowed down to human-levels, Slipstream was still visibly twitchy. They walked in silence for most of the journey, but when they entered the medical bay, she threw caution to the wind and said, "I gotta say, I was really shocked when that Quinlan guy's pirate signal hijacked my television."

Hannah froze.

Majestic's brow furrowed. This was something he hadn't even contemplated being the case, considering the attempt on her life-- "Hannah... did you not hear?"

It was the first time she'd opened her mouth to speak in what sounded like forever. Her voice was a guttural croak, raspy and unsure of itself. "What... are you... talking... about...?"

"Uh, do you--?" asked Slipstream, looking toward Majestic.

He nodded, acknowledging her request to get out of there quickly to update the other Meridian members on the turn of events. "Let the others know we're--"

"Michael... what are you talking about?" repeated Hannah.

Even though Majestic was a thousand times more powerful than her, Hannah stepped up to him. He finally saw her scar-ridden face as her tangled hair parted. It was clear that there wasn't a bone in her body that hadn't been broken over the last ten years.

Her mouth was filled with fake teeth where her real ones had been brutally removed, and despite himself, his intra-vision switched on and he saw through her scarified skin and at the damage done to her on a skeletal level. It was clear that her life the past ten years had been a living hell, and when she wasn't in solitary confinement it had been a cruel free-for-all of which she was on the receiving end.

"Han..." he whispered, shocked by her appearance.

"He framed you!" spluttered Slipstream.

Hannah spun around to face the young speedster. "What do you mean?"

Majestic placed a hand on her shoulder, but she immediately slapped it away.

"Fucking talk to me! Tell me what happened!" she snapped.

Majestic said "Go," to Slipstream-- who vanished in a burst of light-- and then turned his attention fully to his old friend. "Quinlan recorded a video before his death. He outlined how he went about framing you. He cloned you, Hannah. Set your clone up to kill him and his people. That's why the DNA evidence was undeniable. He sent a lackey to trap you in a time loop for the duration of the murders, and then had himself killed to seal the deal. He killed himself to ruin you."

"You... you all thought I did it," she said.

He shook his head. "The evidence..."

"You didn't believe me," she said.

"After everything... what he did to you..."

"What he did?! The monster killed my family! He slaughtered them! My husband! My baby girl! He killed them and got away with it! And then he did this to me! Ten years! Ten years in hell!"

"Hannah, I'm so sorry," said Majestic.

"Sorry! Don't tell me you're sorry! You thought I was guilty! That I was mad! I remember everything you said, Mike. Everything. You told the court that considering what he'd done to me that you thought I had done it-- but after everything-- everything-- I didn't do it!" She pounded his chest repeatedly, so hard that her blistered hands burst, and blood spilled across his white costume. "God, you even had me thinking I did it, but I knew, I knew in my heart, I wouldn't. I couldn't. He killed my family, and I couldn't have killed him. I couldn't even do it..."

"I'm sorry, Hannah. I am. I have so many regrets... I shouldn't... I shouldn't have let them do that to you... I should have believed..."

"Fuck. I thought you finally had enough. I thought you pulled me out of there because.... Because you realised your mistake. But it took him. It took him for you to do it."

Majestic shook his head. "I'm sorry..."

"Stop fucking apologising!"

With that, she threw a punch so hard that it would have broken every bone in her hand, had he not turned aside his face in time to transform it into a glancing blow. Instead, she reeled back, the recoil on impact reverberating through her fist and down her elbow. She hissed at the sensation and turned away from him.

"Hannah..." started Majestic.

"...Where's my brother?" she asked quietly.

"Your brother?" he repeated.

"Where is he?"

He shook his head. "I... I don't know. Let me treat your wounds..."

"No. I want to see my brother."

"I can... I can contact Aleph."

She turned back to face him. "It shouldn't have come to this, Michael. It never should have come to this. But you failed me on every possible level. And for that... I can never forgive you. Get me my brother."

CITIES ON FIRE

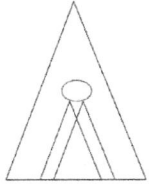

CHAPTER 15: AND ALL THAT COULD HAVE BEEN
LOCATION: ZIGGURAT BLACK - BERMUDA TRIANGLE
SEVEN YEARS AGO:

Three years since they had found her guilty. Three years since they locked her up and threw away the key. Three years and no progress made in the efforts to prove her innocence. Three. Long. Years.

Chris Stone waited patiently in the private meeting room, tapping his fingers against his knee as he waited for the guards to bring him his sister. Previously, he'd visited her in his role as her big brother. This time, he was here in his capacity as Aleph's newly crowned Director of Active Operations. That meant the game had changed.

A loud buzzing noise rang out from behind the door ahead of him which led to the prison cells. He stood up straight and held his hands behind his back, as if he were standing to attention. A few moments later, there was a second alarm, louder than the first, and then the metal doors swung open in front of him to reveal CO Burton, a familiar face from all the previous visits Chris had made to the Ziggurat.

"Hullo, sir. One moment please."

The CO ducked out of the room and vanished around a corner. A few moments later, he returned wheeling an upright gurney in front of him. Strapped down in her very own miniature cage, face covered in a plastic mask and her limbs restrained at every joint, was Hannah. You could see every inch of the wounds inflicted on her face. Where you could see bare skin, you could also see damage. Three years' worth of damage.

"What the fuck is this?" whispered Chris.

"Orders from up on high I'm afraid. She keeps getting into fights, so the warden ordered her in restraints when she's not in her cell. He said he'll review the situation in a month."

"Get her out of that thing," ordered Chris.

"I'm really sorry, sir. Honestly. But it's the warden. He's the boss, and if--"

"It's fine," said Hannah. She was somehow standing outside of the gurney, winding her wrist around where the restraints had, mere moments before, held her in place. She casually removed the mask and tossed it to Burton, then looked over to Chris. "Hello, big brother."

Chris couldn't help but smile. Even though she looked like she'd been through hell, Hannah was still his sister and she had that look about her that put his mind at ease. She was still herself, regardless of her situation.

Burton on the other hand looked like he was about to wet himself. "Oh, fucking hell."

In as calm a manner as possible, she held up her hands. Gently, she said. "I'm not going to hurt you. Put me back in the restraints when I'm done here. But until then… just let me speak to my brother, okay?"

Burton opened his mouth then thought better of it. He placed the mask on the table next to him and said, "Fine. Gonna lose my job, but fine."

After the CO exited, Chris approached his sister and gave her a hug. "You okay?"

"Do I look okay?" she replied.

"…You look like shit."

"Swell. Thanks."

"Can I get you anything?"

"What do you think?"

"Yeah. Okay."

He shook his head. This was how their conversations always went in this place. Pleasantries. Sibling barbs lobbed overhand toward each other. Even in the worst of situations, patterns remained unchanged. Behaviours cycled around and never disappeared from circulation. They just took their time to come back around.

She sighed and looked away from him. "Is there… any word?"

"No. The case has officially been closed. I'm trying to get it put under Aleph's umbrella, but the US government is territorial. They're being hard-line on super crime."

"God, have they put that on any posters? That's catchy."

"Han…"

"I don't care what they say or what they think. I didn't do it."

"I know you didn't. If you tell me you didn't then you didn't. No questions asked."

"Didn't stop them sending in your pal the psychic though, did it?" she replied.

"Henry? He's a good kid, don't be a bitch about it."

"Fuck you."

"Fuck you too. Let it go. His psychic scans were inconclusive. I don't actually understand it, but hey, what do I know."

"He's the son of one of the worst bastards I ever went up against. You think there's some bias there?"

"You think he's in on it?"

She looked uncertain. "No. But… I have to ask the question."

"I don't. But even if Henry was a bad guy, he wasn't the only psychic scanning you. He was just the one in the same room. Aleph had all the big brains in the observation room getting their hooks in. Something about a psychic schism they can't unpick."

"Maybe I was mind controlled…" offered Hannah.

"We've been through this."

"I know… I just… I didn't do it."

"I know. That's why I'm getting you out of here."

"What?"

"Big news. As of yesterday, I'm the Director of Active Intelligence. Suzanne Jordan finally retired. After everything I did with Al-Sheikh and the Meridian, the UN Security Council voted me into the big chair after the Succession Protocol spat out my name."

"Uh, congrats?"

"And with the big chair comes the purview to do whatever the hell I want when it comes to metahuman affairs. Welcome to my remit, sis. You're under it."

"That sounds creepy as fuck."

"Yeah, but pause that. I'm getting you out. Released into my custody. You won't be here."

"But I'll... still be guilty. In the eyes of the law."

"Fuck the law! Fuck the world! You don't deserve to be here! You could leave whenever you want! Let me take you home."

"God, you silly bastard. You just got the job and you're willing to throw it all away? No. I won't let you."

"Won't... won't let me? I'm your brother, Hannah! Your big brother! I'll do whatever the hell I think is best for you, and leaving you here is--"

"I don't want you to visit anymore," Hannah said.

"Is-- is-- Excuse me, what?"

"You've visited every week since the sentence was passed. You're an important man with an important job to do. And now you're the Director of Aleph? Come on, big brother. You're not coming back here. I won't allow it."

"I don't-- I don't think you're in a position to tell me what I can and can't do. And you won't allow it--?"

"Until you figure out how I was set up, there's no reason to be here. I'm in Hell. And I won't leave Hell until they realise their mistake-- until they find me innocent. I put my trust in the law, and I can't turn my back on it now. That's how I know I didn't-- no, how I *couldn't*-- kill Quinlan. I'm not a hypocrite. And I never will be. Not even because of him. You drag me out of here, then you make me what I'm not. And you ruin yourself. You won't be director for too long after that. So, I don't want you to visit anymore."

"Fuck off."

"No, you fuck off. Live your life. I'll live mine. They won't break me in here, Chris. And you've got good work to do out there. So, I'm asking you-- please-- don't come back here. Don't try and save me by making me what I'm not. If there's a way to prove my innocence, you'll find it. But don't ruin your life doing so."

"I'm not just going to stop visiting you."

She scoffed and that. "I'll refuse the visitations. I've already done so with everyone but you and I'm doing this for you, you fucking idiot. You don't need me dragging you down. At this point, that's all I am to you. A fucking anchor."

"Dragging me down? You're not dragging me down! You're my

sister!"

"You just offered to tank your career for me! I'm a liability! You can do more good for me at Aleph than on government unemployment-- which, if you remember, in your line of business involves a mind scrub and being kicked to the curb. I need to aww this through. I need to prove that the legal system works. Even if I have to stay here for a few years, I know you'll figure out what happened and how. You'll find out who framed me. But until then... I don't want you to see me locked up in here."

"I know. I know. You don't keep having to say," said Chris.

"I do. Just so I can hear myself say it too," said Hannah.

Chris sighed. "...I don't want to do this."

"You're going to have to. If there's an answer, you'll find it. But until then... I'm not going anywhere. And I can look after myself. Remember that." She knocked on the door that she'd been wheeled through and picked up the mask she had previously discarded. "...Not like my old one, right?"

"Less terrifying, for sure," he replied.

She nodded and then embraced him for what could have been the final time. "I mean what I said. Please don't come back here. You'll find the evidence that exonerates me. I know you will. But until then... don't let me drag you down."

"You're a fucking idiot. But I'll never stop. I promise," he replied.

"I know. Thanks, big brother."

Seven years later, and he never did find the evidence that proved her innocence. Not that he needed it, after all...

CITIES ON FIRE

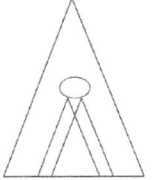

CHAPTER 16: CROOKED FOUNDATIONS
LOCATION: HUDSON UNIVERSITY - NEW YORK

"Keep the press back! Keep them back!" ordered Kristinn Sigurðsson, waving his hand toward the agents under his command as they moved forward to contain the media presence on site.

He was a cold looking man with brutish features, snub-nosed and flat foreheaded, deep groves lining the front of his slab skull. If you saw him coming, you'd cross the road to avoid his gaze, which had been known to make grown men piss themselves where they were chained.

He'd been pulled from the Active Operations field office at Director Stone's request, but this wasn't what he expected to be up to considering his vocation. He killed people for a living. Had done so since his teens. Now he was in his fifties, still willing and able, but reduced to enforcing a cordon while Active Intelligence tried to figure out how to excavate a body that might not even be there. When this was all put to rest, he'd contact Director Zinchenko, and request that AI don't call on him again.

Kristinn watched predator-eyed as someone pushed through the cordon and flashed an ID badge at one of his men. She was beckoned past the line and pointed toward him, so he watched ever impatiently as she headed his way. She couldn't have been thirty, but her tired eyes were darting around as she ambled with clear intent toward Sigurðsson. Her choppy dark hair flitted about her head as the wind picked up, but she didn't seem to mind. She wore a brown overcoat that was wrapped tightly around her body, and if he was a lewd man, he might have thought she was a strippergram. But he wasn't... so he didn't. Obviously.

He cleared his throat. "Can I help you, Miss...?"

"My name is Abstract. I, ah, I was asked to report to the senior agent on site?"

"...Abstract? You're a metahuman?"

"And superhero," she replied, her dark, pillowy eyes squinting as Kristinn's body language changed.

He went tense, something in his stomach twisting as if danger was imminent. No one had mentioned that he should expect a meta on site. He was suddenly acutely aware of the weight of his handgun at his side and wondered if he could reach it in time if Abstract turned out to be someone deserving of a bullet between the eyes.

To their right, another woman rushed over, waving her arms. "Abstract! Yes! Hello!"

Sigurðsson could have rolled his eyes. Special Agent Anushka Rai was leading the Active Intelligence contingent on-site, and she was as scattered as they came. Light flitted about her dark eyes and that stupid smile on her face did nothing to sharpen her flat chin. He wouldn't come out and say it, but he felt actual, inarticulate hate toward this woman.

"Why is she here?" he asked.

If Anushka heard the aggressive tone to his inquisition, she didn't respond in kind. She smiled as if they were best friends and replied, "To help with the excavation, of course! You don't know who Abstract is? From the Crusaders? She can phase through solid matter! When the ground-penetrating radar finds a void in the foundations, she can travel down there and recover the body without causing any damage."

"Hff. Why aren't we just digging the whole thing up?"

"The entire library could be condemned if we dug up the foundation, and I don't think Slatterly appreciated us asking him to consider it. But this is even better! I just wish he stuck around so I could tell him, but he was long gone when I came up with this compromise. You'd think the President of the University would have a vested interest in knowing what we're doing to the foundations of one of his buildings."

"Should've just dug the damn blasted thing up," murmured Kristinn.

"Well, I'm here now, so you don't need to," said Abstract. She looked at him in a way that made him feel like she was seeing right through him. He didn't like it.

The subtle tension between them broke when an agent rushed over and shouted, "Anushka! We've found something!"

Sigurðsson turned to the men manning the cordon and barked, "Keep the press back, no one gets in!", then they headed inside the library.

The agent led the three of them to the back of the massive building and down a staircase. They descended past the basement, eventually joining a group of Aleph agents in the sub-basement, where they were gathered around a large piece of machinery that hummed as it scanned the foundations below them. This must have been the ground-penetrating radar-- GPR-- and they'd already had success with its deployment.

Kristinn looked around the shelves of books that lined the walls of the sub-basement and huffed.

"What?" asked Anushka.

"Quinlan was a mad scientist at the end of the day. And look where we are," said Kristinn, gesturing toward the scientific tomes that lined the units surrounding them. "Everything has to have 'meaning' for these fuckers. They all think they're so smart."

"If Nicholas Quinlan cracked human cloning, then he didn't just think he was smart, he proved it," said Abstract.

"You almost sound like you admire him," said Kristinn.

"God, no," said Abstract. She looked at Anushka. "This is it?"

Anushka gestured toward one of the technicians working the scene, "Sandow?"

Reggie nodded effusively. "Yes! I have no doubt. Straight down, right to the bottom of the foundations. That's where the void-- the body-- will be."

"How far?" asked Abstract.

"Straight down, fifteen metres," answered Reggie.

"Okay, I'll have a look," she replied.

"Do you need anything? A flashlight?" offered Anushka.

"My senses adjust when I go immaterial. I don't even need to breathe," replied Abstract as she shuffled her coat off to reveal her costume. It was brown and tan, centred around a stylised A on the front that started at the base of her neck and ended at her hips. She pressed a button on her wrist and her mask spread from her neck up to her hairline, disguising her features immediately. She handed her coat to Kristinn and gave him a wink. "Please hold this for me."

Then she slipped through the floor, leaving Sigurðsson to toss the coat at Reggie with another huff.

"What if it's not him?" Kristinn asked nobody in particular.

Anushka's brow furrowed. "What do you mean?"

"We all followed the trial. It was unofficially required reading for every Aleph recruit. Everything about that mad bastard came out. Everything. How he led a double life-- supervillain and super-altruist-- under everybody's noses. A sociopath who trained himself to mimic emotions. A diabolical freak of nature. What if this is one of his little tricks? No Kruonis. Just--"

With an audible pop, a bundle of plastic rose from the floor, carried in the arms of the returning Abstract. Within a few seconds, she was back with a human-sized pile in her arms that she gently lowered to the ground.

Anushka turned to Reggie and said, "Get a forensics team in here."

Kristinn crouched down, pulling on a pair of latex gloves. He took out a switchblade from his pocket. "May I?"

Rai's eyes snapped to slits. "You're offering to open up a bag of human stew."

"I know what I'm offering." He twirled his knife around casually. "But we know what the priority is here, and I'd rather get it done now than wait for tech. You may want to put your masks on, folks."

Anushka didn't argue. She looked around the room as she pulled on her mask and watched as others followed suit. Abstract clicked a button on the side of her mask and filters snapped into place from hidden flaps that covered her nose and mouth.

"Then certainly, you know what we're looking for," said Anushka.

"The second confession," said Abstract, taking a step back while she let the Aleph agents do their work. "But why bury it with this guy?"

Anushka held her hands out as she explained, "The advances

we've made will allow us to roughly determine the time of death. The library was built ten years ago, so the question is, how soon before that was this guy--"

"Or gal," said Kristinn, unwrapping the pre-packaged corpse at his feet.

Anushka rolled her eyes. "Sure. Uh, yeah, so how soon before that was our victim killed? That's the question."

Kristinn cut open the plastic and sure enough, scant skeletal remains floated in a thick gloopy stew of human decay. Fragments of an orange and black costume were visible in the swimming muck, though most of the agents had already turned away at the sight. The sickly-sweet smell rushing out from the folds of the plastic was familiar to him, but hard to pin down for the others. It was wholly alien, an unknowable, unexplainable sensory experience that they would never forget. Anushka had it right. Human stew.

Kristinn ignored it like he had countless times before and searched through the pouches on the liquified man's ragged belt. He was surprised when a small USB drive in a sealed plastic bag floated to the surface, ready to be plucked from the death juices that were all that remained of Kruonis.

"Oh, fuck," he murmured.

"It's him, isn't it?" said Abstract.

Anushka held up a mugshot of a battered and bruised Kruonis from fifteen years ago, a power-dampening collar clamped around his neck. Orange and black. "Costume matches."

"Yeah, looks it," said Kristinn.

"ittttttttreallydoessssssssdoesn'it"

A woman, nearly six-feet-tall and wearing a red costume with silver streaks down the side, suddenly appeared between Anushka and Kristinn. She had goggles over her eyes and her skin was slightly smoking. Her voice sounded like a record being dragged backwards as it tried to be played, a long drawl where it should have been a clean rush.

Kristinn pulled his sidearm but the woman's arm was suddenly all the way through his chest, and in her hand his heart spluttered once in front of his disbelieving eyes before he died.

"nowyouseemeeeeeeenowyouuuuuuuuuu"

She vanished again and Kristinn fell to the floor dead as blood poured from the chasm made in his sternum. Anushka reached for her own weapon but Abstract grabbed her wrist before her fingers could grip her pistol.

"Don't--!" snapped Abstract before she was thrown by an invisible force across the room and straight through the wall. Thankfully, her powers activated on instinct at the last second, so she didn't crash into it and break in half.

Reggie was grabbed by the ankle and thrown across the ground, rolling like a bowling ball face first. He landed with a groan against a bookcase that decided to collapse on him before he had a chance to react. The other agents and technicians in the room were tossed into the air all at once, and then the red costumed woman stood in front of Anushka, grinning as the men and women she attacked landed across the sub-basement of the library.

"youknowwhoiam"

"Y-yes," said Anushka.

The woman patted Anushka on the shoulder and then held up the special agent's gun, having grabbed it between the former's blinks.

Another second later and the pistol was dismantled, its pieces scattered across the floor casually by the speedster.

"thensaymyname"

"V-Vel-Velocity," stuttered the agent.

She knew her name, but only scant facts about the woman herself. Velocity was Slipstream's archnemesis, some sort of parallel universe speedster who was as evil as her enemy was good. As sadistic as Slipstream was compassionate.

"goooooood"

She casually wiped Kristinn's blood across Anushka's face before pressing her lips against Anushka's. The agent's face burned on contact with the speedster's mouth, and she flinched backwards in pain and horror. Velocity shrugged and handed her Sigurðsson's heart.

Before Anushka could acknowledge her shock at this, the speedster vanished from the sub-basement, taking Kruonis' body with her.

CITIES ON FIRE

/// UPDATE /// BURGER DON (KIP'S BAY SITE) ROTA - 11/05/2033 (DAY SHIFT)

FRED CLARKE - *KITCHEN*
ROBERT CONTI - *SUPERVISOR*
WALLY EDWARDS - *KITCHEN*
DAVID GANT - *FRONT HOUSE*
GREGORY HAYTER - *KITCHEN*
CHRISTY JIMENEZ - *FRONT HOUSE*
MADELINE LAWRENCE **[ALEPH FLAG]** - *FRONT HOUSE*
   ...
  //PAUSE
   // SEARCH
    >> **[ALEPH FLAG]** - MADELINE LAWRENCE
        TONYA LAWRENCE (MOTHER)
        REGISTERED METAHUMAN
        LEVEL 0 – CHLOROKINESIS
        Low level manipulation of plant matter
   ...
   ...
FLAG SENT TO ANALYSIS TEAM

CITIES ON FIRE

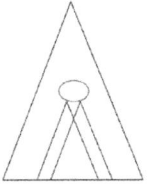

CHAPTER 17: INTO DARKNESS
LOCATION: RUE SAINT-AUGUSTIN - PARIS, FRANCE

Bilal's head swivelled and he saw that Delphine had barely been dragged across the room. It was at that point the entire bar exploded, and he was enveloped in complete darkness. This was it. This was the end.

He cried out as the cold cut into his skin, but he couldn't hear the noise coming from his mouth. Instead, he heard muffled groans, like he was sinking underwater. Was that him? Were those his screams?

He tried to breathe but that just let the coldness inside his mouth and down his throat. It choked at him, filled his lungs, and clasped itself around his machine-gunning heart. He felt like he was drowning. Falling. Tumbling. Completely disoriented and unable to get any sort of bearing, no matter the little good it might do him. He was in hell. He was dead and he was in hell and there was nothing left for him to do because--

He jolted forward, light spiking back into his vision. He lay in the gutted remains of the bar, the wreckage hot but not on fire. Delphine was being helped up by someone he didn't recognise, a woman dressed head to toe in black. Was that a hijab? It was form-fitting, clinging to her body like a swimsuit, so no, he didn't think it was, but still...

"You're all right, you're all right," insisted Delphine, noticing his panicked expression.

Standing beside her, the newcomer's face was neutral in comparison, naturally dark shadows beneath her eyes that gave her an intense, albeit tired, look. She wore no make-up, and her thin lips were sucked in and pursed like she was thinking about something too hard.

If Bilal were pushed to assume, he'd have guessed she was Israeli. The way she held herself, and the visible musculature beneath her costume, suggested she was military-- and highly trained. Who was she?

"What-- what just happened?" he asked.

A smell hung over the scene, smoke and burning alcohol. One moment there was heat, and light, and death, then the next there was this stillness, no fire, no explosion, just these survivors, all scattered around nearby.

"You got lucky," said the black-clad woman.

"That darkness-- that cold-- was that you?" asked Bilal.

The woman nodded once but didn't reply.

"Then… then I guess… you saved my life," he said, extending his hand. "Thank you."

She was taken aback by this gesture, but returned it, shaking his hand once. "You're welcome."

"How many did we lose?" asked Delphine.

"Nine. I could only reach the tables closest to you," replied the woman.

Bilal looked around at the dazed remainders of the contingent who'd been sitting around them moments before. Eleven men and women, all no worse for wear other than the frazzled expressions they wore. Sirens were becoming apparent in the background. He wondered if this were all an elaborate setup, something the likes of L'Armurier would have engineered back in the day.

"That woman… it was Agent Strauss… Julia… she was… she was one of us," said Delphine.

"I don't understand it. Not one bit," said the woman.

Bilal didn't summon the mystical blade of his namesake, but he did tighten his grip around the knife he'd slipped from his belt. If the organisation couldn't even trust its current membership, how could he trust them coming in? Something pin-prickled the back of his neck, and every vigilantism-honed sense in his body pulsed with concern.

Noting his discomfort, Delphine turned to him and said, "Bilal, this is Gavriella Mizrahi, my right hand woman."

Gavriella didn't acknowledge him, she was more concerned with

Delphine. "We need to get you to safety, director. There might be other attackers nearby ready to finish what the first started."

Delphine looked around, then nodded in agreement. "Get the others clear first."

Mizrahi went to argue but immediately knew better. She spun her hands around and a dark portal opened in front of her, a pool of ink black shadows that reflected her own resolute expression back at her. She beckoned the survivors through it, leaving Delphine to look over to Bilal.

"We're leaving. Are you coming?" asked Delphine as she extended her hand for him.

"Does this mean I have to accept your job offer?" he said.

"I'm afraid it does, Mr Ikram," she replied.

What would Shrike do? he wondered. The answer was obvious. Without saying a word, he took her hand, and she pulled him through the portal.

CITIES ON FIRE

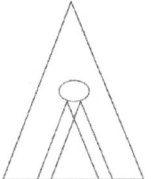

CHAPTER 18: NAME AND NOBODY
LOCATION: ALEPH ACTIVE INTELLIGENCE HQ, NEW YORK

"Can't we just hand the job to this guy?" asked James, pointing at the two photos currently on the screen.

One image showed the prospective new director of Passive Operations in his younger days, perennially grizzled, his thinning brown hair widow's peak-ing up his crown and the kind of blue eyes that could illuminate the dark. Compared to the photo of him in the present, he was positively brimming with youth.

With more lines on his face than not, the photo date-stamped earlier this year showed a man having gone way past grizzled and careening toward hoary. His widow's peak had given up any chance of reclaiming ground and settled for holding the line about two inches higher than the previous photo, his now silver hair wispy and bootstrapping into his thick grey beard.

Arthur Galloway, better known to the public as Professor Ultra, was an international legend.

"Your hard-on for this guy is ridiculous," said Loretta.

Kishana clicked her fingers once, and the pair of analysts turned as she pointed her finger at them. "Can we focus please?"

She sat at Madison's vacant desk, working through her own tasks while keeping an eye on the pair as they went about Succession Protocol. With Director Stone heading back from Washington, she was yet again left holding the baby, making sure Aleph's workings didn't grind to a halt.

Usually, she would have spent this time on the Operations floor, surrounded by dozens of operatives as they went about their duties, but this was her first Succession Protocol as Chris's Chief of Staff, and she wanted to make sure it went forward without a hitch.

"Sure, sorry boss," said Loretta.

"Right, so Arthur Galloway is the second man to take on the name of Professor Ultra. God, choosing a superhero name was so much easier in the seventies. He was eighteen when he took the name. Start 'em young," said James.

"Remind me, did he get permission?" said Kishana.

"From old man Eszterhas himself," said James.

From the thirties all the way through to the fifties, the Hungarian ex-pat Joska Eszterhas helped the allied forces turn the tide against the Nazis. As part of The Trust, and working with the military organisation that would eventually evolve into Aleph, he was instrumental in hammering the final nail in the Eternal Reich coffin, ten years after Adolf Hitler killed himself.

To the rest of the world, the second world war concluded in 1945, but it only came to an actual end in 1956 when the Thule Society was finally routed. This was the secret war-- the shadow war-- known only to those in the highest echelons of power.

After the war, he was given a reward for all his efforts-- and for everything he lost-- and he retired to become a man of leisure. Truthfully, the US government didn't want a man like that out in the world, in case he revealed the true nature of the second world war's conclusion, so he retired to his coastal villa and tinkered away in his lab, until his final days, when a young Irishman sought him out and was granted the boon of his name. That was how Arthur Galloway became Professor Ultra, too.

Loretta sighed. "Did you have his poster on your wall too?"

"The Trust are legends, Loretta. Actual legends... but no, I did not," replied James.

She ignored him and began to skim through the information on her screen. "This is from the dossier Aleph compiled at the time-- 'he quickly realised that the responsibility of maintaining global security in the face of the booming metahuman population couldn't fall onto the shoulders of simply one superpowered team.'"

"He designed the tech that makes up the backbone of the ART units, right?" said James.

Aleph's Armoured Response Teams were stationed at most of their principal field offices and tasked with assisting local law enforcement with controlling incidents involving hostile metahumans. Active Operations had a large contingent of the powered suits at their disposal, as they were the division most likely to be called upon to deal with problems that required them, but it helped to have a number on hand just in case.

"You know he did," said Loretta, as she began to screw up a scrap piece of paper into a ball.

"Yeah, but you hate being reminded about my eidetic memory, so I phrase things I know so you think they're questions instead of answers. You must have noticed that by now."

That wasn't inaccurate to say. Not only did the man have a photographic memory-- though he'd correct you with 'eidetic' if you call it that-- but his pattern recognition skills astounded everybody in the division. With his recall and depth of knowledge, combined with Loretta's own pattern analysis and recognition, the two were the best of the best, and that's why they always ended up with the highest priority tasks.

As much as their banter might irritate Kishana, there were no other two brains she wanted on this kind of thing, and they'd pulled through with the best results time and time again. The Chief of Staff glanced up at the pair and shook her head in mild amusement, then returned her attention to the information streaming down her tablet. Director Stone was in the air and due back within the hour. Lark had received the support team in Ziggurat Black but was requesting a return to home base after everything that happened. Muldair had authorised her agent's return flight, and the plane carrying the drop team sent to bring the prison under control during repairs would get her home in due course.

Even with everything that had happened, the world kept turning, and that meant Aleph couldn't look away from it, not for a second. She only hoped that nothing worse happened today, and gently rapped her knuckles against the surface of the table, as if that would make any difference.

Across the room, Hawkins rolled her eyes and lobbed the projectile she'd made at Johnson's head, punching the air when it bounced satisfyingly off his dome. "Galloway also worked with engineers to build the Ziggurat prisons, of which Black is the highest ranked, security-wise. It's pretty fair to say that if it wasn't for him, we probably wouldn't be here today."

James rubbed his head and said, "Okay, but he's ancient at this point, so as qualified as he is, and as much as the Probability Engine will spew out the best percentage for him, it's not going to happen, is it?"

"No. And sixty isn't ancient. But even if he is best qualified, he'd turn it down. But the suits do love him, so we have to do this song and dance every time. Anyway, I hate to repeat myself, but think this guy might be a real contender," said James. as he threw another profile up on the big screen.

"You've been at this for two hours, and you keep coming back to this guy. Why?" asked Kishana. Her phone buzzed but she ignored it. Any emergency alerts would come through to her tablet, so it was nothing urgent. "Well?"

"Firstly, am I allowed to be absolutely terrified of this guy?" asked Hawkins.

The man on the screen had a narrow face, with a black beard flecked with silver that covered his soft cheeks all the way down to his sharp chin. His bronze skin was intermittently interrupted by thin lines, but his age was indecipherable, though from the look of his dark, haunted eyes that sat deep within hollow, shadowed sockets, he could have been ancient. This was a man who'd seen a lot and paid the price for it, and Johnson nodded enthusiastically at Loretta's question.

"Fucking yes you are!" He cleared his throat and began to read from his screen; "Naasir al-Sheikh. Tiamat's former spy chief and basically a good man... but he betrayed the previous regime due to its numerous human rights violations and the atrocities committed against its own people, only to be exiled from the island when David Liu came into power. He basically handed the keys to the kingdom to the man, then got kicked to the curb for his efforts."

Hawkins sighed. "The previous Tiamat regime was violently anti-Muslim. So was David Liu, but he didn't let it show until he got what he wanted. And al-Sheikh, despite his name, had managed to keep his beliefs a secret. When Liu ascended to the top spot, he thought he could finally be open about his beliefs... and he was fired on the spot and exiled from the island."

"Liu is a monster. Al-Sheikh was lucky not to have been executed there and then," said Kishana.

"Maybe he would have preferred that..." said Loretta. "His wife and two daughters died when they left the country. At the exact moment their boat crossed a certain point, Liu activated the force shield that stands to this day. They drowned on one side of the shield, while Al-Sheikh was on the other, powerless to do anything."

"Clearly not a coincidence," said James.

"Perfectly timed. He was on one side of the boat; they were on the other. He had access to a lifeboat, they didn't. I can't imagine what that must have been like," said Loretta.

"After that, he was granted asylum by the USA and provided a comprehensive debrief pertaining to everything he knew about the country and David Liu. That's how we know about the bastard's real name. He's the sole reason we know anything about the country. And now they want to make him Director of Passive Operations?"

"But you keep coming back to him because he's the most qualified for the job. And besides, it's not up to you to make the final decision. Your job is to clear al-Sheikh of involvement in Murray's death, so we can present him as a viable option for the role. If he's qualified, he's qualified. So, did he have anything to do with Murray's death? You have a rundown of all his movements for the past, how long? Three years? Did he do it?"

"The man upped sticks three years ago and left the USA. Retired to a tiny village in the desert outside of Ni-Hayat Al-Shamal, Saudi Arabia. He's been living in seclusion. No internet connection, no phone line. We only know he's alive because once a month he has supplies dropped off from the local village at the edge of his property. Stone personally ordered drone and satellite surveillance of the property."

Kishana snapped her fingers. "Oh, bollocks, of course. Director Stone debriefed him when he landed in the US, back when he was a field agent. That was a big turning point in his career. After his sister's conviction, he threw himself into his work and that's the case that made him. He got the directorship for his work during that time."

James nodded. "Al-Sheikh made the connection with then-Agent Stone prior to leaving Tiamat. He knew that exile could have become execution or assassination at any point, so planned to turn, turn, turn."

"So, do we think this guy killed the Director?" asked Kishana.

"Ms Muldair!" Jan Tebbel abruptly swung into the room, red in the face and out of breath. "You're not answering your phone!"

Kishana frowned. "What's wrong?"

Jan was a slim woman, and at first glance you'd think the Dane timid, but if push came to shove, she would prove otherwise. With a bob of short, brown hair that was currently frazzled out of place, the lines under her eyes suggested an age older than she actually was, but in fact she was one of Aleph's youngest, and most intuitive, intelligence analysts.

"The Hudson University team were attacked. Anushka identified their attacker as Velocity. Operations Agent Sigurðsson is dead, two dozen Aleph agents wounded, along with civilians Velocity mowed down on her way in and out. She took Kruonis' body with her!"

"Bloody Hell," murmured Kishana. She turned to Hawkins and Johnson. "Finish up your reports. You're on a tight deadline but give me your best. I'll be back."

Accompanied by Jan, Kishana exited swiftly, leaving the pair of analysts to their work.

Loretta looked over to James, who was scratching his chin while pulling a pained expression. "What?" she asked.

"What?" James repeated, only seeing her face but not paying attention to whatever it was she said.

She smirked. "That face. Explain that face you're making."

"I just… I never thought we'd have to do this. I thought we'd vet a candidate when a director retired, not got assassinated."

"You're not happy about having to remove any possibility of a potential candidate killing his or her predecessor?"

"Not particularly," he replied.

"Life is full of surprises, Quiz Boy. We need to have a full report ready ASAP. An Aleph director's seat can't be left open. Not when the world's security is at stake. Shall we?"

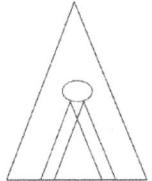

CHAPTER 19: FAMILY REUNION
LOCATION: JOHN F. KENNEDY AIRPORT, NEW YORK

Rain poured down as Chris disembarked his plane, and he immediately regretted not packing an umbrella. He'd changed out of his military dress whilst in flight and was now dressed in a pair of tattered jeans, a white t-shirt and a leather jacket, but that did nothing to keep him dry.

He'd been in the air for just over sixty minutes during the flight from Washington to New York, and as he glanced around the strip of tarmac they'd landed on he breathed a sigh of relief. The team at Hudson were being looked after by the medical team, and no new incidents had occurred. Now, if only he could get in touch with the Meridian and speak to his sister, he might be able to get his blood pressure down.

They'd landed ten minutes prior and idled over to a nearby hangar that was far enough away from the main terminal that they were guaranteed privacy when his boot hit tarmac. He pulled his jacket tight around him and was met halfway toward the hangar by Henry Gardner, who held an umbrella between the two.

"Aren't you supposed to be securing Cobalt?" asked Chris.

"There was another attack while you were in the air. Director Martin was attacked in Paris. I'm informed that she's unharmed, but her entourage took a hit," said Henry. He was shouting, the sound of rain crashing into the tarmac filling the air with interminable audio chaff. He gestured toward the hangar, and the pair made a beeline toward it.

"Any idea who was behind it?" asked Chris.

"That's the thing, according to Delphine, it was one of their own. Someone who passed all the vetting processes we have in place. One

'Agent Strauss'."

"Never heard of her. But an inside job? That's not good. Same MO?"

"Smaller scale blast. Maybe they didn't expect to miss with it? They still took out an entire building, just not a whole block like Murray's attack. We're no longer treating Murray's death as an accident. It must have been a targeted attack. That means you're probably in the firing line too."

"Let's cross that bridge when we need to. I don't want to fear for my life more than I already do on the day-to-day."

"Doctor Thorne is getting impatient-- he wants to take his team to the scene sooner rather than later."

"Magic Department knows the rules. They get their shot once the area is clear. Especially after Ckorda's antics last time. Make sure they stay put until we get the go ahead from the FBI. Anyway. Okay. The directors of Aleph are being targeted for reasons unknown. That's a bit scary. Hey, aren't I a director of Aleph?" He exhaled and shook his head. "Okay, we need to get back to home base. First Murray, now Martin. Have we heard from Zinchenko?"

"Her offices are reporting she's safe and sound."

"But have we heard from her?" repeated Chris.

A shake of the head. "Not directly from her, no."

"Succession Protocol is underway, so Murray's position will be filled within the next day or so. Before that, I want to get the directors together and pick their brains on this whole shit show. Speak to Sokolov. She's on rotation at the minute, isn't she?"

Henry nodded. "Kishana has the viewing room prepped for when you get back."

"Good man. And I'll speak to Delphine about ramping up their psychic screening processes, or maybe Lily Tate isn't up to snuff anymore," said Chris.

"I don't think that's the case. I've worked with her, she's brighter than most. I don't know what it could be, but I think we should probably re-screen everyone we can. What do you think?"

"The attack on Murray.... there's no indication it was one of his people, was there?"

"No. Not at all," replied Henry.

"Fuck. Okay. Pause on that one. The Hudson University team-- how are they?" asked Chris.

"We lost Sigurðsson. The other agents have a few broken bones between them, and severe burns where Velocity touched them when she was at speed. The weirdest thing, though. She took Kruonis' body but left the USB behind. It's currently being decrypted at home base."

"Weird. Why steal the corpse but not the USB? What's the play?" mumbled Chris.

"No idea. I've tasked Special Projects with designing some kind of early warning system for a meta of her powerset, but that's obviously a pipe dream."

They had made their way inside the hangar, and the rain pounded into the hollow metal rooftop, echoing tinny down onto their heads. Gardner shook the umbrella as dry as possible then strapped the slickly wet canopy together.

Standing by the entrance were a pair of armoured guards, their uniforms reminiscent of the suits worn by the COs at Ziggurat Black, while others dressed similarly were patrolling the interior of the hangar. Other men and women, wearing black suits and holding automatic weapons, were near the cars, ready to clamber in after their boss.

Henry closed his eyes, his fingers dancing as his arms hung by his sides. "I can sense some military-grade psychic malware floating on the surface of your brain."

"See, this is why I hate going to Washington," said Chris.

"Nothing penetrated the barriers I put up, and now… it's deleted. Let me just…" Henry put a hand to his temple and waved the other in the general direction of Chris' head. "Yeah, nothing got through. And I can't detect anything else. God, they're shit, aren't they?"

"Just means they'll keep trying. Contact Washington, make sure their offices are clean," said Chris.

"Of course, I'll get one of my people to scan everybody. But, uh, sir, I know we keep dancing around this, but you really need to hire your new STRATOP," said Henry, beckoning him toward the car parked inside the hangar.

"Getting bored of doing double duty?" asked Chris, his voice loud over the hammering rain.

"I'm being pulled too many ways. I need to stand next to you half the time making sure there aren't any secrets being picked from your head, and I'm running the psychic department in the other. When you don't have another second, that means I'm doing both at half-strength. If James was still here... he'd tell you the same thing."

James Winter had been by Chris' side as his STRATOP since he'd ascended to the position of director. An indefatigable bodyguard and one of the sharpest military minds of the century, the super soldier had lived through two world wars and served in a dozen others, always fighting the good fight where he could.

And now he was missing.

"I know the situation. I do. But replacing Winter seems a bit... like an acceptance. And I don't know if I believe he's dead."

It had been six months now, and all the powers of Aleph hadn't been able to locate him. When your main job was the policing of super powered individuals in the world and you happened to lose one of your own, it was a massive point of contention.

"Do you really think that a man like James Winter would drop off the map for this long without being able to get word to us-- or anybody? Somebody?" said Henry.

"I know, I know..."

Against protocol, Chris had left Winter's position by his side open. If the man returned, Stone wanted him to get back on the horse. But the longer the post was empty, the more apparent that it needed to be filled, regardless of whether Winter was still alive.

"And I'm not saying we give up the search. Kishana has Anatoly and Jan working on it, they're combing through as much information as possible. They've put a request through to second the Hamiltons for some field work."

"Okay. Okay, good. Damn. I just... I want to know what happened to him."

The absence of Winter meant that Gardner was working double duty, as he said. Considering the past fragility of his psyche, that was potentially a bad idea. But if the former supervillain took his pills and kept his head on straight, then he'd be fine.

At least, that's what Chris hoped.

"I know you do, sir. So do I. He's a good man. And if anybody's going to be able to find them, it's the team Kishana has put together. But I don't want to let the side down either, y'know?"

"I do hear you. Don't think I'm taking you for granted. I'll... well, I have some ideas. Some plans I want to put in place. When it comes together and I can move forward, I'll let you in on it, okay?"

Henry sighed, knowing full well this was as far as he was going to be able to get today. "You're the boss, boss."

At that moment, Henry's phone buzzed. Muldair's name flashed up on the screen in red letters, indicating the importance of the call. "It's Kishana," he said to Chris, before picking up. "Okay, I'm here. What's happening?"

Stone watched the man listen intently to what Kishana had to say. She was his right-hand, and he didn't know what would happen to his side of Aleph's running if it wasn't for her. He would have been out of the job years ago, probably. Why was she calling Gardner and not him directly?

"Right. I understand. What do you think?" Henry asked Kishana, his hand over his mouth as he spoke in hushed tones that were still loud enough for the director to hear. "Okay, I'll tell him. I understand."

"What's going on?" asked Chris.

Henry grimaced and said, "The Meridian wants to know where you are. Your sister wants to see you. We're just running the transmission through the usual channels to verify, but Kishana didn't want to do all that without looping you in."

You'd be surprised by how many calls Aleph received from people claiming to be superheroes. The Meridian had a dedicated hotline to the organisation, but still...

"I'm here. I'm right here. Tell them," said Chris. He hadn't meant to sound so agitated but even if the world was in the process of ending, the only care he had in it was the retrieval of his sister. Ten years lost to her, all for nothing. All because of a lie.

"Did you get that?" Henry asked Kishana. "Okay. The back-right corner of the hangar is clear. I know they can tell all that with their targeting satellites, but hey." He held the phone against his chest and waved his hand around above his head. "Agents! We're expecting visitors imminently. Over there," he said, gesturing toward the space he'd indicated to Kishana. "Friendlies, but let's not look too comfortable."

Chris' entire body tensed. The air crackled and a blue haze appeared in the far corner of the private hangar they were situated inside. Moments later, Majestic appeared and every single weapon in the hangar was levelled at him-- not that they'd do much good.

Majestic was a Level 4, maybe close to 5. Of all the members of the Meridian, he was one of the few to never be tested on the scale, because once you stop a rogue planet from colliding with Earth, you're clearly not a Level 0.

The hero slowly looked around at all the Aleph agents staring him down and shook his head before stepping forward to reveal that the director's sister was behind him, obscured by his broad shoulders and blue cape.

"Hannah," whispered Chris.

He rushed over and threw his arms around her, holding her tightly. It had been seven years since he'd last seen her, all against his better judgement. All because she said so. And now here she was.

"I'm sorry, Chris... I didn't have anywhere else to go..." she whispered, her head against the crook of his neck.

"Never apologise. Never. I was coming to get you, but he got there before me. I was always coming."

Chris took a step back and took in his sister. Her arms were covered in fresh burns, and blood had scabbed around her knuckles. What had happened to her? Her prison uniform was shredded at the sleeves to reveal scars going up her arms, and when he reached out to move the hair from her face, she flinched, turning away from him. He held his hands up, then looked over to Majestic.

"Thank you for bringing her to me," he said.

Majestic nodded. "She... she refused medical attention for the burns. I absorbed the radiation so there's no risk of sickness, but she shou--"

"I've got it from here," said Chris, interrupting the hero. "You can go now."

"You-- ah-- okay. Well. If you need anything... you know where to find me," said Majestic, before lifting off the ground and flying away, the rain almost parting as he went under the immense gravity of his presence.

"Let's get you back to home base and to a doctor," said Chris.

"I don't... I don't need a doctor," she replied. Her breathing was measured, as if she were making a concerted effort to control every inhale and exhale of oxygen. "I'm okay."

He shook his head. "I'll be the judge of that. I'm your big brother, Han. Let me live up to that mantle, all right? Let me be the asshole who tells you what to do."

Her shoulders were slumped, and he hadn't been able to look her in the eye yet-- not for lack of trying-- but she tilted her head up just a bit and he saw her say, "Okay. This one time."

CITIES ON FIRE

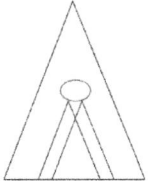

CHAPTER 20: BARNLEK
LOCATION: PINE CITY ORPHANAGE INC - MINNESOTA
TWENTY-TWO YEARS AGO:

It was fifty-five days since Madison's father had died and the immediate aftermath had done nothing to help the healing process.

The family had been on the books at a local doctor's practice in Pine City, just over ten miles away from their secluded cabin nestled deep in the heart of Chengwatana State Forest, and Doctor Edgar, the doddering and eccentric General Practitioner-- who had run the little place for nearly forty years-- never found a problem with the young girl.

"So, your daddy died? So what?"

Ted Myers had always made sure to keep his daughter up to date with vaccinations and he always paid cash to make sure everything was done quickly and efficiently, which the practice's staff didn't mind as that meant they didn't need to chase down insurance companies. Less work for them, less hassle for everyone involved.

Madison was covered in her father's blood when Sheriff Boles and the State Troopers arrived. She was cradling his body, his gutted head resting in her lap as she sat there. Tears streamed down her face, but she didn't make a sound or sob. Shock, the doctors called it. Shock.

The police took Madison straight to the local hospital and the doctors found her to be in perfect health. Unfortunately, Doctor Edgar was so old school that nothing had been digitised since he'd opened the doors to his practice, but after a short conversation with his secretary, they faxed over what little information they had on the patient and there was nothing glaring to report. She was in peak physical condition and perfect health, the only weird thing about her being the lives the Myers lived-- wholly apart from the world unless society dictated their presence.

And then eventually... everybody got bored.

"So, your daddy died? So what?"

There was no mystery. No grand conspiracy. A man had died. He left behind a fourteen-year-old daughter traumatised by a horrific tragedy, and a family pet that quickly vanished into the woods along with any chance of learning why father and daughter lived the way they did.

It was sad, but nothing special. People got shot all the time, and hunting accidents weren't few and far between.

When Boles interviewed the hunters, they were asking all sorts of questions. To their credit, they hadn't tried to hide what they did. Madison watched as they rushed over once they realised their deadly mistake, gibbering like confused children as they thrashed through the undergrowth.

"Why wasn't he wearing a vest?"

"Where did he come from?"

And then they started making loud excuses.

"I didn't mean to! I didn't know!"

"He just came outta nowhere!"

An accidental death. A terrible accident, they called it. But Boles all but accused the deceased of deserving it, considering the circumstances. He'd said all that in front of a traumatised fourteen-year-old who'd just seen her father get a bullet through the head. Why? Because the sheriff had been inconvenienced by having to come so far into the forest to investigate a crime. He'd been yanked away from his fishing trip with his grandson, and when he saw the state of Ted Myers, and the complete absence of fluorescent orange vest, he'd tutted and made his disparaging remarks.

"What kind of idiot wanders around dressed like that during hunting season?"

With no living relatives and her mother long dead, the hospital released Madison into the care of Child Protective Services, who then shipped her to a nearby orphanage. Let her get ground out by the system, that'll sort everything out... right?

"So, your daddy died? So what?"

Betsy Lloyd shoved Madison hard, sending the new arrival into the wall behind her. The other girls jeered and hollered, encouraging the larger girl to continue picking on the smaller. Madison was fourteen, but Betsy was nearly sixteen, and built like a cistern-- hard as steel and full of shit.

If wasn't for the pointed, stabbing words coming out of her mouth, Madison might have found the older girl's dancing Minnesotan accent amusing, the rise and fall of the portmanteau American-Swedish accent new to the sheltered young girl, who was getting used to the world outside of Chengwatana forest.

There was nothing but hate there. Nothing but spite.

"don't," said Madison, her voice a quiet whisper.

She stayed against the wall, making no sudden movements. Her father's words rang in her ears: When they get big and fast, you slow down. When a larger predator zeroes in on you, slow down, or you'll encourage the chase. They won't be able to help themselves. Pursuit predation.

Not yet dissuaded, Betsy shoved Madison again, bouncing her against the wall with force.

"You think you're special? Everybody here has lost somebody. You're nothing. Nobody."

"Shouldn't we do something?" asked Tom Parsons, watching the events unfold from behind a one-way mirror, situated across the far wall of the building's recreational area. He'd worked at Pine City Orphanage Inc a little longer than Madison had been here, and while he disagreed with management's conflict resolution style, they did their best with what little they had.

"These things have a way of sorting themselves out," replied Director Doyle. How many years had she run this institution? How many years spent watching children come and go, off to conceivably better and brighter things-- and how many years had they seen their wards return, no better for their limited time in foster care? Expressionlessly, she turned to Tom and said, "If we go in and break up the fight. Betsy's ill-placed grudge against Madison will just intensify. Let it run its course. Let it burn out."

"I don't know..." said Tom, turning his attention back to the rec room.

"You're a feral piece of shit. Nobody will ever love you. Nobody will ever care," continued Betsy.

"don't," repeated Madison.

"Or what? Nobody cares. Nobody."

"Director…" started Parsons.

Doyle held her hand up. "Just wait."

"Go on! Tell me? What are you going to do?" spat Betsy.

"I don't want to hurt you," replied Madison.

That was enough for the older girl-- it was practically an invitation. She raised her ham-hock hand up, clenched it into a fist and threw a punch that would have knocked Madison's front teeth out. In the split second before she sent it flying, Myers' eyes turned to slits and she moved-- and the punch landed hard against the wall, tearing up Betsy's hand. The crowd of girls stopped shouting and fell silent at the sight.

"Holy crap," whispered Tom.

"Fuck! Fucking hell!" screamed Betsy, clutching the bloody knuckles of her hand.

Madison hadn't gone far. She had simply side-stepped the punch, but no one had expected her to move so quickly. She stood beside Betsy, no sign of exertion, and leaned over so her mouth was next to the older girl's ear.

"What is she doing?" asked Doyle.

"I've never seen anyone move so fast," said Tom, leaning close to the glass. "She's not a, y'know, metahuman, is she?"

In the rec room, Betsy had no choice but to listen to whatever Madison whispered, and when the smaller girl was finished, the bully's face had gone white. She fell to one knee and then vomited all over herself. Once she was done with that, Betsy sobbed loudly, and pulled herself into the foetal position.

"We ran all the usual tests. All negative. She's just fast. And nasty. Look at her."

As Tom and Doyle watched, Madison slowly walked away from the vomit-ridden mess that had been Betsy, and through the parting crowd of previously bloodthirsty girls. She approached the one-way mirror and considered her reflection for a moment.

"She can't see us," noted Doyle.

Tom didn't sound convinced when he replied, "I know."

"This room is sound-proofed," added Doyle.

"I know," replied Tom.

Madison tucked a stray strand of blonde hair behind her ear, then went to turn away. Tom and Doyle sighed in relief, but then Myers abruptly looked back in their direction, and flipped them off.

CITIES ON FIRE

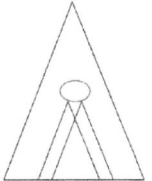

CHAPTER 21: MIND CRIME
LOCATION: ALEPH MEDICAL FACILITY, NEW YORK

Aleph had numerous facilities across the globe, each purpose built to deal with metahuman medical incidents. When one of their own were injured in the line of duty, they were rushed to one of these facilities over local medical centres, and the doctors on staff would do everything in their power to restore them to health. They didn't have access to the Meridian's adaptive alien technology, but they stayed as close to the cutting edge as budgets and research would allow, and Charlotte McQueen was hoping that would be enough to save Leon Cobalt 5's life.

They'd been sat around for hours outside the surgical suite, twiddling their thumbs, and waiting for news, and while Charlotte was content to play Snake on her cell phone as a way of pretending not to worry about the life and death situation surrounding her friend, Madison was engrossed in whatever she was looking at on her personal tablet.

"What are you up to?" asked Ronnie, pausing her game and leaning to her right so she could look over Madison's shoulder.

"A three-dimensional map of the crime scene," she replied, holding up the tablet to show the intricate intersections of blue lines and red. A before and after of the explosion that had rocked Kip's Bay, New York. "I'm trying to figure out what kind of explosive was used."

"Yeah? Shouldn't you save something for the bomb techs to do? Stevie will have something for us when they're done working the scene."

"Stevie?" repeated Madison.

"Oh, yeah. You're new. I keep forgetting somehow." The former superhero smiled slyly and leaned back into her seat. "Our driver. Stephanie Cross. She's still back at the blast site, remember?"

Madison shook her head. "We weren't introduced. I thought that's what you were there for, but apparently not."

"Funny. You're getting it."

"What, humour as a coping mechanism to deal with the absolute horror of the situation? Yeah, not hard to miss," replied Madison.

"Okay, okay, talk me through your findings. I could use the sleeping aid."

"Right, well, firstly, Hawkins and Johnson aren't returning my calls. We're stuck on babysitting duty for Cobalt 5, so I thought I'd make myself useful and I can't get through to my... support team? Is that what we're calling it?"

"There are all kinds of names. I'm sure you'll have a chance to read the employee handbook when the world stops ending."

"Oh, so never?"

"Exactly. Anyway, I wouldn't be surprised if Kish has them on something important. With Murray dead, there's a void that needs filling. When we're not on the clock, let me tell you all about Succession Protocol and how much of a ball ache that is."

"I can assume from the name," she replied.

"Excuse me, is this homeless woman bothering you?"

The pair were approached by a tall man with blond hair combed back into a pompadour. His dark eyebrows crested over his pale blue eyes and he spoke with a lilting German accent. His angular jawline made it look like his entire face was framed, and his thin lips were curled into a smile.

Charlotte cut the moment off before it could get any more awkward. "Tomas, you bastard, shut the fuck up and come here!"

The two embraced and patted each other unnecessarily enthusiastically on the back.

When they parted, he said, "Still wearing those stupid glasses indoors I see. Have I told you I hate them?"

"Many times," she replied.

"Oh, great," murmured Madison. Old friends. More awkward familial banter to endure.

Shaking her head like everything was one big joke, and still patting her friend on the back, Charlotte said, "Tommy, this is Madison. She's new. Madison, this is Tommy Hochburg. He's a dangerous bastard but more bastard than dangerous."

"I have on occasion kicked young Miss McQueen's ass," said Tomas.

"Yes, he most definitely has. But I took my licks and gave back some kicks," said Ronnie.

"I'm so happy for you both. You're our back-up?" said Madison.

"Ja, I am indeed. Sorry it took me so long to get here, but with the attack downtown, the feds and local PD have put roadblocks up all around the place. Flashing my badge only got me so far."

"Well, you're here now. We're just talking about explosives. Or maybe the lack thereof," said Charlotte.

"What does that mean?" asked Tomas. He sat down against the wall opposite where the pair had been located and shuffled his elbows onto his thighs, bending as far forward as he could without falling off his chair.

"There was no trace of an explosive device of any kind at the scene," noted Madison.

Tomas shrugged dismissively. "Maybe the device was completely obliterated when it exploded?"

Charlotte held up her hands. "No, okay-- I don't mean to interrupt Mads-- but hear me out on this. I used to run with Leon back when we were both in the Crusaders, okay? I've seen him take bullets to the face, seen him clamp his hands around a grenade and contain the blast, I've seen him take a high dive into molten lead and I've seen him survive the worst fucking things you can imagine, all without a scratch. This bomb... if it was a bomb... shouldn't have been able to get through his force field."

"That just means that the bomb was even more powerful than anticipated, too powerful for his suit... all this, it doesn't mean shit, does it?" said Tomas.

"The bomb techs will be able to confirm our suspicions," said Madison.

"Or prove them wrong. Who are you again?" said Tomas.

Madison felt her stomach clench like a fist. Was that how it was going to be? "I'm somebody who knows what they're talking about."

Tomas looked her up and down and then slowly began to smile. "Okay. Okay, maybe you're right. No bomb, but an explosion. You're thinking... what? That the attacker was a metahuman?"

"Maybe. This could be linked to Tiamat's metahuman development program, y'know? It could be a series of metahumans with explosive powers acting in tandem. You heard about the attack on Director Martin a few hours ago? Same MO, same explosive effect... same metahuman? I don't even know where to begin. But it's a thread, and how can you not pull it to see where it leads?"

"Okay, you're one of those. Good to know," said Tomas.

"One of those?" asked Madison.

"Intense and inquisitive. You'll go far," he replied.

Ronnie chuckled and took a swipe at Tomas, but the rugged man dodged it and threw his hands up like he was in an eighties ninja flick. After matching his pose, she said, "You're being an ass, man. God. Anyway. You know what I had to do before I ran straight toward the aftermath of a terrorist attack?"

"I mean, it wasn't as dramatic as you're making out," said Madison.

"Well, we know that now!" exclaimed Ronnie. "Jeez, you're getting into the rhythm now, and you've only been on the job for two minutes. No, right, okay, I had to arrange a fucking babysitter. I thought moving back to NY would be a break from all this shit, but oh, no. Instead, it made me agent of choice for these kinds of horror shows."

"It shouldn't have been you. It should have been one of mine," said someone.

The trio turned toward the other end of the corridor, where a man stood with his hands in his pockets. He was a lithe man, craggy lines around his eyes and a thin moustache over a sharply pinched mouth. His eyes were small and dark, pricks of light visible if you looked close enough. His hair was styled upwards an inch or so higher than it needed to be, and he was currently floating a half inch off the ground, which explained how he managed to sneak up on three highly trained agents.

"Oh, fuck me, this we don't need," murmured Charlotte, rolling her eyes.

"Who's that?" asked Madison.

She sighed. "Meet Jason Hackman. Director Murray's TPOP."

"Nuh-uh. That would be the current Director of Passive Operations," corrected Jason.

Tomas shook his finger at him. "Nuh-uh right back at you, my friend. Maybe that's true until the Succession Protocol is finished, but after that, you're back down here with us little people. Don't even think of telling us what to do."

Jason smiled, and his small teeth became visible between his pale lips. "Blah, blah. I'm here now. I'll take care of my man. You're excused."

Charlotte disagreed. "I'm afraid we can't leave yet. Leon is in emergency surgery. 80% of his body is covered in third degree burns, and we've been ordered by Director Stone not to leave his side until he's out of danger. That means we're going nowhere, and you're not going in."

This time it was Jason's turn to shake his head. "He's my opposite, and I'm his. If he's out of the game, I'm in. Don't care what your boss says."

Madison watched as Charlotte took a step forward. "Henry Gardner is on his way. When he gets here, we can sort all of this out. But come on, man. You know we can't just stand down. You're mad to even suggest it."

"Leon Cobalt falls under Passive Operations' remit. That means he's not your responsibility. Get that? He's out of your jurisdiction and under mine. So, you can stay out here, but I'm going in there. I still have time to take information out of his head before he dies."

Ronnie waved her hands in front of herself in a further futile effort to defuse the situation. "Whoa, whoa, whoa. Couple of things. Firstly, that sounded hella creepy. Secondly, and I'm sorry to say, but Director Murray is dead. That means you're not exactly attached to any position right now. Interim director. Acting director. Whatever you are, it's not enough to make hard decisions. Succession Protocol means they're choosing a new Director as we speak, so by the time I finish this sentence, you might even be out of the job. So, like I said, let's wait until Henry gets here, but until then... take a seat and wait with us. I'll let you play Snake on my phone."

"...You all think I had something to do with this," said Jason.

Ronnie laughed out loud. "What? No! No, I don't know who arranged this. Thing is, Director's travel itinerary was changed at the last minute on a need-to-know, and you were in that loop. So, there are a few questions that we need answering. Now, I'm being really Fonz-style cool about it, but you're a notoriously irate person, so how about we all take a chill pill, and we don't fight outside a surgical theatre, yeah?"

"You really think we'd fight?" said Jason.

"I think you'd lose," countered Tomas.

"Guys, please, let's not escalate this," said Madison. "Why do--"

"I don't think we'd fight," interrupted Jason. He sighed and rubbed his chin, as if he were considering some grander point. The trio opposite him were frozen in place. "Actually, I think I just locked down your bodies' motor functions so you can't move, and I think you should have a trip down memory lane. The past is a great learning tool."

With a click of his fingers, Madison, Charlotte, and Tomas collapsed instantly into unconsciousness, and he simply walked over their prone bodies toward the surgical ward.

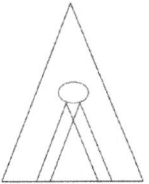

CHAPTER 22: OLD FRIENDS
LOCATION: ALEPH ACTIVE INTELLIGENCE HQ, NEW YORK

As soon as they had made it to home base, Chris had rushed Hannah to the medical bay, where the doctors immediately began treating her wounds. Doctor Sumner actually winced when he saw the injuries inflicted on the director's sister, but said nothing. He merely got to work, cleaning and dressing the wounds on her hands and forearms, before saying something about needing to perform more scans to identify the extent of the damage.

"I need to go speak to the other directors. But I'll be back. I'll come back as soon as I'm done," said Chris, crouching down in front of his sister. There was an eight-year age gap between them, but the horrific murders of their parents had galvanized their relationship. There was no room for sibling rivalry when all they had was each other.

"Don't rush. Not for me," she murmured.

"I'll do whatever the hell I want. Do what the doctor says. Don't beat anybody up," he said.

Despite the debilitating events of the last decade, she cracked a smile. Broken teeth and cheap replacements were visible, and when she saw the shocked expression-- he gasped despite himself-- her crooked mouth clamped shut.

"Don't rush," she repeated. "No need."

Chris grimaced and turned his attention to Sumner, who had been talking to a nurse about the scans they'd need to perform. The director gave him a glare that said, "look after her" and the doctor responded with a look that said "obviously".

"I won't be long," Chris said again, and then he headed out of the medical bay and marched to the elevator that would take him down to the holographic meeting room, ready for his parlay with the other directors. He was determined, frustrated, and above all, he wanted to get to the bottom of what was going on across the world.

Three floors down, the elevator stopped, and he cursed. To his surprise, Kishana slipped in. "You're a hard man to pin down."

"And yet, you always manage to track me down," he replied.

"I've got the nose for it. How's your sister?" she asked, tapping her nostril.

When Stone had ascended to the top spot, one of the first things he did was assign Muldair to an off-the-books investigation into his sister's alleged crimes. They'd been partners back when they started in Aleph, and the pair were both in the running for the directorship, but after everything with Al-Sheikh, he'd pipped her at the post.

There was no animosity between them. They'd been through hell and high water together, and the understanding was that she would eventually replace him. He'd already put the Succession Protocol amendments in place in case of his unfortunate demise or retirement. She had all the ammunition to tank him-- not that he ever needed much help doing that himself-- but she'd never fired a shot.

"I don't know. We haven't even been able to start... talking... about the whole thing. I need... okay, there's a lot I need to do. But officially, Hannah Stone is in Aleph protective custody. She's up in medical. She's..." His shoulder fell forward, like he momentarily lost any ability to keep his head up about the whole affair. "She's a mess, Kish. She's an absolute mess."

"You'll do what needs to be done, Chris. You always do." Unsure of what to do, Muldair decided it wouldn't be awkward at all to reach out and pat him tentatively on the shoulder. "And you have all our support. You know that."

Chris looked at her hand, still resting on him, and chuckled. "That's so patronising."

She shrugged. "You taught me well."

The elevator door pinged and opened on the level that held the holographic conference room.

" I hate all this rushing," said Kishana, as she hurried after him.

"Hey, you're the one who wants to speak to me, you could have waited."

"Oh, no, not this. Chasing after you feels like one of my major responsibilities since I joined Aleph. What I actually mean is that the Succession Protocol is being pushed through mega-fast because 'a seat can't be left open' for too long, but we know that's rubbish. We can tick over as long as we need to, that's how the organisation is designed. Ah, whatever. We'll have the results on your desk before the night is through."

"Great. Any suspects in the pile?"

"None. We've got a list of ten men and women all highly qualified for the directorship, and none of them-- best we can tell-- had anything to do with the attack on Murray. Or Martin."

"Thank goodness. I could really use my new co-worker not trying to kill me."

"Funny you should mention that. You've been rushing around, and I haven't had a chance to tell you before now-- Naasir Al-Sheikh is in the running."

Chris froze mid-step. "...You're kidding."

"Nope. Not about this," she replied.

"Wow. That's... that's definitely interesting, isn't it?"

"That's one word for it. When was the last time you spoke to him?"

"Seven years, maybe. Then he went into retirement. Seclusion. Self-imposed exile. Whatever you want to call it. God... talk about a blast from the past."

The pair came to a stop outside the holographic meeting room and Kishana gestured toward the door. "You ready?"

"Face the music? The firing squad? I don't know what I'm getting ready for. I just know half of us have been targeted and we don't know how or why."

"You need to choose your new STRATOP. If you get targeted, you need somebody by your side that can help you dodge the bullet. Or take it for you. I spoke to Mizrahi and it sounds like that's the only thing that saved Martin, and half her agents."

"Henry was saying the same thing, but that's because he's exhausted."

"Yeah, he's been more frazzled than usual these last few weeks, but you've got him running around doing double duty. Running psi-division was supposed to give him down time, but now he's doing that and acting as your STRATOP too. He's burning the candle at both ends."

"I hear you both. I'll finalise the position this week. I think the events of today have proven I'm going to need one. Speaking of, do we have any technopaths available locally?"

"Uh, I can find out, why?" asked Kishana.

"Because if somebody is coming at me with a suicide vest, I want a technopath stood next to me who can say 'Please don't detonate', and it not be a fruitless gesture."

"Good shout. I think Special Agent Leung is in New Jersey. I can have her here within the hour. And I'll have Witwer from Henry's lot join you too. If there's a chance we can have the bomber psychically locked down before he even thinks to pull the trigger, all the better. "

"Good idea. Make it happen. Thanks, Kish."

"Yeah, well, good luck in there. You'll need it," she replied.

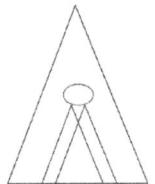

CHAPTER 23: JUDGEMENT CALLS
LOCATION: ALEPH ACTIVE INTELLIGENCE HQ, NEW YORK

"All right, let's get back to it. The algorithm has thrown this blast from the past into the mix," said James, sending the image on his computer onto the big screen.

The man's thin lips were curled down into a scowl and his flat nose had clearly been broken once or twice in his lifetime. His wide head was topped with a thatch of blond hair that bordered on gold, and his grey eyes peered out from almost hooded eyelids.

Mackenzie Ransom. One of the most insightful and qualified voices on the metahuman community, mainly due to him being part of it for much of the last thirty years. Before he retired over a decade ago, he'd operated as the Grey Hood, the hard-hitting defender of New York, and since then he'd acted as an unofficial liaison between certain parties in the community and law enforcement agencies.

"Didn't he get put up for it last time? And the UN shot it down?" asked Loretta.

"I don't think they ever liked the idea of someone being bigger than the directorship," said James.

"And that's how we ended up with Director Stone," said Loretta, clicking her fingers.

He shrugged. "The Security Council preferred to promote from within. And now Ransom is being considered for the other side of things. Interesting."

"Bigger than the job... I mean, I always respected his balls. He was one of the few who took his mask off on his own terms. Didn't have it torn off like Shrike."

"Look though-- he made plenty from it. Managed to pivot from one type of fame to another."

James typed away, churning through reams and reams of data. First they had to prove Ransom had nothing to do with Murray's death, and then evaluate his suitability for the role of Director of Passive Operations. He had the smarts, that wasn't in doubt. On top of that, he had the connections, and he had the trust of a community renowned for closing ranks to outsiders.

But James and Loretta's predecessors had been in this same position before, seven years ago. The UN Security Council simply didn't want a man like him in a role where he could make an actionable change in the balance between humanity and metahumanity.

Suzanne Jordan retired and Christopher Stone ascended to the top spot. Did Ransom ever know he was in consideration? He shouldn't have. But the man did wine and dine with ambassadors and diplomats. The churn of data that came with Succession Protocol highlighted key details of meetings between him and persons in positions of power.

Could he have been behind the suicide attacks, all in a bid to get a top spot in Aleph?

James leaned back in his chair. "Y'know, I remember when the media always positioned Quinlan and him in opposition to each other. Who was the most charitable of the charitable men? The most philanthropic? Thank god for the social media influencers we've got nowadays, am I right? That's the kind of fame I aspire toward."

"You were fourteen when Quinlan bit the dust, right?" said Loretta.

"Yeah. Why?"

"Oh, nothing. Hey... did you see this?" she gestured to the screen. Aleph's surveillance unit covered all the prospective candidates for any major position in their infrastructure. If you made the list then you were assigned to an observation team, and that meant you had a shadow. It also meant your calendar and schedule were gone over with a fine tooth comb.

There was a photo on the screen of a charity function, where Mackenzie was laughing along with the current president of the UN Security Council, Ambassador Naoko Kidani.

"...Huh," murmured James.

"So they're friends," said Loretta.

"Sure looks it. But that doesn't mean anything. We do a data churn on everything available. We pick apart what we can. The Probability Engine tallies it all together and then spits out a well-informed percentage guess on whether or not the person did the deed. That's all we can do."

"First Al-Sheikh, now this guy. Fun," said Loretta.

"Come on, let's move onto the next name so we can get the Probability Engine running," said James.

Loretta scrolled back to the old newspaper clippings of Quinlan and Ransom from over a decade ago. The pair would glad-hand and play nice in public but the analyst wondered how much the latter knew about the former. "It's crazy though."

"What is?"

"The way their rivalry was framed in the newspapers. All friendly competition or whatever. But really, with hindsight, it was good versus evil, wasn't it? Quinlan hid behind his mask of philanthropy and used all the charitable efforts he put forward as bricks and mortar for the wall between the rest of the world and the truth. It's fucking disgusting. And the media played right into it."

"Nothing we can do about that now, though. All we can do is look to the future," offered James.

She sighed. "Fuck. Just fuck. Right. Who's next?"

"The last major name. CIA Director Elena Kincaid," said James.

Two photos flashed onto the screen. The first was from a Washington fundraiser a few months back, the kind of dull affair that Loretta hated and James savoured. She'd been invited to a few in her short life but always declined out of principle, while he remembered the days when he was a fixture at them. Days long since past, unfortunately for him.

"Hey, do you think she's ever met Ransom?" he asked.

"Probably, looks like they run in the same circles," said Loretta.

In the still, Elena stood surrounded by men and women in tailored suits and dress uniforms. She was clearly holding court, and the facial recognition software slaved to the Aleph computers flagged them as various Generals, myriad CEOs, and miscellaneous power brokers from all corners of the world. And they were all deferring to her, the CIA Director who claimed to know everything they needed-- or wanted-- to know as well

She had a strong jaw and cheekbones that made one hell of an impression. The photographer had caught her wearing a slight smile, but neither James nor Loretta could be sure if it meant anything good. The photo beside that was from her CIA personnel file, black and white and with her demonstrating an intense glare that popped right through the screen and caught both the analysts by surprise.

Loretta glanced down at the reams of data on her screen. "Ten years in the top spot over at Langley. She spearheaded the integration of metahuman operatives in the organisation with huge success. But she's also pushed for more CIA oversight of domestic metahuman affairs, away from the Aleph umbrella."

"You can hardly blame her. We do swoop in and have all the fun," said James.

"The details of her missions are redacted within an inch of their life, but the one thing you can't ignore are the results," said Loretta.

"What do you mean?"

"Well, I've never seen a CIA Director decorated so much while still being in charge. She served in the army and was awarded the Purple Heart after being injured in the Az Zudiyah conflict. But did you see how she was injured? In the course of an ambush that decimated her squad--"

"Killed ten percent?" interrupted James.

"Don't start. She was shot three times-- once in the fucking head-- and managed to hold her team's location in the middle of the desert for seven hours. Seven hours. Five men died, including the squad leader. Three were severely injured. And then there was her. I think she's my hero, man. My absolute hero. After the army, she ended up at the CIA, and in the course of her time there, she received George H. W. Bush Award for excellence in counterterrorism... the Intelligence Medal of Merit... and that's just to name a few. She's received honorary doctorates from six different universities, on top of all the ones she earned before and after her stint in the military. She sounds like a boss."

"Youngest ever CIA Director, and clearly the most qualified," said James.

Loretta's brow furrowed. "One problem though. She was in charge when Hackman was at the CIA. She spearheaded the Remote Action Taskforce that let him cut loose and get on Murray's radar in the first place. RATs... the psychic assassination squad. For all her bonafides... she was the brain behind that, right? So she's not a particularly nice person, right?"

"This is the modern age of espionage, Retta. Nobody's particularly nice."

"Maybe she's the kind of bad we need then..."

CITIES ON FIRE

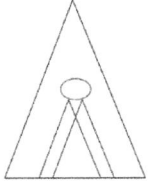

CHAPTER 24: QUEENS AND A KING
LOCATION: ALEPH ACTIVE INTELLIGENCE HQ, NEW YORK

Chris entered the room and surveyed the scene. There was a large table with a single chair waiting for him at the head. Above the seat was an elaborate lamp-like device that glowed with a dim purple light.

This was one of Aleph's holographic conference rooms. In each of the directors' secure locations there was a room like this, and when they took their place at the table a holographic projection of their equals appeared in the relevant position.

Due to the rules and regulations of Aleph, directors weren't allowed to be in the same place at the same time due to operational security. If the four heads of the four divisions that made the organisation were sat in the same room and, say, a metahuman decided to unleash their powers in said location, then the United Nations' global superhuman policing force would be obliterated.

Chris took his seat and the dim light brightened, enveloping his entire body, and a few seconds later he was projected across the globe to two classified locations. At the same time, two figures were cast into his classified area, and for the first time in months, all three surviving members of Aleph's leadership were together.

"How are you holding up, Delphine?" asked Chris.

"I've had worse champagne hangovers," she replied.

Chris smiled. "And you, Zoya? Have you been targeted?"

Zoya Zinchenko sighed. She was not a conventionally beautiful woman, but with long, narrow eyes that seemed to radiate a pale blue, she was instantly alluring. A walking enigma that had defected from Russia nearly two decades ago and become a member of the Meridian, only to shift gears and move into the world of espionage.

When the Active Operations seat opened up, she'd proven herself a worthy prospect, and to the surprise of everyone in the UN Security Council, the Russian ambassador pushed for her ascension to the throne. It had been too late to realise that the entire situation had been a two decade long con to get one of theirs in the top position, but she'd immediately alienated President Kozlovsky and his ex-KGB lackies by refusing to push their anti-metahuman agenda when she took control.

"No. Not as of yet. But I assume I will be. That seems to be the trend," she said.

"Yes, with the attack on Delphine, it's clear that these are organised strikes at the heads of the organisation," said Chris.

"You seem to have come out of it relatively unharmed," noted Zoya.

"As have you," he replied. This was always the way with the Russian. She poked and prodded. Tried to elicit a reaction where none was necessary. She had lived a long life of subterfuge, so it was second nature to her. She loved discerning lies because she was so adept at weaving them herself.

Zoya shook her head. "Don't make me laugh."

"Ha. Ha," replied Chris, deadpan.

"People. Please. Niceties. We lost a friend today. The least we can do is not snap at each other's throats."

"How did you escape, Martin?" asked Zoya.

Delphine cupped her hands together as she spoke. "Agent Mizrahi was on hand."

"Lucky."

Delphine gave a fake smile. "Not particularly. You read the prelim report. It was one of my own that tried to kill me. I know we expect that kind of behaviour from your people, but mine actually like me, Zoya."

"What precautions are you taking to ensure no one else is trying to kill you?" asked Chris. He didn't mean for the question to sound so sarcastic, but he couldn't temper his tone with that one.

Delphine arched an unamused eyebrow and said, "You too?"

"Following the line of conversation," replied Chris.

"I'm holed up in my quarters with Gavriella and a new recruit. If it weren't for him, I would be dead right now."

"Good way to ingratiate yourself with someone. Save their life. Makes it easier to take it later on down the line," said Chris.

"If you knew who it was, then you wouldn't say that," said Delphine.

"Oh?" said Chris, the question of the new recruit's identity asked silently.

"A conversation for another day. We're awaiting Lily's arrival so we can begin systematic scans of all personnel. Might I recommend you do the same in your departments?"

Chris nodded. "We're beginning to put together a plan of action."

"As are we," said Zoya. She impatiently rapped her fingers across the table on her side of the world, and added, "This is the highest priority of all departments. I appreciate that Tiamat was about to come under closer scrutiny, but if we're removed from the board, then there's no stopping any threats to the security of the world."

"This could be Tiamat," said Chris.

"Perhaps. We don't have the full picture yet. And until intelligence-- that would be yourselves-- provide us with said picture, operations-- that would be me-- can't act," replied Zoya.

That was the way of Aleph. Martin and Stone's role in the organisation's balance of power was to provide actionable intelligence for Zinchenko-- and previously, Murray-- to act upon. That was the mandate they fulfilled. Operations could not take place without intelligence to back it up. Intelligence couldn't overstep their mandate and operate without oversight from their opposite. An ever-folding origami shape that provided accountability and order in a chaotic world.

"My people are working the scene. Delphine's are supporting," said Chris.

"All of them?"

"Excuse me?"

"Are all of your analysts working the bombing?" said Zoya.

"Most. Succession Protocol is underway, so we have a team on that," said Chris.

Zoya smiled. She'd set a trap and was about to spring it. "And what about your sister? Are you dedicating manpower to her situation?"

Before Chris could respond, Delphine stepped in. "Two entire divisions of Aleph are focused on the assassination attempts. I nearly died, Zoya. My people are working on the data, and so are Christopher's. We are an international endeavour. If 98 teams are investigating the data instead of 100… that's still 98 of the greatest analysts and investigators the world has ever seen. Please stop trying to get a rise out of him."

Zoya simply waved the point off, as if it were nothing. "How goes the search for Murray's successor?"

Chris stifled an outburst. Instead, he remained calm and said, "Succession Protocols are nearing completion. We'll know who they are once their candidacy is ratified by the Security Council."

"Wonderful. I can't wait to meet them. I have other places to be. I shall await your findings, so that we may go to war," said Zinchenko. "Director, out."

The holographic projection of Zoya Zinchenko snapped into nothing but stray photons, leaving Chris and Delphine alone, projected into each other's bases of operations.

"…Are you all right?" he asked.

"I would have died if it weren't for Gavriella. Are you sure you're safe?"

"I'm putting measures in place just in case. I wonder if this has something to do with the Passive divisions? I wonder if that's why you and Murray were targeted…"

"Perhaps. Murray's travel plan was only finalised minutes before they left. He changed it, remember? At the last minute. That means only his STRAT and TPOP were aware as they coordinated his travel, and then they would have disseminated that information to need-to-know parties only."

"That doesn't explain how you were targeted though…"

"I know. It's one piece of a larger puzzle. Leon Cobalt was on-site and survived the attack though, correct?" she said.

"Yes. I've sent Henry to see if he can glean anything from him psychically. If he was the perpetrator, then he's doing well to obfuscate his guilt. He took an explosion to the face. We have no clue if he'll make it through the night."

"And Hackman?"

"We're giving him the run-around, but he's gone quiet. Maybe he's accepted that he's not going to get anywhere with us. We're just running the clock until he gets the boot."

"Jason's a dangerous man to play games with, Christopher. If there's a way to find your people, to find where Leon is stashed, he'll find it."

"I'm sure my people can look after themselves. He's just one man."

"One of the most dangerous men alive. Regardless, with the travel plans behind changed, it might be an inside job. But also, the attacks have taken place outside of our secure locations. That means that whoever is striking against us does not have access to them. Leon or Jason or whoever could have planted a bomb under our desks if they wanted to do us in quick and easy. These attackers… these assassins… they're out in the world, and we're safe where we are right now."

Chris tapped his knuckles on the table. "Let's not jinx it."

CITIES ON FIRE

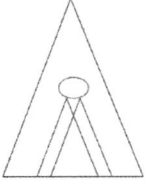

CHAPTER 25: WORDS CARVED IN TREES
LOCATION: ROANOKE ISLAND, NORTH CAROLINA
TWELVE YEARS AGO:

Hannah Stone could never claim to be a student of history. Not unless the history lesson had something to do with any one of the many martial art techniques she mastered during her time travelling abroad from her teens into her twenties. Not even her brother knew the extent of her experiences, the adventures she had, the lives she led, and she intended to keep it that way. The knowledge of her time spent amongst the Brotherhood of the Shard was hers to bear, especially considering the massacre that wiped them from the earth.

Despite being unable to ignore the horrible smears of crimson and black meat across the sidewalk, she tried to think of other things. History. Happenstance. Lives led and experiences had.

She could recite all the dialogue from The 36th Chamber of Shaolin in its original Mandarin-- as well as the dubiously dubbed English. She memorised the fight choreography from every film in the One-Armed Swordsman trilogy. She also mastered the real-life techniques behind Kill Bill's Five-Point-Palm Exploding-Heart-Technique, because why not. She'd never used it, mind. She'd never killed a man with all the accumulated martial knowledge available to her. That's what made her all the more terrifying, because... she could. The only thing stopping her was the thin line of morality that separated her from others, the line that kept good from becoming evil.

Regardless, there was always one story that stayed with her, even long into her adulthood, way past the quiet time in her life that she'd been taught all about it. and that's why she was here now, among the dead.

The one history lesson she could never shake was the story of Roanoke's Lost Colony. A settlement in the then 'New World'. Eighty men, seventeen women, and eleven children left the old behind in search of something new. Over a hundred people vanished off the face of the earth, the only clue to the reason behind the disappearance the word 'CROATOAN' carved onto the wall of a building, and 'CRO' carved into the bark of a tree.

Prior to his supply run back to England in 1587, the colony's governor instructed the settlers to carve a Maltese Cross on a tree nearby, along with the location they had fled to if they had to abandon the island. He left behind his daughter and her husband, as well as their daughter Virginia, the first English child born in the Americas.

There was no cross when he arrived back in 1590-- his return was delayed by the British Empire's need for ships to defend against the incoming Spanish Armada. No cross, no sign of foul play. Just the name of a nearby island etched into wood.

The governor was unable to conduct a search of the island, and the colony was declared lost... and nobody knew what happened to the lost settlers. There were rumours. Hearsay. But nothing concrete. He lost his family. His world. He died three years later, after a retirement spent contemplating the evils and unfortunate events that had led to the loss of daughter and granddaughter, forever holding out hope that they might still be alive...

...But there was nobody left alive on Roanoke Island today.

There had been yesterday, of course. It wasn't as if the failure of a colony over four hundred years ago would prevent something like progress. Yesterday, around eight-thousand men, women and children thrived on the island, living their lives, doing their best with the hand dealt to them.

It started slow, but that didn't last. She wondered if the ones who lived the longest suffered the most, but it didn't matter in the end, and it did nothing for her mental health to dwell on those kings of questions. They were all dead by the end of it.

Today, they were all dead, their lives coming to an end in the most horrifying and gory way imaginable. Within a matter of hours, the population had keeled over with hematemesis-- they violently expelled all the blood in their bodies in a handful of agonising minutes. Even though FEMA were contacted when the bodies started piling up, they couldn't identify the cause and they couldn't be sure what the source was either, so they called in the Meridian, and Majestic and Shrike arrived immediately, with the rest of the team following shortly.

"God..." murmured Shrike. She looked around the centre of town, bodies sprawled out on the sidewalk and roads. Men and women had dropped dead behind the wheels of their vehicles, and the island didn't have manpower to clear them. All it had taken was a few hours from the first sign of infection, and everybody was dead. No signs of life. "What did this?"

She was safely-- and hermetically-- sealed inside her armour, but her stark white outfit was already dotted with blood. The streets were caked in it, and it hung in the air to give a scarlet tinge to everything around them.

"Are you getting all this?" she asked.

Starlight had erected an energy shield in a fifteen-kilometre perimeter around the disaster zone, while FEMA based themselves on the other side of the Croatan Sound-- the length of water between the mainland and the island. They were hooked into the cameras built into Shrike's helmet, and she'd also provided them with a live data feed from her suit's various sensors and scanners. Whatever she knew, they knew too, and it felt like the best bet to share everything around this tragedy.

The organisation had blocked off the Virginia Dare Memorial Bridge while Meridian members Tempest and Undine had stilled the waves to prevent any boats holding potentially contagious contraband from reaching North Carolina or heading out to sea.

Slipstream was back at the Nautilus, coordinating the efforts of the team. His speed abilities could be disastrous if combined with an airborne pathogen. He could spread it across the globe in a matter of seconds, so they'd made the decision for him to hold back. He was apprehensive but knew that his scientific knowledge was best served in the lab, not on the scene.

FEMA finally responded, a crackle of delay punctuating the start of their transmission. <"We're reading you, Shrike. Metabolic scans are analysing the blood as you go. There's a strange mutagenic strain that we can't identify in the air. Any sign of the source?">

"Not yet. We're going to head further in," she replied.

There was a no fly-zone currently in place, enforced by the USAF and the tandem of Penance and Zyj, who soared below the clouds, searching for anybody that might try to fly out from Dare County Regional Airport. The only flyer allowed on the island was Majestic, who wore one of the team's forcefield survival suits, a medallion-shaped disc that clung to his chest and prevented exposure to the virulent killer. Alien in nature, they were cobbled together from what was left of Zyj's native technology, and by far the safest thing to wear in the current situation.

Zyj had only managed to construct one so far, but the alien royal had remained behind in the Nautilus to build more when it became clear that there was an immediate need for them on Roanoke.

Majestic held up his hand and she froze. He pointed his palm forward, toward the centre of Manteo, the larger of the two townships on the island. "There's a build up of the pathogen over there." His voice sounded like he was talking through the blades of an air-fan, distorted due to the forcefield keeping the deadly viral strain away from his body.

They moved forward, trying their best to ignore the enormity of the disaster around them. Thousands dead. A recovery effort epic in its scope. Hannah would contact her brother after the Meridian had done all they could, and see what Aleph's response would be. He was a senior operative for the group, working his way up the ranks. If the organisation could contribute to the relief effort-- to collecting the bodies-- he would tell her.

Shrike stood in front of Manteo Elementary School, and Majestic floated nearby. She glanced at him, and she could see the pain on his face. "Are there--?" she began to ask, knowing the answer would be 'No', because there was no way whatever had been unleashed here, killing thousands, would have spared children. He looked down at her, and closed his eyes. There was her answer. An unspoken, mournful, 'No'.

A moment passed as he collected his thoughts, and then after a deep breath he pointed past the school. "There's a... cemetery... back there. I can see a concentration of the pathogen hanging in the atmosphere."

"Someone's sick sense of humour," murmured Shrike.

Majestic didn't reply.

The breadth of the man's powers fascinated and terrified her. She'd witnessed him stop a rogue planet from colliding with their own. She'd seen him discern the truth from the fluctuations in a madman's blood pressure by ear. He could fly faster and think quicker than anybody she'd ever met, and the fact that he was so kind and decent to all they came across, with all that power flowing through his veins, surprised her to no end.

Shrike bounded over the roof of the school, trying to focus beyond the dozens of bodies littering the playground out back. Corpses too small to be adults and just the right size to be--

Hannah closed her eyes and looked away.

'No,' she thought, 'don't think about it like that. Don't think about them like that.'

The corpses were huddled together on benches-- people of indeterminate age trying to seek comfort and safety in their final moments-- while other bodies had fallen far from the school grounds themselves. They had run. Tried to escape death. But the thing killing them was already inside. Poking holes in their lives. Letting the best of it drain away. One minute they were whole, the next they were empty. Dead.

She pushed past it. Physically. She moved across the narrow field separating the concrete of the school grounds and the treeline at the edge. But mentally? It would stay with her. Images she'd never be able to forget. A massacre beyond any she'd witnessed before, through all her lives. She pushed past it. She moved past the treeline, and walked across the empty road separating the school grounds from the cemetery across it.

In the graveyard itself, Majestic stood in front of a tree, his fingers brushing up against the bark. Shrike could see the forcefield flicker at the point of contact, a static buzz reminder that for all his powers, there was a lack of certainty if he could survive exposure to the pathogen.

"What is it?" she asked.

"A message," he replied.

Shrike's eyes narrowed behind her mask. She approached the tree hesitantly, and saw what had drawn her colleague's attention.

The word 'CROATOAN' was carved into the bark.

A message to those who came after, just as it had been centuries prior, a message left etched into the wall of one of that abandoned settlement's buildings.

There was no cross, but the populace's exit from the island-- and the land of the living-- had been anything but peaceful.

"I can see a concentration of the pathogen in the grooves. Whoever carved the message, they're the ones who released the virus. It started here. Next to a school."

"Inside a cemetery," said Shrike.

"Somebody's idea of a joke. Who do we know who would do such a thing?"

"...There's a short list. We can follow it up immediately. Did you catch all that, FEMA?"

<"Affirmative. Please can you retrieve a sample? If this is the first in a series of--">

"I understand," said Shrike, cutting the speaker off. There'd already been too much death, she didn't want to contemplate follow-up attacks. She calmly scraped away at the seams of the letter C so that filaments of contaminated bark fell into a small vial she'd taken from her belt. "But now what? We don't know who did this. The entire air is full of... of poison. It can't be allowed to spread any further. We're just lucky the winds were still--"

"Lucky? When something like this happens, when does luck ever factor into it?" said Majestic.

"You think this could have been planned, weather and all? Something to keep the spread contained? That would take... resources. Basilisk maybe... one of the science terrorists groups... and whoever did this is still out there, unless they're among the dead." She paused. "Where's Grimm? We could use his brain on this. Might be worth bringing him in."

"He's unavailable," replied Majestic. He was closer to the Grimm than the others on the team, and if what Shrike heard was true, it made sense that the dark avenger wasn't available for a Meridian mission. He had more important things to worry about, much closer to home.

She sighed. She could really use a second opinion on this. Her small fleet of golf ball-sized drones swooped back into sight and she extended her arm so they could reattach to her sleeve. "I've got a full topographical map of the island as is uploaded to my suit. I'll upload it to the Nautilus servers once Starlight's shield drops--"

Before she could finish the thought, the ground rumbled beneath her feet. Even as the quaking slowed to a shuddering stop, and the symphony of silence was punctuated by car alarms in the distance, her suit was analysing the situation. Its internal sensors pinged inside her helmet as the seismological readings were instantly taken, and she was shocked by the information fed to her as the earth finally stilled. "That was a 5.6 on the Richter Scale. But this area only gets hit by 3s, tops, and even then…"

"It's localised, and there's no movement in the water," said Majestic, glancing around. He looked up, past the shield, and said, "Starlight, what are we dealing with?"

<"Weirdness, that's what. I've scanned the entire state with my bands, and there's no movement in any of the nearby fault lines. That means whatever it was, it wasn't a damn earthquake. I've scanned the entire island, and other than… well, y'know… there's nothing. It happened. We felt it. But other than some minor damage to some of the smaller buildings, you wouldn't know it happened. Damn weird.">

"I don't like this," said Shrike. "Mysterious earthquakes? Deadly plagues?"

"You're thinking biblical?" said Majestic.

"No, I'm thinking, this feels like the kind of thing that brought us together in the first place. It feels like a coordinated attack."

"From another world?" said Majestic.

She nodded. "This could be a shot across the bow. Start small, just like the orchids."

"There's no extra-dimensional energies in the air. Just poison. Just death. If it was anything like two years ago, we'd know. Starlight's cosmic early warning system alone…"

"I know. But still…" said Shrike.

"Say no more, I understand. Starlight, scan for extra-dimensional energies again. Check across the entire spectrum. If you find anything-- no matter how small-- you let us know."

<"Sure thing, hoss.">

The silence filled the town again. The pair of heroes knew that it wasn't just this small township that was devoid of sound, but the entire island. When they faced interdimensional titans, there had been nothing but noise, nothing but chaos, and Hannah almost felt like that might be preferable to this. She corrected herself-- it definitely was. Sound and fury, sturm und drang, those were things you could fight against. If they were facing a monster taller than the New York skyline, something with twenty-seven hungry mouths and a thousand piercing eyes, designed only to kill their world, they could beat it into submission and save lives. But this? A monster smaller than the eye could see, capable of stripping life from an island within a handful of hours? That wasn't a fight they could win. Only an aftermath they existed within.

"We need to clear the area. Wipe the pathogen away. We can't allow it to spread," said Shrike.

"Agreed. Starlight?" said Majestic.

<"Nothing yet, but I'm still working through the spectrums,"> said the interstellar hero situated on the other side of the shield.

"Thank you, I appreciate that. We need you to isolate and eradicate every trace of the pathogen. No part of it can be allowed to survive in the open air."

<"I can do that. Shouldn't affect my scans either. You want that now?">

"Please," said Majestic.

The air shimmered. The cosmic energies focused through the bands Starlight wore on his wrists had a distinct signature, and this was them at work.

Shrike watched as the air popped and fizzed an indescribable colour, an effect she'd witnessed before when Starlight had performed similar acts. Be it when Basilisk unleashed a chemical attack on Paris, or when the bloated corpse of one of Xegar's mutations burst with poisonous gas after it ended up beached off the Sydney coast, if he could comprehend a solution, then the day would be saved.

In this instance, as the virus was wiped from the atmosphere, it was eight thousand lives too late. Starlight's energies, derived from some distant, alien power source, descended upon the dead town, and she watched as it washed across her gloved hand. Within a matter of seconds, the entire island was washed clean of the contagion.

Hours to kill. Seconds to clear.

She exhaled. Eight thousand dead. Her drones held a map of the entire island. She had a sample of the pathogen in her belt, and now all that was left was the autopsy. Autopsies.

Eight thousand dead and no clue as to why. They wouldn't find out for a decade.

CITIES ON FIRE

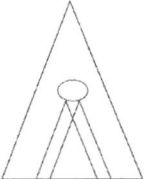

CHAPTER 26: PUNCHING IN A DREAM
LOCATION: AN UNNAMED ISLAND IN
INTERNATIONAL WATERS
FOUR YEARS AGO:

Blood flew from Tomas' mouth in a ragged bolt as he took a punch to the face. He had seen it coming so he'd managed to roll ever so slightly with the blow, but not enough so that his lip and the inside of his mouth didn't split open, the red metal taste violently spilling through him. He fell to one knee and sneered, hocking blood and internal fluids out of his mouth and trying to get his bearings.

The elderly judge raised a flag and the baying crowd jeered. He'd lost a point. If he conceded two more, he'd lose the bout, and the entire International Tournament of Death event. He'd also forfeit his life, his death then the responsibility of the man who defeated him.

Tomas had gotten so far, fought for days on end in the ancient tournament dedicated to deciding the most skilled fighter in the world, and even though it had taken him everything, he'd made it to the final.

"Get up," growled Zhǎngwò Dàshī, the broad shouldered and anvil-fisted master of the Cruel Murder Style style of combat. Which would have been funny to Tomas if it wasn't for the fact he was on the receiving end of it.

Zhǎngwò was the defending champion since last year's tournament, having won the title by first tearing the eyes out of Tomas' father, Gerhard Hochburg, then ripping out his throat.

Tomas was the challenger. He had a buy-in to the tournament through rite of blood and vengeance, and he'd left a trail of bodies behind him to meet his father's killer in the ring.

Three days ago, he'd punched the West African Damba master

Asmau so hard the man's heart exploded in his chest, killing him instantly. That was after two hours of careful consideration and sparring, both men weighing up the best method to kill each other.

Two days ago, he'd collapsed the throat of the Mexican lucha libre El Diablo Negro with the heel of his foot and watched as the masked man slowly choked on his own blood. A short death that felt like it lasted for hours.

Yesterday, during a brutal semi-final against the Kapu Kuʻialua purveyor Vasilisa, he had struggled to defeat an opponent who targeted his nerve clusters and pressure points without mercy. She was bigger and stronger than him, but he had one thing on his mind and that was vengeance. With one arm hanging useless at his side, he'd kicked her in the leg so hard that bone came out the back of her knee. She spat obscenities as he locked her in a choke with his good arm, and even though she lashed out with everything she had, he just synched in his hold until she died a pathetic, spluttering death.

Zhǎngwò Dàshī had experienced a much easier path to the finals. He'd brutalised and mutilated all comers. In the friendly sparring sessions that signalled the beginning of the tournament, what was supposed to be a performative demonstration of each fighter's skill against potential future entrants in the competition ended when he slit the throats of three prospects with the edge of his palm.

And then he wiped their blood on his chest and declared himself the greatest fighter that ever lived.

Without saying a word, Tomas had watched his father's killer from the old, wooden bleachers that surrounded the chalk outlined ring. He knew he had to win. He had no choice but to win. He had to win because then he could kill the man who'd killed his father. No questions asked.

"Did you not hear me, white boy…?"

It had taken thirty minutes for Zhǎngwò to win the first point against Tomas. And the smugness exuded by the master martial artist dripped off him along with the sweat from the day's feverish atmosphere. It was midsummer on Dì Yī Quán Island and the heat was unrelenting.

"…Or are you going to sit there and die like your father?"

Zhǎngwò's body was a tapestry of the violent repercussions of his chosen fighting style. Scar tissue covered every inch of his muscular body, but he moved as if unburdened by the training of his past. He punched and kicked and tore at his opponents. During the quiet moments he ran his mouth, jabbing and testing with his words instead of his limbs.

Tomas stood and smiled. "Come on then, dickhead. Hit me with your best shot."

Zhǎngwò was momentarily thrown by his opponent's apparent confidence, and shot forward, faster than most of the spectators could follow. But Tomas tracked his movement like his father had taught him to, and when the Cruel Murder Style master got close, his hand swiping down like a blade, the German fighter punched him under the armpit, the sudden shock of impact causing the Chinese martial artist to trip and somersault forward-- he caught himself mid-motion and landed perfectly, while Tomas backed off, watching the elderly judge raise a flag.

"Didn't you hear me? That was an invitation," said Tomas.

For all his apparent confidence, Hochburg was concerned. He had hit him with the same amount of strength as he had Damba master, and it had only staggered the powerful martial artist. What should have been a heart-exploding killing blow was a minor inconvenience to Zhǎngwò.

The Chinese martial artist cursed in his native tongue and straightened up. He gestured at the judge aggressively, but the old man shook his head dismissively. Zhǎngwò wouldn't get any sympathy from him.

"I killed your father. And I will kill you the same," he said.

"Please. Try," replied Tomas, beckoning his father's murderer towards him.

The pair rushed forward and when they met in the middle of the ring they started trading blows, but it became obvious-- very quickly-- that the fighters were evenly matched. Punch was followed by parry was followed by punch, the speed of the exchange a blur to those watching in eager, baying crowds.

Tiger punch-- block. Dread hammer-- block. Dragon kick-- block. Terror claw-- block. Mantis strike-- block. Block, block, block, shins, and forearms bleeding where they'd been used to defend the body, and neither man gained an advantage over the other.

Dàshī growled and went to lock up, collar and elbow, drawing Tomas into his centre so that he could land crushing knee strike to his stomach, but before he could connect with the change of tact--

--Hochburg vanished.

No-- he was suddenly on the ground-- performing a full set of splits-- and he drove his hand straight for the groin of the Cruel Murder Style master. It was the same move Zhǎngwò used to tear the throat from Tomas' father but applied in such a way that when his hand withdrew, he was clutching the fighter's severed penis.

Zhǎngwò howled, and Tomas sprang up and reached into the man's throat, taking his tongue out in the same manner he'd demasculated his father's killer. The man half-gargled, half-screamed as blood spewed up from deep inside him, but the hole inside him was suddenly plugged as Hochburg shoved the man's cock down his throat as a replacement for his tongue.

Dàshī staggered backwards, clutching at his throat, but Tomas wasn't finished yet. As dishonourable a death as this, as mocking and sadistic as it had ended up being, it wasn't done. Tomas drove his fingers into the man's eyes, blinding him instantly. At that point, his victim belched up blood and his own member, but he still refused to die. Tomas kicked him in the gory hole between his legs and then tore his ears off, then his nose. He picked and plucked at his prey, but it did nothing to fill the void in himself.

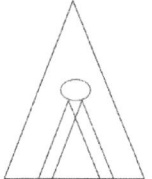

CHAPTER 27: EXPECTING
LOCATION: AL QASILIAH HOTEL, ALEPPO
TWO YEARS AGO:

"Fuck!"

Ronnie threw the pregnancy test across the room with such force that it disintegrated on contact with the wall. It was the third she'd taken, and they'd all come up positive.

Taking her frustration out on them made the most sense, because it was not like there were any other healthy outlets available to her.

She groaned and kicked at the plastic fragments littering the bathroom floor before flopping onto the unmade bed in the other room.

I've fucked it now, she thought.

Except she'd fucked him and now she was fucked, even if she had enjoyed every minute of it.

"Every hour of it," she corrected herself. She smiled before realising that kind of thinking wasn't helpful right now. There was no point in making light of the situation because she was well and truly fucked. She cursed again, and rolled over, thinking over her options. "Fuck."

Across her hip was a surgical scar, two years old and healing ugly. Before she'd left America, the folks at Touchstone had pinned metal rivets to her hip. The bolts were composed of an element that negated the addictive effects of narcotics, so that no matter how much she shot up, the biological need to keep shooting up wouldn't occur.

That didn't help with the psychological aspect of addiction. The mad hot rush of pleasure that came with the right kind of drug. Her body didn't scream for more, but her brain did… and that need might have killed whatever it was growing inside her.

Enough was enough. She had to pull the plug on the operation. She had to get out of this cesspit and back to America.

There was a knock at her door before she could think any further.

She kept a pistol under her pillow but that was because of the business she found herself in, not because she was an undercover Aleph agent. She was Charlotte McQueen, sure, but the outside world thought of her as Charlotte McQueen, former superhero, current disgrace, and active Basilisk devotee. She pulled the weapon and stood behind the door.

"Who is it?" she asked.

"Who do you think?" came the accented voice.

She smiled. Then caught herself. This guy. This guy was the reason she was in this mess.

She unlocked the door and let Naga in. This guy, codenamed: The Money, was the target. She was told to follow the money and that's what she did, all the way to his bedroom. Then back to hers. Then back to his and rinse repeat and now look where she was.

He was a ruggedly handsome man, his features expertly carved as if by a master sculptor. He smiled when he saw her and leaned in for a kiss, but she turned at the last moment and his lips grazed her cheek. He pulled back slowly, confused by the lack of affection. Realising how out of sorts she must have looked, she yanked his tie forward and kissed him hard and fast, and if he had any doubts about her, they were gone in an instant.

His hand found hers, and in her hand was her gun. "Expecting the bad kind of company?"

"I'm a stranger in a strange land. Hold on." She quickly stepped over to the bed and placed the weapon on her bedside table. "There. Now it's just us."

His eyes were inquisitive by nature, heavy-lidded and seemingly half-tired most of the time. She didn't know his real name, even though she'd asked on occasion. Screaming 'Naga' at the top of her lungs as she came made her feel uncomfortable, no matter how good his cock felt inside her.

Everyone she'd met while by his side knew him as Naga, the snake who had come out of the woodwork in recent years to provide funding for Basilisk. It was her job to find out where he was getting the money from and cut the head off the snake before they could strike out at the world.

Basilisk. A doomsday cult condemned by global powers across the planet, whose leaders were shrouded in mystery, but whose destructive tendencies combined the homicidal devotion previously seen in the likes of Japan's Aum Shinrikyo, Nigeria's Boko Haram and Peru's Shining Path, and multiplied it tenfold.

They believed in a specific apocalypse, an event they called Apolíthosi. Non-believers weren't privy to the details of the final days of man but suffice to say... Ronnie had put together enough to realise that if the end times wouldn't come at their own pace, then Basilisk would ensure that their prophecies were self-fulfilling.

"I missed you," said Naga. The two stumbled back and he kicked the door closed as he pushed her toward the bed. "I missed you a lot."

"I missed you too," she replied. She'd be lying if she said that wasn't partly true. She'd been undercover going on for two years, her staged fall from grace leading her to this very moment.

Aleph had seen an opportunity after her public disgrace. She'd fallen off the wagon, the tape was leaked, and she'd already died once after shooting up a potent strain of heroin on a dare. Her friend from the future had brought her back, but someone had leaked photos... and the Crusaders kicked her off the team.

Aleph had swooped in before her brother, the Meridian's own Tallyman, could arrive on the scene, and they detoxed her hard. That was the first time the physical need for narcotics was expunged from her system. When she was sober, the psychics stepped in and flipped a switch in her head to block the psychological component of addiction. It was a temporary measure, they'd told her. Only she could make the change permanent. All they could do was help her along the way.

Then they'd outlined their plan. A deniable ops mission to take down Basilisk. The group were recruiting metas of all stripes, and a high-profile target like Sneak would be a great find. They could create a psychic shield in her head that would disguise her thoughts to the group in case they had their own telepaths, giving her the appearance of someone who'd had enough. Someone who just wanted to live her own life. Who wanted to be bad, because being good wasn't doing it for her anymore.

She knew how bad her life had gotten. She knew she needed a second chance. And this… seemed like the best way to go about it. So, she continued her fall from grace, but this time, it was controlled. Contained. And then she had punched Tallyman at a joint Crusader / Meridian press conference that she 'crashed' and left the country under a black cloud.

Basilisk came calling soon enough, and two years later…

"I bought you something…" continued Naga, searching the inside pocket of his jacket and then pulled out a small bag of cocaine, "…To make tonight a bit more interesting."

Something in her stomach seized. "We, ah, we don't need that," she said.

"I thought you liked the way it made you feel?" said Naga. He sounded hurt. The two had spent many a coked-up night together, fucking until dawn and then carrying on until noon, only stopping to hydrate and snort a few more lines. "I mean, we don't need to…"

"No, no, it's just… I have something else in mind," said Charlotte. She was left wondering what that was, exactly. "Do you trust me?"

"Of course," he replied.

She shoved him down onto the bed and mounted him, removing her tank top to reveal her tanned and freckled breasts. She'd taken to basking nude on the roof of the hotel in between the business deals her lover attended, and he said he loved the way her skin tasted of the sun afterwards. Her bosom fluttered. She was a little out of breath. A little bit nervous.

Was this what a panic attack felt like? she wondered.

He moved to meet her nipples with his lips, his movement a juddering, premonitory motion of anticipation, but she shoved him down and began to unravel his tie.

"What's your name?" she asked.

"Naga," he replied.

"Your real name. Tell me your real name," she pressed.

"I can't do that, my love. You know I would if I could…"

She yanked his head up by his hair and leaned in close. "You could. If you wanted to. Hold your head up." Naga did as he was told, and Charlotte wrapped his tie carefully around his eyes. "No peeking."

"Of course," he said, enjoying the jolting thrill of the encounter.

"Do you trust me?" she asked again.

"Always," he said.

She pointed the gun at his head.

"Good."

And then she pulled the trigger.

CITIES ON FIRE

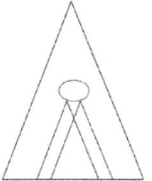

CHAPTER 28: THE GOOD OLD DAYS
LOCATION: PIER 101, SAN FRANCISCO
SEVEN YEARS AGO:

Leon Cobalt sat in the sofa-lined partition of the meeting room in the Crusaders' high-rise headquarters. The curtains closed and the lights turned off, he tucked himself away in a corner so that nobody would see him if they poked their head inside, and while it would have been smarter to lock himself away in his bedroom, he also didn't want to separate himself from his team like that, even if he didn't want to be downing shots with them in the common area two floors down.

Without his costume's batteries running, he always found his full costume weighed on him, so he discarded various components of it on his way to the sofa and sat with his tunic part way open, revealing his black tank top beneath. The team hadn't stopped moving since the early hours, and his body was reminding him of that with each ache and pang.

After his ransom demands were ignored, the Anarchitect had followed through on his promise to make a mess of the city when he transformed Union Square into an elaborate maze with his geography-warping abilities. Not only did the Crusaders have to rescue the trapped shoppers who were there trying to take advantage of the Black Friday deals, but they had to track down the Anarchitect himself and get him to revert the changes he'd made to the city.

While Abstract, Sneak and Cobalt evacuated the affected citizens, Cere-Belle gave the villain a psychic push to see the error of his ways-- a temporary measure, as madness couldn't be placated by even her considerable abilities-- and then Kid Valiant knocked him out once Union Square reverted to its previous state.

Statements were given, evidence collected, and before the team left the precinct Valiant had already sent out the mass text to all their friends and fans, inviting them down to Pier 101 for an afterparty. It was now four hours in, and it stopped being fun for Leon three hours and fifty-nine minutes ago.

Pier 101 was located on the northern edge of Hunters Point, and from Leon's vantage point, you could open up the curtains and look out across San Francisco Bay and see the lights blinking off in Alameda and the lights blinking on as planes landed nine miles away at Oakland International Airport.

To his right, warm hazes of light began to creep in from the hallway, and the sound of people having fun in other areas of their home followed suit. He craned his neck around the corner and gave Sneak a wave as she entered the room, her bare feet silently padding across the floor.

"I thought I'd find you up here," she said.

"Yeah, the party was getting a bit loud for me," he replied.

"All parties are a bit loud for you, Leon," she said.

"…There's that too."

Ever since he had fallen down the centuries and landed with a bang in the present, large public gatherings had made him feel uncomfortable. He wondered if he had always felt this way, or if this sudden onset of social anxiety was a side effect of the mind-bending method of time travel he utilised.

His memories were fragmented and scattered, key details of his personal history and reasons for the jump still missing, with no indication of when they might return. He thought of his personality as a still-recovering injury that made decisions tentative and actions hesitant. What kind of man had he been once, before he took the leap into the past? Would he ever remember who Leon Cobalt 5 was before his arrival? Even his own personal UFO couldn't shed any light on the proceedings. It had grown to the size of a Land Rover since his arrival, but the memory banks were as barren as ever. It was currently floating above San Francisco Bay, its cloaking system keeping it out of sight and out of mind until the Crusaders needed to get somewhere flashy and fast.

Charlotte sat next to him and put her feet up on the opposite sofa.

In the middle of the room behind them was a meeting table, a gift from the Meridian themselves, along with a wall-sized screen 'crime monitor' that aggregated information and displayed it for their consumption.

They were more reactive than proactive, firefighters rather than hunters, and the group agreed that this was the best way for them to operate. If they started acting like superpowered bounty hunters then the legal grounding would be shaky at best. Better to stand and protect, rather than seek and destroy, as Kid Valiant said.

"So, something on your mind?" she asked.

Noncommittal, he replied, "Ah, you know. The usual."

Sneak knew what he was referring to and sighed, "I don't think sitting in the dark is going to jog your memory."

"Well, we don't know that, do we?" he replied.

She shrugged. "...I'm pretty confident though."

He laughed and shook his head, and she smiled as his dour demeanour lifted, even if it was for only a moment.

"It's just," he started, beginning what was clear from his tone would be an unloading of emotional baggage that had been at the tipping point of his tongue for a while now, "Every time we save the day, I wonder if that's it. If that's why I came back to this time. What if today was a domino that led to my future? Do I even have a future? Have I changed everything by simply being here? I mean, fuck… it sends my brain spinning."

Sneak patted at her pockets then checked behind her ear, until she found what she was looking for. "Try this, it'll make you feel better," she said, as she handed Cobalt her unlit spliff. In her other hand, she held a silver-cased zippo lighter, which she dangled in front of him as he considered the joint.

Without putting up much of an argument, he accepted it and allowed his teammate to light it for him. "This is your answer to everything," he said, watching the paper burn at the tip.

"I'm a superhero, bro. Enhanced reflexes, enhanced strength, enhanced braininess, and that means the come down from a fight hurts just that little bit more. This takes the edge off." The air between them was sweet and fragrant, undertones of warmth throbbing through as they shared a breath. "Unless you want me to get hopped on prescription painkillers instead?" she added.

"When you put it like that..."

He took a long drag and handed it back to her. She leaned back and closed her eyes, savouring her inhale. In the same moment, she moved her legs back onto their side of the sofas and tucked her feet beneath her thighs, swivelling slightly so she was facing him. Eyes still closed, she said, "All we can do is our best. Every day. You're here for some reason. We know that. So, do your best. Every chance you get, do your best. And if you remember why you're here, then act on it, but in the interim..."

"...Just 'do my best'. I wish it were that simple," said Leon.

She brushed his jaw lightly with her fingertips, and Leon felt a charge between them. He turned away from her, but could feel her eyes upon him. Quietly, delicately, she said, "I can't begin to imagine how you feel. But I do know you've put the entire weight of the world on your shoulders. The world, and I guess, the future. But you don't have to carry that weight alone. The Crusaders are a team because of you. We're here to help you through this. You don't have to carry all that weight alone."

"I'm not meant to be here..." he said.

"But you are here. The whys or whatever don't matter. You're here." Sneak fell silent for a while, then said, "Leon. Look at me."

Hesitantly, he did as he was told, and she leaned in to kiss him. He pulled back at the last second and breathlessly asked, "What about... you and... Valiant?"

She recoiled in shock. "Me and--?"

He looked around, searching for the best way to put it, "The two of you, you're..."

She finished the thought for him, punctuating it with a long drag on the toke. "Fucking? Yeah, sometimes. Because it's fun and we're both single, so why not? But right now he's trying to turn the party downstairs into an orgy and while all the power to him, I want nothing to do with it. Abs and Cere have already gone home, they had to feed their cats."

"Oh, I just... well..."

"Future Man, you are an awkward prude and for some reason I find it a massive turn on. Now, are you going to let me kiss you, or is this not happening?"

He didn't need to think twice. He grabbed her by the shoulders and pulled her into him, then placed his hands on either side of her face as they kissed. She allowed this to go on for a few seconds, before pushing him back then down onto the sofa. She mounted him effortlessly, and it was then he realised that she was just that bit stronger than him, and he had no problem with it at all. She placed a hand on his chest-- and her head cocked to the side in surprise when she felt his heart racing. She finished unbuttoning the front of his tunic, yanking the top part of the uniform down so his shoulders were caught in the material. With his arms secured at his side, she proceeded to unzip the front of her costume, revealing her sports top beneath. That peeled off with ease.

"I just think," said Sneak, watching as Leon craned forward, attempting to kiss her bare breasts. She pushed him back down with one hand and rolled her hips forward on his crotch, enticing a groan from her prospective lover. "I just think... if there are certain things you can't remember... then why not give yourself some experiences you'll not want to forget?"

"You sound pretty sure of yourself," he replied.

Sneak leaned forward, her lips a breath away from his, and said, "Oh, I am..."

CITIES ON FIRE

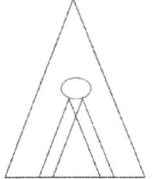

CHAPTER 29: OF SOUND MINDS
LOCATION: LARGAS, CARIBBEAN SEA
SIXTEEN YEARS AGO:

"Do either of you know what remote viewing is?"

The General was not a particularly chatty man, so the question posed to his minders caught the pair off-guard. The old man had wandered over to the drinks cabinet, taken out a crystal decanter of whiskey, and poured himself a glass, then turned to await their response.

"No?" he said.

"No, sir. Sorry," said Carlos, known colloquially as 'The Tall One'. Six and a half feet tall and gifted with the thickest beard you could imagine, he'd been on the General's detail going on two years now, shuttling him from appointment to appointment. The cranky bastard had never so much as looked his way, let alone asked him a genuine question, so he was confused by the strange, but ultimately painless enquiry. He'd been told that his job was to keep the General alive-- which he'd obviously done well at since taking on the job-- and not to engage him in small talk.

"A shame. And you?" asked the old man, turning to his second bodyguard.

The General's military coup had been a short, bloody affair. When he'd taken control, the civilian population had revolted against him, but he had the firepower to make sure that kind of resistance didn't last long. There were still pockets of unrest, but, since he'd taken control of Largas-- an island nation off the coast of Venezuela, a few hundred miles west of Dominica-- he'd been in complete control.

Carlos turned to his comrade, Lupo, referred to as 'The Short

One' even though he was six-feet tall, and furrowed his brow. Lupo took this as a sign to give his own answer. He shook his head and answered, "No. I'm afraid not, sir."

The General took a sip from his drink and exhaled loudly, savouring the harsh alcohol sting. *"It's an absolutely fascinating phenomenon. There are certain scientific circles that believe that a subset of those with psychic abilities have the capability to cast their thoughts far and wide, inserting their astral selves into places that they might usually not be able to access. The CIA have apparently recruited metahuman psychics of various skill levels to explore this. So far, to little actionable success, but still... the possibilities are vast."*

"General, sir, are you feeling well?" asked Carlos.

"Of course. Another day in paradise," said the General. He finished the whiskey and wiped his mouth with the green sleeve of his military uniform, then slammed the glass down on the cabinet with enough force that a crack shot up the side of the container.

Carlos and Lupo glanced at each other, then the Tall One asked, "Will that be all, sir?"

"No, I have another question. Did you know that it's possible for other psychics to send their astral minds across vast spaces and assert control of lesser psyches? You must have heard of mind control."

"Yes, sir. That one I have heard of," replied Carlos.

"Good. Then you can tell the Devil what happened when you wake up in Hell," replied the General.

He pulled his pistol and fired three shots into Lupo's head, three small entry wounds forming under his right eye. Brain matter spewed out the back of his skull, but for a singular moment, before the Short One keeled over into a pile, he looked as if he was crying red. Carlos didn't even have time to react fully-- by the time his hand was nearing his holster, the General had pulled the trigger another three times, with one bullet tearing through the Tall One's larynx, the second sliding effortlessly through the meat and bone under his left eye, and the last one plucking the actual eye out of his head on its way through.

The two bodyguards were dead, and the General still had enough bullets left in his gun to finish what he'd started. His feet dragging, he pulled himself over to a nearby mirror. When his heavy head lolled upwards, the reflection looking back at him wasn't his own, but the face of the man who'd taken control of his body. It was a horrifying sight, seeing another man where your own face should be.

"*We finally meet face-to-face, you dirty bastard,*" said Jason Hackman. His mouth moved but it was the General's own voice speaking the words.

He smiled as the tendrils of his mind further entangled the General, but in an act of contempt, he loosened his grip ever so slightly so that the old man could finally scream after being locked inside his own brain by the psychic's machinations.

"What -- what-- what have you done to me?!" howled the General.

"*I watched you. And then I wore you.*" Hackman raised his fist and the old man did the same. The psychic threw a straight punch at his own face, and the General split his own lip when he copied the action. "*Stop hitting yourself,*" said Jason, repeating the move once, twice, three times, all the while mockingly hissing, "*Stop hitting yourself.*"

The General coughed up blood and broken teeth. Every part of him screamed to fall to the ground, but he wasn't in control of his body. Instead, he held the gun he'd used to kill his two bodyguards up to his temple, and watched as a telepathic image of Hackman leaned toward him, from inside the mirror.

"*The CIA doesn't appreciate you going off script these past few years, General. Looks like you're just as bad as the man we helped you depose. That's an awful shame. Guess we'll just have to start all over again.* Don't do this! I can give you money! Drugs! Women! I can give you anything you want! *That's the problem, General. There's only so much sin we can overlook before we start to suspect you're not the right man for the job. And all I want from you... well...*"

The General pulled the trigger and Hackman opened his eyes in Caracas. The night air was warm and sticky, but he couldn't help but smile. The psychic residue of whiskey was still there on his lips, and he could smell the blood and smoke that came with a triple murder.

But that was two hundred miles away, in the Largas royal palace, and he was held up in a 2-star hotel in the Bolivarian Republic of Venezuela's capital.

"You get the job done?" asked Agent Blue.

That wasn't his real name, but when you were deep cover CIA assets operating in a foreign state, aliases were a must. Jason knew everything about Blue, because when he got bored at night he would pick at his handler's thoughts, looking for anything juicy. He'd swiped a few good fuck memories without him knowing, taking them into his own brain and erasing them from Blue's.

"Of course. I don't mess around," said Hackman, rubbing his eyes. He had projected his mind hundreds of miles, across the ocean and into a rogue nation that would now, slowly but surely, come back around to being an ally to the United States. All thanks to him hitching a ride and pulling a trigger seven times. The snapback to his body was abrupt, like someone had suddenly hit the brakes when they were travelling 100mph down a straight, but he liked the feeling that came with it. That, combined with taking a look inside someone's head as they were dying, was like mainlining the best kind of heroin right into your veins. Not something he ever shared with the debriefing team back at Langley, of course.

"The guns are with the rebels, the General is dead. Let the diplomatic corps do the rest," said Blue. He took out a beeper-- low-fi was sometimes the best-fi-- and sent an acknowledgement code to their ex-fil team to get the plane ready for immediate exit from Venezuela.

"They always have all the fun," sighed Hackman.

"Pack up your shit and let's go. The sooner we're out of this cesspit, the better," replied Blue, his patience wearing thin with the psychic he'd been saddled with for this mission.

Jason smirked again. Later when Blue wasn't looking, he'd reach inside his head and erase the memory of his darling wife's date of birth. That would teach him for speaking to him so poorly.

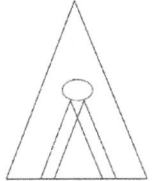

CHAPTER 30: INTO THE WILD
LOCATION: CHENGWATANA STATE FOREST
TWENTY-TWO YEARS AGO:

Madison drew back the bowstring and held it there. She hadn't nocked an arrow, nor had her father given her one with which to do so. He'd simply told her to pull back the bowstring and wait. Almost immediately, in the cold winter Minnesotan morning, her arms began to strain. Her father was crouched next to her, his eyes near slits as he surveyed the woods. If he noticed the tension growing on her face he hadn't said a word.

"Why are we doing this again, dad?" she asked.

"We're diversifying your skillset, kiddo. You know how to use a rifle, so where's the sport? The bow takes considerably more skill. And strength."

Her father was not a tidy looking man. He was an imposing figure, scruffily dressed in drab greys, with eyes that matched. He perpetually appeared to have not shaved for days, but even though he was intense in action, he was just as gregarious in character. Madison never knew her mother. She'd died in childbirth. If this were a sadder kind of story, Ted would have blamed his daughter for the death, but he could never have done such a thing. If he did, his wife would have come back and killed him for it.

Regardless, he explained to Madison when she was old enough to understand that after his wife's death, he'd up sticks and moved them to Chengwatana, a supposed 'ghost town' on the edge of Minnesota, where they would live a quiet life, shooting and hunting.

Training, her father had called it. When she asked what for, he never had a good answer.

For what's to come, he had always said cryptically. But what did that mean? It would take years for her to find out the truth. But now? Fourteen and on the very cusp of teenage rebellion, she simply accepted her father's word as law. They lived a peaceful, unassuming life, one unbroken by the outside world. Until one day in the future. One morning. A stray bullet and the end of her father's life.

"Y-yeah, about that..." said Madison, visibly struggling to hold the bowstring in place.

"I know it hurts but hold it. Isometrics. Hold the weight in place. I built that bow to be optimised to you. Draw weight of 35 lbs. You have to work for this, Maddie. You have to be strong."

"I know, I know."

"...What do we say?" he asked.

She cleared her throat and quoted Sun Tzu: "Appear weak when you are strong, and strong when you are weak."

"That's my girl," he whispered.

She straightened her back and grit her teeth. Her arms stopped shaking. She held the bowstring in place and gripped the bow aloft immediately in front of her. But then something dawned on her. This wasn't particularly difficult, was it? She'd done it a thousand times before. Cold Minnesotan mornings. Hunting for food-- never for sport. Just Madison and her father.

"...Oh," she whispered.

"What's wrong?" he asked.

"...This isn't actually hard. I remember it being hard. But now. Today. It's not," she said.

"What do you mean?"

"When I was fourteen. This hurt. I hated it. I hated all the mad shit you made me do. But today, because of it all... it doesn't hurt. I don't feel it in my actual bones. I feel it in my memory. This isn't real."

She slowly returned the bowstring to its resting position and looked at her dad. She couldn't help but feel sad. He'd been dead for decades, but here he was, in her mind, a confused expression that she'd seen time and time before. The last time she saw that face was the last time she'd seen him alive. Just before those stupid hunters took the wrong shot at the wrong time and killed him instantly.

Her father stood fully, and he towered over her. She was still fourteen. Still looking up at him. "Okay, then. What do you feel? Talk it through. Maddie."

She breathed in slowly and considered her situation. Then, methodically working through the checks in her head, said, "My heart rate is 20BPM. I'm asleep. I'm not in the forest. I'm on the floor of a hospital. The hospital. Aleph. Looking after... oh, hell. It was Hackman. The psychic. He put me to sleep. Trapped me in this memory."

"And walked right over you," noted her father.

"But he didn't factor in something," she added.

"What's that?" asked her father.

"You. He thought you'd be a distraction. You'd keep me here. But you taught me everything you knew and that means I can't be held here. I can't be trapped in a memory."

Her father nodded and suddenly she was looking him in the eye. She wasn't fourteen anymore, but back to normal. He smiled at his grown daughter, a sight he never got to see in real life, and asked, "Then what are you waiting for?"

She threw her arms around him and every warm memory of him crashed together. "I missed you, daddy."

As he began to fade away and the real world came back into view, she heard her father say exactly what she needed: "I love you, Maddie. Now go kick that psychic bastard's ass."

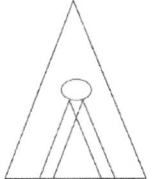

CHAPTER 31: WAKE UP, PLEASE
LOCATION: ALEPH MEDICAL FACILITY, NEW YORK

Madison jolted upright soundlessly. The transition from the psychic dreamscape she'd existed within moments before back to cold reality was one she exerted all her willpower over. She didn't want to gasp or scream or give any sign that she was awake again.

Her father's words echoed in her head, more Sun Tzu, more snippets of ancient wisdom: {Attack him where he is unprepared, appear where you are not expected.}

He wouldn't be expecting this.

Beside her, Charlotte and Tomas were unconscious and twitching, still caught in whatever nightmare Jason had thrown them into. She could wake them up, but there was no way she could guess how they'd react, and she needed all the elements of surprise she could manage.

{I've got your back. He won't hear you.}

There was a commotion coming from inside the operating theatre. She pulled her service weapon and exhaled. She moved slowly toward the entrance and hung back just out of sight. She heard Jason bark orders at the doctors, his voice rising with every word. Clearly, she'd only been caught in the psychic space for a handful of minutes, even if it were like reliving a whole lifetime while she was in there.

"I'm taking operational control here!" shouted Jason.

"He's-- he's in critical condition!" said the surgeon.

Madison had exchanged words with the doctor prior to Cobalt being prepped, and she hadn't been optimistic of the downed agent's chances. Now she sounded terrified, and rightly so.

Another voice piped in. "Nearly all his body is covered in third degree burns, he won't survive unless you let us do our work!"

Jason scoffed. "I don't need him to survive to do my job."

Myers peered inside and saw him reach out toward Leon with his left hand, while putting his fore and index finger against his own temple.

{He's about to initiate a psychic connection. Now's your chance. He'll be distracted.}

Madison crept inside the room, keeping her weapon aimed at the back of Hackman's head. Her footfalls were silent, and she watched the mad agent twitch as he pushed invisible tendrils of psionic energy toward his fellow telepath.

Then she drew the butt of her weapon down on the back of Hackman's head with enough force that he fell to the floor. He cried out in outrage, and spun around to stare daggers at his attacker.

"How-- fucking-- dare-- you!"

"Stand down! You're done here! Stand down!" she ordered.

"Fuck off, am I," growled Hackman. He whipped his hand out in her direction but she didn't move. She had her pistol aimed squarely at him, and wasn't going to be deterred by shows of force.

"Wait… why can't I… why can't I get inside your head?"

{That would be me…} "…Stand down, Jason," came a calm, unassuming voice behind Myers. She recognised it immediately. She'd heard it in her head at her interview. She heard it mere moments before. The newly arrived Henry Gardner stepped forward, his hand also outstretched, pushing his own powers toward Hackman. "Stand down or you're going to get hurt."

"Fucking hell. They sent the wimp," said Jason.

Henry shrugged. "Sticks and stones. Your brain is scrambled, Hackman. You're concussed. Your psychic powers are on lockdown and I'm in control. Do as Agent Myers said: Stand down."

"No!" spat Hackman. "Cobalt is my second. He was on duty when Murray was attacked. It's my job to pick up the reins while he's down and out. If I don't scan his mind now, we might lose precious intel! This is my job. This is my responsibility. Get out of my damn way and let me do my work!"

"I'd have a better time listening to you if you hadn't downed my men," replied Henry.

Jason growled and shook his head. "I don't know why I'm wasting my time with you. You're the son of a fucking mass murderer. A fucking super villain! I know all about you! I know all about what you've done! Me? I'm American-made. Better than--"

Hackman was cut off as both McQueen and Hochburg riddled his chest with sedative pellets from their pistols. They both looked pissed off, and Tomas was bleeding from his left nostril.

"No... no..." Jason stumbled and tried to reach out with his mind, but Henry beat him to the punch, and sent him all the way to the bottom of an ocean of sleep with a colossal mental shove.

"That'll be the difference between you and me. Forever and always. You always have to do everything on your lonesome. I've got my team," said Henry, kicking him in the side to punctuate his point.

"Bit harsh, don't ya think?" asked Charlotte.

"You don't approve?" said Henry.

"I think she's sad you didn't offer her the opportunity to kick him while he was down," said Hochburg.

"Can-- you-- get-- out--!?" asked the surgeon.

"Getting," replied Charlotte, as they dragged Jason out by the feet, his head bouncing off the door frame as they went.

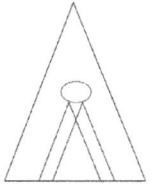

CHAPTER 32: SPEED LINES AND FLASH BACKS
LOCATION: ALEPH ACTIVE INTELLIGENCE HQ, NEW YORK

Anushka Rai held Kristinn Sigurðsson's heart in her trembling hands. It continued to beat and splatter blood across the agent's front, but she was frozen. Anushka didn't know what to do with the mess of muscle, valves and arteries that the vicious speedster Velocity had tossed into her cupped palms.

And now the villain, her red and silver-streaked costume a distorted blur, was moving toward her, appearing on one side of the library and then the other, as if trying to stay in the same place for any one moment was an effort.

Anuska couldn't speak. Tears ran down her cheeks, but she couldn't do anything in the face of what was about to happen. Velocity clamped her hands on either side of the agent's head. Anushka's skin physically trembled at the touch, as if the speedster was holding a pair of impact drills at the same time as making contact with the agent. Finally, Velocity went in for a kiss, and when their lips touched, Anushka's head went up in flames.

Anushka woke up screaming in the medical bay of Active Intelligence's headquarters, the sudden spike of activity causing a pair of nurses to rush over to her bedside.

"It's okay, you're okay, you're safe," said Nurse Amanda Roe, who tried her best to restrain the panicked agent as the nightmare she awoke from receded back into her head. "Anushka, you're in medical, you're okay!"

"The-- the-- the--" spluttered Anushka, looking around frantically. She was in an open ward, and beds were filled with other agents who had been working at the campus earlier that day. Broken bones and bruised egos were among the ailments being treated, but she had been face-to-face with a monster, and she could still feel the surprising weight of Kristinn's heart in her hands. "I-- I can't-- I can't--"

Kishana Muldair rushed over from talking to one of the doctors and clasped her hands around Anushka's. "Nush. Listen to me. You're safe. Velocity is long gone. Just breathe."

Anushka took a few seconds to lock onto Kishana's words, but when she did, her panic began to fade and she did as she was told. Her lips hurt, and when she went to touch them, Roe gently redirected her hand.

"You've got burns on your mouth, best you don't touch them. We've applied a salve that should mitigate damage, but it tastes like crap, so just be careful," said Roe.

"Velocity is a sadist. Makes sense she would do something like that. Probably thinks it's funny," said Kishana.

"Well, I'm... I'm not laughing," said Anushka. She tried to resist the urge to daub her bottom lip with her tongue. She could taste metal and rust at the edge of her mouth and didn't know if that was the burns or the salve doing its work. "Velocity took the body, right?"

"And left us with the USB. Data Analysis are going through it now," said Kishana.

"Anything useful yet?" asked Anushka.

A voice cut into their conversation from across the ward, saying, "That's what I want to know."

Abstract limped over from where she had been listening to their conversation. Her torso was heavily bandaged, which made sense considering Velocity had thrown her with such force that she had to phase through a wall to not pancake on impact. Wherever she landed on the other side must not have been comfortable.

"Laura, glad to see you're up and about," said Kishana.

"Yes, no thanks to Velocity," said the hero. She looked at Anushka. "How are you feeling?"

Anushka shook her head, "Awful. So, the USB?"

"Come on, let's see where the eggheads are with it," said Kishana.

"Feels like all we've done today is watch TV," said Julia.

"Speak for yourself, I got beaten up by a supervillain," said Reggie. He looked like the human embodiment of road rash, half his face moiled with friction burns after being thrown across the ground by Velocity hours earlier. Thankfully, that was the extent of his injuries, and just like his partner, he requested to get back on the job immediately.

"Reruns. It's all just reruns," said Julia, ignoring him. She unpaused the footage hanging in static on the screen in front of them. The past played out once more.

"Are you recording?"

"Yes. Is that a problem?"

"No, but... uh, if you don't mind me asking... why?"

"I want there to be a record of everything that happens next."

"But isn't that evidence of... well... everything?"

"Only if it falls into the wrong hands. It'll be safe. Stored somewhere no one will think to look. And then when it's found, we'll both be untouchable. Don't worry. I'm going to take care of you."

"I appreciate that. You're paying a lot. And, well, you're the boss, after all. Never thought we'd be sat in the same room, but you're the boss."

"As long as you remember that."

"Pause it there."

In Nicholas Quinlan's office, the titular supervillain sat opposite Kruonis, like two old friends meeting up for a catch-up and a coffee. The former was in his standard black business suit, while Kruonis wore his brown and tan costume under a nondescript hoodie. The footage fizzled, though the date stamp-- mere days before Nicholas' elaborate suicide plot-- was visible throughout.

"It's real then," said Anushka. She stood behind Abstract and Kishana, the latter leading them into the office and giving instructions to the pair of data analysts at work parsing through the footage recovered from the USB found on Kruonis' body.

"Nush! How are you feeling?" asked Reggie, rising from his chair.

"Particularly terrible, but what's new. You're okay?"

Reggie tentatively daubed at his contusion-mottled cheek and said, "I'm pretty high on painkillers right now, so I'm feeling pretty good. Feeling better than I look, definitely."

"Enough questionable small talk, what're we working with?" asked Kishana.

Julia cleared her throat. "It's everything. We've gone through all the footage at speed, but yeah, it's the entire sordid affair. There's a couple of conversations between these two, pretty damn incriminating, and then they slap a body camera on Kruonis for the rest. Everything he did for Quinlan, it's on there."

"Then let's get started," said Kishana.

Julia pressed play.

"Oh my fucking God. You're serious?"

Quinlan revealed the transparent container holding Hannah Stone's clone. She was suspended in liquid, with a breathing apparatus intubated down her throat. Various tubes were trailing into her head just above her ear through the entry point cut into her brain. She twitched every couple of seconds as her muscles were electronically stimulated.

"Deadly. I am going to ruin her life. It took years of work, but I'm a patient man. And now I'm ready."

Quinlan's hand lingered on the tube in front of Hannah's face.

"You're talking suicide, man. You're going to ruin her life, but at the cost of your own! Isn't that a bit... severe?"

"It's wonderful, isn't it?"

"If you say so. But uh, why are you showing me all this? No offence, but you're like... nobody knows who you are. Nobody sees you. I feel like the other shoe is going to drop and this is going to be some kind sting, you know?"

"I assure you, this is real. The money I'm paying should prove how serious I am. Now here's what I want you to do--"

Kishana cleared her throat. "Show me the murders."

"Yes, chief," said Reggie.

"Are you sure about this? I can pause everything, we can get out of here," said Kruonis. The camera was mounted on his chest, but you could extrapolate his position in Nicholas' office with ease.

Nicholas looked over from his desk. *"You're here to watch. And <u>then</u> to act. You've already tangled Hannah Stone up in a temporal knot at her home. This is the most important moment of all our lives. Just get ready for your next part."*

You could hear murder outside the office door. And then the Shrike arrived. She looked at Nicholas, and then toward Kruonis in his corner. It was like she could see him, even though he was hidden between the ticks of the clock. But if she could see Kruonis, he wasn't her priority. The criminal backed up anyway, unsure of what exactly would happen next.

She looked back at Nicholas as he stood up from his desk. The camera could barely keep up with her next movements. The knife was out and driven into Nicholas' torso, then she took it to another level, the blade stabbing in and out of his chest with a ferocity reserved for prison hits.

Kruonis' hand covered the camera for a second, and you could hear him retch at the sight of his employer being murdered. *"This is... this is mad... absolutely mad..."*

Shrike tore off her mask and took a breath. Hannah Stone's face was clear for everybody to see, but angled so the security camera recording the events from the opposite corner to Kruonis couldn't see the incision behind her ear. There was no indication this wasn't the Shrike the world knew. No suggestion this was some sort of clone.

She spat on Nicholas' corpse and then headed toward the window, replacing her mask as she did so. Kruonis waved his hands around when she was out the window and out of sight of the cameras, and caught her in a temporal bubble. She was frozen in place, seventeen floors up, floating above the world, and Kruonis knew what he had to do.

"What's he doing?" asked Anuska.

"Oh, my God," whispered Abstract.

Energy swirled around the Shrike, and her blood-stained costume began to warp and crack. Parts fell away and disintegrated into nothingness as Kruonis turned the dial up on the local time within the temporal bubble. You could see her skin shrivel, her body age. Blonde hair grew out and then turned white, then fell out. Kruonis was accelerating her life span, removing her from the equation by ageing her to death and beyond. By the time Kruonis was done, there was nothing left of the clone, not even protoplasmic dust.

"There goes all the evidence," said Kishana.

"Yup."

Kishana checked her watch. "Get me a full breakdown of the events. We've got a technopath coming in that might be helpful, Shelly Leung from New Jersey. Put her to work when she arrives, but I might need her on short notice. I've got somewhere to be." Her phone began to ring. "And I've got to take this. Get to work, people."

She exited.

Julia pressed play.

"And just like that... I'm a multi-millionaire," said Kruonis. The attaché case he had been handed contained three million dollars in untraceable currency. The world slowed to a stop outside his immediate vicinity as he took the time to count it all, bill for bill. It took him hours, but he savoured it.

A male voice from behind him asked, *"Please can you hand me the camera?"*

"Of course. Hated having this strapped to me all the time," said Kruonis. He removed the camera as it continued to record, things got blurry for a second, and then the camera was pointed at Kruonis himself. *"Half up front, half after the act. I can retire now. All it took was... well, everything, I guess."*

Behind Kruonis, a woman pointed a pistol at the villain's head and pulled the trigger, killing him instantly. The attaché case was removed from the room. The camera recorded the dead villain as blood and brain pooled out of his voided out skull.

"Download all the footage onto the USB. Throw it in a bag and put it in his pocket. They're pouring the foundation tomorrow, so we'll dump the body tonight."

"I can't believe the boss went this far," said the man.

"Turn off the camera. Just remember our orders," said the woman.

"Huh. Who the heck are those two?" asked Anushka.

CITIES ON FIRE

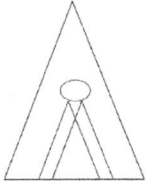

CHAPTER 33: SOMEWHAT DAMAGED
LOCATION: ALEPH ACTIVE INTELLIGENCE HQ, NEW YORK

Much to his surprise, Kishana was standing by the door of the holographic conference room when Chris finally exited. "Fancy seeing you here," she said, as if it was a casual meeting, almost a surprise, rather than something she had clearly planned.

"Have you been outside here the entire time?" he asked.

"Nope. Just got back down actually. Report just in: Hackman went off the rails. Took out Hochberg, McQueen and Myers and clearly jeopardised Cobalt's recovery. Thankfully, Myers broke free from whatever psychic nonsense he put her through and rattled his brains. Gardner arrived just in time to help shut him down. He's currently being pumped full of sedatives to keep him off the board."

"What the actual hell...?" said Chris.

"They're keeping him under and Henry wanted permission to mine his psyche for answers."

"I assume you already gave the greenlight?"

"Of course. Another thing: There's something about Myers. She was able to shake off Hackman's psychic trap and she's no worse for wear. The others are a bit out of sorts. He threw them into their own memories, according to McQueen. That's all she said."

"They can speak to the counsellors in the morning. Are they okay to stay on assignment?"

"What do you think?" she asked.

Chris sighed. "I love these stubborn bastards."

"They remind you of yourself?"

"How could you tell? Any word on Leung? And Witwer, was it?"

"He's upstairs chatting to his wife. You know Linda Witwer?"

"Sure, the analyst," said Chris.

"Yeah, she's a smart egg. Might have found something weird with one of the staff at the burger place. She's going to chase down a lead with the NYPD"

"Weird?" repeated Chris.

"We're just waiting to see if the weirdness forms into something a bit more concrete. I'll tell you everything when that happens. Anyway, Leung is thirty minutes away."

"And Succession Protocol?"

"My guys have nearly finished vetting the list. Hawkins and Johnson know their shit."

"I know they do. You recruited them, after all."

The two continued to talk idly as they rode the elevator back to their respective destinations, two old friends back in a casual rhythm, even with the chaos of the day infiltrating their lives. They eventually fell into silence, and Kishana began to sway back and forth on the balls of her feet, before asking, "You're checking in on your sister?"

He nodded. "I need to see what Doctor Sumner says. He should have finished putting her through the wringer. I need to make sure she's okay."

"Ten years in maximum security hell… you need to be ready for anything, Chris."

"I know. She got burned pretty badly by Scourge… Majestic said he drained the radiation from the wounds, but she's… dismissive. And really… radiation burns? That's going to be the worst kind of hurt. I'm really concerned but I know if I show it, she'll shrug it off."

"You're doing the best you can." The elevator dinged and Kishana stepped off on the analysis floor. "I'll catch up with you later."

He gave her a salute then continued back up to the medial floor. When he arrived, his sister was sitting in the isolation ward. She had changed out of the mangled remains of her prison uniform and was wearing a pair of black sweatpants and a white tank top, sitting cross-legged and barefoot on one of the beds, her eyes closed and her hair pulled back behind her ears as she breathed in and out slowly.

She was meditating again. Chris noted the bandages from her elbows down to her fingertips, and he once again saw the damage inflicted on her across the decade. He'd last seen her seven years ago, and it hadn't been anywhere near as bad as this. He made a mental note to contact Warden Stonewall and find out what the hell kind of operation they were running on Ziggurat Black.

Instead of making a beeline to her, he looked around for Sumner and found him in his office, where he was poring over the results of the examinations they'd performed. He occupied a spacious area that was littered with books and papers, and there were windows on each wall, one that looked in the main ward where a handful of agents were receiving treatment, one that looked into Hannah's isolation ward, and another leading to a laboratory Sumner utilised.

"How's she looking?" asked Chris.

"Not an easy question to answer," stammered the doctor, somewhat surprised by the sudden appearance of the director.

Joseph Sumner was taller than you might expect when you were told about a doctor who specialised in metahuman medicine. African-American and with the build of a line-backer, he dressed like he'd never set foot on a football field before, but that was as far from the truth as you could imagine. He'd put himself through university on a sports scholarship, surprising everyone when he went into medicine and not into the major leagues.

But he had his passions, and he understood the concept of a means to an end. Sat at his desk, he was currently sporting a pair of grey slacks and polished black shoes, as well as a purple checked shirt that he wore under his lab coat. His glasses slipped down his nose and he pushed them up with his middle finger, and shook his head as he shook Chris' hand.

"At one time or another over the last ten years, nearly every single bone in your sister's body has been broken. And whatever kind of medical attention she received was substandard because they have healed terribly. The amount of accumulated scar tissue across her body... I've never seen anything like it."

Chris grimaced. "She... she, ah, put her body through hell even before all this, back when she wore the cape."

"I considered all that. At least when she was Shrike, she had better medical care. A third of her teeth have been cracked or knocked out. They replaced some, but after a while, just stopped. Even then, the work they did do? Seven dental implants, all rather haphazardly applied. The damage to her nerves is substantial, and the dental work to repair it will be ridiculous and painful. Painful as all hell. But that's the thing… the amount of pain she's in now should be monumental. Poorly healed fractures to the orbital bones above both eyes, breaks in her jaw in three different places. Perforated eardrum by what I can only assume was a screwdriver of some type. She's deaf in one ear, sir. And the damage to her hands from today alone…"

Chris looked through the window. She was still sitting, legs crossed, eyes closed, breathing slowly in and out as she centred herself. "Some of the people she trained under… They taught her how to control her experience of pain. Meditative techniques. All the time I've been with her since she's been out… that's what she's doing."

He thought back to the drive over when she'd close her eyes and try to manage her breathing. He remembered the footage from when Scourge attacked her in solitary. All this time, she was meditating, trying her best to push the pain she was in all the way down, somewhere deep where it couldn't get to her.

"…I should have noticed. Fuck."

"I can give her something for the pain, but we need to start looking at… well… at least seven root canals. We can replace the dentures they gave her in there with something a bit more substantial. I'll have to re-break the jaw and wire it back into place so it heals properly, or that'll just get worse. I'm thinking that at the least, we'll need to pin bones and maybe put some rods in place to ensure they heal correctly. Her hands and forearms will be covered in scars from the burns today, but at least the radiation was removed from her system immediately or we'd have… we'd probably have to amputate, as the tissue would've necrotised. The eardrum… I don't know what we can do there. An implant, perhaps. Dozens of operations. Not a dozen. Dozens. Sufficed to say… she won't be the same. Even after we do all that work, the rehabilitation… she'll never be the same. They really did a number on her, sir."

Chris turned away from the doctor and moved his back to the glass in case Hannah could see him. He gripped the top of an empty chair and dug his fingertips in so deep that it hurt. He tried to consider his options, what he could do for his sister, and then something occurred to him. "...What's the progress on the Reiki Project?"

"Nothing new to report, sir. But I don't-- oh. Oh."

Chris nodded slowly. "I'm considering our options here. The computer projections are optimistic, but the side effects... we could do without. Are we any closer to testing?"

"Months, maybe years, sir. With the projected side effects, there are massive issues with the Non-Proliferation treaty."

"We're not here to build metahumans, doctor. We're here to build a better tomorrow. What samples do we have available?"

Sumner rubbed his chin. "I've synthesized a series of doses for study, derivative of the Murray sample. But we're nowhere near ready to start human trials. I want to try and create a more dilute version of the serum and see if the projections are less... problematic. But the biochemical composition means doing so is another trial unto itself."

"I'm not committing to anything, but I want the option. I need to speak to my sister now. Clear the isolation ward of your staff. We don't need to rush anything. But I'm just thinking of the wider implications."

"Of course, sir," said Sumner. He took an old-fashioned looking beeper from his desk drawer and pressed a button. Chris watched as a nurse in the main ward glanced at her hip when her own buzzer went off, then gave her a nod as she looked through the glass. Seconds later, the entire medical bay was empty.

"Clones," said Chris, clicking his fingers.

"Excuse me?" said Sumner.

"Quinlan claimed to have cloned Hannah, and the evidence will come out about it. But if he got his dirty fucking hands on her genetic material once, there may be more out there, and I want to be prepared. This is my sister. Get something together that makes sure we know. That we'll always know."

"I can, ah, come up with something. Let me get to work on that now," said Sumner.

"Thanks, Joseph," said Chris. He put his hand on the doctor's shoulder and nodded slowly. "I don't want anything to happen to my sister now. Not ever. This is the most important thing to me, and I won't let monsters like him ruin her life any more than he already has. Help me do this. Please."

"Of course, of course," said Sumner. He headed out of his office and into the anteroom containing his lab, leaving Chris alone.

The Director of Aleph's Active Intelligence division shivered. Now to have one of the hardest conversations he knew he'd ever have.

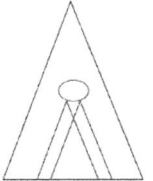

CHAPTER 34: NIGHT FLYERS
LOCATION: ALEPH MEDICAL FACILITY, NEW YORK

Eyes closed and concentrating, Henry had his fingers gently resting on the temples of Hackman. The psychic was sifting through the mangled thoughts of the psychotic telepath who'd tried to scrape out the mind of Leon Cobalt 5, trying to parse through the man's psychosis, the drugged-up haze, and the truth. Even if Henry were feeling 100%, it would be a difficult task.

As soon as they'd knocked him out, Henry had a nurse inject Jason with an above-average dose of the psychic inhibitor Tetrapanadol. Even if he were awake, he would have been powerless to get inside their heads anymore, but it was better to be safe than sorry in instances like this.

Searching through the inebriated remains of a telepath's mind was a draining exercise and even a few minutes in, Henry was already feeling rough around the edges, but he knew he had a job to do: Find out what Jason Hackman had to do with the murder of Jonathan Murray and the attempted murder of Delphine Martin.

"Are you getting anything?" asked Tomas.

The martial artist paced around the edge of the room like a tiger in an undersized cage. For someone so in tune with his body and so centred with himself, he sure was impatient. They'd set up shop in one of the private rooms, the stupefied Hackman strapped securely to a bed while Henry did his work.

McQueen and Myers were sitting outside surgery, waiting for the results of the doctors' labours. After the distraction provided by Hackman, the attending staff had doubled down on their efforts, working tirelessly to save the ravaged man's life.

"Surprisingly... nothing... questionable... yet..." said Henry.

Tomas cocked his head to the side. "Right. So, he's just a bastard?"

"Pretty… much…" replied Henry, beads of sweat wending their way down his pale face.

Tomas shifted his head to the opposite side. "I shouldn't distract you, should I?"

"Nope…" said Henry.

"…And you're not worried he's going to wake up and kick our asses?"

Henry opened his eyes. "You helped pump him full of power suppressants. Even if he did manage to wake up from the sedatives, he'd be dangerous, but he couldn't harm us psychically. You could take him pretty easy, considering your skillset."

"Sorry. I was distracting you. But thanks for the compliment."

"No, you weren't. I was done. The man is a paranoid psychotic with an unwavering loyalty toward Director Murray. Looks like he didn't have anything to do with the attacks, which is just… frustrating. I thought we'd followed this all the way down the rabbit hole and actually got a result."

"So, his plan for Cobalt?"

"Equal parts wanting to do the same as us-- getting to the bottom of the situation. He also suspected his second of being responsible in some part, so mix that in with the aforementioned psychosis…"

"He didn't care if finding answers killed him," said Tomas, finishing Henry's sentence.

"Exactly. You're good at this," said Henry. He reached out and rested his hand on the martial artist's shoulder.

Hochburg glanced down at Henry's hand, and then up at his face. He smiled and was about to say something when the entire bunker shook. Instead of whatever he was going to say seconds before, he blurted out, *"thefuckwasthat?"*

Henry put two fingers to his temple and reached out into the facility, linking with Charlotte and Madison's brains, and seeing through their eyes. "Holy shit," he said.

"What is it?" asked Hochburg.

"We need to move!" said Henry. He led Tomas outside and motioned for the guards positioned at the door to continue watching

Hackman, and then the pair rushed down the hallways, until they came to the surgical ward. They burst in and were surprised by the blinding light that spotlighted where Cobalt 5 had been laying. Now he was floating upwards, and even though he was caught in the cone of light, they all saw the extent of the damage on his body-- the majority of his skin was gone, just charcoal and exposed musculature and bone left on there. If this was where he was currently, no wonder the surgeons were stressed out.

Both Myers and McQueen had their weapons drawn, but Ronnie had her hand over Madison's pistol as she stared up at the source of the noise. "Don't panic!" she shouted.

"Jesus Christ, what is that?" asked Hochburg.

"Give me a second," said Ronnie, never taking her eyes off the light flooding downwards. Her green irises looked black; her pupils dilated to such a degree that you might think she was high. But no, she was focusing her enhanced vision on taking in every detail of what was occurring above their heads.

Above the operating theatre, a borehole had formed linking them to the street level, seven floors up. A spotlight caught Leon Cobalt and was floating him upwards, his body limp. All the IVs and equipment hooked up to him had come loose, but his chest was still rising and falling, he was still alive.

"Ronnie! Answers!" shouted Tomas, pulling out his own weapon.

"It's... it's his ship. The Orb. Its radar cloaked, so we wouldn't have spotted it coming in until it was... is... on top of us, but I'd recognise it anywhere."

Henry's head whipped around. "Who's piloting it?"

"It's run by an AI called Madrox-- Fuck! I should've thought! She's linked to his vitals. She's probably been searching for him, and we took him underground, where the signals would've been harder to penetrate..."

"We can't just let him leave," said Henry.

"What do you even suggest?" asked Madison.

McQueen continued, "...Her pilot is sick. Near death. She's come to collect him. The future tech onboard... she might have a better chance of saving him than our docs."

"No, no, no," mumbled Henry. They were losing a lead, and so he focused all his psionic powers on the unconscious mind of Leon, trying to glean as much information from his anaesthetic-hazed consciousness before it was too late. He reached out with all the psychic might he could muster, racing the projected tractor beam as it carried Leon aloft to his ship. . A fraction of a second later the porthole sealed shut, cutting off the shaft of light before both vanished altogether.

Ronnie cursed, "We won't be able to track it. As soon as the cloak is up, it'll become invisible to even the most advanced radar."

"Then we just lost our best and only lead," said Hochburg.

"Not… not necessarily…" said Henry, blood dribbling from his nose. "I've taken an… an impression… from his mind… direct download into my head… I'll…" He suddenly collapsed, his body twitching uncontrollably.

"Holy shit, what did he do?" asked Madison, rushing to aid him.

Tomas had gone pale as he followed suit, dropping to his knees and checking Henry's vitals. "Fuck! You heard him-- he just downloaded information from Leon's brain-- and Leon was on *fire* six hours ago!"

It was the kind of realisation that had never even occurred to Madison before, but when it did, it was a punch to the face. She realised what the psychic must have been experiencing and felt sick. In a world where sentiments like 'I can only imagine what you're going through' were rife, this was something else entirely. This was the real thing. Henry couldn't help but experience what Leon had been through. One man had been caught at ground zero of a catastrophic explosion, skin turned to ash and flesh to charcoal, and the other? He felt every single cell of his body-- Leon's body-- their body-- revolt against the inferno that engulfed him-- them-- and there was nothing Henry could do about it.

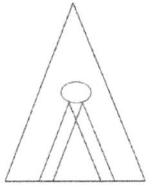

CHAPTER 35: ALL OF US CAST ASIDES
LOCATION: ALEPH ACTIVE INTELLIGENCE HQ, NEW YORK

It was just the two of them now. That old story. Brother and sister, alone in the state-of-the-art medical facilities located at the top of the underground headquarters of Aleph's Active Intelligence division. He sat opposite her, and she hadn't opened her eyes yet. But she knew he was there. Even when they were kids. They always seemed to know where the other was, even when one of them didn't want to be found.

"How much pain are you in?" Chris finally asked.

"I'm fine," she quickly replied.

Hannah definitely earned the eye roll she caused Chris with that. He pitched his voice higher and replied, "'I'm fine'," mockingly, then continued, "Really? And who taught you that mantra? The White Lotus? Tsurugi Mao? Which of the many sensei you studied under taught you to lie to your brother like that?"

Hannah opened her right eye. "...All of them."

"Well, they're not here now but I am. I've spoken to the doctor. He told me what's going on with you. So, 'I'm fine' doesn't exactly cut it. Let me help you. Talk to me."

"You already did. You got me out," she replied.

"Not soon enough, I didn't."

She closed her eye again. "What do you want me to say?"

"The truth."

She scoffed. "The truth. Amazing."

"Hannah..."

"Listen, it doesn't hurt if I don't think about it, okay?" she spat, indignation seeping into her words.

"And are you thinking about it?" he asked.

"Of course. All the damn time."

Her body shuddered, as if the admission allowed a crack to form in the dam that held back the physical manifestation of how much she was hurting.

"...What did they do to you?" pressed Chris.

"Everything. Anything. It was a real free-for-all. The inmates had their turn and then it was over to the guards. Nobody likes a superhero. Nobody likes a super-hypocrite. Unfortunately, to them, I was both."

"Doctor Sumner says he can help put things right. It'll take time, but--"

She touched her face, her fingers brushing against the rough bumps and thick scars left over from a decade's worth of torment. "Do you think Ben would recognise me? Or Ginny?"

Chris had walked his sister down the aisle. Eight years between them, and she'd known him longer than she had the chance to know their parents. Nothing else made sense to her than to ask him. He wore his dress blues and she wore white. Ben-- her future husband and future father to their future daughter-- had tears in his eyes as she approached, and Chris had leaned toward his sister's ear and whispered, *"Wimp."*

He remembered how she'd tutted quietly and said, *"You just wish you had a woman like him in your life."*

"This is true," he'd replied, squeezing her hand ever so slightly.

In the present, he shook his head vehemently. "Of course. Don't be stupid. You're still you. Nothing will take that away from you. Now, listen. I spoke to the doctor. It'll take dozens of operations to fix the damage done to you. Months, if not years of rehab. And even then... there's no guarantee that you'll be back to 100%..." Even though he'd told himself he wouldn't say it, he sighed and suddenly changed course, "Hannah... you should have contacted me... you should have reached out..."

Her voice dropped to a low growl. "Are we back to this? That was never an option for me. And I don't want to hear you say it again. Y'hear?"

"...Fine, but my point still stands. You don't deserve what's been done to you. Nobody in your position does. Not even the worst actual criminals that were in there for you."

"Are you about to go on a rant about prisoner rehabilitation and criminal justice reform?" she asked.

He cut her off with a gesture of his hand. "Stop. Stop deflecting. We've been working on something. Applying everything we've learned from our experiences with metahumans into a solution to wider problems. Sumner's proposal was about looking for cures to diseases like Alzheimer's and MS-- incurable diseases-- with a derivative taken from Erkalite-activated metahumans."

"Right... okay.." She nodded, following his train of thought but unsure of where the tracks ended. "I don't have the meta-gene, Chris. Even if I wanted superpowers-- and I most definitely do not want fucking superpowers and never have-- Erkalite wouldn't work on me."

"Here's the thing-- Sumner has managed to create a serum that effectively installs the meta-gene into the human genome. The next step is to strip the extraneous power manifestation and isolate the healing qualities of the process. Our projections tell us that right now we can't do both. The serum can-- in theory-- eliminate cancer cells, but it also has the side effect of making the patient a superman."

"Which goes against the NPMD," noted Hannah.

"Why do people think I'm not aware of the Non-Proliferation treaty? That's why we're not releasing our findings yet. We need to get past the unintended consequences stage and arrive at the cure-all stage. Then we work on making it available to the world. No more unnecessary deaths. No more lives cut short by disease."

She slid off the bed and turned her back on her brother. He watched as she shook her head, her shoulders shuddering as if with laughter. "Get real. You're buttering this whole thing up. You want to give me superpowers, right?"

"...Basically, yes," he replied. She always could see right through him.

"No," she said.

"No? Hear me out--"

Much to Chris' surprise, she swiped the accumulated trays and equipment on a nearby surface onto the ground, the clattering crescendo punctuating the point she made as she spun to face him, her finger jabbing at the air between them with every step.

"No. Never. I am enough. Me. Not me-plus-superpowers. Not me-plus-something-else. Me. Every skill I've mastered, every battle I've fought, everything I've endured, I did it being me, not because of some magic god damn rock!"

"I get that, but--"

"No, I'm not done! I survived hell. I can survive this. So, no. Keep your damn superpower miracle drug. I don't want it. I never will. It should be used for somebody who truly needs it, not wasted on someone like me."

"Wasted? Are you hearing yourself? This isn't about trying to improve you. This is about getting you healthy. It's not about changing you, it's about helping you. You joke, but I saw the damage done to you. I can only just begin to imagine the amount of pain you're in."

Chris paused, but the sudden silence hit him harder than he expected. He swallowed, took a moment to collect himself, and continued talking, his voice quieter and sharper.

"This isn't about my superpowered sister. It's about fixing a problem. But, y'know what? I've not seen you for seven years. Your fault, mind. Not mine. I don't want to argue! So, we'll shelve it for now. For now. Fucking hell. You always make me so god damn mad. Right. Fine. Do you want something for the pain?"

"Finally, a question I wanted to hear asked. Fucking yes. Can I please get an aspirin, because you're giving me a god damn headache."

"Typical. Absolutely--" He turned away, only for her bandage-wrapped hand to clamp around his arm. When he turned back, she was looking at him on full beam, her eyes wide and glassy with tears. "...Hannah...?"

"Chris, I am grateful for everything you've done. For all you offered to do. Don't think I'm not. But... this is me. I am my experience, for better or worse. And while I appreciate the medical attention... I've been buried alive for ten years. Locked up in the dark at Ziggurat Black. A whistle stop trip under the sea to the Nautilus. The most I've been outside is inside an aircraft carrier and then in the back of a tinted window car only to get sent down here.

Can we go outside? Please? I just wanna feel the sun on my skin."

Chris checked his watch. "It's 10pm."

"Fuck you. The stars then."

"This is New York," he said.

She threw her hands up in the air. "Oh, my god! I just want to be outside!"

He smiled. "Let's get you some painkillers first, then we'll head topside, okay?"

"My favourite kind of deal," she replied.

CITIES ON FIRE

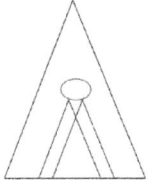

CHAPTER 36: LA MER A BERCÉ MON CŒUR POUR LA VIE
LOCATION: FESTUNG SHAMBHALA, ANTARCTICA
THIRTEEN YEARS AGO:

Stood with her hands resting against her hips, Hannah sighed as she marvelled at the view. "I don't know how you do it, Lumi," she said, awe quietly wending out alongside her words.

The icy outcropping that the platform was built upon was positioned so that it looked out across the frozen wastelands, all diamond bright glaciers and untouched snow. Hannah's costume was reinforced and insulated, with internal heating keeping things a cosy 21°C-- cool enough to ensure she didn't overheat during her vigilante exertions, and warm enough that the frozen wasteland of the Antarctic didn't put a dent in her smile.

If Hannah was simply comfortable, then her friend Lumikki was positively basking, wearing nothing but a bikini, along with a pair of sunglasses. She basked in that winter sun like it was the kind of weather you soaked in by the pool, but it helped that she was a formidable magician, and that one of her distant ancestors was a member of the water-dwelling Homo Aquaticus. Thanks to a fluke of genetics, that meant the cold didn't have the same sort of effect on her as it would an average joe in the same situation.

She tipped her sunglasses down her nose and looked over to Hannah. "What, live in an abandoned Nazi laboratory at the bottom of the world?"

Beneath their feet and beneath the ice, was a vast underground complex constructed under duress by thousands of long dead prisoners for the 'glory' of the Third Reich. Countless rooms made space for numerous machines; vast, intricate devices capable of god knows what. It had taken decades for any of their experiments to come to fruition, and when they did...

Undine had killed the surviving Nazi occultists alongside her husband, Tempest, when the ghosts of world wars past activated a device deep inside the subterranean lab. It had threatened to tear the world and sea in twain, making way for something old to move in on our dimension.

The machine was described in the scientists' notes as 'Geistangetriebener Weltbrecher', an engine powered by spirits to break the world. To break the world. The reason they learned the name of the device from journals and not from the scientists left was because none were left alive after the fact. Tempest had been plain in his intention: None who could dream up such a device, and power it with such suffering, should be allowed back into the world.

When Undine admitted that it wasn't difficult to end the lives of the decrepit members of the Thule Society, Shrike had been taken aback. They may have been Nazis, but they were still humans, if by a matter of degrees. How could the couple do what they did and be so nonchalant?

"Because they wanted to kill the world, Han. And when it comes to stakes like that, I don't have a problem making the hard choices."

In the aftermath-- and once they'd finished burning the bodies of the Nazi occultists in a pile outside the fortress-- Undine endeavoured to put to rest the restless spirits of the long dead prisoners whose tortured souls were powering the Geistangetriebener Weltbrecher. Hannah had watched the Danish witch combine her immense force with young Temperance Lloyd-- the exuberant medium from England-- and send them to their final resting place.

They successfully prevented the end of the world, and Undine liked the views from the uppermost tower in the Nazi's fortress-- dubbed Festung Shambhala by the unimaginative dark magicians that made up the Thule Society membership in the final days of the war-- so Tempest, regent of the underwater realm of Lemuria, made an official land claim that was quickly granted, thanks to a large payoff to the Norwegian government, and the couple made the icebound fortress a holiday home of sorts.

She later admitted that aesthetics wasn't the true reason they'd set up shop here. This was a bedevilled place. Tainted by the decades of occult practice committed by the Thule Society. Nobody could be allowed to take advantage of the mass of magic scar tissue left like a picked scab by the German's meddling. Undine was there to safeguard the future. Better to set up residence there and watch over the enchantments put in place to keep the hole full of malevolent magic plugged up, than demolish it and hope no one thinks to journey south and start their own evil work.

The ever-smirking Lumikki Villadsen had taken the name Undine after spending days trying to come up with an original enough superhero title. She had piercing blue eyes that seemed to change shade depending on the shifting weather, which was the first clue to her parents that she had inherited the ancestral powers that run on her mother's side of the family.

Lumi was of the Kloge Folk-- the Cunning Folk of old-- practitioners of ancient mysticism with a penchant for elemental manipulation. She had powers, so she had to do something with them, and the strong moral centre imposed by her mother and father meant that a career in superheroics was almost inevitable. You'd have thought that super crime wasn't prevalent in Norway, but soon enough, Undine had made a name for herself, and when the world needed heroes, she was there to defend it during the crisis that led to the formation of the Meridian.

Just like the weather around them, she was icy, all pale Danish skin and hair, with an angular face and cheek bones that almost carved their way down her face to accentuate her curling lips. She never looked unhappy, and even in her most serious moments, there was a glint in her eye, the kind of look that suggested she saw past whatever catastrophe had befallen them, and saw a brighter future beyond it.

"Kinda sorta," replied Hannah. She smiled and took a seat next to her friend. "No, just… this. It's all so much. It's amazing. And in the world we live in… don't you think it takes a lot to amaze nowadays?"

"You need to take me up on that tour of Lemuria some time," replied Lumi.

"Ooooph, don't even. I've only just turned twenty-five and I'm a founding member of one of the most powerful groups of people in the world. Going down to the Nautilus is one thing, but Lemuria? An entire underwater continent? I don't think my feeble mind could take it."

"Oh, to be twenty-five again..." chuckled Lumi.

"You know, I never did find out how old you were," said Hannah.

"There's a reason for that," replied Lumi, tapping her nose.

"And you still haven't told me how you and Atlatesh met..."

"So many questions! I have to save something for later, don't I?"

"Lumi, you're my best friend and I barely know anything about you other than you're awesome. How are you going to be my maid of honour if you're not going to open up to me?"

Lumi rolled her eyes. "Well, firstly--" Then she realised what Hannah just said. "Hannah Stone." She sprang out of her chair so fast that her right breast nearly popped out of her bikini. "You're finally tying the knot?!"

"I mean, I'm twenty-five, it's not like I'm an old maid," replied Hannah.

Lumi jumped up and down and pulled her friend in for a hug that nearly squeezed the life out of Hannah. "Oh, god, when is it? What happened? When did he propose? Wait, did he even propose? Was it you? Oh, it was you, wasn't it?"

"No, surprise, surprise, it was Ben. He caught me completely off guard. Got down on one knee and everything. He even asked Chris for permission, the old-fashioned idiot."

"What did Chris say?" asked Lumi.

"Ha, well, typical Chris, he said that Ben didn't need his permission, as long as he made me happy. Then he threatened to have him renditioned if he broke my heart. Standard big brother stuff."

"But Lieutenant Christopher Stone can do all those things..." said Lumi.

"Well, I didn't want to belabour the point. So, that's a yes?"

"Of course it's a yes! I just thought you wanted to take in the view, if I'd known you were going to ask me something like this I would have-- oh, well, the wine cellar is fully stocked. All the good stuff is stored behind the Nazi gold..."

Hannah covered her mouth in amused shock. "Lumi!"

"I'm joking! But there's some champagne in the fridge and I think if there's ever an occasion to uncork some of the hubby's sunken treasure, now's the time!"

"I knew I wouldn't regret asking you this," said Hannah.

"You've not been on the hen-do yet, my dear," said Lumi, gently poking her friend on the nose. "But first, champagne! And celebrations! And later, probably, strippers!"

"And you're the queen of an entire underwater continent, how?"

"Well, if I'm your maid of honour, I guess I have to tell you now, don't I?" replied Lumi. "But on the other hand...."

CITIES ON FIRE

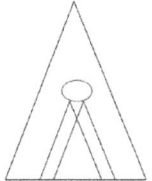

CHAPTER 37: SUSPECT BEHAVIOUR
LOCATION: APARTMENT OF DANIEL AND TONYA LAWRENCE - BROOKLYN, NEW YORK

The doors closed and reopened as a hand wave prevented the elevator from leaving. Linda Witwer struggled with the papers she was carrying as she rushed inside the compartment. The two detectives-- Scott Shapira and Mariana Lupo-- were waiting impatiently for her, even as she apologised profusely. She was in her late-thirties, her blonde hair was tied back in a ponytail, but long strands had gotten loose and she looked frazzled.

"I don't see why you need to come with us," said Scott. He had clearly opted to take an aggressive stance to the situation, his irritation never in doubt. He was stocky in that Coney Island wrestler kind of way, broad shouldered, a bulge above his belt where his round belly liked to say hello when he was hungry, and the kind of hairy backed toughness that came with a more rough-and-tumble upbringing than most would prefer.

"We've been on this all afternoon, we could just send you our report," said Mariana. She was trying to be diplomatic. She had aspirations beyond the NYPD. If she played her cards right, impressed the right people in Aleph, then that might be the best place for her to end up. She was born and raised in the Bronx, and found herself playing peace-keeper for her new partner the same way she had to do for her brothers.

"Th-there's, sorry, one second," Linda finally had her papers in order and placed them in her satchel. "Right, Daniel Lawrence is a professor of theology, Tonya Lawrence owns a boutique florist. Two kids; Madeline, the eldest, who we're here about; and Elyse."

"Okay, but that's not an answer," said Scott.

"There's a flag against the victim's mother on the Aleph database. She's a metahuman. Lowest level, but a flag is a flag. That's the main thing."

"A meta? We can handle a meta, that's just part of being police in New York," said Scott.

"Oh, I'm sure," said Linda. The spike of sarcasm raised both the detectives' eyebrows, considering how wholly untogether the Aleph agent was seconds prior.

"What do you mean by that?" asked Mariana.

Linda cleared her throat, then went straight at it. "You've only been partnered with Detective Shapira for seven months. In that time you've only passed one case over to Aleph due to suspected metahuman involvement. But before you were partnered up, Detective Shapira pushed seventeen cases to Aleph in the year preceding. So, while I think *you're* more than capable of being involved in metahuman cases, I do think your partner should be realistic, and a lot less antagonistic. I'm here to help."

The information rolled out of Linda with ease, no hint of her earlier awkwardness. She looked Shapira in the eye as she spoke, clear and concise, and she felt like she proved her point when the vein at his temple popped out for the world to see. The detective took a step forward, as if he was going to do something stupid, but Mariana put a hand on his chest.

"You, uh, shouldn't throw accusations around like that," said Mariana.

"They're not accusations, especially when Aleph's non-mandate crime stats-- you know, the ones that are there because our agents are investigating crimes where the perpetrators aren't throwing energy bolts around-- are up because we have to deal with stuff outside our remit."

Linda took a breath. The elevator pinged and the doors opened. She stepped out, leaving the two detectives to stew on what she had said.

"You need to chill the fuck out," Mariana quietly hissed at her partner.

"Bitch called me lazy, called me, I dunno, inept or some shit, I don't have to take that," he replied.

"Yeah, you kinda do, especially if it's the truth. Buck up, try not to embarrass yourself-- or me-- and let's get this over with, all right?"

Scott grumbled, and the elevator door nearly closed on them. Linda's hand prevented that from happening. "Do you want to know the other reason I'm here?"

"To piss me off?" offered Scott.

Mariana rolled her eyes and cursed inwardly.

"No, but nice guess. You've been busy today doing the worst work imaginable-- telling people that their loved ones are dead. How far down the list are you now?"

"This is the seventh," said Mariana.

"The seventh out of fifteen employees who worked at a restaurant that exploded quite publicly *today*, at *lunch*. It's evening now. Do you know how many times Madeline Lawrence's parents contacted the police since then?"

"...Uh," said Scott, a non-starter of a contribution if there ever was one.

"They've *not*. Other folks on your list: David Gant's parents didn't stop calling the NYPD until they got an answer. You know that. Greg Hayter's parents are separated, and *separately* they both turned up at One Police Plaza for word on their son's condition. You know that too, because that's where you spoke to them. Christy Jimenez's parents are both deceased. Her aunt and uncle went so far as to contact the FBI for an update. You know that, because you were just at their apartment. But Madeline Lawrence's parents? Happily married? Two kids? Lived together in this building for thirteen years? Not a word."

"Maybe they, uh, had some kind of falling out?" suggested Scott.

"How did you make detective?" replied Linda.

"Look here, miss--" started Scott.

"It's Mrs, but to you, it's Special Agent. I've done my time in boys club institutions like the NYPD. I was a detective in the Baltimore PD for twenty years before making it to where I am today. I don't like the stink of your shit and I never will." Linda looked at the shocked Mariana. "You'd be best served requesting a new partner at the earliest opportunity, because trying to keep him in check is a sure fire way to never get to where you want to. Now, you can both stand there and process everything I've just said, or we can have a conversation with the Lawrences."

"I'm... I'm going to complain," said Scott.

"Good. Luck," said Linda. She knocked thrice on the front door of the Lawrence family's apartment, and her entire demeanour changed when Daniel Lawrence answered. "Good afternoon, sir. I'm Special Agent Witwer with Aleph. These are Detectives Lupo and Shapira with the NYPD. We're here about your daughter."

"My daughter?" said Daniel. He was well into the six-feet-tall, all gangly arms and knocking knees. His hair was thinning but he had a kind smile and tired eyes.

"Does Madeline work at Burger Don, over at Kip's Bay?" asked Mariana. She took a step forward, while her partner remained behind her, opening and closing his mouth as he tried to process everything that had happened before the door opened.

"She does, yes," said Daniel.

"Is she working there today?" asked Mariana.

"Yes," said Daniel.

"Please may we come in?" asked Linda.

"Oh, of course, of course," said Daniel.

He beckoned them into the hall of the apartment. A vase of wilting flowers were situated nearby, and the place smelt of the sea. Wet, salty and slightly cold. He led them into the kitchen, past two bedrooms, one clearly belonging to the parents, and the other belonging to Madeline. In each room there was a vase of poorly maintained flowers.

"Can I get you a drink? Tea? Coffee? Water?"

"No, thank you. Is your wife home?" asked Linda.

"She's running an errand. Please can I ask what this is regarding?"

Scott finally caught up with the conversation, and had decided against cussing out Linda. Instead, he asked, "Didn't you hear what happened earlier today? The explosion at your daughter's place of work?"

Daniel blinked. "Oh, is she all right?"

"No, I'm afraid not," said Mariana. "We fear that she is among the fatalities."

Daniel blinked again. "Do you know what happened?"

Linda interjected, "Do you mind if I look around your daughter's bedroom?"

"I can tell you everything we know," said Mariana.

Daniel gestured down the hallway. "Uh, yes, yes, that'll be fine. What happened to my daughter?"

Linda left the detectives in the kitchen and slipped into Madeline's room. The curtains were closed. Everything was in order. Worn clothes were in the wash basket, waiting to be cleaned. There was a half empty glass of water on the bedside table. A damp towel was on a cold radiator. There were books on her desk, a laptop open but turned off, and the general flotsam that came with being in your twenties and living at home with your parents.

Linda pulled on a pair of latex gloves and began to open drawers in the bedside tables. There were the usual kind of chotskies you would expect from someone who hadn't yet left home. Half-used make-up palettes, fake rings, photos of friends and random bits of twee. Birth control pills, an open box of condoms. Nothing of particular note.

Finally, Linda stared at the bed for a bit. at. "If I…" she mumbled. Lifting up the mattress was easy. The covers and pillows fell into a pile on the opposite side of the bedroom. Situated between the wooden slats of the frame was a simple black diary. She removed it, and began to flick through the densely written pages. There was an account on every page, for nearly every day, going back to last year. She looked at yesterday's entry:

…Mom didn't come home today. Dad says she's visiting friends. He's still acting weird…

She flicked back a few pages, speed-reading the entries as she went, picking up a sadness and concern in the young woman's writings as she travelled back days into her life.

Last week:

...Dad still isn't eating...

Linda looked around the bedroom. On Madeline's desk was a pink frame, and in it, a photo of a sunny looking matriarch, a stout patriarch, and two younger women. Written in a blank space beneath them was the note, *Barbados - Summer 2032*. The Lawrence family on holiday a year ago.

Daniel Lawrence had lost a considerable amount of weight between the holiday and the present day.

An entry from two weeks ago:

Dad came from his research trip and is acting strange. He looks like he's lost weight. He came back without his suitcase, said he gave it all to the church as a gift. All he had with him was his passport, wallet and a small black book I've never seen before. When I asked him about it, he snatched it out of my hands and said it was private. The cover was black, and felt weird. There was a symbol on the front, a gold triangle with a circle inside it. I've tried searching online for it but there's nothing. He apologised for being so abrupt, but I've never seen him like that before.

"Special Agent Witwer?" Mariana stood in the doorway, waiting for Linda to face her. "Mr Lawrence is a bit out of it. I think he's in shock, but there's something else to it. Scott is with him now."

"You're sure it's a good idea leaving your partner with him?" asked Linda.

"Scott... isn't a bad guy. He's just a bit... coarse," said Mariana.

"Men like that are anchors, Detective. They either hold you in place or drag you down. You're not naive. I can see that. You don't have to make excuses for him."

Mariana sighed. "Have you found anything?"

"Just weirdness. Look at this," said Linda. She held up the photo. "Notice anything different?"

"Is that Mr Lawrence? Jeez, he's lost a lot of weight," said Mariana.

Linda nodded. "He went on some sort of research trip, and came back with the pounds dropping off. I think we should--"

Daniel Lawrence entered the room without a sound. He was moving quickly, his body rigid and uncomfortable, and before Linda or Mariana could question his sudden arrival, he drove a steak knife up through the bottom of the detective's ribcage, straight into her heart, and twisted.

Linda cried out in shock and took two steps back, pulling out her gun as she did so, but Daniel didn't stop moving. He yanked the blade out of Mariana's body and she flopped down dead as blood poured out the tiny slither beneath her sternum. Daniel threw the knife at Linda and it cut into the side of her gun-wielding hand. Her digits spasmed and the weapon fell from her hands.

Covered in Mariana's blood, Daniel rushed toward Linda, kicked the dropped gun backwards under the bed, and shoved her back against the desk. She dropped the diary then grabbed the laptop with her other hand, swinging it hard across his face, but this only staggered him. She reeled the laptop back for another go, but he grabbed her by the wrist and twisted, causing her to drop it. He was strong. Stronger than he had any right to be.

She kicked him, and the desk shunted back again as she used it for leverage, causing the window to shatter. She swiped back and caught the diary in her arc of movement, sending it flying through the broken window and down into the street below.

Daniel grabbed Linda and tossed her into the hallway. He took one last look at his daughter's bedroom, and then followed after the Aleph agent. She had smashed into the wall, plaster cratering on impact, but managed to pull herself up. That was just in time to be punched in the stomach, then in the face. She fell into the kitchen.

Strewn in the corner of the kitchen was Scott, the sounds coming from his blood-filled mouth frantic, shallow and wet. He was shaking toward the verge of a seizure, the knife still embedded in his chest, his fingers cupped around the weapon even as blood poured out of the wound.

Daniel grabbed Linda by the throat and pinned her against the wall. Next to him was a rack of knives that he paid far more attention to than the agent he was restraining. She kicked at him, driving her foot into his crotch, but the attack didn't faze him. She dug her nails into his wrist but it was like throttling a lead pipe.

There was zero give, and it did nothing to distract him from the delicate consideration he gave as he pulled the knives from the rack.

The wall immediately next to Linda's head exploded suddenly, brick, paint and plaster spraying out, and she winced as Daniel turned to see Scott shakily aiming his pistol at him. The detective was pale, drenched in sweat, with seemingly more blood outside his body than in. He squeezed the trigger off one more time, and Daniel's head creased to the right of his forehead as the bullet entered. It travelled through, fulminating out on the other side, blood spewing in the direction the bullet travelled. Bullseye.

With that act, Scott finally succumbed to his violent injury.

And yet, Daniel managed to turn back to face Linda. Tiny threads of inkly black matter journeyed out from inside the hole in his forehead as the wound closed. Barely able to breathe, Linda managed to smash her elbow downwards onto his nose, but all it did was dislodge his face, smearing it down and to the left, as if a mask he wore had slipped. More black matter became visible under his eye, between his lips and teeth, but there was no blood, not anymore. The damage to his face was undone.

Daniel punched her in the face repeatedly, until she couldn't fight back anymore. Ideas that she held concrete in her head had been reduced to rubble, and she found it difficult to think. He released her throat, and then grabbed her by the wrist, holding it up above her head. Daniel took the cleaver from the block, and considered his victim. And then he went to work.

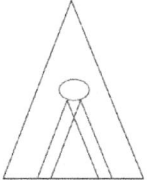

CHAPTER 38: DISCOVERY
LOCATION: ALEPH FIELD OFFICE, WASHINGTON

She rolled the bronze sobriety coin across the knuckles of her left hand while fiddling with a pencil in her right. She liked to keep her hands in motion when she was thinking, though there was the occasional clatter when inspiration hit and she literally dropped everything to attack her keyboard.

"What... what... what... *what...*" she murmured, staring at the encrypted data package Nicholas Quinlan had dumped online posthumously, in tandem with his pirate signal hijacking the television stations.

Analyst and codebreaker Gemma Vessey had worked at the Washington field office going on two years now. She'd transferred out from headquarters in New York thanks to a stellar recommendation from Kishana, who'd been in the trenches with her a few years prior. The pair agreed that a fresh start was probably best, especially considering Gemma's apartment was heavy with memories of the time spent there with her now ex.

Vessey was a short woman with a round, freckled face that was perfectly complemented by her dark eyes. Her thick lips were consistently caught in a befuddled pout, and her crazed head of black curls were always too tangled to even begin to consider doing anything practical with. So she let them sit wild, and went about her day. Who cared what people thought of her? Definitely not her.

The two data packages landed online simultaneously on every torrent site and dark web nook and cranny you could imagine. Before he died, Quinlan must have pre-programmed the releases to become available on whatever the most trafficked websites were at the time.

Or there was something a lot more sinister going on. Conspiracies and clones. Who knew how far down that rabbit hole went?

One package held every single piece of scientific research the mad science villain ever put together, and had already been downloaded over twelve million times in the last seven hours. That made it the most torrented file of non-pornographic content on the internet, blowing past whatever episode of the sexy swords and sorcery prestige TV epic was currently airing behind a paywall. A ticking time bomb of fringe science that was suddenly available to any Tom and Dick with a router and the know-how to deliver on its promise. An Anarchists Cookbook for the new age of bleeding edge science terrorism.

Getting less attention was the second package. An elaborate puzzle box of encryptions that nobody in Aleph had been able to decipher. If any of the other intelligence agencies had figured it out, they'd kept schtum about it. The agreed upon free flow of information meant that if the CIA or FBI or any other agency untangled the Gordian Knot in their laps, Aleph would find out eventually... but eventually didn't mean immediately.

"What... what... what..." She reared her head back and looked around the office. The day shift was winding down-- her shift-- and the night shift would shuffle in like the nocturnal animals they were in a few hours. Everyone was working a different angle of the Quinlan case, as promised by their boss to her boss. Her partner was out sick so it was just her, pulling her hair out, fidgeting around her cubicle like it was full of ants, with a package of data that nobody else could crack.

She pulled up the digitised evidence from the Quinlan murder trial. She ignored the video footage. Everyone had watched that a thousand times each, so what was the point of watching what was now revealed to be a clone stabbing a self-confessed supervillain to death?

No, she wanted to know how Quinlan's brain worked. She brought up the private papers the police had recovered-- anything digital had been wiped from his personal servers some point before his death. Now they knew that it hadn't been wiped but moved, and the only thing standing between her and that trove of juicy information was this encryption.

"There you are, you weird beautiful thing..."

She clicked into the digitised copies of Quinlan's private journal. Nothing but numbers and symbols. Nothing but nonsense. She allowed her sobriety coin to slip through her fingers and then snatched it before it could fall to the ground.

"What... what... what... if?"

Her screen lit up and she slipped out of her chair in surprise. Other members of the day shift lazily looked over to her, but nobody really paid her any heed. She was a weird one. Good, but weird. That meant they gave her a wide berth, regardless of how whip-smart she ended up being.

"Holy crap. I think I did it," she murmured, pulling herself to her feet. "I god damn did it."

"What did you do?" asked Deputy Director Cross. She was stood behind Gemma sipping from an oversized coffee mug, along with Signe Wasner, who exuded the kind of ice cold lesbian energy that ticked all sorts of boxes for the queer codebreaker. "You fell out of your chair. You don't normally do that unless it's something good."

"I, uh, I broke the code," said Gemma, running her hands through her muss of crazed curls.

"You did what?" said Signe.

"The encryption on Quinlan's supersecret data-dump--"

"You're sure you did it?" asked Cross.

"Well, yeah, look at it, the data is unspooling, but it's everything. It's massive."

"Great work. Slave your computer to the briefing room. Let's take this private."

Gemma looked around. "Uh, sure." She quickly typed something on her keyboard and the briefing room's screen lit up as Wasner swung the door open and abruptly pulled the blinds down.

Cross yanked her forward, and the three of them were alone in the briefing room, Gemma's findings projected onto the big screen.

"Talk us through it," said Wilhelmina.

Gemma stood in front of her screen as the data from the encrypted data package continued to download. "Do you remember how his journal came out during the trial? How the contents were all nonsense, strings of numbers and symbols, some kind of elaborate code that no one could break? We digitised it early on, had it running through all the breaking software we had available, but we never got a result. I just-- okay, it was actually really surprisingly simple-- I just ran it through the data dump, and--" She clicked her fingers. "--It unlocked everything. The journal wasn't a code; it was a key. Well, it was both things, but you follow what I mean?"

"Another domino he set up ten years ago to fall today..." noted Signe.

Cross watched in silence as the data continued to scroll down the screen.

Gemma continued, excited by the flow of information coming through her. "Exactly! There are reams and reams of data we'll need to parse because this looks like it might be his actual journal." She turned her back on the senior members of the department and randomly scrolled down the page, pausing every now and then to take in the treasure trove of information they'd uncovered. "Fucking wow. He recorded his thoughts, his feelings, there's so much... it's mad. But I think... if we look carefully... yeah, look," she pointed at the screen, her fingertip stubbed below a series of coordinates in plain black and white: *ROANOKE ISLAND - LAB A (UNDERGROUND)*

Signe shook her head incredulously. "Roanoke? What's he... what's he got to do with what happened at Roanoke?"

"There's more," said Wilhelmina. She pointed at the screen. "What's that say?"

"Er, right, okay... '*I always had a fondness for the mystery surrounding the first settlers on Roanoke Island. Whatever happened to the men, women and children who bravely journeyed there, hoping to make a better life for themselves? I could think of no better place to build a monument to my <u>own</u> achievements in the shadow of that place, but of course, over four hundred years later, the island is populated by thousands. I don't think they appreciate the magnitude of the place. I think I should take it from them. I'll make them their very own Lost Colony.*' God, the guy likes to talk. There's hundreds of thousands of words in each subsection of the database. Look at the database tree."

She indicated to the vast file directory on the screen-- a simplified breakdown of what was downloading, row after row of section and subsection folding out from one another, the file sizes ticking over with every passing second.

Signe looked to Cross and said, "We never knew what caused the outbreak of influenza on the island. Nearly eight thousand people died. The entire island is cut off now-- it's a no man's land... so, he killed them for real estate?"

Cross nodded slowly. "That's what it sounds like."

"Yeah, if it wasn't for FEMA and the Meridian working in tandem, the epidemic would have spread to the mainland," noted Gemma.

"We know where his lab is. That's where the clones will be," said Wilhelmina.

"Certainly looks that way," said Signe.

"Right. Call in the night shift early and get the day shift up and at 'em. All hands on deck, nobody leaves unless they want their walking papers. Gemma, you take the lead on this. I want you to coordinate. We're going to mine this for everything it's worth. We'll be uploading the entire thing onto the Aleph servers so HQ and the rest of the field offices have access, but let's get what we can out of it right now."

"Yes, ma'am," said Gemma, heading back outside.

Signe caught herself at the door and looked back at Cross. "What about you, Bill?"

"I'm going to contact the director. I want him to hear it from me first. We've got the bastard. If Quinlan was actually telling the truth, then all we need to prove it is in the middle of Roanoke."

CITIES ON FIRE

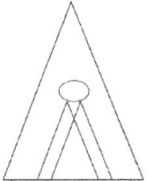

CHAPTER 39: UP THEN OUT
LOCATION: ALEPH ACTIVE INTELLIGENCE HQ, NEW YORK

"Everything all right?" asked Hannah.

She had been left leaning against the wall outside the medical bay while Chris took an urgent call from Washington. All she had to occupy herself while she waited was to roll the bottle of ultra-strong painkillers she'd been given from hand to hand.

Doctor Sumner had given her strict instructions on how many she was supposed to take and when-- explicitly stating that they were a short-term solution and that surgery was the long term one-- but she ignored him, shook four out of the container and ground them between her teeth so they started working faster. A few minutes later, her brother returned with an uncertain expression on his face.

When he didn't respond, she immediately grew concerned and quietly said, "...Chris?"

He took a breath. He seemed to strain against the act of speaking, as if he knew he had to say what had happened but didn't want to, and it was a tug of war between the conflicting feelings. He finally gave in and said, "The Washington office cracked the encryption on Quinlan's data package. We know where his lab is."

"...When do we leave?" she asked, pocketing the painkillers, and placing her hands impatiently on her hips.

"'We'?" he repeated.

"Did I stutter? You're not keeping me out of this. Of course I'm going!"

And this was why he was hesitant to tell her. He immediately went on the defensive and retorted, "You're in my custody. You go wherever the hell I say you go!"

"You think you can keep me out?" Hannah punctuated her point by stubbing a bandaged finger against his chest.

Chris swatted her hand away. "I could tase you."

"You wouldn't fucking dare," she snarled.

"You're right. I'd *have* you tased. But... fuck... let's just take it down a few notches. You wanted to go outside, we're going outside. I'm just... this is all very fresh. Very raw. You're an exposed nerve and I guess I am too."

She slumped forward, tension once again lifting from her. "Okay. Sorry, yes. You bring out the worst in me, you dickhead. But... sorry."

"I get it. I do. Because you're the worst god damn sister in the world."

She chuckled. The pair were falling into old routines, for better or for worse. She quietly added, "Every time you mention him. Every time it comes up, I'm just... god, what if it's all a setup? What if there's no evidence? What if I have to go back?"

"You're not going back."

"Ten years already gone... already lost..." She touched the wall next to her and sighed. "Okay. Outside. Up and outside."

"Yeah, and I think..." Chris trailed off as he saw Kishana standing at the end of the hallway with Robert Witwer-- one of Henry's psychics-- and a young woman he didn't recognise, who must have been the technopath he'd requested. "...I think we're ready to go." He beckoned them forward. "Is this...?"

"Special Agent Leung, as requested," said Kishana, gesturing toward the young woman beside her. "And you know Rob Witwer."

"Morning, boss," said Witwer. He was an average looking man with a long face and a round chin, and his lazy smile when he greeted Stone was typical of him, as was his generally unkempt appearance, and the scattershot stubble that came with too many nights on the town in a row.

"It's gone 10pm, Robert," said Kishana.

"Ah, well, time has no meaning when... ah... okay, I just woke up," he admitted.

"Sleeping in your wife's office again?" asked Kishana.

"How did you know? Have you heard from her by the way? She's not answering her phone," said Robert.

"Not yet, but she's on assignment. She'll check in when she's finished," said Kishana.

Robert nodded, unconvinced. Across from him, Leung looked like she was barely in her twenties, if she was even out of her teens. Her delicate features contradicted her sharp eyes, and her black hair was tucked behind large ears. She gave Stone a slight wave then said, "Good evening, sir. You can call me, umm, Shelly."

"Only if you call me Chris. No need for formalities here, Shelly," he said. Regardless of how sheepish she appeared, and how clearly hungover Witwer was, Aleph didn't hand out badges and titles frivolously. If Kishana said Leung knew her stuff, then she knew her stuff. No questions asked. "This is my sister, Hannah. I'm sorry for pulling you both into this at such a late hour, but with your skill set, it was a must."

Witwer waved off the apology, partly because he knew that Chris wasn't actually sorry. It was just part of the job, and he'd accepted that long ago.

"It's absolutely fine." Shelly smiled and shrugged at the apology. "It's not often I get contacted, so, well, it makes a change. Does this have something to do with the Manhattan bombings?"

Chris nodded. "Connected tangentially. Kishana?"

Muldair explained, "The directors of Aleph are being targeted. Director Murray is dead. That was the Manhattan attack. Director Martin was also attacked, but she managed to escape."

"The Paris bombing?" offered Leung.

"Exactly. What we've been able to determine so far is that the attackers are using suicide vests. We need you to stand next to Director Stone and if you 'hear' anything that sounds like an incendiary device in the vicinity, ask it not to detonate. And Witwer, same goes for you. If someone approaches with malicious intent..."

"I'll sort it," he replied.

Shelly considered the assignment, weighing it out in her head as she balanced her metahuman abilities to the task at hand. "They'll need to be close for me to... 'hear', like you say."

"That's fine. As long as you're quick on the draw, then it's fine," said Chris.

"We're putting a lot of stock in this girl's ability to talk fast, aren't we?" said Hannah.

"That's why I have these," said Kishana. She held up four belts made up of small zippo-sized plates of metal. Wires were visible connecting each, and a small power pack was affixed to the back. "Forcefield belts."

"Uh... they look pretty ramshackle," said Hannah, eyeing them up. "The Meridian have survival suits that are stored in discs, don't we-- you, sorry-- have anything like that?" Then she paused. "...I'm not being used as bait here am I?"

"No, but we have to be safe," replied Chris, as he took the forcefield belt and pulled out his regular leather one from his trousers. He threaded the new belt through his belt hooks, holding his shirt up so Kishana could check the power pack. She gave him a nod and he lowered his shirt back down.

"We don't have access to the same tech as the Meridian. Zyj's Dierlullian stuff is lightyears ahead of what we have access to, and the team aren't comfortable sharing their advances until the world gets their shit together. Standard."

"You seem remarkably relaxed about this," said Hannah, her voice growing quiet as she looked over to her brother.

Chris shrugged. "I trust my people. Do you trust me?"

She immediately shook her head but held her hand out to Kishana for her own forcefield belt. "Nope. But do I have a choice?"

"That's certainly not the spirit, but I'll accept it," he said.

While everyone finished attaching the belts, Doctor Sumner popped his head out of the medical facility. "You're still here. Good, good."

"What do you have for us, doctor?" asked Chris.

He held up a syringe gun filled with a transparent liquid, then looked at Hannah. "It's a genetic tag. To make sure we always know you're you."

"I'm... always me?" said Hannah, a crack showing.

Chris nodded. "I asked the doctor to put something together, to make sure that Quinlan can't fool us again. There won't be any doubt that you are who you say you are."

"How do you know I am me right now?" she asked.

"You think he'd let a fake go through what you did?" said Chris.

"...You have a horrible point," she replied.

"Okay, I just need to inject this, it'll bind to your DNA-- no, no, don't worry, it's harmless," said Sumner, noting the look of concern that appeared on everybody's faces. "It's like..."

"It's fine, honestly," said Hannah.

Sumner motioned for her to move her hair away from her neck and she did so, then after dabbing the skin above her jugular with a small swab, he plunged the needle of the syringe gun in, and injected her with whatever it was he'd concocted.

Chris noted Shelly winced while Witwer drank from a bottle of water he'd been carrying. Kishana looked on, indifferent, which felt right considering everything he'd been through with her. It took a lot to faze a woman like Kishana Muldair.

Kishana finished attaching the power packs to the belts as Hannah rubbed the spot on her neck that Sumner quickly covered with a plaster. Content that his work was done, he promptly excused himself and left the five of them to walk into the nearby elevator that clunked as it ascended toward the surface.

A few moments of silence later and Chris said, "Hannah, this is Kishana Muldair. She's my second in command."

"I was wondering when you'd actually introduce me," said Kishana. She extended her hand and Hannah accepted it.

"Let me guess," said Hannah, "He wouldn't know his elbow from his ass without you."

Leung's eyes opened with the same abruptness as the comment, though Kishana smiled and nodded in agreement.

"Basically. I've not heard it put so eloquently before, though," said Kishana.

"Behind every great man..." murmured Chris.

Witwer snorted.

Ignoring that, Kishana smiled at the sentiment. "We're going to get on, Hannah. But okay, listen, here's the situation. You're headed topside and we've got the entire block under surveillance. Here," she handed the foursome a set of transmission-receiving earwigs. "We'll keep you in the loop if anything weird happens, but we're not expecting anything. Standard operating procedure now is that any high-ranking Aleph officials must wear protective clothing at all times-- body armour is mandatory, forcefield belts where possible."

"Where possible?" asked Leung.

"They're extremely expensive to make and we only have a handful per castle. These four are yours and another two are currently in for repair. But remember, the explosives being used are extremely powerful. Strong enough that they got through Cobalt 5's suit. You wear these, but we're under no illusion that if you are at ground zero of something like what hit Manhattan or Paris, you're a blast shadow."

"You're so upbeat," said Hannah.

"I'm a realist. Anyway, these are all precautionary measures. Nothing should get near enough for you to need them."

"And yet, we're wearing them. Colour me relieved," said Hannah.

"You wanted to go outside," said Chris.

"I've been in prison for ten years," retorted Hannah.

Leung's eyes swivelled over to the younger Stone. "You've been where? Oh my god, are you Shrike?"

Hannah sighed. "Nothing gets past this one, eh?"

"Do I have time to call in sick?" asked Witwer.

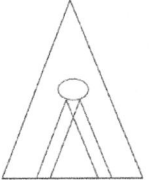

**CHAPTER 40: FIRST FLIGHT
LOCATION: MANHATTAN, NEW YORK
SIXTEEN YEARS AGO:**

Full moon. That was about right.

She remembered the night her world ended. The night the knock sounded at the door.

The night her parents died.

There was a full moon then as well. Synchronicities. The monks had explained that the more she learned, the closer she'd become to the inner workings of the wheels of circumstances. The more she knew, the more she'd see. The more she saw, the more she'd be able to do. The more she could help. That's what this was about. No one should suffer as she suffered. No one should lose what she lost.

High above the streets of New York, Hannah Stone reached her fingers out across the void beneath her, white gloves crunching as she closed her hand into a fist. Everything that had come before was leading inextricably to this moment. And all she had to do was take one step.

Everything that had come before. A thousand lives lived, condensed down into one. The present. Her current. She had been a ghost. Immaterial, but now she was made manifest. She'd returned stateside under an alias, using the credentials given to her by Mackenzie Ransom. He was the only one who knew about her return, providing the start-up funds she needed to begin an operation on the scale she was planning. Thank god for vigilantes and their willingness to invest in wars against crime.

Chris was still in the dark. She wondered if he thought of her. He had already left their aunt and uncle's home when she decided to follow her own path. He followed in their parents', joining the Air

Force. Taking flight on his own terms. Soaring above the problems-- the horrors-- that defined the later years of their childhood. She was about to take flight too but in a much different way.

<*I am as infinite as I am singular,*> she said, her voice distorted by the voice box built into her mask. The mantras and chants of the monks rang in her head. She didn't remember the details of her legend. Only knew that she'd lived it. The Sisterhood of the Shard took her in, and it was then that her training culminated, deep in the mountain beneath their monastery.

Then she smiled, an old tune breaking in over the solemn utterances of the women who helped her become her present self. <*You're the master of your own destiny... so give and take the best that you can...*>

Her cape flapped gently. Her mask's HUD showed her temperature of the air outside, cold enough that she'd have shivered if it weren't for the regulating systems that lined the interior of her suit. She looked down at herself one last time. The suit obscured any physical features and filled out space around her torso and hips, all so you wouldn't have known she was a woman if you saw her silhouette.

She'd made the suit herself. Reinforced in all the right places, flexible enough in others. She wanted to be a mystery-- an enigma. The shape of the mask, the colour scheme, they'd come in a dream that signified her return to existence after being broken into pieces beneath the world. A deadly bird of prey as cold as the most gibbous of moons.

She had spent countless lives learning how to fight, how to strategize, how to win, and now she was back in the city that had birthed one of the most monstrous of men, back to take revenge on all those who would seek to take from others what was taken from her.

No one needed to suffer as she had. No one should lose what she'd lost.

Hannah Stone was no longer just a woman, though there was no shame in living that life. Instead, she had become something more-- something bigger. Travelling the world since she was sixteen, Hannah learned everything she could from the masters of dozens of martial arts. She had spanned infinity thanks to the Sisterhood of the Shard and the thing buried beneath their monastery.

Hannah Stone was no longer just Hannah Stone. Putting on the costume. Wearing this armour. Everything that came before culminated in the now. And all she had to do to make her personal reality the reality of the rest of the world was to take the first step... and fly.

<*Nobody. Never again. If I can-- I will,*> she said. A solemn vow. An impossible promise. She threw the grapnel line across the chasm that spanned the length of New York and beyond, and as she took flight across the void, her legend became real.

Hannah Stone was no longer just Hannah Stone. Now... she was the Shrike.

CITIES ON FIRE

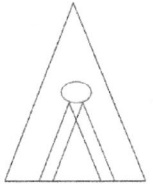

CHAPTER 41: THIRD TIMES AND CHARMS
LOCATION: ALEPH ACTIVE INTELLIGENCE HQ, NEW YORK

<*"Four quadrant overwatch-- status-- North?"*>
<*"Clear."*>
<*"East?"*>
<*"Clear."*>
<*"South?"*>
<*"Clear."*>
<*"West?"*>
<*"Clear."*>
<*"You know the drill, boys and girls. Eyes open and sharp."*>

The voices of the sniper team performing overwatch whispered into their ears like sweet nothings. Every angle surrounding the garden was covered by armed men and women who were fully prepared to pull the triggers on their rifles given the right circumstances.

Technopath Shelly Leung hung back as the siblings strode off into the secluded garden to the east of the Aleph building, while Robert Witwer played Snake on his phone. Trees obstructed any lines of sight curious pedestrians might have, and there were no visible markings to distinguish the site from any other nondescript building somewhere in New York.

"You okay?" asked Shelly.

Robert shrugged. "Linda-- my wife--she should've called by now. She's as tough as nails, but that doesn't stop me from worrying."

"I'm sure she's okay," said Shelly.

Robert shrugged again. "Never stops you from assuming the worst though, does it?"

Bordering the winding pathways of this secret garden were beds of luxurious flowers not native to the city, cultivated and preserved by a team of gardeners. All in all, it was a lush space to relax in, and there were various benches and picnic tables set up in the area. You could hold one hell of a barbecue here, and if Hannah knew her brother... he probably had at one time or another.

"Mind the gap," said Chris. He gestured toward a gaping muddy hole in a nearby plot, far enough away for it not to be an issue, but safety first in all things...

She glanced down toward it. "That's deep. Did you pull a tree?"

He smiled. "Not personally, no. I was told something called 'heart rot' set in. Left the gardeners no other choice," he said.

"Well... I'm sorry for your loss," said Hannah, pouting as sympathetically as one could whilst also making it abundantly clear that she was being as sarcastic as a sister could be.

"Okay, dickhead," replied Chris.

In the distance, cars could be heard in motion, but for the most part, the urban sounds that came with being in the centre of one of the most vibrant cities in America were subdued. Leung kept a wary eye out and kept clearing her throat and talking to herself, but Chris didn't pay her any heed. He assumed she was practising speaking clearly and concisely, but he had no reason to question it. Those kinds of people had their way, and so did he. What else was there to it? Witwer meanwhile cursed quietly and pocketed his phone, frustrated at a pixel snake smashing into a pixel wall when it shouldn't have. Game Over.

<*"North?"*>
<*"Clear."*>
<*"East?"*>
<*"Clear."*>
<*"South?"*>
<*"Clear."*>
<*"West?"*>
<*"Clear."*>

"You know... we take all of this for granted," said Hannah.

She had closed her eyes tight, her arms open at her side in a forty degree angle , and was enjoying the feeling of the cool evening air against her skin. She took a few steps forward, her fingers brushing up against the leaves and petals in the flower beds on either side of her, and for the first time since they'd been reunited, she actually looked somewhat like herself, rather than the battered shell she'd been earlier in the day.

Chris hadn't noticed it before due to the sterile lights they'd been interacting under for the last couple of hours, but her skin was painfully pale, an assumptive result of being locked underground for a decade.

"In this life, you barely get to stop and enjoy the little things," he replied.

Eyes still jammed closed, she said, "You should do something about that. Have you spoken to--"

"Nope." Chris cut her off with a swiping gesture, an ineffectual karate chop through the air between them that did nothing but momentarily amuse his sister. "Don't want to talk about them."

"Okay. Okay," she replied, raising her hands up higher, half stretching, half conceding a point. She changed the subject. "How far away from the Manhattan bombing are we?"

"Just over ten kilometres. Why?"

"Wondering. And we travelled north to get here from the airport. Are we in the Bronx?"

"…Yes. How could you-- oh, I always forget about you and your obsession with maps," he sighed.

<*"North?"*>

<*"Clear."*>

<*"East?"*>

<*"Vehicle slowing on approach. Hold. Hold."*>

<*"Adjusting…"*>

<*"One second-- ah, crap, my cam just glitched-- okay, sorry, vehicle moving off, no exits. Clear."*>

<*"I'm keeping East in view. South?"*>

<*"Clear."*>

<*"West?"*>

<*"Clear."*>

"Yeah. I just like to know where I am. You held the world together when I wasn't in it, so I assume my geography skills still hold up. What's your plan? With me and... and the whole damn thing?"

"I don't know. I was actually with the President when all hell broke loose earlier. He's speaking to the Attorney General and they're looking at overturning the conviction. It's either that, or a presidential pardon, and he's amenable to either option--"

"I don't want a pardon. I did nothing wrong," countered Hannah.

"But! We'll cross that bridge when we come to it," said Chris, cutting off his ever-defiant and individualistic sister.

"Fine, fine. I didn't expect it to be easy. How can you take the word of a self-professed supervillain? There's more to it. There's always going to be more to it."

"Yeah. But we'll get there. I promise."

"Thanks, big brother," said Hannah. She squeezed his offered hand and they shared a smile. The moment between siblings was interrupted by a gate opening with a loud, authoritative BEEP at the far end of the walled garden. Hannah looked at Chris and asked, "Who's that?"

Linda Witwer stumbled through the gate on the east side of the walled garden. Her clothes were drenched in blood, and her terrified looking face was covered in welts and lesions. She nearly fell over immediately, but fell against the wall behind her. Her right hand was shoved in her pocket, while she used her left hand to prop herself up, though her knees looked like they would give in any second.

"H-Help me," said Linda.

"That's--" started Chris, but Robert knew his wife when he saw her. His brow crumpled like paper and he started moving toward her.

Shelly went to follow after the shocked psychic after he began running over to his wife, but Hannah reached forward and grabbed the back of her coat, stopping her in her tracks. The technopath looked back at the director's sister, but she could barely see her face. What expression she could see was unreadable, until Hannah said, "Not yet."

Chris nuzzled his neck into the microphone pinned to his lapel "Linda Witwer just entered the garden from the east, does anybody have eyes on her?"

<*"Sir, I'm looking directly at the entrance, but there's nobody*

there-- Robert Witwer is approaching, but other than that--">
<*"Can confirm, there's nobody there!">*

"There's clearly somebody there," said Chris, grimacing. He didn't like this, not one bit.

Robert reached Linda, and could see the extent of the damage done to her. Her right eye had flooded red after a violent burst of blood vessels. He delicately touched her battered face and asked, "Honey, what happened?"

"I don't... I don't remember... there was... a man..." whispered Linda.

Her voice was lower than anybody who knew her remembered. The words formed lazily and tumbled out of her like a dropped bowl of rice. Nothing was what it was supposed to be. Nothing about the situation was right. But Robert's eyes were wide and his heart overriding common sense. That was his wife. Of course it was. Who else could it be?

"It's okay, it's okay, let me help, okay? Let me help," said Robert.

When she opened her mouth to reply, Robert could see broken teeth and shredded gums. He brushed his psychic powers against her mind, thinking that it would be easier to process the information directly without forcing her to articulate the horrors, but instead of seeing what happened in the Lawrence apartment, he immediately reeled back.

Memories-- a victim's eye view-- of a man-- an attacker-- a villain-- a monster-- whose mouth opened far too wide to be human. More animal, or insect, or serpent or squid, than a man. Terror caused the memory to vibrate with an adrenaline-flavoured tinge of a lived experience. The skin at the corners of his lips tore wide as a pulsing, throbbing muscle of a thing tried to climb out from down his throat and inside his mouth. Its skin was slick and shiny like a seal's, but black, an absence of colour you could only experience on the dark side of the moon. It moved with the slug-like determination of a one-muscled invertebrate, pushing and pushing out from the man, as it gained purchase from his oesophagus, more and more of the creature becoming visible as a retching, vomiting sound followed with it. To the victim's right, a bloody stump, a large knife embedded in the wall, blood everywhere. Eyes front and seeing eyes sunk, eyes sunk into sockets, spheres of seeing-jelly tumbling backwards into the skull as tentacles began to push out from somewhere inside. Movement visible in the nostrils, but pulling, pushing, projecting, and suddenly the black thing that lived in the man was externalised, and climbing into the victim, and then the memory snapped as the victim was completely subsumed and all that was left was

"--Nothing-- there's nothing-- there's just--" spluttered Robert, reeling away from his wife as vomit began to bile up in his throat, threatening to spill over into the real world and out his trembling mouth.

Linda smiled and shoved her hand, palm up, between the gap under her husband's nose and above his top lip. Her fingers moved through his skull like it was a propeller through water, with a speed and ferocity one might expect from an unthinking engine, but definitely not from one's wife. And her smile didn't fade even as healthy teeth came loose at the root and blood began to pour freely from her husband's mouth.

Robert screamed discordantly as the top and bottom half of his skull separated. He tried to grab at his face but before he could do anything, before he could even think of holding the damage together, Linda closed her hand whilst it was still embedded in his skull and shredded the base of his brain into pulp. He let out a piercing death cry that combined with his telepathic powers to trigger a shockwave that sent everybody in the garden flying backwards.

Chris performed an elaborately uncomfortable-looking backward roll, but managed to stop himself from falling into the deep trench that the arboriculturists had left behind when they pulled the garden's oldest tree. He managed to steady himself in time to shout, "Fire on Witwer's last position! Fire! Fire!"

Sniper fire rained down toward the eastern gate immediately. None of the snipers could see what they were aiming at, but the door was torn to shreds within seconds. The wall sprayed mortar, the ground churned to mulch, and Linda was somehow lucky enough to be missed by all but one shot-- it caught her in the left shoulder, and caused flesh and bone to vaporise on impact. She spun in on herself, dancing awkwardly in a red mist of her own making. During this flurry of movement, her severed right hand fell out of pocket, landing on the garden floor with a pathetic thud.

"Oh my god," whispered Shelly.

Linda rolled her mangled shoulder. Gore had settled into place, but there was a shimmer where flesh should be. A sort of idiosyncratic heat shimmer that appeared where it shouldn't. The garden, nor the city, was particularly warm. There was rain in the clouds wanting to fall, but they were constipated and refusing to budge. The air was still and chilly, and yet a gaping wound in this woman's shoulder was making the eyes of those present *hurt*.

She took a step forward. Blood had dried all around her mouth. Her lips parted and she said, "Why did you send me to die, Director Stone?"

"Shelly, do your thing. Do your thing *now*," said Hannah.

Shelly managed to pull herself out of her shock and shouted "D-do-- *do not explode!*" while pointing her hands at Linda. If there was anything on her body electronic, anything that conducted electricity from one end of a wire to another, if there was a suicide vest beneath the blood-soaked coat, it would do whatever Shelly told it to do.

Linda tilted her head to the side, as if questioning the action undertaken by the Aleph agent.

And Shelly realised something that caused her stomach to sink. "There's no bomb. There's no bomb. Whatever this is-- it's *her*."

"Linda, I'm going to need you to stop right there," said Chris, holding up one hand while his other unbuckled his holster. He then spoke into his lapel mic, "Get an ART here *now*. Keep firing, two metres from where Richard Witwer's laying, directly in front of me."

"B-but why, sir? You sent me to die. *You sent me to die*," said Linda.

She twitched. There was a sound, a quiet shriek that started like an insect in flight, that started to ring in the bones of those present. It didn't come from Linda's mouth, but it came from around her, like a vibration. It grew, from a shriek to a scream, and then the fully lit garden sank into darkness as all the lights switched off without any fanfare. The receivers in the agent's ears buzzed and then shorted out, and the lapel microphones fizzled and popped, no longer fit for purpose. Their forcefield belts shimmered, but remained active... for now.

No more sniper shots flew. Chris didn't know, but the communication equipment the team were hooked up to was overloaded to such an extent that the sound-- that horrid, violent sound-- knocked them out before they could disconnect. The only thing preventing the same thing happening to those in the garden were the forcefield belts, and they were barely operating, so what next? No protection, no back-up, and no idea of what was coming for them next.

"What... what was that?" asked Hannah, trying to dislodge the ringing in her ear by slapping the other side of her head.

Shelly had some sort of answer. "Nearly all the electronic signals in the immediate area just went dead. These belts just went from 100% power to 5. We're in a blackout zone. I've never... I've never felt anything like it before. I can't hear anything nearby." Blackout zone meant no electricity, and no electricity meant no elevator from the Aleph base beneath the surface. No elevator meant no back-up, meant no ART to come to the rescue. It was just them. Alone. Against whatever this force of horrific nature was that wore Linda Witwer like a human suit.

"I'm sorry," said Chris. Every alarm bell in his body was ringing, and he could feel the ticking clock of his life rushing toward the final seconds. They were in the sudden death phase of the game, and it turned the adrenaline in his veins into electricity, every motion and movement an acute sensation in his body.

Hannah had crossed the distance between Linda and the rest before he could shoot. She unleashed a flurry of punches at key pressure points across the agent's upper body-- both eyes, parotid node, jaw and brachial plexus-- and when Linda went to retaliate, Hannah backed up immediately, keeping a distance between them as she calculated her next move.

Each of the punches she threw should have done debilitating damage to the woman, ending the fight if she was a normal person immediately. But it was abundantly clear that this woman was next level, perhaps even some sort of metahuman, and it would take a lot more than close quarter combat to take her down.

Chris cursed. Linda smiled, bloodied gums and broken teeth visible. Hannah grimaced. Shelly tried to hold back tears.

With the open distance between Linda and his sister, Chris fired three shots-- head and head and head again. He was aiming for the brain stem-- instant kill. On impact, the woman spun around and then fell to the floor. Hannah flinched at the POP POP POP of his gun going off, raising her arm up to hide her face, but keeping her eyes on their failed assassin.

"Fuck!" swore Hannah.

"Get away from her!" shouted Chris.

Before Hannah returned to her brother's side, she heard a horrid gurgling noise coming from where Linda had fallen. The dead woman grabbed her by the ankle and threw Hannah upwards, before Hannah came crashing down a second later, the air out from her lungs, her ribs rattled on impact.

"Oh fuck, *fuck*," mumbled Hannah, rolling onto her back and trying to move, but finding her body unable to do as her brain asked of it.

Nearby, Linda began to stand, even though there were three holes in her head that should have stopped that from ever happening again. Her limbs moved in staccato freestyle, every gesture and movement like stop-motion as she glared toward Chris. Blood dribbled in black rivers from the hole in her head and forked as it reached her nose. Two branches of darkness slipped past her nostrils and into her mouth, having joined the stream from the wounds above her lips.

"Oh my god," whispered Shelly.

Chris didn't need any more excuses. He decided to empty his clip into the woman then and there. With the first shot, he took out her eye, one slug caught her at an angle and tore her nose off in a ragged spray. You could literally see through her face to the garden behind her. One eye still blinked. Her face, even if it was caved in by Chris' shots, still wore an amused expression. Teeth were shattered, gums gone, a visibly gored tongue torn to pieces.

"You... sent me... to die..." said Linda. Except it came out more like "*Yuh - shun - mush - shuh - duh*," due to the state of her mouth.

Her intention was clear. Black lines began to form across her skin where she hadn't been savaged by bullets. Black lines that vibrated with an unearthly light the more they spread. She began to raise her left hand. Not like she could do what was to come next with the stump left where her right hand had once been.

Hannah blinked. She could take a hint, even if it was one she had never witnessed before. She rolled to her feet and sprinted back toward her brother.

Chris didn't see her. Linda had started vibrating, and as hard as it was hard to look at her, it was even harder to take his eyes off her. Hannah tackled Chris and grabbed Shelly on the way down, shoving the pair into the nearby hole as Linda finally clicked her fingers, and exploded.

Hannah screamed in absolute agony as her back was caught in the blast, and Chris cried out for his sister as her dying forcefield belt immediately failed completely. She tumbled into the hole with them, as her body was shredded to bloody burnt bits by the blast that originated from somewhere within Linda Witwer's dismantled body.

The heat of the blast washed over the hole, but soil and mud slapped downwards, adding another layer of fortification along with their still functioning force fields and protecting them from the brunt of it.

Chris couldn't get a good look at the wounds Hannah had received, but she had passed out, and he did everything he could to protect her from any more injury. He'd failed ten years ago, he'd failed again, and now they were in a hole in the ground. They were drowning under the earth, and it was all his fault.

Chris tried to speak, but the words were replaced by earth as it spilled into his mouth. The hole filled with a churning torrent of dislodged soil and detritus, and soon all he could see was darkness. His body seized up as his premature and violent burial rite continued. He felt his sister's hand wrenched away from his own, but even if he could see her, he couldn't even move to reach her again.

Buried and lost. All that was left for them was to die.

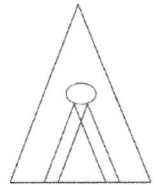

TO BE CONTINUED

Printed in Great Britain
by Amazon